YIDDISH *for* PIRATES

Also by Gary Barwin

⁺⁺

Poetry

Cruelty to Fabulous Animals
Outside the Hat
Raising Eyebrows
frogments from the frag pool: haiku after Basho (with derek beaulieu)
The Porcupinity of the Stars
The Obvious Flap (with Gregory Betts)
Franzlations [the imaginary Kafka parables] (with Craig Conley & Hugh Thomas)
O: eleven songs for chorus SATB (with music by Dennis Bathory-Kitsz)
Moon Baboon Canoe
The Wild and Unfathomable Always

Novella

The Mud Game (with Stuart Ross)

Short Fiction

Big Red Baby
Doctor Weep and other strange teeth
I, Dr. Greenblatt, Orthodontist, 251-1457

Books for Younger Readers

Seeing Stars
Grandpa's Snowman (illustrated by Kitty Macaulay)
The Magic Mustache (illustrated by Stephane Jorisch)
The Racing Worm Brothers (illustrated by Kitty Macaulay)

As Editor

Sonosyntactics: Selected and New Poety of Paul Dutton

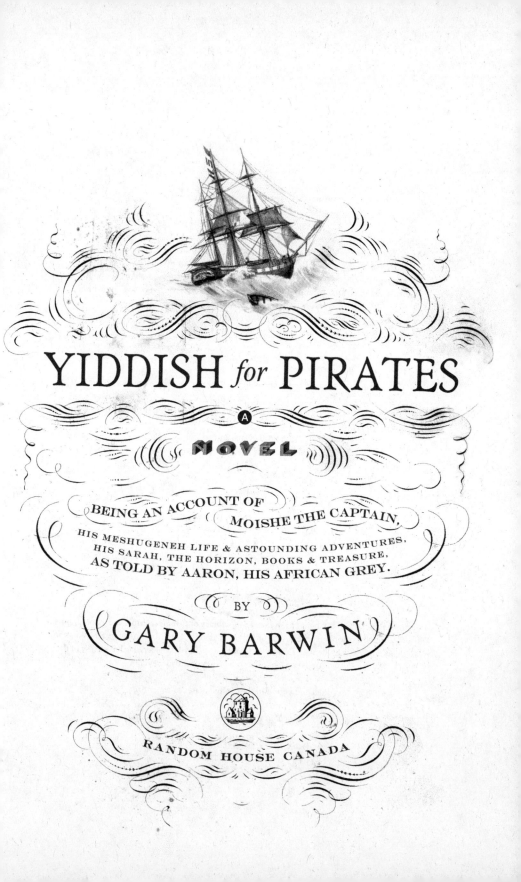

YIDDISH *for* PIRATES

A NOVEL

BEING AN ACCOUNT OF MOISHE THE CAPTAIN,
HIS MESHUGENEH LIFE & ASTOUNDING ADVENTURES,
HIS SARAH, THE HORIZON, BOOKS & TREASURE,
AS TOLD BY AARON, HIS AFRICAN GREY.

BY

GARY BARWIN

RANDOM HOUSE CANADA

PUBLISHED BY RANDOM HOUSE CANADA

Copyright © 2016 Gary Barwin

www.penguinrandomhouse.ca

Random House Canada and colophon are registered trademarks.

Library and Archives Canada Cataloguing in Publication

Barwin, Gary, author
Yiddish for pirates / Gary Barwin.

Issued in print and electronic formats.

ISBN 978-0-345-81551-4
eBook ISBN 978-0-345-81553-8

I. Title.

PS8553.A783Y53 2016   c813'.54   C2015-905824-4

Book design by Five Seventeen
Cover image © C.M. Butzer
Interior images: (ship) © Charles H. Keith, 1846. Library of Congress Prints and Photographs
Division; (flourishes) Topographical Atlas of Jefferson County, New York, 1864, by S.N. Beers and
D.G. Beers, and Atlas of Steuben County, New York, 1873, by D.G. Beers, both courtesy of the
David Rumsey Map Collection, www.davidrumsey.com

Printed and bound in the United States of America

2 4 6 8 9 7 5 3 1

Penguin
Random House
RANDOM HOUSE CANADA

For the whole mishpocheh, both fore and aft.

We are going to a different world . . .
and I expect it is the one where
all goes well.

VOLTAIRE, *Candide*

Hello. Howaya? Feh. You think those are the only words I know? Boychik, you don't know from knowing. You ain't seen knowing. I may be *meshugeh* crazy, but I know from words. You think I'm a fool shmegegge? I'm *all* words.

Hello? If you want the story of a life, don't wait for your alter kaker old gramps over there to wake up. Maybe he'll never wake. But me? Listen to my words. They tell some story. Because I remember. Sometimes too much, but I remember.

So, nu, bench your fat little oysgepasheter Cape Horn tuches down on that chair and listen to my beaking. Come all ye brave lads, and so forth. I'll tell you the whole megillah story from fore to aft.

What's it about? Pirates. Parrots. Jews. Jewels. The Inquisition. Gefilte fish. Gold. A girl.

Boychik, I was a pirate's parrot, and had I not noshed from the Fountain of Eternal Youth hundreds of years ago, I would rest beside my scurvy captain and Davy Jones hisself at the bottom of the sea where the soulless creatures crawl. And then where would you be?

Without a story.

That life. It was a book made into a life. A wonder tale. The glinty waves. The deep jungle. A world I wouldn't have believed if I hadn't sailed right into it. And for a time, that world had but one shoulder, blue and fussy with epaulettes hanging off the rigging of a stolen frock coat, a cutlass of a collarbone covered in flesh like mangy beef jerky.

My captain's shoulder.

Feh, these days no one wants to hear. Maybe not even you. They treat us like leftovers—wizened chicken-gizzard pupiklech in this birdhouse of leftover Yids. But nu, it's true, most of us look like yesterday's chicken or its gizzards. Though look at these feathers. A young bird would be proud of such grey.

The Shalom Home for the Aged.

Shalom? In Hebrew, "shalom" means hello, goodbye, peace. Imagine the crazy farkakteh waving of some poultry-skinned geezer on the fifth floor, squinting out from between the orange curtains. Is he waving hello or goodbye? Ptuh! It's an old age home, so who knows? Maybe the shlemiel thinks he's in a crow's nest and is warning of an invading armada. Alav ha'shalom. Peace be upon him, old nudnik.

But what does peace look like? Is it better to be careened tsitskehs-over-tuches, nipples-over-nethers in dry dock, the dangling clams of your ballsack scraped daily for barnacles by some balmelocheh know-it-all nurse, or lost somewhere on the seventh of the seven seas snorting the scent of new flowers and the soft jellyfish pazookheh breasts of beautiful sheyneh maidens?

Too often, stories in this library of lost people are told in the farmisht confused language of forgetting, but I speak many languages and I'm fluent in both remembering and forgetting. Though, nu, it's easier to tell the stories you remember.

Or pretend to. And what you don't remember, the stories tell for you.

Ach. I talk too much. I've got myself twisted fardreyt with words turncoating again, thinking about my bastard mamzer captain himself. But what do you expect? Five hundred years old, I'm an alter kaker geezer of the highest degree, with a brain like a cabbage roll. A parrot brain like a chameleon on Jewish tartan.

The horizon, I once told a Spanish painter, it gives you a whole new perspective. It doesn't exist except from far away. The horizon is always a story, and as soon as we get there, it's somewhere else.

The horizon, it's a line we crossed just to see what we could see. And believe me, we saw many things, some things that wouldn't just stay over the horizon.

They wanted our souls for eternal barbecue so we travelled with Columbus into that braves' new world as if across a vast and chilly Jordan. An undividing Red Sea. And what did the ancients find? A promising land. Thousands of years of history. Regret. Happiness. The future.

And what did we find? Ach, this is a pirate tale I'm telling you, so it has to be treasure. So, nu, you ask, what is this treasure and where is it buried?

This I'll try to answer. As well as another, the big question of all stories: And then what happened?

Yes, it brings mazel for a pimply boy like you to hear about blood, kishkas—guts—dangerous books, and shtupping. It puts some hair between your ears and above your skinny-dick shmeckel.

You'll like it.

So, nu, in the beginning what was there?

A beginning.

Introduction

We're on a ship and high above us, the pale full moon—keneynehoreh—pus-coloured, to be frank, streaked semen-silver across the shawl of the sea. The clouds bulging dark, spun fat over the slate grey sky. The world is a slow breath. The cool sea air, the quiet ship deck, the crew sleeping below, except for a few rum-soaked shikker and unconscious seamen collapsed against the capstan. The flap of the sails like the wings of a giant seabird, the steady lapping of waves against the hull somewhere far below. Where are we? *Ver veyst?* Who knows. We could be anywhere, between one place and another in the long night, heading toward another horizon.

"Gevalt!" the watch calls out suddenly from the wheel, waking from his near stupor. "Galleon! At two o' the clock." There's sudden action from below deck. The dishevelled quartermaster strides onto the scene. A rigger, monkey-like, runs up the main to the crow's nest. Seamen scatter about deck and rigging. We've been waiting for this.

I'm quick aft to the poop deck, landing on the skinny rigging of the captain's shoulder. He's squinting through the spyglass. I totter, almost falling off as he grepses. His breath is like pickled rat.

"Spanish," he says.

The rigger runs down from the crow's nest.

"Spanish, Cap'n," the rigger says.

"For that, I could have saved him the trip," the captain says, shrugging.

Moishe.

My captain. He was born to cross the Ocean Sea. Which is what we used to call the Atlantic before we knew what it was. His young mother died soon after he'd sailed from her safe inner sea. Then he was thrown like dreck into the river. No basket. No pharaoh's daughter for him to sail to, unless she be Death's rat-skinned, sweet and toothless princess herself.

His father, the great boot and sword, the hot snorting breath of a pogrom.

But he was rescued, a barely moving, pink conch-flesh baby. A young Jewess beating the laundry on the rocks downstream fished him out of the water and brought the poor little farshtunkeneh back home—finally in a basket—where he was named Moshe. Moses. Moishe. He who is drawn from water. He who was circumcised soon after.

Years later—it's the beginning of another story—he named me Aharon. Aaron. Brother of Moses and he who spoke his words.

But I should keep my tales straight. I was telling you of a galleon.

"*Mach shnel!*" I called to no one in particular. "Hurry up!"

It would take us some hours to catch up to our prey. Already the bo'sun had the men hoisting and securing the sails, netting the wind like a dreamcatcher, the ocean gleaming past us as we ran toward the horizon. With any luck we'd take the Spanish by surprise, hit them in the beytsim before they were even fully awake, and gonifs that we were, have their gelt-laden chests aboard our ship before dawn.

And so we sailed.

In the east, a bruise in the sky, the horizon's bleeding lip. We approached the Spanish caravel. Putzes. They didn't see us coming, the farshikkered crew rum-addled, the shnorrer captain drooling beneath his poxy sheets.

From the orlop below deck, the powder monkeys began scrambling, that stilted scarecrow scuffle, careful not to spill powder. The gunners made ready with our eight pounders. We hove broadside to the galleon and Moishe, calling the carpenter surgeon to him, instructed the man to take his greatest drill and bore broad holes in our ship's sides, an invitation for the ocean to rush aboard and quicken our men's valour.

"Captain?" the surgeon inquired.

"With no ship to 'scape back to," Moishe said, "it'll put a spring in the shleppers' steps."

The surgeon did as he was ordered, and soon a cry of panic came from below to which the captain, ever laconic, replied, "Unless you're Yoshke—Jesus—and can run home on water, we've no choice but to take the ship with haste and commend the Spaniards directly to their maker."

Soon as we heaved ourselves close with grappling hooks, the crew roared aboard with their dirks and daggers, their cutlasses and bucklers, their marlinspikes, boarding axes, and flintlocks, and most of all, their complete lack of foresight.

From my perch in the modern world, I'd say—hapless if endearing shlemiels that most crews are—there was nary a frontal lobe between them, save the captain, the quartermaster, and the surgeon.

And my captain, though he'd lost his foreskin to the moyel at seven days, had yet enough foresight to go around. Before boarding, he'd taken a moment to tie limewater and saltpetre fuses into the long scrub-bush of his beard and hair. These he lit and let burn as he stood in the middle of the galleon, firing his flintlocks and shouting fearsome instructions to his men, while the smoke of hellfire itself rose about him.

It wasn't much of a battle. The Spanish, surprised and afraid, surrendered quickly. There was the customary disembowelling, cutting off of noses, hands, and of shmeckels. Some were taken prisoner to be sold as slaves. Men, not shmeckels. Some—those whose pleading was especially plangent—were left to their fate on the first island we sailed by.

"Why worry?" Moishe said to them. "*Abi gezunt*. As long as you have your health."

++

We were triumphant conquistadors and we'd taken the Spanish ship like a continent. For now, we had a new home unencumbered by its former residents, the shtik dreck Spanish. The men revelled in the plenty of their new found land. There was some freilich music from pipe and tabor. Bungholes from rum barrels were unstopped and drink flowed free. Food stores were opened and the crew fressed on the abundant supplies of salt pork.

Except for us Jews. Moishe might celebrate good fortune and the Lord's bounty with a nafkeh—a whore—or two, keneynehoreh, those times ashore, but by reason of custom rather than belief, he wouldn't nosh pork, nor would he, unless compelled by the situation, fight on the Shabbos.

The situation? More gold than usual.

And usual was often none.

We dined on hardtack and salt fish washed down with the Spanish captain's private store of Madeira. There was a small supply of nuts for me, Aaron, the captain's familiar. Under his breath, Moishe said the brocheh over wine and then for bread.

"Amen," I said, between bites. "Amen."

We ate and Moishe looked at the Spanish charts, a treasure as valuable as gelt for a mensch like him.

Pirates change coats as do snakes, snails, thieves, and Jews in these times of hate. They shed ships and gain others. They shed past lives, identities, names. But: even with a different skin, they still have the same bones. The North Star is always a yellow star.

So, you ask, how did this shell-less cheder-bocher—schoolboy—drawn from the waters of Ashkenaz find himself on the Spanish Main, the blade of his sword pressed against the quivering kishkas of Spanish captains? How did Columbus, the Inquisition, and the search for some books cause us to seek for life everlasting?

And, come to think of it, how did I, an African Grey, become his mishpocheh, his family, and he my perch, my shoulder in the world?

That, wherever I begin, is the story.

And you want to know?

Okay. So I'll tell.

Part One:
AIR

Books are emigrants, and belong in the place where they arrive.

MANUEL RIVAS (trans. JONATHAN DUNNE)

Part One:
AIR

Books are emigrants, and belong in
the place where they arrive.

MANUEL RIVAS (trans. JONATHAN DUNNE)

Chapter One

Moishe as a child. He told me stories. Some were true.

At fourteen, he left the shtetl near Vilnius for the sea. How? First one leg out the window then the other. Like anyone else. Before first light. Before the wailing of his mother.

A boychik with big ideas, his kop—his head—bigger than his body. He would travel beyond the scrawny map of himself, and beyond the shtetl. He'd travel the ocean. There were Jews—he'd heard stories—that were something. Not rag-and-bones shmatte-men like his father, Chaim, always following the dreck of their nag around the same small world. Doctors. Court astronomers. Spanish lords. Tax farmers. Learned men of the world. The mapmakers of Majorca. They were Jews. Rich and powerful, they were respected by everyone. They could read the sky. They knew what was on the horizon and what was over the horizon. Jews had trickled through the cracks of the world and had rained upon the lands.

He'd travel the globe. He'd travel to the unknown edges of the maps, to where the lost tribes had built their golden cities, where they knew the secrets of the waters and of the sky.

And nu, perhaps along the way there might be a zaftik maideleh or two, or his true love, who knew secrets also.

So this Moishe put the cartographer before the horse and left.

Luftmensch, they say. Someone who lives on air, someone whose head floats in the clouds of a sky whose only use is to make the sea blue.

The world is wide because the ocean is wide. So, nu, he'd had his Bar Mitzvah, why shouldn't the boychik sail west on a merchant ship, some kind of cabin boy, learning not to be sick with the waves? A one-way Odyssey away from home, his mother weaving only tears.

And where had he heard the stories? On the shmatte cart, making the rounds with his father. The sun rising, they travelled from home. They didn't fall off the edge of their world, they circled around it, until by nightfall they were home again. Moishe's old father, the bent and childless man who had taken in the drownedling, spoke to him of the great world that they shared. Moishe's father, grey beard, wide black hat, stooped back. The world, he said, was a book. A great scroll. Like the Torah, when it ended, it began again.

Everything began again. Each week with its Shabbos of silver candlesticks and braided challah. Each year with its seasons, festivals, Torah readings. Child, father, child. It was a Moebius strip. At the end of the story, the story begins again and so we live forever, his father said. His father was a mensch. His mother also. Good people. But though they spoke of it, they never tried to find out "and then what happened?" They knew. Second verse same as the first, a little bit more oysgemutshet worn out, a little bit worse.

Before he climbed out the window, Moishe left a letter for his parents.

If the world is a book, I must read it all.

He had packed only his few clothes, some food, a knife, a book he had often examined when alone, and two silver coins that he took from where his mother had hidden them behind a stone of the hearth. He sewed these into the waist of his pants.

He had come across the book by accident, this book that had a beginning and an end. Playing at a game of catch-and-wrestle with his friend Pinchas, Moishe had slid under his parents' bed and pushed himself against the wall where he hoped he would be invisible behind the curtain of the embroidered bedspread. Breathing hard, attempting to remain quiet and undetected, Moishe felt its shape beneath his hip. When he was eventually discovered—after he'd deliberately released a prodigious and satisfying greps, a gaseous shofar-call alerting his friend to his location—he left whatever-it-was beneath the bed to be disinterred and examined later. He knew it was somehow important and secret, so better to wait until he was alone and his mother out at the mikveh.

When he unwrapped the old tallis—a prayer shawl—that surrounded it, Moishe was surprised to discover a book. An ancient book. Grainy brown leather with faded gold lettering and pages the colour of an old man's hands. The script looked like Hebrew but it was the language of some parallel world, gibberish or the writing of a sorcerer.

Most intriguing were the strange drawings. Charts that seemed to diagram the architecture of heavenly palaces or the dance steps of ten-footed angels. Mysterious arrays of letters, the unspeakable and obsidian incantations of demons. And, most captivating of all, what appeared to be maps of the parallel world itself, filled with ring upon ring of concentric circles, rippling out from the beginning of creation and the centre of everything, as if one fine morning God had cannon-balled down from everywhere and nowhere and into the exact middle of the primordial sea.

But perhaps, Moishe wondered, these maps represented the actual earth, the alef-beys of cryptic markings, boats floating upon the waves of a vast ocean, searching for the edges of hidden knowledge.

It was as if Adam and his wife, Eve, had found a map instead of an apple, there in the centre of the garden. Instead of good and evil, they had discovered a map of Eden, the geography, the secrets, the true limits of Paradise and the Paradise that lies beyond.

Maybe that is why his father kept this book hidden where no one— not the rabbis or the shammes or the other men—could find it.

So Moishe took the book and left.

He followed the wide road to the market town of Kaunas and from there to the seaport of Memel. The sea was the widest road. He would follow it, a bottle looking for a message and new shores. Great ships filled the harbour, men crawling over them like flies on a shipment of modern-day pants or—*abi gezunt*—sailors on a shiksa. Decks were swabbed, rigging secured, barrels and chests heaved along docks and over gangplanks. Men with fruit-leather faces and pigtails close-talked with great weaselly machers in greasy coats, furtively scanning the docks for other great weaselly machers in greasy coats as they exchanged shadows for shine. Broken-toothed taverns lined the wharves, and farmishteh shikkers stumbled in and out, not knowing which direction was up, yet maintaining an unsteady relationship with down. Vendors held stickfuls of pretzels and bagels, stood beside barrels of brine or behind braziers roasting meat. There were other boys shlepping sacks containing all of their world that was worth carrying, seeking a shipboard life as a cabin boy or powder monkey. Several boys, stooped low with their sacks, entered one particular frowsy tavern tumbled between others and Moishe followed.

They formed a shlumpy pack before a table where a huge sailor held court, leaning back, pork-hock hands on his enormous thighs.

"Boys. Why should ye be cabin boys on my ship?" His bristly steak of a face shook as he spoke. "Tells me and maybe ye shall be one."

Ten boys, tall and short, smooth-faced or pocked, had gathered 'round.

"I'm a strong boy and honest you can be sure," said a tiny pisher with all the resolution his unbroken voice could muster. "I'll serve true and learn well," he said, standing tall.

"You're a hearty lad, I's can tell," the sailor said. "Spoke right up. Ye be welcome. Look to *The Sea's Pride* early tomorrow and ye'll sail with us."

"You," the sailor said to another. "D'ye have some teeth?" The boy grimaced, showing such teeth as he had. "My father went to sea, and this I aim also."

"Family," said the sailor with a grin wide as a plank. "We're all barnacles stuck to the rump of family. Tomorrow. *The Sea's Pride.*" He waved the boy away. "And you?" he pointed at Moishe. "Ye be a big lad."

Moishe wasn't a Jew.

Until he spoke.

"Vell," he said. "A *ponim yeh*. It seems."

As soon as he said it, Moishe realized how foreign his words sounded. Like having a mouthful of something you just realized was treyf, not kosher.

The big man paused.

Moishe was about to run.

"We never had a Chosen People on board. Ye do something nasty? Need to make a quick exodus from Egypt?"

"No ... I ..."

"You Jews are clever and I don't knows I trust ye. But there be no baby's blood on board and if you turns out not honest, we'll beat you till ye bleed like the baby Jesus hisself."

That night Moishe slept under a pile of sticks and broken bottles in the lee of a dung heap behind the tavern. At first light, he made his way to *The Sea's Pride* to leave the solid earth behind.

Chapter Two

To be new to the sea is to have your kishkas become the waves themselves. For days it was white water inside of Moishe, and a team of pugilists bailed out his insides with their convulsions. He'd be a new man, keneynehoreh, for nu, what could be left of the old one after such puking?

The Sea's Pride was sailing for Portugal, laden with cargo and a crew of the feckless, the brave, the poor, the drunk and the honourable both, as well as seasoned sailors preserved by salt, farmisht first-timers, and the master, purser, quartermaster, bo'sun, the captain and his parrot, an African Grey, he who has lived to tell the tale.

Moishe's commission was to serve the master, the big macher sailor who had hired him. In his cabin, the master had created his own private Versailles. Instead of a crew's shambles of piss buckets, hammocks and a salmagundi of sailors' chazerai, he had stored an abundance of liquors, sweetmeats, sugar, spices, pickles and other things for his accommodation in the voyage. He had also shlepped a considerable quantity of fine lace and linen, baize and woollen cloth. Not for him the usual shmatte slops of the everyman mariner. And besides, these things could buy him passage on the fleshy sloops of night women or be traded without tax or duty for gold or drink in port.

The master was good to Moishe and taught him much, though his was a pedagogy based on exhaustion and the definite possibility of a mighty zets to the ear. In addition to his work below deck, on deck, and climbing the rigging, working on booms, gaffs and spars, Moishe was a manservant to the master, serving his every wind-changeable whim.

But he asked and, if his work was done, was allowed to gaze at the maps and charts. Even as they took him away, they recalled his home and his longing to leave. His quick mind pleased the master.

"Ye shall be a sea artist good and true, right ye will. Your paint shall be the shiny stars in the sky above and your canvas the waves of the salt sea."

You think Moishe had any idea what such words meant? Gornisht! Nothing. Nada. Bupkes. Not that boychik. Until he met me, he didn't know his shvants from a sloop, his dick from a deck.

Was I good at language? Let's just say Polly's been a nautical boy for most of his long life. Since I was press-ganged out of Africa covered in pinfeathers, I've been parrot to a whole shipload of shoulders—Arab, Portuguese, English, Spanish, German, Polish—but none like Moishe.

And I taught the young bubbeleh something other than the mother tongue mamaloshen.

Hogshead. Rumfustian. Hardtack. Turtles.

Baldric. Blunderbuss. Muskatoon.

Cutthroat. Tankard. Stinkpot.

How d'ye do?

In nomine Patris, et Filii et Spiritus Sancti.

Yes sir, very good, sir.

Captain. Ocean. Syphilis.

Pirate.

He was a good mimic, that sheygets, though no parrot.

"Farshteyst? Do you understand?" I'd say.

"I oondershtand," he'd reply.

I took an immediate liking to him. His narrow shoulder, his earnest face, his kindness, his credulity.

Ech. A parrot is a one-person bird. I saw Moishe and the boychik was soon imprinted like words in indelible ink on the farkakteh page of my brain. Who decides such a thing? Like waking up the morning after shoreleave with an anchor tattooed across your hiney, it isn't, emes, exactly the result of choice. But I needed to be needed and this poor shnook needed me.

His pleasant demeanour and obvious intelligence attracted the attention not only of the master but of the captain, who took a shine to him, would take him under his wing, though not parrot-permanently as I did. He soon had him managing that part of the ship's stores that were for his private use. Guns, gold, dainties, drink and good meat. If the master's stores were Versailles, the captain's were the Vatican. Moishe kept them neat as a marlinspike, free from vermin, insects, and the salt scum that encrusted everything aboard ship.

"Yes sir, very good, sir," he'd say.

He knew on which side the holy toast is buttered. Farshteyst?

Moishe was kept busy running between the captain, the master, and his other responsibilities. The crew began, if not to trust him, then at least increasingly to regard him as one of them. Mostly they left him to his own devices, dedicated to appearing occupied while diligently avoiding their own chores. Occasionally they'd call for him to help haul on a halyard, or throw him a broom when they were swabbing the deck.

"Aye, lad, it's the only thing we sailors wash," they'd laugh.

He'd gather round for rum, stand as an equal in surly and superstitious congregation for Sunday prayer, and share the inscrutable mystery of galley stew, though he'd leave what he was able to identify as pork. He'd station himself nearby to listen to the long ramble of their narratives or mewl and warble soprano with their morbid tavern-hacking choir on the choruses of their songs, whether he understood them or not.

> I wish I was back in my native land
>> Heave away! Haul away!
> Full of pox, and fleas, and thieves, and sand
>> Heave away! Haul away, home.

Sometimes, as Moishe stood middle watch between dusk and dawn, insomniac sailors, their gigs adrift with drink, staggered onto deck and confided their tsuris woes to him. They were grown men, their brains and skins turned to leather by years out on the open sea, and Moishe was only a boy, his beard barely more than the nub of pinfeathers on his girly skin. Still, though he knew little but his native tongue, he knew the universal language of the nod, of the hmm.

And though each day his Yiddishkayt became increasingly submerged, thanks to a certain mensch of a parrot and his lexiconjury, the other cabin boys kept to themselves, not trusting Moishe and the farkakteh way he spoke. Association with him, they had surmised, would turn out to be a liability. They were, after all, ambitious young lads and engaged in professional networking with those both before and behind the mast, hoping to seek advancement in their chosen vocation.

Was Moishe happy to have finally left the firm land?

Is milk happy coming out of a mother's tsitskeh?

The sea, Moishe exulted. I *am finally at sea.*

Take a small, dark shtetl. Paint it with the swirling blue and foamy white of the moving waves, the endless blue and curly white of clouds and sky. Hold the edges like a sheet and toss it up and down like a child's game, the breezes flapping above you, the gust blowing the tang of salt across your face. Your house, the rag-and-bones path of flesh and blood, ever hopeful as it floats toward the beckoning horizon, free from the gravity of ground. To be at sea is to know vastness, to understand the flight of clouds, the reach of the stars and of invention. He was riding the expanding ripples of God's great cannonball. Moishe felt as if he were travelling in every direction at once, each direction away from home, toward story.

It didn't take long for the milk to sour.

It was an afternoon of little wind and the crew, having had their food and drink, were becalmed. Moishe shloffed in his hammock below deck, dreaming maps. I had flown up to a spar, my own kind of crow's nest. In the still air, his master's voice rose, gramophonic, clear to me, though he was speaking low to an old sea dog on the fo'c's'le. I flew down into his cabin and bit Moishe's ear.

"*Gey avek,*" he moaned. "Get out of here."

"Listen," I said. "Listen." He needed to hear what the master was saying.

"The wits and limbs of my little Hebrew are keen, aye they are," the master was saying. "I's reckon I be able to trade him for a few bright pennies on the wharf. That and his wages will add a little fat to my sack and me golden balls'll swab the deck as I walk."

The taller the prophet, the greater the fracture of the falling tablets.

"Gonif," Moishe cursed. He was ready to swab the deck with the master's beytsim all right, but he knew there was nothing he could do. He'd be swinging from a gibbet, or hacked into lobscouse if he tried anything.

So, nu, what do you do when everything's farkakte?

It didn't take long for Moishe to turn what was smashed into a dirty shiv and to spit on the niceties of moral details. After a man is condemned, how could it hurt if he steals?

Moishe took to helping himself to comestible advances on his pay and to availing himself of the captain's collection of maps. The maps were of distant places, of waters more like legends than actual destinations.

And a little gold, a drink or two of the captain's fine wine, a bit of meat serves to ease the pain and evens out what the world owes you. The captain was almost the same thing as the master—a horse cares little to whose cart it's tied; besides, the captain would never notice the filching. There was so much and he was casual with his riches, unlike the master who kept a close eye.

But, a few days later, the captain noticed.

"Curse the hot piss of the devil himself!" he shouted as he stormed from his quarters. "I'll have the skin of the man who did this for a sail."

Clearly he had a different conception of the equitable redistribution of resources, both savoury and liquid, for the wages of cabin boys.

He ordered the crew on deck. "No Christian sailor would steal from his own captain," he hissed, "for he fears the devil hereafter and the lash before. There shall be neither sup nor grog until the man who did this speaks of it to me, or his mate tells the tale."

Chapter Three

*I*t was then that Moishe learned a new word, but not from me.

The crew had little notion who was the gonif who'd been grazing on the captain's wares, but when the afternoon's rations were withheld they went sleuthing for the lost luxuries. Mostly the interrogation was accomplished by the fist, though there was some cross-examination effected by the knee. The crew searched each other's measly lockers and bestowed smart zetses and slaps upon each other's chins. Moishe searched also, or did his best to appear engaged in time-sensitive tasks of critical importance.

But soon the cabin boys began considering Moishe's hobbled and palsied recitation of newly acquired words. Un-Christian hoodoo incantations and organs-on-the-outside spells, they said. The Bible turned backwards. Harelipped prayers that led clubfooted only to sacrilege, damnation, and punishment both eternal and maritime. Naturally they were keen to avoid a messy tryst between their freckled backs and the captain's daughter, and so little time passed before they attributed the theft to Moishe. Their attribution was, of course, perfectly sound, though they had not a snail's leg of evidence on which to base their accusation. What was evidence to them? Bupkes. So, nu, they should wait two hundred years for all good sailors to be apprised of the Enlightenment, the scientific method?

"Heretic," they called him, and the captain, betrayed by this strange boy whom he'd planned to help, invoked the Inquisition.

The Inquisition. That Swiss Army–knife trump card of a final solution.

You're only the same until you're different.

Moishe's spice-rich accent. His un-Christian curses. His porkless-ness. Not that it had been his intention to assume a role as anything but Jew.

Differently Christianed. Jesusly challenged.

"You, my greedy-fingered lad, will burn at the stake the day we arrive in port. And then we'll offer your ashes the opportunity to repent." The captain's eyes like two fires, condemning him to hell.

When the going gets tough, the goyim get tough, too.

There was no escape. In the cold sea it would be water instead of fire that would steal the breath of life from his mortal body. He pled with the captain to spare him, wailing and protesting his youth.

"Common thievery, and from the captain, no less. The crew has spoken of your ungodly babbling, your pagan psalms. You have recited our Gospel with a forked and goat-footed tongue. You gather with us to pray yet you'll not eat pork. This is a Christian ship and there shall be no heresy. If Jew you ever were, your Hebrew soul was flayed to dust by demons, and now no spirit but the devil takes residence in your bones," the captain said.

Religion a trump card in a game where the captain is king.

"What shall I do?" Moishe wailed later as he lay in his bunk.

"The master," I said. "Remember the sagging sack he would fill with gold in exchange for you? You are an investment. Men protect their investments as if they were the twin baby moles of their own tender between-the-leg sack."

Next watch, with both broken voice and tongue, Moishe begged the master to intervene.

The master weighed the matter on the scales of his own greed, then agreed to speak to the captain.

Chapter Four

The captain was in his cabin at table before a silver plate of meat. "Captain," the master purred. "My captain, I's thinking, this boy's trip should not yet be done. Let us steady his keel, weather his daring by our own hand on our own grim vessel. I'd wager that the prize you seek can be won with but a few drops of red, and then"—the master paused at this point to grin conspiratorially—"at the nearest port, we can sell him, as he were . . . off the rack. What says you, sir?"

The captain, reaching deep into his sea chest of compassion and jurisprudence, replied, "Torture, my good man. It's as effective as truth serum. What's flayed onto the back speaks more plain and true than lines found in the hand."

He would have Moishe stripped, the better to see the naked shmeckel of his immortal soul. Then he'd let the cat out of the red bag that hung from the impressive manhood of the mainmast. He would flog the boy—who was, naturally, free at any time to present a cogent refutation of the accusations against him—until he bled like an innocent saint or a pestilent piss-veined devil. Certainly, the lash spilled stories from the accused, but those who first confessed would still be flogged so their tales, tanned into their backs, became incorruptible and permanent as leather.

They waited until dawn appeared blood red on the new sky of the next day. The morality play of punishment made more acute by a vivid setting. The crew gathered, the other cabin boys making box seats of barrels for a close view. Moishe's clothes were rent to rags on the deck, then he was bound to the mast.

"Sir," he began to wail. "Very good, sir." He had command of few words that they'd understand, and most of those learned from his heymishe parrot.

The bo'sun, a desiccated and diminutive mamzer with rings in his twisted, labial ears, lifted the cat and brought it down hard on Moishe's back. A crack as of lightning splitting a great tree. A moment only and then rivers of blood seeped from the raised banks of the boy's flesh.

"Hogshead," Moishe cried, bursting open his meagre word horde in desperation. "Rumfustian."

The bo'sun struck again.

"*In nomine Patris, et Filii et Spiritus Sancti*," Moishe wailed.

At this the bo'sun paused. Who could flog man or boy who was saying prayers? And in Latin.

At least what man who feared offending the captain? The bo'sun would have flogged Jesus himself since it gave opportunity to sear flesh with the lash and draw a rich red city map of fresh blood on the mortal canvas of his Lord's bare back.

"He knows his Mass, Cap'n," he said. "What should I do?"

"We've drawn the Christian out," the captain said. "It's like tenderizing meat. Perhaps we have saved the boy."

No one, except for the master, knew what they'd saved the boy for. He'd be sold soon as they anchored.

They untied Moishe, who could hardly stand, though he'd received thirty-seven lashes less than Moses' law, the usual prescription. Salt water was poured from a waiting bucket to stave off infection. He could walk no more than an eel and so, frogmarched below deck, he was deposited wet and sloppy into his hammock.

Sleep. Silence save for a few moans.

Nightfall.

Moishe woke and covered himself with an abundant and foamy tide of his own puke.

Chapter Five

By the next morning, the dawn sun was but a pallid cue ball beside the raging red rising on Moishe's back.

"Get your dog's body out of bed, boy," the master shouted. "Unless you seek another lashing?"

Moishe staggered to his feet. Soon he was struggling to lug an enormous piss bucket up a ladder, stale urine sloshing over his cross-hatched flesh.

"Over the larboard side, you thieving piss monkey," the master said. "Into the wind."

There were no chains binding him. The ship was restriction enough. If he jumped overboard, the waves would snatch him in their wet paws, Moishe their plaything while it pleased them. Then—*mazel tov!*— he would be pulled down into the lair of blind fish and luminescent cucumbers, where the contents of his lungs would find their way to the surface while he died.

And like most sailors, he couldn't swim.

Did the captain provide him vittles for a sultan's nosh? Feh. He was fed only enough to keep the bones around his marrow. Who needs such decoration as that provided by the ostentatious hoo-hah of flesh and blood?

One doesn't re-shoe a horse that is to be glue.

The bucket emptied, he collapsed on the deck. He was roused, made to return down the ladder, then haul up another bucket of farshtunkeneh bladder-rum squeezed from the syphilitic shmeckels of his bunkmates.

"Lad, the spume of the sea be cruel, but spurn the sailor's code and we be crueller."

All morning Moishe was compelled to toil. By afternoon he collapsed on the deck and fried like a side of Yiddish bacon under the griddling sun.

The dog's watch bells rang.

As if conjured from the silken sleeve of the duplicitous ocean, three ships appeared close behind, moving quickly. They flew the red St. George's cross.

A shout from the crow's nest. "Caravels. At seven o' the clock."

The master and the captain appeared on deck.

"English, I's reckon," the mate drawled. "They fly the Genoese ensign and pay the doge for the privilege."

"Unless in truth they hail from Genoa," the captain said.

"Then curse their devilled privates fo' it's like then they be privateers." All able-bodied seamen—and Moishe, the Cain-bodied—were called to prepare. The ship's few four-pounders were rolled by the gunners into position. The powder was readied in the orlop. The crew made busy adjusting sails and preparing smaller arms.

Before long, the caravels were arrayed broadside and close. Their guns fired into rigging and across decks.

Gevalt. They were Genoese. It wasn't to be a bucolic romp with falsely dressed sheep. We'd soon be muttoned and shtupped with holes.

I flew to up to the foremast spar, hoping to get above the meshugas like an eagle above a storm.

But the thunder and flash soon rose to surround me. I looked down on a sea-borne village on fire, seeing nothing but the flicker of flame amidst billows of black smoke, the booming blasts of the guns.

Shouting. Movement. Fire. The boys running with powder. Men loading muskets. Cannons filled with shot and powder. A call of "clear," then the lit fuse and the frame-shaking blast. The crack as the cannonballs splintered both ship and man.

Screaming. Chaos. Explosion.

Repeat.

I could not find Moishe in the tumult.

A Genoese ship rammed against us.

Gezunterhayt. Let us both die in good health. See if I care.

A massive crack and the foremast below me was rampiked as if by lightning. A forest fire on the ocean. The sails were aflame. My goose—whatever part of a parrot that is—was soon to be cooked.

I'd not be poultry nor part of any recipe.

Death waits for no man, and neither would I.

I called, "*Gey kakn afn yam*"—"go shit on the ocean," the traditional curse of the irate at sea—and then took to the air.

Here's hoping we were near shore.

Chapter Six

This is what I know of seagulls: It is not "where there's a will there's a way," but rather "where one finds seagulls one finds shore."

Exhaustion had taken flight from my wings, but as I struggled on I saw below me a severed piece of ship's plank, floating in the waves. I fell from the sky and sought respite and safe harbour, a smoke-damaged surfer, riding in to the sand.

It was night.

I hoped for seagulls.

⁑

Seagulls.

My idiot brothers. Squawking shlemiels farshraying the sky. The Keystone Kops of the air. If only they were silent.

They can no more think than a brick could weave water into rope.

A story. Once there was a meshugener who was so brainless he thought he needed a new brain. On the way to the market he met a merchant who offered him the choice of three bird brains he had for sale. "It's true that they're not very big, but that's good: they're very portable, and not too heavy so they won't strain the neck," he said.

"Great," said the brainless one. "How much?"

"Five kopecs, fifty kopecs, and five hundred kopecs."

"They all look the same," the meshugener said. "Why such different prices?"

"The first is the brain of a nightingale. Good singer, but not too smart. The second belonged to a parrot. Very intelligent, spoke six languages."

"And the last?"

"A seagull's. The most expensive."

"I didn't know that seagulls were that clever."

"They're not. The brain's never been used."

+-+-

By morning there were seagulls.

The scene: me, a farmisht flotilla of broken wood, seagulls kvetching moronically above me, and a bedraggled youth, draped like seaweed across the remains of half a barrel.

Moishe.

He'd survived, keneynehoreh.

Good thing I'd been there for him.

But as far as I could determine, given the uncooperative chawing of the waves, the youthful jetsam beside me was tall, red-haired, and strong. Compared to him, Moishe was short, svelte as prayerbook paper, and with hair black and curly as the broadloom that had—in honour of his Bar Mitzvah—sprouted above his shvants.

The buoyant roytkop was clutching a bundle of rolled papers as if they were the things keeping him afloat and not the barrel.

We were churned by the sea, but always the tide pulled us as certainly as lust or regret. It concluded our passage by beaching us without comment or ceremony but tossing us blanched and exhausted on the soft sand. The red-haired sheygets had collapsed with half of himself still in the sea. He'd crawled just enough to ensure his rolled charts were beyond the dissolute criticism of the lapping waves.

I flew low and landed on a sodden seaweed-veiled timber. Around me, the sand was stippled with human, avian, and nautical debris.

The distinction was not entirely clear.

Down the beach, in the shallows before shore, an oysgedarteh skinny beluga of a boy was embracing two fractured flagons. He washed up and down with each foaming wave. A wrinkled white shmeckel between two broken beytsim.

The pekeleh? It was Moishe.

I hadn't realized how worried bazorgt I'd been. He'd become a barnacle stuck to where it chaffed.

I flew over. "So, nu, vos macht a Yid? Come here often?"

He was motionless.

So I spoke to the sky. "O Adonai! Creator of the Universe, thank you for saving this boychik's life. But I've just one complaint: he had a hat! How could you forget his hat?"

"I had no hat," Moishe murmured.

It was good he could speak. Hat or no hat, he was alive.

The red-haired man pulled himself to his knees. He held the rolled parchment to his chest and crawled further up the beach. When he noticed Moishe roiling in the shallow water, he staggered to his feet and approached. "Stand, sailor," he said in Spanish. "With these maps I have made, I shall show you marvels."

"He's half-drowned, like a noodle in soup. And he speaks as much Spanish," I said.

He looked at me, incredulously.

"What?" I said. "Is it my accent?"

He did what people do when they encounter something entirely alien. They pretend there's nothing out of the ordinary.

So I spoke intelligible Spanish. Of course: this Polly is something of a polyglot.

As a parrot, I'm a man of the world.

The water continued to wash up on Moishe. "In any case, I could use some help hauling him," I told the mapmaker. "Look. No hands."

He stumbled up the beach and secured his maps beneath a knot-holed plank. He grabbed Moishe under the armpits and hauled him to safety on the short grass far above the tide line, a sack of wet, semi-conscious Jew beside some damp charts—his father would be so proud.

"Thanks," I said to the mapmaker. "Business or pleasure: which brings you to the beach?"

I could tell that he was still somewhat fartumelt, a bit shore-shocked, though he spoke with a stiff formality, like jello served on a silver plate.

"A letter of marque from the Doge of Genoa made us privateers. We sought the sweet cargo of the Alboran Sea. Our three ships came upon a vessel..."

"My vessel," I said.

"My father is a weaver and I began travelling to sell his wares, and to study maps and winds. But I am paid better than weaver's wages to sail, and sometimes to board merchant ships. I am sorry for your loss. It is, unfortunately, as my father says: 'Quien no sabe de mar, no sabe de mal— He who knows nothing of the sea, knows nothing of suffering.'"

Who was this haughty, geshvollener young man, with his father's Ladino sayings and Ashkenazi "I-am-sorry-for-your-loss" consolations?

He continued with his silver patter.

"And as for myself, though I be a weaver's son, my warp and woof are the waves. My home is nowhere, but my heart is everywhere. Soon I shall be an admiral as indeed another in my family has been. And before I die, I intend to sail both the charted and uncharted places of this world. The isles wait for me. Marvels, also."

Moishe groaned and then rolled over. "Vi heystu?" he moaned.

"What does he say?" the weaver's son asked.

"Who are you?"

"My name," he replied with a flourish of self-importance, "is Christoval Colon."

I translated the name for Moishe. "Christopher Columbus."

"I'm supposed to know him?" Moishe asked, and put his head back onto the green grass and passed out.

Part Two:
FIRE

my flesh burns with history

QWO-LI DRISKILL

Part Two:
FIRE

my flesh burns with history

—QWO-LI DRISKILL

Chapter One

$\mathcal{C}$olumbus stood over Moishe's inert body. "It is because of me that he has arrived here," he said. "He should thank me for his good fortune."

"If he knew he was anywhere," I said, "my master would indeed be grateful to be there."

"Lisbon is a place of bounteous opportunity," Columbus continued. "I myself am bound for the studio of Bartholomeo, my brother, whose maps grace the courts of popes and philosophers, the chambers of captains and kings."

One could do worse than follow the route of one who makes maps. Besides, these several months past Moishe had sought to chart a course from shtetl cart to court cartographer.

We agreed that we would set out together, the three of us, once Moishe had regained himself.

✛✛

The pickling in the ocean had changed Moishe.

Azoy bald—so soon?

Ay, it was a kind of briny baptism.

"From now on, like a knife in a boot, I'm keeping my Jewishness hidden," he said. "It's safer if no one knows. So, nu, I need a new name."

"Miguel," I said. "It's Spanish and Portuguese. But you need a last name too. You can't be Miguel Ben Chaim."

"So what should I be?"

"Rich. But in the meantime, you could try Levante. It means 'where the sun rises': the east."

Moishe tried it out. "Miguel Levante. Yes. I could be him," he said.

It was late in the morning when we began walking the road to Lisbon. Or rather, they walked and I rode on my now customary shoulder.

The sun was a gold piece against the smooth ocean of sky. The three of us, having nothing, carried nothing, save Columbus's charts and Moishe's book, concealed in a shouldersack worn under the clothes like a prayer shawl. My tatterdemalion companions appeared washed up, dredged like seaweed from the bottom of the sea. I, adorned in my usual crepuscular feathers, appeared no different than if I were a parrot king dressed for his coronation. By noon we needed a nosh, so stopped at a farmhouse to beg some bread.

The farmer eyed us suspiciously.

Moishe was dark, curly haired, but as long as he did not speak he was no more Jew than Portuguese. His head was uncovered—ach, he had no hat, remember?—and his clothes were faithless rags. Columbus was bedraggled, yet his supercilious bearing impressed the farmer and so he believed our story. "Just this morning, we were beaten and robbed on our way to an audience with the King."

"And he," I said, indicating Moishe with a nod of my beak, "lost his hat."

The farmer brought bread, grapes and wine to the table. Miguel, under his breath, made the brocheh for both bread and drink. Soon, his inner Moishe would learn to sound like someone else.

Who better than a parrot to teach such a thing?

Chapter Two

A cool night breeze. We sat outside the farmer's cottage with Columbus and a flagon of the farmer's wine. The self-actualized liberators of libation, we'd helped ourselves, for as Rabbi Hillel said, "If I am not for myself, who will be for me?" The ancient sage clearly knew a thing or two about schnapps.

Moishe set a bowl of wine on the sandy ground. I drank.

"They say that I shall be nothing but viceroy of a continent of water, an admiral of seaweed and fishes only, but I have studied the maps. I have made the calculations." Columbus spoke as if he could guarantee a thing by speaking boldly.

He explained his plan to sail west across the Ocean Sea to Cathay, Cipangu, and the lands of the Great Khan.

"I have studied the ancients. Their books mark out the miles—the Ocean Sea is not so large as we imagine. If we approach from the west, we do not need to crawl like Polo over the hackles of the world."

Columbus spoke of Marco Polo's account of his travels. A book, written while Polo was imprisoned, had been later chained to the Rialto Bridge in Venice so all could read its marvels.

"I will spend some years attaining complete mastery of the ways of the tides and winds. I will sail to Thule, to Galway, and south to the new territories of Africa. And then I shall seek a king who will provide me ships and the mariners to sail them, and who shall grant me governance of the new lands that I shall discover on my great voyage."

Of course he would stand astride the world. With such beytsim, he could bring his legs together?

"What of the dragons and the monstrous whirlpools which hunger for your ship?" Moishe said.

"Some also believe the woods filled with witches, ghosts and demons, but these are only shadows or squirrels made infernal by fear." Columbus emptied his mug of wine with a flourish and sleeved his mouth. "A traveller with a good stick can easily manage these travails."

He stood up, the better to continue his enthusiastic oration to the crowd of boy and parrot.

"Not long ago, they thought a book could only be made through the crablike crawling of the human hand, but Gutenberg showed us a new route was possible. Soon they will take their moveable type and print books with my name in them. Histories and new maps of the world with 'Columbus' written over the western seas."

Then this lord of the new ocean listed toward the barn where he would collapse beside pigs and chickens.

"Do you think that what he says could be true—that the world is a snake with its tail in its own mouth?" Moishe asked. "Could he sail to the Indies?"

"I'm sure by now that that balmelocheh has the chickens ready to wager their eggs on it. But *ver veyst?* Who knows? Here am I, an African Grey, speaking to a boy, five thousand miles from where I was born. Could my mother have dreamt this when I was hatched from the egg?"

Later, as he staggered toward sleep, Moishe took his father's book from its hiding place beneath a bundle of rags. Columbus's words reminded him of its circular maps. But, unwrapping the cloth that protected it, he discovered that the book, waterlogged when he was wrecked off the coast, had dried into a paper brick and would not open.

Perhaps all it needed was another good dunking. The hair of the dog that fressed upon it.

Early morning. The sun squinting bloodshot over the droop-eyed horizon.

An early exodus along the coast road. We were to work for the farmer in exchange for food and lodging, but planned to be far away by the time he came looking for us. You're no one's worm if you're earlier than the early bird.

The two of them held their heads and shielded their eyes against the daylight and the effects of wine. I sat on Moishe's shoulder and closed my eyes.

A worn path through the rolling hills, the beaches and the steady breaking of the waves far below. We walked between dusty boulders and stunted trees, the only sounds the shuffle of their feet and the occasional bird. Then low murmuring, but, half asleep, I imagined it nothing but the rumble of Moishe's belly.

We continued over a small rise and along a curving cliffside road.

"I was thinking..." Moishe began.

But then the unmistakeable scrape of a blade drawn from its scabbard. Three men jack-in-the-boxed from behind the rocks. A thin youth soon had a dagger across Columbus's chicken neck. The older and thicker two stood in front of us. All were wrapped in rags.

"Money," the one to the left said darkly. An orator, his demands were expressed with near-classical economy.

Moishe had nothing but the book tucked into his shoulderbag and one remaining silver piece sewn into his waistband, the other having being lost in the escape from the burning ship.

I had nothing but my keen wits, my good looks, and my treasure trove of many words.

Columbus, of course, had untold riches.

Just not yet.

I have not found ruffians to be at ease with the concept of IOUs.

It was not long before Columbus was on the ground, the knife ready to carve him into brisket.

One of the shtarkers held Moishe while the orator punched him in the kishkas, hoping, one assumes, to have him puke money.

I took this moment to attempt an old trick. A parrot, desirous of pecking-order dominance, doesn't futz around with pecking. He stretches his wings wide and swoops clawfirst and topples the rival parrot.

The orator's head, perched on his shoulders, would be the rival parrot.

I flew up and began my swoop.

If his head didn't fall off, at least I'd make a nice borscht of his face.

"Avast!" the skinny thief warned and the thick thug let go of Moishe. Moishe slid the book from beneath his shirt and gave the pugilating orator a mighty *klop* on the head. It did not fall off, for it was attached like a dingleberry to the thick tuft of his neck, but the orator collapsed.

Then Moishe heaved the book over the cliff. "Money," he yelled. The two standing gonifs, taking the bait, ran after the book as it fell toward the sea. I rerouted my attack and hit the skinny thief in the face. Moishe rushed forward and grabbed the knife. Columbus lay still on the ground like an uninhabited island awaiting discovery.

Moishe had boyhood experience playing catch-and-wrestle. And this time he had a knife. The kosher way to slaughter an animal is to slit its throat and let the blood run out. Moishe was the shochet and he had the skinny one ready to be turned to deli meat.

"Money," Moishe said again, this time into the ear of the skinny youth, and I noted that his pronunciation was rapidly improving. Fear had already drained the blood from the youth's face. He reached into his pocket and produced a small sack. We heard the muffled chinking of money.

"Money," Moishe repeated with an ironic smile, tucking away the sack with his free hand. "If you want a job done right, you have to do it yourself," he said, demonstrating casual mastery of the idiom.

By this time Columbus was on his feet. Moishe's blade was still at the youth's throat. Columbus put his face, with its sea blue eyes, close to the youth's. "Go," he said.

The single syllable was sufficient. Moishe removed the knife and the youth fled back along the road like a bullet trying to return to its gun.

Columbus said one more syllable, this time to Moishe.

"Thanks."

Columbus owned little. Evidently, he had to be frugal, saving even his gratitude as we had saved his life.

Chapter Three

*M*oishe was learning of the world outside the shtetl: it was the fifteenth century. Bandits were expected roadside attractions. There were no signs that said, "Last mugging for twenty miles," but *du farshteyst*, you get the idea. You couldn't trust the eyes in the back of your head not to wink coquettishly at misfortune, once in awhile.

We resumed walking.

Moishe now had a chance to look back and be scared in retrospect at the rush of events. And though it had been unreadable, the worlds in its maps unreachable, Moishe mourned the loss of his father's book. It had been a tangible memory, a written familiar from his past.

Ach, but he still had me. I might sometimes be a tosser, but I was untossable. I was a flying language guide for travellers, and as we plodded on, I continued to teach. I imagined myself like the chirping feygeleh that landed on Pope Gregory's shoulder and whispered Gregorian chants in his infallible, pontifical ear.

Who knew what words they would use to offer this Polly a cracker, or a bite of a pretty zaftik morsel? But, nu, it'd certainly be in a language meant for Miguel and not Moishe.

Miguel would need to be ready.

Columbus spoke little. The rudderless coracle of his thoughts bobbed elsewhere. Except when Moishe inquired of his brother's charthouse.

"My good brother Bartholemeo is a writer and merchant of charts and texts. There are many learned men from Granada to Galicia, from Portugal to the Pyrenees who learn who and where they are by purchasing his finely drawn maps and his well-bound books."

When the subject was himself or his brother, Columbus did not use one word when two were possible.

Like some parrots, he was—ech—his own echo.

Moishe listened with visible wonder as Columbus roiled on about the beauty and scholarship of his brother's wares. He spoke of currents, shorelines, Ptolemy and Africa. Of carmine-coloured writing and even of blue. Of inks created of vitriol and black amber, of sugar, the lees of wine, fish-glue, and isinglass, this last being especially appropriate for nautical charts, made as it was from the dried swim bladders of fish.

"My father's book," Moishe began enthusiastically, "filled with strange, unreadable writing in beautiful script. Diagrams and drawings of unknown places. The world made larger because drawn on a page."

"What was this book?"

"I don't know. I couldn't read it though its letters were Hebrew . . . I mean of course I couldn't read it . . ." Moishe stammered, realizing he had said too much.

"A book of the Jews?" Columbus asked.

Moishe had inadvertently revealed his true background. He quickly began to cover it in false dress.

"My father could not have known what it was. He had meagre learning and read little. He had faith in the teachings of the Church. He was no heretic . . . he prayed frequently and crossed himself often . . ."

"I myself am much interested in the ancient holy books," Columbus said. "The First Testament of the Jews. The Books of Ezra, Joshua . . ." Then he muttered, as if looking toward the distant Holy Land itself, "God willing, Jerusalem will soon be wrested from the infidels and returned . . ."

He became lost along the vague trails of imagination and desire.

He hadn't noticed anything Jewish out of the Christian ordinary. Nu, he saw no light but his own shadow.

"But of course," he said, suddenly returning, "I also read navigation, history and cosmology. Ancient writings from Ptolemy to Pliny, the travels of Sir John Mandeville and Marco Polo. And the works of Church Fathers from Cardinal d'Ailly's *Imago Mundi* to Pope Pius II's *Historia Rerum Ubique Gestarum*.

"And yet there are many books that I still wish to read. Once, I heard my brother speak of a book of the Jews, written in ancient Aramaic; perhaps your father's was, also. It tells of a fountain that flows from a crack in the edge of the world, a fissure between earth and sky. Its elemental waters bring life eternal. I would travel and drink there, carry away its waters more valued than gold."

A Fountain of Youth, Columbus? That emes was a wet dream. Time is the only river and it makes you grow old. Or at least, that's what I thought then. Ach, what did it matter, we now needed water from a more quotidian puddle, for the sun demonstrated an interest in hard-boiling our pates, and so, when we observed a small cluster of buildings at a crossroads a mile away, we quickened our step. We expected to discover an inn, both sustenance and shade. With some gelt from Moishe's newly acquired money sack, there would soon be plates of meat and cups of wine before us. Me, I was chaleshing for fruit, seeds, and an ocean of fresh water.

Several grey mules, a few bent horses, and one impressive black stallion were tied up outside and tended to by a scrawny boy. The inn was called Dom Venéreo, and it stooped like an old nag, leaning oysgeshpiltedly toward the glue pot. A door sagged open to a dark place of pockmarked tables and wine. An assortment of men with their heads in their hands, faces sombre and brooding. And a tall, handsome man with a red feather in his impressive hat. He was undoubtedly the stallion owner.

We set our course for a table below a shelf cluttered with seashells and wooden mugs. Before our tucheses made landfall, Columbus had already called for food and drink from the barmaid who, it seemed, had been sewn together some time ago from old leather and duck meat.

He left us at the table while he went to speak with the man and his ostentatious hat.

A red feather. Someone I knew?

The barmaid arrived with a wooden plate of amorphous stew, a jug filled with wine, and some bread. Moishe tore some breadcrust for me and held a mug of wine to my beak. Columbus was fathoms deep in words with the man when he motioned to Moishe to bring some money. Moishe fished out two small silver pieces and went to the table.

Moishe had saved Columbus's life. He had mined the thief's money sack from its youthful source. Yet, somehow, Columbus assumed the role of captain. As if it were as natural as his haughty self-absorption and blinkless faith in himself. As if he had not been born wet and slippery, but was from some other place. A place where the worth and fame of his future deeds were assured.

Moishe put the money on the table and Columbus pushed the coins toward the man. A game of checkerless checkers. The man promptly lifted the silver and stowed it in a pocket of his embroidered waistcoat with a small twitch of a smile.

We were to ride two mules to Lisbon.

Chapter Four

The scrawny boy stood smartly at attention as Red Feather strode from the inn door, his boots billowing small clouds of dust with each imperious step. A few curt orders and the boy began untying the mules.

Columbus, with the air of a grand knight setting out on a grail quest, took the reins and mounted the mule as if it were a great stallion.

Moishe climbed aboard his mule as if clambering out a window. He had no experience with great horses, but his father's swayback carthorse was like an old and simple uncle to him and Moishe had taken joyrides about the yard on its rickety back.

We set out along the road to Lisbon. Moishe, the mule and I—mule surmounted by youth surmounted by parrot—resembling the fabled Musicians of Bremen, that motley vertical parade-across-species.

By late afternoon, we saw the broad blue expanse of the Tagus River as it widened into a virtual inland sea before flowing into the ocean. I remembered a *fado marinheiro* sung by a sailor intoxicated with nostalgia and loss, a feeling the Portuguese call *saudade*. "My hair is getting white, but the Tagus is always young," he sang. And, ach, the sadness and wonder at witnessing a great river opening out into the sea. The current flowing purposefully forward, the always-young river suddenly lost in the endless, bankless vastness of the directionless sea, the stories of the lands that border the river diluted like so much salt.

Soon the lanky towers of the royal palace, the Alcáçova Castle, rose above the city.

Gotenyu, Moishe was gobsmacked. He'd never seen a city of such vastness.

Me, I'd travelled the sea from fort to raft and had seen much. Still, there is that excitement that builds at the approach of a city. The great hive buzzes with its citizens, the energizing mix of honey, work, romance, shtupping, horse dung and thieves.

The Tagus was filled with grand ships leaving, returning, bringing news of new regions of Africa, bringing gold, spices, textiles and slaves.

You know what they say about being a slave: it's a terrible job, but at least you have job security.

We entered the city proper, guiding our mules through streets filled with a chaos of traffic. Then Columbus stopped. He began explaining to Moishe how to find his brother's shop.

"You will travel elsewhere?" Moishe asked.

Columbus had a speech ready, in case history were listening.

"Convey my affectionate greetings and regrets to my brother. Though born a weaver's son, I would be a man of the greater world and, by Jesu, have been granted this chance. Today, I trade weft for wharf and warp for wave. The gentleman met in the Dom Venéreo Inn has a brother who requires mariners for Iceland and Africa. He who wishes to find his way through the labyrinth of the western seas must first learn the winds of the whale roads and the warm waters of Africa. We sail this same day and so you must present yourself before Bartolomeo with this message: you will help him with his maps in my stead. Perhaps together you will chart the new lands I will find."

And with that, Columbus turned down an alley and was gone.

We were marooned in the great ocean of the city with nothing but a mule and the empty net of Columbus's words.

A *shaynem dank dir in pupik*, as they say. Many thanks to your belly button. Thanks for nothing.

Perhaps not exactly nothing. Mapless, Moishe had travelled in search of maps and those who read them. From the narrow river of his birth, he would soon enter a larger sea. And, takeh, it's true: what was unmapped for Moishe was maps.

Maps did not lead one to navigate with the eyes only. Reading maps led to following them. Before long, you wanted to be aboard that tiny caravel inscribed on the goatskin sea, blown by the favourable winds of commerce and curiosity, looking with a miniscule telescope at the islands of ink and the monsters that swam about the vague shores beyond.

And the roots of mountains, friable with gold.

Whatever the path, maps led to mariners.

Columbus's brother, Bartolemeo Colon, lived and worked in a small building bordering on the Jewish quarter of Lisbon. A dun-coloured globe hung from a gibbet sticking out above the door.

A knock and then we were inside the dim room cluttered with books and charts both rolled and laid flat, piled on shelves, tables and the floor. A white-bearded, bent-backed ancient was stooped as if davening—praying—before a large map, dipping the dried-out hook of his nose into the ocean of parchment.

"Bartolemeo Colon?" Moishe asked, though surely this rebbe was more like the brother of Columbus's ancestors.

The *alter mensch* wheezed a sound between leaves and a handful of phlegm and a young man appeared from behind a tottering shelf. His clear blue eyes revealed him to be the true brother of Columbus and he took us to the small courtyard behind the building.

We sat at a small table and he poured wine from a clay jug.

We were not surprised to learn that Bartholomeo did not actually own the shop but was rather an apprentice to the old man, Angelino Dalorto, a much-celebrated cartographer in his day. We had suspected that Columbus's art consisted of embellishment, confidence and poetry in equal measure. All codpiece and no cod. All chop with no liver, Indians without India.

A pirate tale without pirates.

Yet.

And Bartholomeo was not surprised that his brother's path had veered to the sea, that he'd sent Moishe as his proxy.

"My ambitious brother. One day when he is famous, they will say he was a self-made man who loved his creator."

Chapter Five

We were a week there, amidst the books and charts. Moishe did what he was asked. Sweeping, lifting, carrying. Drawing water, not on maps but only from the well, though he was taught to decipher portolans and to box the compass from Tramontana to Maestro.

We accompanied Bartholomeo on business, learning something of the alleyways of both the city and the language, the mapmaker's world. The Jews of Lisbon were unlike any Jews that Moishe—Miguel—had seen. With their Moorish hats and bright flowing robes, they lived in their own quarter of the city. Through the Arco do Rosário was a new world: La Judería. Some were immensely wealthy, merchants and bankers living in grand big macher houses. Indeed some were mathematicians, physicians, cartographers, astronomers, or treasurers employed by the court.

What was familiar were the occasional snatches of Hebrew—prayers, oaths and chochma sayings—like flashes of colour from beneath slashed sleeves. But their Ladino language was an alluring and exotic spice, plangent and musical, russet red and nutmeg against the chopped liver and guttural blue breakers of Yiddish.

One Friday evening, Bartholemeo led Moishe into the shop. The old master and his older, more shrivelled twin were sitting in the unsteady light of the guttering Shabbos candles. The man waved for Moishe to sit down. His face was so abundantly cross-hatched with wrinkles, it appeared he had been shattered, the fragments only held together by a scaffolding of wispy beard. Still, there was a twinkling bemusement in his expression, and he spoke to Moishe in Yiddish.

"Bocher," he said. "You like it here?"

Moishe nodded.

"See? One doesn't forget the mamaloshen," the old reb said. "Not like the foreskin."

The rabbi made a scissors motion.

Moishe inhaled sharply.

"Sha. That's language you don't forget either. Now I know for certain you're a Yid."

"What made you suspect?"

"Words and how they're said are maps also. But *nisht gedayget*—don't worry—you're safe. You're a hindl, a chick, among chickens."

Miguel had become Moishe again.

"A hindl with a feygeleh—a bird—on his shoulder," the rebbe mused. "You're just the boychik for us. We have a bisl job for you. A delivery."

The mapmaker, sitting beside him, smiled wanly, though it wasn't clear if he knew what was being said.

The rebbe explained about the Inquisition. "It's like the old inquisition but worse," he said. Ferdinand and Isabella, rulers of the combined kingdoms of Castile-León and Aragon, had created a made-in-Spain solution including threatening to withdraw Spanish military support in the war against Turkey—they had received the Pope's blessing by way of a Papal Bull.

"Ach," the rebbe said. "It's still kosher to be a Jew in Spain, if you don't mind an occasional pogrom. Or to be accused of blood libel or witch-craft, whenever anything goes wrong. Or—as in Seville—you're ready for the foot-on-tuches invitation to leave your city and all you know."

Many had converted to Christianity. "But you'd better make sure there's smoke coming out the chimney on Shabbos, and on Friday, to eat a bisl fish. You want it to look like you've had a relapse? That's heresy. But," he said, "there's a cure for that. It's called death."

Those converted were called *conversos*: "New Christians." Some families had been Christian for over a hundred years, converting after a previous outbreak of pogroms and persecutions. They'd left their Jewishness behind like a distant and half-remembered homeland. Some were more recent graduates. At any moment, the Inquisition might ask you to produce a *Limpieza de sangre*—documentation of blood purity. It was how many discovered that they had a Jewish great-grandmother or grandfather. This was tantamount to discovering fatal traces of peanuts in your nut-free lunch.

After you've had a bite.

Some conversos were hidden Jews, Marranos, crypto-Jews, practising their faith in secret. The Jewishness that dare not speak its name. They lit Shabbos candles in cupboards, shared Passover meals in cellars, whispered blessings as they walked through doors. Studied the Talmud and davened from prayerbooks late in the night. Hebrew books, Jewish books were treyfeneh bicher: verboten.

"So, Migueleh," the reb said. "We want you to shlepp some books to the secret Jews in Seville. But no one can know. It would be fatal. Farshteyst? You understand?"

Moishe nodded.

"But you're not a Jew. You're a goyisher sailor from Lithuania. You were almost sold at port but you escaped."

No so far from the truth.

"Besides, what do they know from Ashkenaz?" the reb shrugged.

"You'll have a horse, something to nosh, a letter of introduction, and a small sword," the mapmaker said in Portuguese. "You'll be paid, enough. There are those—like Reb Isaac Abravanel, the treasurer to King Alonso—who have the money to support such things."

"And if there's trouble, maybe you'll let your parrot do the talking," Bartholomeo said. "As far as I know, there is no Inquisition for birds."

"At least not yet," the reb said. I said nothing, but wondered, nu, what's the right word for snatching parrots like feathered fruit from their perches in Africa?

Your new life, a procession of cages, jesses, clipped wings, and exile. Starved and poked until you speak the language of those who did it. Converso parrots singing our Lord's song in a strange land.

But, as they say, there's job security.

And, after awhile, the words we spit in rage are the words of those we rail against.

Feh.

Eventually, all that's left is words.

Chapter Six

A day later we gathered our few things in both sack and saddlebag, and shtupped our pockets full with bread and dried fruit.

"Boychik," the old rebbe wheezed. "Sit." The rebbe put his shaky spiderweb fingers on Moishe's shoulder. "There's news."

The story had travelled west, through a network of Jewish learning and trade, taking many months to arrive on this furthest European shore.

There had been pogroms in the distant east. The east which had been Moishe's home. Shtetls had been plundered then torched. Jews raped then killed.

Cossacks like pirates boarding the landlocked villages.

Moishe's shtetl. Was it on the banks of the Nevežis near Panevezys?

Ash. Chickens. Lost and baleful dogs.

No one survived.

His parents?

Ha-Shem yikom damo. May Elohim avenge their blood.

꘎

It was a week along the road to Seville, a connect-the-dots route of small villages drawn together by dirt roads, scattered stones, and an assortment of travellers. The thought of his parents burned in Moishe.

53

"They were the centre of the compass. Where I was travelling from. What do I have left—an accent and a memory of my father's book?"

Moishe described a shul ceremony. On the bima, the dais, the Torah was passed hand to hand and embraced from *dor l'dor*, generation to generation. He recalled his father telling him that Jews were "the people of the book"—books were akin to blood, something that allowed them to live forever.

"So what did I do? Pitched my father's book into the sea. *Zay gezunt*, eternal life. Hey, sea cucumbers and shiksa mermaids, here's all you need. I might as well have dropped my parents into the sea. Never mind eternal life, they have no life and where was I?"

Near Andalusian territory, a shlemiel with a stringy beard stood by the side of the road and invited us to kick his tuches for the price of a few small coins. I suspect he was often compelled to give away his service for free. We stayed overnight in a selection of inns or, to tell the emes truth, in their barns. Each night, after an evening observing the rich variety of human knots becoming unravelled at the inn, we found our way to the sweet scuttling of the barns. Sometimes there were others there: a variety of the bedless and transient, those shlumpers left trailing behind the promise of their own better futures. I encountered no other parrots, but we're not usually companions for those bound inland, unless they're buoyed by the jewelled palanquin of privilege and can afford feathered marvels.

Moishe paid with Don Abravanel's coins, never allowing more than one to be visible at a time. He kept some in his shoes, some strapped to his leg, some beside his own family jewels.

Outside the city, with the sun still seeping like a wound over the Andalusian mountains, we came across what we thought to be a festival procession, loud with bright colour and the wailing, singing and shouting of thousands. Enormous crosses held high, a parade of priests, monks, and the powerful riding in carriages and on huge horses dressed in silks and resembling cantering four-poster beds.

A bright and horrifying line followed. What appeared to be a troupe of clowns savagely beaten and now muttering, weeping, mad, or silent.

They trudged barefoot, arrayed in red, yellow or black sacks covered in a bestiary of demons emerging from amid the lewd tongues of painted flame, pointed and insane. Each clown surmounted with a peaked hat emblazoned with still more fire. Some robes were drawn-and-quartered by a gash-red cross, as if Father-Son-and-Holy-Ghosted by sword. Man, woman and child, each carried a green or yellow candle, and walked with a noose around the neck, macabre neckties dressing them with a grim and dark formality. At the end of the procession, several men, beaten until barely more than stew, carried in cages pulled by mules.

An auto-da-fé, part of the newly created made-in-Spain Inquisition. Bartolemeo's master had warned us about this, but, oy, a broch, this was persecution dressed like the birthday party of the boy Satan.

People lined the streets bawling religious songs.

"The Jews," a man shouted. "Those vermin caused the plague."

We pushed our way into the crowd, wishing and not wishing to see more of this demonic circus. A girl, but a season older than Moishe—dark curls beneath a coloured scarf—sobbed beside us, tear-soaked face half-covered with a handkerchief.

"My father," she whispered. She gestured toward a rickety man in one of the cages. He gripped the bars, held himself in a crouch. His frail head with its wispy beard and sallow face bobbed as the cage moved forward. He was saying something, singing weakly, but in the din we could not understand.

Moishe turned from the procession, looked steadily at her, but said nothing.

Ach, what could you say?

Sorry?

As long as you have your health?

I lost my father, too?

Men, women, children. All threw rotten food and dreck that dripped from those in the cages. The girl's father did not respond but kept muttering, clinging to the bars.

The crowd walked alongside the procession and Moishe, the girl and I followed. We arrived at a large square outside the city walls.

On a large platform, the rich, the aristocratic, the clergy.

Four huge statues of Old Testament prophets stood mutely at each corner, their blind eyes staring grimly into the crowd.

The quemadero. The place of execution.

"The architect for this place," the girl said, indicating a tall man in a black robe. "But a Jew first."

A priest in red robes climbed the few stairs to a raised dais on the platform, and began to proclaim, "If a man does not keep himself in Me, he becomes dead and is severed like a dry branch; such branches are taken up and put in the fire and burned. John, chapter fifteen, verse six. We know what should become of these heretics."

"Laudamus Te" from the choir. The crowd joined in. All around us: "We praise, we bless, we worship, we glorify."

Several of the condemned fell to their knees, weeping.

Perhaps they did not like the musical selection.

Then they confessed their heresy, the secret Judaizing of their deeds and hearts, their repentance.

"We accept the Lord Jesus Christ as our saviour for the wages of sin are death but the gift of God is eternal life through Jesus Christ our Lord."

They collapsed before the platform, watering the ground with their tears.

Soldiers strode toward the centre of the quemadero.

"Stand," a sergeant ordered. The penitants staggered up or were hauled. Then briskly, the soldiers reached around their necks with a red silk cord and strangled them.

May they rest in peace. *Aleyhem ha'shalom.*

The soldiers: their time will come.

When parrots and Jews take over the world.

When is that?

When the Messiah comes to earth and shines my shoes.

When I get shoes.

My luck, they'll be horseshoes.

The garrotted bodies were carried by pairs of soldiers, then secured to stakes planted throughout the square in a mockery of trees. Then a marquesa stepped from the platform, her brocaded skirts fluttering behind her. A priest passed her a lit torch, and, after a nod from another, she made the sign of the cross over her own mortal body and touched the torch to the kindling at the foot of the stake. The pyre ignited, a burning bush inverted.

The greatest pain wasn't apparent in the quickly sagging body, curling in the heat, the yellow sack now florid with real fire. It was in the burning horror on the face of the girl, on the faces of the still living, the about-to-die.

A shout like a *shtoch in hartsn*, a stab in the heart, from somewhere in the crowd. A brief commotion as someone collapsed. The soldiers looked over. The crowd attempted to become invisible. The commotion stilled.

Another brocaded dybbuk descended the stairs and received a lighted torch. Then another. The faces of the living burned even more fiercely. The girl gasped for air, her shoulders heaving.

The living bound in ropes. The broken taken from their cages, each carried then tied to a stake. This time several of the lords stepped from the platform and received torches. The girl sank to her knees.

First one, then several of the bound began to sing in desperate voices, the Sh'ma, the central affirmation of the Jewish faith.

"Hear, O Israel, the Lord our God, the Lord is One . . ."

"*Adonai Eloheinu*, the world ends. Soon the Messiah will come," a man beside us shouted. He was quickly overpowered, brought down by the fists and feet of a band of cursing men.

The girl sobbing on her hands and knees.

Moishe crouched close to her.

In the middle of such tsuris, such misery, she was the painful centre of the world. And beautiful.

Moishe's mind became a syrup of ragged light and electricity. I could almost see the girl being imprinted into the brain of this boychik, like this boychik had imprinted on me.

"Moishe," he said to her. It was a naming, a consolation, an explanation for something he had no other words for.

An affirmation.

Then he turned and ran, a loud snap behind him as kindling at the foot of the remaining stakes burst into flame and the crowd cheered.

Chapter Seven

We ducked into an alley. It's a paradox if a parrot ducks, but in this case, it would have been a good idea because:

Blam!

A *shtik fleysh mit tsvey oygn*—a piece of meat with two eyes—hit me right in the punim with his fist and I fell off Moishe's shoulder. They hit the bird when they want the boy. I fell to the ground and our narration almost ended here, with me farkakte, looking up at the thin blue sky above the alleyway.

A gangly shmendrick of a man looked down at me.

"Splinterwit," he said. "You ran into my fist. Who are you running from?"

"The wrong person, obviously," Moishe said.

The shmendrick pointed at the small shuttered window of a goldsmith's shop. "I was breaking in. If it weren't for your stupid bird, I'd've been inside already."

I attempted to return to Moishe's shoulder but I'd hurt my wing.

Moishe held out his hand. I climbed on and he lifted me back onto his shoulder. His other head. His second thoughts.

"Miguel," Moishe said, introducing himself to the shmendrick. "I'm . . . a sailor. They were going to sell me but I escaped."

"They call me Diego," the shmendrick said.

And perhaps it was true.

···

Diego gave us directions to the place where we would meet the secret Jews. The Catedral de Sevilla, the enormous cathedral that stood over the city. An old mosque dressed in Christian drag. We didn't require the convolutions of complex directions: its bell tower, La Giralda, once a minaret, pointed like a giant finger toward heaven. We're number one.

But, nu, perhaps it was a middle finger flipping the Christian bird toward a displaced Allah.

In the Rabbi's letter of introduction, there was a fragment of a two-hundred-year-old poem by Judah Halevi, the famous Spanish-Jewish poet. Moishe would say the first line and the contact would answer with the second.

A Jewish password.

Save my beard from a haircut. Two bits.

The plan wasn't to walk up and shpritz old poetry at just anyone. Moishe was to find the man who tended the candles beside the largest of the cathedral's five naves.

The cathedral was big as Babel, a vast Ararat looming over the city, the largest man-made thing that we'd ever seen. And still, after nearly a century, they hadn't finished building.

Like that joke that is itself older than creation: Lord, it took only six whole days for you to create heaven and earth, but even you had to wait for the weekend.

Nervously, Moishe walked through the vast front doors. A fully rigged ship could pass through such doors, if the captain could get the crew to shlepp it.

We plunged into the candlelit twilight of the cathedral. The aurora borealis of stained glass: our brainstems replaced by kaleidescopes.

It was the inside of a huge city square, the vaulted ceiling unreachable as heaven. Each stone block in the vast walls was a square meal, an unfed belly, a tangible monument to what the church had and the people did not.

And, takeh, I wasn't thinking incense.

We walked down the main nave toward the rumble of prayer and distant singing. Toward the altar, there was a sea of candles, each flame a bright wave.

Even the dried-out beef-jerky soul of an alter kaker parrot became dazed by the intoxicating lotus-scented pong of Mother Church in such a Xanadu of thurible-fumed fantasmagoria.

Nu? Isn't it time for a thurible pun?

"As the sea rages, my soul is jubilant," Moishe muttered to an ancient stooped beadle. He stared blankly back at us, then motioned to the candles, offering Moishe the opportunity to light one.

"Crazy? Then try faith," the beadle might have been thinking.

Another man stepped out of a shadowed archway.

"As the sea rages . . ." Moishe began.

"My soul is jubilant," the man continued. "For my ship draws near to the sanctuary of her God." The lock clicked. The right key in the right lock. The man began walking away. The light was dim at the far end of the transept.

A Madonna, large as an ogre and made of dark wood. The man made sure the coast was clear, then touched his hand to the smooth underside of Mary's foot, and extracted a key, a heretical splinter hobbling the Mother of God.

"In the other foot, a mezuzah," he whispered. "The lady, she is our doorway. Come with me." As we walked by, he touched the mezuzah foot and murmured a prayer. We followed him behind the statue where he unlocked a small door. We stood together on a landing. He locked the door behind us. The right key, the right lock. We were in darkness.

"My name," he said, "is Samuel."

We felt our way down the stairs.

Our final step was into a soft uneven floor.

"Sand," Samuel said, "so we make no noise."

We crossed the room in the twilight that fell from an opening above. Another door and we had entered a room bright with menorah candles and torchlight.

Moishe looked amazed at this subterranean synagogue.

"The fox doesn't look for chickens in his own foxhole," Samuel said.

Half a dozen men sat around an immense table.

"Our souls should be quite jubilant today," Samuel said to them. "Look what washed up."

At the end of the table, a desiccated figure stitched from driftwood, a cloud, and an old saddle. Standard issue ancient rebbe and the doppelganger of the rov in Lisbon. Rabbi Daniel.

"You brought a friend from Africa?"

He meant me.

"We can trust him? In Ecclesiastes, it says, 'A bird of the air shall carry the voice, and that which hath wings shall tell the matter.' And this particular matter is highly secret." The rebbe eyed us intensely.

"I wouldn't want this bird to trade our lives for a cracker. Unless it were matzoh. Ahh, that I could understand. I could be Judas myself for a bisl matzoh."

He smiled, then offered Moishe a seat. "You're a brave boy. The officers of the Inquisition are everywhere: the thousand faceted-eyes of an excremental fly."

We were brought some bread, wine and soft cheese. "Eat." Moishe set me down on the table and tore off a shtikl bread.

The men looked on approvingly as we noshed.

"And now, " the old rabbi began. "The books. It is as they say, if you drop gold and books, pick up the books, then the gold. So, show us."

Moishe reached around to take the books out of the shouldersack that he'd hidden beneath his smock.

A look of shrek horror. Oy Gotenyu! The sack was gone. He had had the books when he rode into the city. A broch—the horse! He'd abandoned the horse, tied up near the quemadero. In his horror, he'd run without any thought of old dobbin. Without any thought at all. By now, some gonif had rode off with the nag.

But the books?

Before we'd dismounted and went to watch the auto-da-fé, Moishe had hidden behind a wall, taken the books from the saddlebags and stuffed them into the concealed sack. But the sack was gone.

Rabbi Daniel and the other men looked at Moishe expectantly. He looked from the old rabbi to the floor, considering what to do.

"I . . . I must find the books." He scooped me up and ran to the stairs. "Diego," he whispered hoarsely. "The cutpurse must have robbed me when we klopped into him."

It was the oldest trick in the book. *Here, would you like to buy these flowers?* And while you were leaning in, snorting their scent into your shnozz, you were relieved of the responsibility of your gold. Only it was the pretty pink flower of Diego's fist that went up my beak, and he had swiped something more valuable—and more dangerous— than gold.

We were in the dark at the top of the stairs. Moishe grabbed the handle but the door wouldn't move. *Vo den?* Of course. It had been locked behind us. For safety.

"The books?" Samuel was behind us. "Where are they?"

Moishe burbled an explanation.

"If the Inquisitors find them—and they generously grease the hands of those who place such things in their grasp—then we will— you will—be in great danger. They will search for you and your end will not be good. Was there anything beside the books? The letter?"

Moishe felt for the small pouch that was tied inside his pant leg. Ach, but the letter was stowed between the pages of one of the books. Still, he could hope. One can wish for a leak in the tub of the firmament when the flood begins.

"It's gone," he said.

"We will talk to the rebbe," Samuel said. "We will make a plan. There was already great danger. Now this danger knows where to find us."

We waited in silence in the dark at the top of the landing. Only the sound of Moishe not breathing.

"The letter says 'meet in the Catedral,' but not where," I said.

"The Inquisitors would think it only a place of rendezvous. For now, keneynehoreh, they don't know what goes on behind the back of their Virgin."

We returned to the cellar with all the enthusiasm of a cow being led to the shochet, knowing that soon it would be brisket.

And why was I worried?

I was a bird. I could not be brisket.

But Moishe was my family, my mishpocheh. The only family I had, Oy Gotenyu. God help us.

"Sit," the rabbi said.

Moishe sat.

"We are not Israelites, or Hebrews," the rabbi began. "We are Jews. We are Jewish wherever we are and with whatever we have. Do you know when the first time this word—Jew—was used?"

Moishe did not.

"The Megillah. The Book of Esther. You remember in Persia, the Prime Minister—"

"Haman," Moishe said.

"He who convinced the king that all Jews should be killed."

"But they were saved," Moishe said. "By Esther."

"Yes. The Jewish queen. Since the beginning, they have tried to kill us Jews, but ha-Shem—God—gives the story a little, what you would call, a drey, a twist, and then somehow, we aren't destroyed. Until the next time."

"And each time," Samuel added, "we make a new holiday to remember."

"Purim," Moishe said.

"Soon the calendar will be filled up with festivals," the rabbi said. "Adonai will have to forge us another year. A whole year just for these days of remembering."

Samuel shrugged. "We remember, but then we eat."

"And so we survive," the rabbi continued. "Though we must hide. One of the stolen books was the Book of Esther. They tried to destroy us then, but did not. Perhaps they will fail again."

Rabbi Daniel's plan. Moishe would lead them to where Diego had taken the books. They would try to buy the books back. One who speaks for money, listens to money.

Then Moishe would be hidden in a house where he would be safe. When the Inquisitors became less inquisitive and thoughts of Moishe and the books had faded, he would leave Seville.

Of course, if they couldn't find Diego, or he had already taken the books—and the letter—to the Inquisition, then the story would be different.

The world could be a dangerous library. For a book or a Jew.

"And Moishe," Samuel said, "We'll give you new clothes. You need a disguise."

"So get rid of the bird," Rabbi Daniel said.

Nu, they didn't have a disguise for a bird?

Feh.

They can take the bird out of the story, but the story stays in the bird.

They gave Moishe a long brown cape, green leggings, and a red hood. He put on the leather boots that belonged to one of the cathedral Jews. To look like a gnome, that was his disguise?

But his right shoulder—my shoulder—was to remain unadorned.

"What else can I do?" the shoulder shrugged.

Zay gezunt. Be well.

We'd meet again.

I knew it was right. Moishe had to go alone. Together, it was like waving a talking, grey-feathered African flag.

They didn't leave the cellar all at once. First, two climbed the stairs, speaking quietly to each other. Next Moishe, the rabbi, and Samuel. And then a few more. They blew out the candles, extinguished the torches. I was left alone in the dark, save for the dim light coming from the ceiling of the first room.

How many parrots does it take to change a light bulb?

That's okay. You go out and enjoy yourself. Who needs light? Just leave the door a bisl open. Don't worry about me.

I waited, wondering what to do.

They would return.

Eventually.

I tried my wing. Gevalt. It didn't hurt like hell. It hurt like much of which happens before that.

But I could still take to the air, if only for short hauls. I didn't need to fly to heaven. Just into the cathedral. A Christian way station.

The light in the first room came from a chimney shaft in the ceiling. It led either outside or into another part of the Catedral. I emerged from this stone cloaca, smoke, a farshtunkeneh cloud, a pipe dream with claws.

Now what?

It was to be Parrot vs. World.

The world that I was now born to was small, musty, and bounded by shadows: I was in some kind of cloakroom. Dark red capes lined the walls; above them, like a butcher shochet's wet dream, hoods hung from hooks.

Some Hebrew letters at the room's dim far end. Hebrew books of some kind.

Since I was invited out of Africa, I have learned many words from the pretty, poxy, scurvy, or sweet mouths of mariners, princes, brigands, maidens, nebbishes, shlumpers and shlemiels, but nothing from their pens.

Nu, what words would I have had if I'd not been snatched from my parrot life in the scintillation of leaves high in the African forest? I was but a fledgling taken straight from nest to mast and knew little beyond the nutritive regurgitations of my parents—halevay if only, what would they have been like? I would have learned but a beakful of words for rotten fruit and cloacae, for a thousand shades of green and the little wings of my pinfeathered offspring.

I'd have been a different bird.

Still with holes in my head, but different holes. In a different head.

And still, I'd have wanted to get out of this room. And to find Moishe.

There was a door. Plain as the nose on my face. Azoy, as the breathing holes in my beak.

But it was locked.
A broch.
But then I noticed a small window.
Open.
Escape.

Chapter Eight

I wasn't outside but found myself behind the altar. Bells began to ring. Nice of them to celebrate my freedom. I flew up into the vault of the nave. The light was startling and I bumped into the diamond-shaped panes of the leadlight windows several times before I adjusted. One of them was open and I flew out and above the slate roof. The city was a vast ocean around me, Moishe a tiny craft adrift in the narrow alleys between its waves.

I flew in a large circle, unsure which way to go. There were few people out in the streets. Because of the plague, they kept out of public places, except when absolutely necessary, for example, to perform their civic and religious duty in the witnessing of a good life-affirming stake-burning.

I saw one of the men—I remembered his name as Avraham or Abraham—from the secret basement talking furtively in a nearby square. I landed on a roof to listen. He was speaking to a red-robed priest about a stash of books. Jewish books. Moishe's books. They were negotiating a price.

How did he get the books? Did it have anything to do with Diego?

There are advantages to being a bird.

Flight.

Feathers.

Enticing little feygelehs with pretty wings.

The ability to play dumb.

I flew down, landed on Abraham's shoulder and tried to look stupid. So, nu, not such a stretch for me.

"Hello. Howaya? Hello." I imitated first-rate parrot repartee.

They were both surprised. They may have thought I was an idiot, but I was exotic, more unusual than your Generalife-garden variety idiot.

"How did it . . . ?" Abraham began. "Stupid bird." He was worried that somehow I might compromise the negotiations. If they went awry, instead of being served a hearty helping of gold he could end up as Jewish barbecue himself.

"Hello," I said. "Howaya? Hello."

They hurried through their discussion, not wanting me to draw attention to them.

Their plan: Abraham would meet up with the other hidden Jews and produce the books. Then the priests of the Holy Office would burst in and the red-capes would catch them right-to-left-handed with the forbidden books. They were supposed to have been New Christians, converted Jews. To set eyes on anything but the Gospels was heresy and would certainly mean death by fire.

Unless they repented. In which case, as I'd just seen, they'd be killed twice. First by strangulation. Then fire.

Choke and smoke.

The Catedral wasn't going to be the meeting place. They wanted to preserve it as a trap for the future. For now, the books would be both lure and hook. Abraham would arrange a meeting in a "safe" place.

The two men parted. The priest in the blood-red Inquisition robes strode confidently across the square. Abraham slithered furtively, checking over his shoulder.

"Hello," I chirped from his other shoulder. "Howaya? Hello."

As soon as the priest was out of view, Abraham slapped at me. "Leave, vermin," he said, and I obliged, flying up above the gables, following him like the conscience he didn't have.

The priest navigated his jagged way forward through the illogical, dark and narrow alleys.

He must have been navigating by faith.

Like that priest who walked into a bar.

There's a few Inquisition guys playing cards and they invite him to join them.

He asks, "What's the ante?"

"Ten silver pieces," they say.

Priest says, "I'm gonna get burned at those stakes."

So, nu, I lost Abraham as he walked under some awnings and, before I could find him again, he slipped into—I think—a building attached to the Catedral. Me and God. We can't think of everything.

By now it was dark; it was doubtful I'd find Moishe. I'd flown to where I'd gone head-to-knuckle with Diego and then to the quemadoro, where there was nothing left but ashes and shadows instead of people. The grandstand stood mute and fraught with expectation, a psychopath waiting for another touch of those silk-covered tucheses.

If I didn't find Moishe and the hidden Jews, by next week they'd be the entertainment, the puffs of sweet human smoke that the Sevillano audience would breathe as they cheered.

Chapter Nine

Next morning as I flew over the city, searching for Inquisitors or wine merchants, hidden Jews or Moishe, I spotted the rabbi and Samuel walking down a narrow alleyway. At the corner they ducked under a low archway and through a battered green door. No one else arrived. Ten minutes later the door opened: three unkempt men and a shlumperdikeh woman singing and staggering with what appeared to be a generous filling of good spirits. A tavern, I deduced, marked only by these doddering processions.

I waited. After half an hour, Samuel and the rabbi emerged from the green door. They sang too loudly, slurring their words. It paid to be seen not Judaizing, but instead, having a good Christian mug of unkosher wine. They walked through a complex plait of alleys, eventually entering a building beneath a sign carved with images of wine barrels. I slipped through the back door and flew along a narrow hallway piled high with casks. Voices spoke indistinctly. In the dim light, I followed stairs down to the cellar. I walked along the top of casks that filled most of the room, keeping close to the wall, remaining invisible. I would first understand what was going on.

And whom I could trust.

The centre of the cellar: the rabbi, Samuel, and others around a table. Jugs of wine, decks of cards. A mixture of kibitzing, davening, and, if you can use this word for Jews, pontificating. Where was Moishe? Ach. It was better he wasn't here. They didn't know it, but they were like animals gathered at a watering hole, not knowing that the red silk lions were ready to pounce.

At one end of the table, a young woman. The pretty girl, the sheyneh maideleh, from the auto-da-fé, listening gravely to the men. I tried to get a better view, and knocked over a few corks. They fell to the floor, a muted explosion. The men, absorbed in talk, didn't notice but the girl looked up.

Me, I'm dangerous. And except for my tail, the colour of twilight and unknowing. A creature of darkness and mystery.

So I'm grey, and hard to see in dim light.

She squinted behind the barrels where I was attempting my shadowplay.

"I've seen you before," she whispered.

"Hello," I tried. "Howaya? Hello." Best not to brandish the bright blade of my considerable eloquence.

"You were with the boy. Moishe," she said almost inaudibly. "At the burning."

"Hello," I said again, idiotically. "Howaya?" Any moment now she'll offer me a piece of matzoh.

"I know you understand," she said. "I am named Sarah. He gave me a letter. I was to watch for you." She glanced over at the men speaking at the table in the centre of the room, then took a scrap of parchment from the pocket of her apron.

"He's safe. They've hidden him with Doña Gracia de la Peña. My father used to say there's safety in numbers if the numbers mean large sums of money. The Doña has plenty of those kind of numbers."

Was this a trick? Moishe knew I couldn't read.

"My uncle—Abraham—works for her. As I do. Last night, though I wept, I did the washing. I saw Moishe brought to the Doña. She agreed to hide him. I came here to say prayers for my father. My uncle doesn't know. It's no place for girls and women but the rabbi took pity."

She unfolded the note. "Your Moishe asked me to read this for you. The letters are Spanish, but the words are in the Jewish of your village."

She read haltingly and without understanding, only parroting the sounds the letters spoke:

Arie: I'm safe, keneynehoreh. For now.

The books are gone. No sign of the mamzer Diego. But still I must hide.

Don't know what he'll do. They pay well for exposing Marranos.

The girl is as beautiful as the seven worlds. Already I dream of her arms and other places. She'll show you Doña Gracia's, where I am hidden. The Doña is a powerful and wealthy Jew. A trader. She will take us to safety.

Don't speak. They tell me not to trust anyone. Even them.

M.

It was a bittersweet trick, having her read how pretty she was when only an Ashkenazi—or his parrot—would understand.

But every language is bittersweet to those who don't know it.

There was a new voice, speaking at full volume from the foot of the stairs. The men around the table stood.

"I have something. You'll be happy." It was Abraham. He was cradling Moishe's sack of books.

Sarah ducked behind the barrels to hide.

Her uncle walked into the centre of the room, opened the sack and spread out the books on the table.

The men held their breath. As if they were looking at a pile of rubies, their first-born sons or the shadow of the Messiah himself. The people of the book needed their books.

Rabbi Daniel began to pray. "*Baruch atah Adonai Eloheinu . . .*"

"*Omein,*" the others sang as he finished. They all sat and the rabbi positioned a book before him, stroking its cover as if the idea that it could exist in the same physical world as him caused both tender sadness and great joy.

He opened it and began to read out loud.

His passionate, hypnotic voice. The murmuring of assent by the men. The flicker of the candlelight.

Then the sudden thud of boots on the steps as if we were inside a Golem's vacant heart.

The men scrambled to gather and hide the books. They picked up cards and tried to look natural, a few friends, some wine, the Ace of Cups hidden up one of their sleeves.

Two Inquisition priests and half a dozen soldiers stood in the sand at the bottom of the stairs.

"*Dominus vobiscum*, the Lord be with you," the rabbi said and crossed himself, hoping to mimic the Christian piety of discovered gamblers.

The priest did not reply, "*Et cum spiritu tuo*, and with thy spirit," as would be customary, but rather, "*Ecce Homo*, Behold the Man." The words of Pontius Pilate presenting the thorn-crowned Jesus to the crowd. In this case it meant: "I'm going to crucify your Jewish tuches."

Abraham stood up and motioned to the books concealed beneath the table. Two soldiers held the rabbi, another two held Samuel. Then a lanky soldier with a greasy moustache pushed past a small man still clutching a hand of cards, and crawled under the table. He emerged embracing a stack of books. The second priest lifted one off the pile and opened it.

"Hebrew," he spat.

"Heresy!" the priest hissed, playing his part with high drama, as if this hadn't all been arranged. "Converso Judaizers! You shall burn."

From behind the barrels, an involuntary gasp from Sarah. Her uncle's duplicity had condemned these men to die. Immediately, two soldiers rushed to look between the rows. They grabbed her arms and roughly dragged her into the centre of the room. Weeping, she shuddered between them, unable to stand. I squeezed out of sight between a barrel and the stone wall.

Abraham seemed entirely taken aback. "Sarah?"

"You know this girl?" a priest said.

"My niece."

"The girl will come with us," the priest said. "But, because you have been helpful to us, we will give you a choice."

"Yes," the second priest said. "We will take her. Unless you want to go in her place?"

Abraham looking steadily at Sarah.

Sarah sobbing.

"Take her," he said.

The others looked at Abraham but said nothing. The soldiers then hauled them up the stairs and to a jail cell that would give them a taste of where they would spend the rest of their eternally damned lives. As if what they had just experienced wasn't enough of an amuse-bouche.

The sound of great tumult after they left. The few short candles burned down. Leaving dark cellars was becoming my speciality.

If I didn't know better, I would have thought that upstairs looked like the result of a Bacchanalia. It was a cooper's nightmare of smashed and splintered casks, hogsheads, firkins, puncheons, pipes, butts and breakers intermingled with wine spilled everywhere like blood. A man lay dead near the back door, real blood running from the corner of his mouth and spreading from a dark wound in his side. I flew through the open door and over the city. Moishe was a hidden Jew, hidden even from me. But Doña Gracia, whoever she was, I would find.

And before Abraham and his red-caped fathers.

✢

In Seville one was allowed to be a Jew the way one was allowed to be a leper: somewhere else. The Inquisition was for New Christians, heretics, Moriscos, and all those once baptized who, like addicts, had returned to illicit Judaizing. And the Inquisition was for money. For nu, what's the intoxicating draft of organized hatred without a chaser of profit?

But where to find former Jews?

I flew toward what had once been the Jewish market. It wasn't hard to find. I looked for a tall building that had a cross on it, but where you could see, like a healed-over wound, the scar of what had once been a Magen David. The Jewish star.

The old synagogue.

And in front of it: the market.

Flying between stalls, I beheld untold riches of nuts and fruit. Overripe pears and oranges fallen onto the cobbles and singing a hungry parrot's song. Delicious almonds held in the open hands of children so I could nosh and delight and amaze. For this, I was happy to play my part. But I was watchful of the slices of melons and other morsels their parents offered me, for just as a cap and a ball on a stick can be sold for amusement, so too can a captured parrot. Even more than losing Moishe, I had little fancy for the clipped wings, the jess and leg-band of the kept parrot.

It wasn't long before I heard the name of Doña Gracia amidst the confusion of vendors' songs, gossip, and the convoluted stories with their ay-yi-yi's and laughter. She was the richest converso in the city, and so in the market many repeated her name. I flew about until I found someone in her employ: a man carrying an armful of bread to her kitchen. And so I followed him.

Chapter Ten

*D*oña Gracia's house was a grand affair, an appropriate dwelling for such an important balebosteh, with decorated terracotta archways onto the street, and leadlight windows high above the street. The man pushed open a bright blue door with his shoulder and then backed in with his armload of bread. He couldn't touch the mezzuzah on the door, but he did say a quiet blessing.

"Hello, pretty bird," a woman said as I flew in behind him. "You've brought a friend," she said taking some of the loaves from the man's arms.

"She's been following me," he said.

"She must want some of this lovely bread," the woman said.

Why is it that people think some animals are male and some are female, as if we don't come in both flavours? So was I going to explain my noble ambitions regarding procreation and the love of a good parrot maiden?

Not yet. I had found it best to wait until you really know someone.

The woman broke off some crust and offered me a nosh. Really, I'd had plenty at the market, but I received her kindness with what I considered a manly grace and delicacy.

"Thank you," I said.

"Miguel," I said. "Miguel."

"Miguel! How pretty!" the woman said.

The man broke off some more bread. "Funny name for a girl parrot."

"Why don't you bring Miguel to the painter? Maybe he'll put her in the new portrait of Doña Gracia?"

Likely the painter was closer to the action than these two crusty bread breakers, so I was quick to jump at the opportunity. I hopped onto the offered forearm of the man and we walked further into the house.

House. It was more like a galleon planted in the ground. A palace.

We walked down many halls, up countless steps, past innumerable rooms.

It was a small world but who would want to paint it?

We entered a hall lined with colourful tapestries depicting seas of curling waves, great ships balanced on the foaming cowlick peaks. A man in a spattered red smock, his white beard itself like ocean foam, had rolled out many painted canvasses on the floor and on the dock-sized oak table in the centre. He was speaking solicitously to an impressive lady dressed in furs and a fine brocade robe.

Doña Gracia.

Tall, dark, full, her hair plaited elaborately above her, like the dark red leaves of an autumn tree.

The painter pointed at the canvases. "My Doña, the hills of Tuscany behind this prince, the Grand Canal behind this Pope's nephew. Each painting tells its story not only in the faces of these noble people—a small curve of the lips, the stage play of the eyes, the angle of the nose and forehead—and not only in finery of their dress and jewels, but also in the landscapes behind them, stretching out over the unreachable horizon of the canvas."

Doña Gracia examined the paintings dispassionately.

"Doña Gracia, I would paint you before an ocean teaming with boats, the wind bulging full in the sails, the barques sunk low with the rich prizes of your trade."

She remained impassive.

"Doña," he said, suddenly quiet, whispering conspiratorially, "you would appear so strong and beautiful, so haughty and so rich, that the King and Queen of almost-all-the-Spains would wet their Catholic britches and despair."

At that, Doña Gracia smiled broadly, the bright sparkle of a diamond twinkling where an incisor once was. And then she began to laugh, which made her appear all the more strong, beautiful, haughty and rich.

"Señor Fernandez," she said, "you paint a pretty picture with your tongue, and more than a portrait of me, I would rather relish this picture of Their Almost Spains in their sodden bloomers."

She then caught sight of me and clapped her hands together. "Señor painter, is this your ghost-grey Polly? Something flown out of a painting? Speak, Polly!" she said to me.

As I have said, I know on which side of the brain the bread is buttered.

"Doña Gracia," I said. "My gracious greetings, Doña Gracia, hello. Hello. Howaya?"

She nodded gracefully at me and then turned to the painter and smiled wryly. "You're a sly old brush slinger, canvas-monkey," she said. "You've brought me a courtier to speak pretty as if I had my own court. To make me puff like a sheet in a gale."

"Miguel," I squawked. "Miguel."

"Indeed, painter-Polly," Doña Gracia said. "I had that thought also."

She turned back to the kitchen servant, on whose forearm I rested.

"This will keep the boy busy until we make arrangements for him," she said. "Take the bird to Miguel and tell him to teach it to pray. When we are all gone, at least the parrot will remember our prayers."

The servant bowed once, then together we walked through a neighbourhood of hallways and down a hillside of steps. Eventually we arrived at a large wooden door that led from a courtyard, in the middle of which was a fountain in the form of a fish.

The man opened the door with a large and rusty key attached to his belt by a rusty chain. We walked into the room.

Moishe.

He stood up, beaming. I flew from the man's arm onto his shoulder. My shoulder. The light shone in from a high window and so my shadow fell where it should. Across Moishe's skinny chest.

A bookmark without a book doesn't know where it is. Moishe was my slim volume, my scrawny story. My shoulder.

And he radiated joy and relief. If he could have hugged me, he would have.

"Whips. Sinking ships. The Inquisition. Someone doesn't want me to have a parrot."

He scratched my neck and it was pure delight. I became an idiot chicken.

"Pretty girlfriend you've got there," the bread man said.

"Thanks," Moishe replied. "His name is Aaron."

♣

We told each other our stories, Moishe explaining how they wandered the streets looking for Diego, Moishe like a dowser, trying to lead them to the alleyway, following only his intuition and the nervous beating in his chest.

"I knew I was near," Moishe said. "But after awhile, the corners all looked the same, like the corners of a circle. And I knew if we kept wandering around, we'd be discovered. So we gave up and they brought me here."

I told him how Abraham, like Judas, had betrayed us. How he had betrayed Samuel, the rabbi, and even his own niece. About the wine that was blood after the raid of the merchant's cellar.

"Ptuh!" he spat. "That mamzer Abraham is the one that deserves blood and fire. And since he won't save his own niece, I will. And the others, too."

Since we'd been apart, it seemed Moishe had had his Bravado Mitzvah. His chutzpah was impressive. It had taken root and had been growing since he'd held that knife to the thieving youth's neck. And like me, he was a bit of foygl too. A wise guy.

He looked around the room and up at the high window as if he were imagining escape.

"But I have no idea how."

I told him about how the room filled with red capes and Hebrew books.

"So, nu, how will the rabbi and his Jews fly from their prison?" he asked.

"Red wings," I said, spreading my own grey ones impressively. "Not a wolf in sheep's clothing, but sheep in red silk. Catholic wolves. We'll dress them as Inquisition priests."

"You molodyets of a bird," he said. "You clever rascal. An impressive plan.

"Especially the part where they're still locked in a dungeon, but just better dressed."

We agreed that there were some details that remained to be worked out.

There was a knock on the door. "Perhaps it's the Messiah," I said. "Our prayers are answered."

Nu, it was the bread man telling us that Doña Gracia wanted to see us.

Chapter Eleven

*H*e led us along a covered hallway and into a small inner courtyard. Doña Gracia was sitting by a pool with another fountain, surrounded by greenery. Broad leaves, hibiscus flowers, palm trees, and twittery birds with the brainpower of flowers.

It felt like home.

Doña Gracia received us like a queen.

Moishe bowed slightly as he stood before her, and so, whether I intended to or not, I bowed also.

"I see you and the bird have become friends," she said.

"Yes, Doña Gracia," he said. "We've had a few minutes together. He's taught me all he knows."

She laughed but then added gravely, "Flight should be something on your mind. Even with my gold, it will be hard to keep the Inquisitors satisfied without you. They are not planning to bother themselves with even the pretence of a trial. On Friday they intend to burn those they have already taken."

"Like Shabbos candles," I said without thinking.

What a pisk I have sometimes. A big mouth.

"You have taught this bird not only davening, but about Shabbos candles, too?" Doña Gracia looked at Moishe with some amazement.

"He needs to know. For his Bar Mitzvah," Moishe joked, covering for me.

"And similes?" she said. "You taught him similes?" She was a clever bird herself. She knew.

"Once I had a husband," she said. "He was a smart man. Even when he was alive, he never disagreed with anything I said. But I'm told that when the opportunity arose and he was called upon to make his own decisions, he had a mind of his own. I suspect that it's this way with this parrot. That's good. We can use him."

What was I saying about being press-ganged?

"You can be of great help in rescuing our friends," she said to me. And then, businesslike, she moved on, evidently believing it best not to question intelligence in this time of folly.

A prominent merchant from a family of hidden Jews, her husband had been murdered by zealots. Since then, the Doña had sworn to help Jews or conversos escape. They'd be taken on as extra crew or cargo on her trade ships that sailed for Morocco. The ships would return with a new Moroccan crew and fruit, wheat, slaves, copper, iron and African gold—gold-embroidered caps, golden saddles, shields and swords adorned with gold, and even dogs' collars decorated with gold and silver.

Jewish freedom was all collar and no dog. And the dog that wasn't there was free to roam the streets of Fez, Marrakech and Rabat.

It was only a matter of time, she said, before all Iberian Jews and the sincere or expedient New Christians would be as the Jews of Egypt in ancient times: slaves, servants, and builders of monuments to their masters. The Jews of Andalusia had been expelled, ballast thrown kippah-first off the kingdom's bow, but even this treacherous fate wasn't available to conversos. The Inquisition would poke and prod for signs of the vermin-taint of continued Judaizing, take their money and property, but not let them leave, save through Death's door.

Doña Gracia wouldn't wait for the waters to part to help them escape these plagues. She had a fleet.

Moishe and the condemned Jews would travel to Morocco—to Fez—where the houses were finely built and curiously painted, tiled and roofed with gold, azure, and other excellent colours, some with crystal fountains and surrounded with roses and other odoriferous flowers and herbs. And where they could be safe.

When she had helped the last of the hidden Jews to escape, she would set sail herself for Morocco, an elf at the end of a difficult Age.

Her plan: We knew that most prisoners were held in a dungeon that had been created below a certain church. She would have someone ply the guard with drink. It was a typical escape story. Moishe would help me get through the bars. I'd get the key from the guard and carry it in my beak. The taste of freedom in a jailbird's mouth.

I suggested we bring the red capes so that the prisoners, as the saying goes, could be disguised in plain sight. In those times of heightened security, Doña Gracia thought it would be a good idea.

I looked at Moishe with I-told-you-so eyes.

"But it will be impossible to get the capes from the Catedral," Doña Gracia said. "Do you expect that we can just walk out with them?"

Now it was Moishe's turn for the I-told-you-so eyes.

But then: "I know of a way," he said. "My father told me this story. Each evening, a servant was seen walking home from the court, carrying a silver plate covered by a cloth. 'Leftovers,' he said. The guards at the portcullis began to get suspicious. 'He's stealing from the king,' one said to the other. 'Let's search him.' And so they did. They lifted the cloth from the plate, but there was nothing but a few scraps of ill-used food. Each day for a month the man walked home with a plate and each day the guards found only scraps. At the end of the month, the man did not return to work. The news quickly spread throughout the palace that thirty silver plates were missing from the royal kitchen and the shyster was nowhere to be seen.

"So, my plan: sneak into the Catedral and walk out wearing two red capes. Return wearing only one. Repeat until we have all the capes we need. It's perfect. Who would think twice about a priest walking in a church?"

"Another priest. Maybe you could put on all the capes at once and pretend to be a fat shnorrer of a priest," I said.

Doña Gracia laughed. "And then if you were stabbed, like Queen Isabella's overdressed ladies-in-waiting, no knife could reach you," she said.

"So, my idea needs work," Moishe said.

Chapter Twelve

*M*idnight. The streets of Seville empty as the wind from either end of a shlemiel. The sky moonless but for a luminous blade disappearing behind cloud. We exit through a small sally port in the west wall of Doña Gracia's and into an alleyway. Moishe is Red Riding Hood, carrying a basket of food. Not for his Bubbie but for fairy-tale Christians, the secret Jews held prisoner by red-hooded wolves.

What drink goes best with dungeon food?

The Merlot of Human Kindness?

Molotov cocktails.

We'll get to that.

Some of the larger homes had night watchmen but more often than not, their beat was the jurisdiction of Nod. Still we crept quietly and kept close to walls.

"Sarah. This sheyneh maideleh, this beautiful girl," Moishe whispered. He could name her, but didn't know what came next.

There were guards before the gates of the church, but a behindback such as ours necessitated an unorthodox approach.

Moishe slithered on his kishkas toward the barred windows at the back of the building. He pushed his face close, his shnozz between the bars, but he could see nothing, only smell the rat-ripe dankness of the dungeon.

The prisoners were in darkness. We dared not call them for fear of the shtarkeh guards. I slipped between the bars. It was the deep black of the jungle at night. I navigated by the give of air at doorways, the thicker air as I approached a wall. I went through a doorway and along a hallway lined with cells.

"So, nu," I said. "Come here often?"

I heard breathing. They hesitated, disoriented in the dark.

"We have food for you. And wine," I said. "From Doña Gracia."

"Strange that you didn't knock, but yet do not intrude." It was the rabbi.

"Gracias," someone else said.

Moishe was at the window. They were in cells. How to get the food to their mouths? I'd be the mother bird, feeding her chicks. "Es, es, mayne feygelech." Eat, eat, my little birds.

Moishe reached inside the window and dropped the food to the floor. I carried each piece of bread, each portion of cheese from window to cell.

"Aharon. Aharon." A small voice called my name. A girl's voice. "Tell him there's a gap in the stone of my cell. I must speak."

Moishe, a church mouse against the wall, crawled until he found a face-sized hole. "I'm here," he whispered. "Moishe."

A few minutes of breathing only.

Then: "My father's books. Will you save them?" Sarah said. "In his memory. For mine."

Torquemada, the Grand Inquisitor, had ordered the burning of Jewish and other heretical books.

"Libricide, lexicution, biblioclasm. To save our Catholic Spain," he'd said, "we must first destroy heresy."

"All Jewish books were condemned," Sarah said. "So the community brought their books to my father."

"As I'd taken one from mine," Moishe said.

"They knew he would keep them safe. They knew he would preserve their history and their future."

Sarah's father's hidden library. As he'd been a hidden Jew.

For years her family had lived in secret. They went to church. Received the wafer and the wine. Baptized their children.

But still, the hands over the eyes and the blessings over candles in the cupboards. The whispered words when walking through doorways.

And a library of Christian theology. Inside some books, in the compartment cut into the pages, smaller Jewish books.

As their Judaism was hidden inside each member of the family.

Like a devil or an angel child. Depending on which midwife you asked.

Each boy learned his true identity upon Bar Mitzvah. Each girl, usually when she married. But Sarah was an only child and her father taught her as if she was a son.

There was a priest. Padre Juan Lepe. A good man. A friend. He had known and had helped.

"He told me a story," Sarah began. "A man told a rabbi he would convert if the rabbi could explain Judaism to him. There was a catch, though. The man would stand on one leg. The rabbi had to explain everything before the man fell over. The rabbi sent him away, chastising him for insulting God with trivial gymnastics. Later, the man came upon the great sage Hillel and presented him the same challenge. Explain all of Judaism while I stand on one leg.

"'Left or right?' Hillel asked.

"'Either. Does it matter?'

"'Tell you what, you jump in the air and while you're there, closer to God, I'll explain everything,' the sage said. 'Ready? Jump!'

"And what did Hillel say while the man left the ground?

"He said, 'What is hateful to yourself, do not do to your neighbour.'

"'That's it?' the man said as he returned to earth.

"'That's the whole Torah,' Hillel said. 'The rest is commentary.'

"And that, the priest said, is why I help your father. When someone is looking for their footing here on earth, we Christians, Jews and Muslims, have the same things to say. When I jump, I don't ask religion to tell me how high. I think of this story.

"As the poet said, 'Where they burn books, in the end, they will burn people also.' That priest," Sarah whispered, "died the same day as my father. I will soon join them. My mother also—*aleha ha-shalom*—whom we lost in childbirth. The priest and my father had planned to take the books to safety outside of Spain."

"But they were discovered," Moishe said.

"Betrayed," she said. "And now I know: my uncle."

"I'll get the books," Moishe said. "Where?"

"The Catedral. It's where all the forbidden books are taken. Padre Juan told me before he was captured. He'd found a coffin there—they'd already taken my father—the padre was going to fill it with books and have it carried to safety. It is too late for my father. You cannot rescue the rest of us. Save at least these books."

There was noise at the other end of the hallway. A key rattling in the barred door. A man's farkakteh singing. I was back at the window, ready to fling more food into the cells. In the Torah, the manna just fell. Here, I had to shlepp it, loaf by loaf. And after thirty trips, I'd rather carry even a schmaltzy tune myself than some cheese.

The door scraped open and a priest fell in, wine-shikkered and staggering like each leg didn't know the other was there. He was dressed in hauberk and helmet. Why a priest needed chainmail wasn't clear. His lamp swayed like he was on the deck of a storm-wracked ship.

Those in the cells became silent. Hid their unfinished crusts in their clothes. Moishe lay flat against the ground, not daring to look between the stones.

"There's a pretty little bird here," the priest drawled. "And I shall have some dark meat."

At first, I thought he was here to fress on my bones, to have parrot pot pie for a late night nosh, but then I understood.

It was Sarah he was after.

"Little bird," he said. "Little bird." He shone his lurching light at the doors of the cells, looking for Sarah.

I considered our options. Moishe was outside. Perhaps he could sneak through the church doors, slip past the grobyan guards and klop the priest from behind.

"L'chaim, Father."

Blam!

Maybe with a chair or a silver church tchatchke. A candlestick.

A boy of fourteen. Two guards and a shikkered helmeted priest intent on knish.

Ach. Dreams.

It would have to be me. The mighty sparrow.

I didn't risk flying. He might hear. I crept like a rat toward him.

"Little bird," the priest said.

"Stay away from her," a man shouted from his cell.

"The caged bird sings," the priest said. "But can do nothing."

I'd lost sight of Moishe. He might have remained prone and invisible on the ground. Perhaps he was entering into strategic negotiations with the guards' fists.

"Little bird," the priest said. The lamplight crept over Sarah.

The priest put his key in the lock.

This was my chance. I leapt with my claws before me. I would turn his eyes to raspberries.

Sarah shrieked. The priest heaved open the cell door and I crashed into it and fell to the floor.

✣

When I came to, I heard weeping and the prayers of those around me. I did not know what they were praying for.

For Sarah. For themselves. For the Messiah. For another world.

For the priest, may his beytsim be rat-chewed until the Messiah comes. Then may the Messiah continue with His teeth of broken wedding glass.

May his soul gnaw on itself through each of eternity's endless nights as it thinks about what he has been and what he has done.

Sarah was on the floor of her cell. Sobbing.

I had been as powerful as a raspberry in her protection. I was bupkis as a hero, the protector of but a small patch of floor.

There was a draft from the end of the room: the priest had left the main door open and so I flew through the darkness, up the stairs, and into the church.

I had few ambitions: Find Moishe. Burn everything. Escape.

I entered the transept, the church's stubby wing. A barely visible light glowed at the altar. A candle. Someone kneeling before a cross, praying. His clothing shone with dappled light, the sun on shallow water. The priest in his chainmail.

I landed in the open hand of a marble saint and waited, considering what to do. One thing occurred to me immediately: Here, Saint Chutzpenik. Let me fill your palm with grey-white dreck, an extruded offering in payment for your sacred chutzpah. Why did you not help us, you stone bystander?

Before the altar, the priest shifted in his genuflections and began mumbling a new prayer.

A sound in the other transept. The brief shine of metal from behind another unmoving saint's back.

Moishe lowering the blade of a halberd slowly in the darkness, readying its sharp end.

He crept forward and hid behind a pillar, ten feet from the priest and his pin-cushion back.

So, an ethical question:

Boy. Back. Sharp stick.

A priest on his knees, praying.

Is it kosher to skewer one who is davening, maybe even repenting? What should I do?

The priest was about to be caught on the horns of a dilemma.

And so I recalled that we are all birds, festooned with feathers, lifted equally by the breath of God. From the wren to the swan, we are a single flock. Whether we congregate and are called a brood, a brace, a murder, or a clutch. All of us, whether we gather into a wisp of snipes, a wisdom of owls, a wing of plovers, or remain like a single regretful priest on his knees before his God, we are one and it is not for us to decide another's fate. Unarmed truth and unconditional love will have the final word.

Did I think this?

Of course.

Me, Yeshua, and Gandhi.

Really, I thought only, *Give him a shtup he will not forget, my Maccabee.*
Stab your murderous blade into the hymen of his immortal soul until Sarah is
revenged with robe-red blood.

And then Moishe charged. The priest, hearing footfalls on the stone
floor, raised his bowed head and turned half around. A moment of intimacy: Moishe's eyes and the priest's connecting.

Moishe found a gap in his chainmail and penetrated the priest's side.

Pork on a spit. His God would provide fire.

Moishe recoiled from the weapon as if it were already hot with
flame. Moishe and the priest: the same horror-torqued face.

The priest was pinned to the cross.

Then Moishe turned and ran.

What had happened?

I can explain it while standing on one leg: Do unto others as they
have done unto you.

So, nu, that's not exactly it. An eye for an eye lacks foresight, but
what about an eye for twenty eyes? For a hundred, a thousand, for as
many had suffered?

Sha. That is visionary.

And what did we care that the priest had been praying?

The Inquisition had given Moishe his first letter of marque. His first
murderous thrust at death.

I flew off to find his shoulder as blood pooled around the knees
of the priest. There were no guards at the door. The priest must have
excused these protectors of the church and possible witnesses.

⊹

It was already tomorrow. Nothing like hastening someone's entry into
the hereafter to make time pass quickly. Moishe and I stole through the
streets, the pinks and reds of dawn seeping like a wound. The colours of
regret, and of moving on.

Were we regretful?

Does the braincleaving broadsword of a Visigoth wish it were the doily-delicate scalpel of a soft-handed surgeon rending the spine of a man into two symmetrical servings of dog meat? We were silent conquistadors returning from an El Dorado of revenge and glory. We would eat and boast, then find our beds until night when we would plunder the books from the Catedral.

"Sarah," Moishe said softly.

What could I say?

Nothing. I said nothing.

We made plans to enter the Catedral and retrieve her father's books. The red hounds of the Inquisition would be sniffing around the church for whoever skewered the priest. They'd not be expecting book liberators in the Catedral. We ate some breakfast in Doña Gracia's kitchen and then slept.

Chapter Thirteen

*I*magine: the Inquisition is everywhere. You are a known trafficker of forbidden texts and a helper of hidden Jews. You aid those who are imprisoned under orders of the Pope and the King and Queen of Spain. You are hunted as a murderer and a violator of the holy church and a heretic. You have plans to steal some hidden books. So, nu, how do you sneak into a cathedral?

Through the front door.

It wasn't locked.

We arrived late in the night—after even the most energetic of lotharios had slipped back into his cassock—and returned to his cell.

Moishe opened one of the Catedral's front doors a parrot's-width and I flew to a distant corner and onto the beams below the painted ceiling. I began mumbling what I hoped was the frightening preternatural blarney of Spanish spooks.

A word doesn't have to know what it means to mean something. A bird, either. I chanted these creepy lokshen noodles of nonsense until a sexton heard. My meshugas wasn't a raven's "Nevermore," but it had the same effect. The sexton's lantern did the trembling dance of the less-than-happy shades over the dark cathedral as he began his fearful search for the source.

He soon retreated only to return with another sexton. While these two doughty men braved the vivid conniptions of their own baroque imaginations, Moishe was able to find the Madonna and her hollow lucky foot, then open the door to the Jews' secret chamber. Once on the landing, he lit the candle hidden in his pocket.

Sha. And you thought he was just happy to see me?

I spoke a few more meshugeneh sermons from various rafters around the church, found the entrance to the room of books behind the retablo of the altar, and disappeared. The two sextons, gibbering their own narishkayt nonsense to the saints, had become self-sufficient: they now generated their own fear.

Once inside the room, I heard my name rising from the shaft in the floor.

Was it the devil himself, maybe? Takeh, his hacksaw voice of blood and sex and velvet had beckoned me to the basement many times before.

Nu, who else? It was Moishe.

Sometimes one is struck by a great idea. I pulled the silk cords like worms from the waists of a few red robes and knotted them together. I tied one end to a table and dropped the other down the shaft. The cord klopped Moishe on his Yiddisher kop. Moishe rubbed his head, then began to climb.

Which reminds me:

Two lengths of thread meet at the end of the tallis—the prayer shawl—of the Chief Rebbe of Warsaw.

"Hey, sweet string," one says to the other. "I've been looking for a single bisl of tassel just like you. Are you unattached?"

"I'm a frayed knot," the other says.

So, you've heard it. Still, a story helps you not to brech when times are tough. It keeps your kishkas inside, where they're supposed to be.

Moishe pulled himself out of the shaft. "The coffin is below," he said,

"Empty?" I asked. It wouldn't do for our books to share their berth with a corpse.

He looked at me. "Gevalt!"

Sha. He had the chutzpah to offer early retirement to a member of the clergy but not the beytsim to open a forgotten casket in the nether dark of the cathedral? But it's as they say, Az *di bubeh volt gehat beytsim volt zi geven mayn zeydah*. If my grandmother had them, she'd be my grandfather.

We proceeded with our plan. If the coffin were occupied, we'd wish its resident *zay gezunt* and commend him to the floor.

Moishe gathered the imprisoned books into a sack that we'd filched from Doña Gracia's pantry. Then he lowered it into the hole and shimmied down the rope. He was soon born again and back at the shelves refilling the sack. Three more times and we were both in the basement ready to screw our beytsim to the sticking place and open the casket. We were quite like the two sextons: afraid of the shadows cast by our own fear.

There was a scuttling as Moishe lifted the lid. A rat ran from behind the coffin and into the darkness. Thanks God, the casket, *Got tsu danken*, was empty. The only thing worse than finding a body in a coffin is finding half a body.

Moishe filled the coffin with the books. He left a small space.

I flew in.

He began nailing the casket closed.

A terrible sound.

I hoped—keneynehoreh—it was the only time that I heard it from this side. But, takeh, what's worse than hearing your own casket being nailed shut?

Not hearing it.

Moishe donned one of the robes and pulled the cowl low over his face. Then, disguised as Padre Moishe, he went to speak to the two trembling sextons.

Moishe, newly consecrated canon of the Chutzpenik Church.

"This very night, I have received orders from Torquemada himself," he told them in a deep, Inquisitorial voice. "The heretical body in the casket is a cancer on the Church. It must be removed and buried in unconsecrated ground immediately.

"And how could you have been so derelict in your duty to Their Highnesses, His Holiness the Pope, and indeed the Father, Son and the Holy Ghost Itself not to have noticed the secret chamber of the Judaizers right beneath your incense-breathing noses and behind the back of the Holy Virgin Mary, as if she didn't have enough to do being the mother of God?"

They would question less if accused.

Soon I heard voices. Then the coffin was lifted from the floor.

"By Santiago, if this sinner doesn't weigh as much as two Jews."

"You're certain there's just one in here?"

"He must be have been filled up right to bursting with heresy."

My pallbearers hauled the coffin up the stairs. Several sharp turns as we manoeuvred out the door and around the back of what I assumed was the Virgin.

"This sinner," Moishe said, giving two smart knocks on the lid, "died without confession and shall soon take transit to hell."

As planned, I began to voice the sounds of the dead, an ominous below-deck creaking and shuddering.

"Ghosts and demons fill this box," a sexton said.

"I expect it is its damned and undead body stirring, for it wishes to confess and repent," Moishe said. "We must open it."

I redoubled my groaning. A dybbuk was gnawing my kishkas with its stumpy teeth.

"*Dimitte mihi*, forgive me," the other sexton said. "I am afraid." I heard the quick steps of his retreat. His mother would be surprised to see him at this hour and at this age, and with his nappy needing changing. But we had expected that both sextons would run. We would have to improvise.

"Open it," Moishe commanded. The remaining sexton knelt down and began prying open the lid. I burst out, shrieking.

The sexton fainted.

Moishe quickly removed the books. He replaced them with the insensate sexton and nailed the lid back on. In the morning, there would be more shreking and shraying—from the sexton waking inside the coffin; from everyone else when they heard him.

Later, Moishe confessed that he had given the poor boychik some assistance in leaving his fears behind: he'd been kind enough to administer a mighty zets to the back of his head with a silver crucifix.

♱♱

A list of properties and dramatis personae present in the current drama:

A Sexton, comatose and in a coffin.

A Second Sexton, fear-footed, courage-lost, whereabouts unknown.

Heretical books piled higgledy-piggledly inside a cathedral.

Brilliantly insightful African Grey. Strikingly plumed in shades of dawn light. Much admired.

Fourteen-year-old Litvak. Male. Proto-pirate. Unarmed.

The sun. Life-giving. Carminizing. Currently rising.

The scene begins: the books must disappear even as night is disappearing.

Moishe hid the books in flour sacks behind the sty-fence outside the Catedral. Doña Gracia would soon send men to take them to her ships. In the meantime, the powerful nose-patshing dreck of the pigs would protect the books from discovery. Moishe removed the red silken robes, stuffed them into the flour sacks, and hid them behind the fence.

And then we walked off into the early morning world of fishermen, bakers, homebound carousers, and privateers of the book.

Curtain.

Chapter Fourteen

*I*n the kitchen, breakfast was waiting. A sweet hormiguilla of honey and hazelnuts. Blood oranges. A mug of cider.

Doña Gracia waited for us also. It was clear from the deferential scurrying of the servants that she was not often in the kitchen. They brushed their food-stained clothing apologetically, bowing as they hurried to bring succulent shtiklach before her, early morning delights for their Maris Stella Esther.

"The pearls have been hidden from the swine?" Doña Gracia asked.

"Four sacks directly under their priestly noses," Moishe said.

"Soon there will be the morning delivery to the Catedral," the Doña said. "The books will be recovered and taken to the wharf to begin their exodus to Morocco. They will again find freedom on Jewish shelves."

Then the Doña asked for a reckoning of our safety record. She knew about the previous night's Jack in the pulpit.

We told her about this morning's Jack-in-the-box.

She laughed, but then became serious. Moishe must leave on the boat. With the death of the priest, it was too dangerous to remain in Spain.

"I will sail only with Sarah and the Jews of the Catedral. Another Moses helped the people escape, and so, too, will I."

"There's Moses and there's Moses," she said. "You're a brave boy, but he fought with God in his gloves."

"The back of a guard's head cannot distinguish between ha-Shem and a rock," Moishe said. "Besides, I know how we may fight fire with equal fire."

Crowds would gather around the quemadero. Soldiers. Horses. Priests. Carts. Citizens.

People carried bread and fruit and wine. Nothing like a little nosh before conflagration and death. Food for thought or torture.

Men would also bring something to fill their snoot. Bottles of wine and of liquor. If these bottles were filled with oil, and if, all at once, this oil was used to set alight the many carts filled with straw or the hay bales used for seating, it might be that a rescue would be possible amidst the Judgement Day–like agitation of souls, the excitement of bodies, and a mob flashing mad with a fire-ignited panic.

Fighting fire with fire, Moishe had invented a kind of medieval Molotov cocktail.

The condemned would be taken to a ship before the Inquisition was able to distinguish ground from sky.

"Torquemada travels here, to the Seville Catedral, to celebrate an Easter mass with other Inquisitors. You are at great risk. If you will not leave, I will allow you to remain in my home, but only as long as you stay hidden inside and in the room I have given you. Else, you risk discovery and torture and execution for both of us."

"I will stay hidden," Moishe said. "But help me to save the Catedral Jews from the stake. Allow me this."

"You will stay hidden," Doña Gracia said. She would not allow Moishe to play a role in the escape that she was planning. "Then successful or not, you will leave for Morocco on that day."

Back in our room, he said, "I will remain hidden here, as the Doña wills it. So hidden that she won't know when I leave to find Abraham, the shtik dreck uncle of Sarah. Perhaps he suffers from regret. I intend to spare him such tsuris, such woes."

"And how will you do this?"

"A heart that does not beat feels no pain."

"Emes," I said. "It's true."

✛

Like owls and murderers, we slept through the day, waking only when the world was dim and without doubt. Besides, we were so tired we didn't have the energy to go to sleep. Luckily, it came to us.

Some food and then we slipped into the moonless night, seeing little but the shapes of the less dark against the deeper dark. Lit only by certainty, we crept like shadows along the alley walls.

So, emes, it was Moishe who had such certainty. I did not wish to leave our hiding place, to risk our lives, to think only of revenge, but sometimes, thoughts grow legs and carry you forward and you find yourself sneaking through the streets on the shoulder of an impulse, intent on the hunt. All you can do is hold on, try not to end up on the cobbles.

Abraham.

What would we do when we found him? Does a dog wonder what it will do when chasing the car?

"Sarah. She'll know where he is," Moishe said.

We slid along the skirts of the church.

"Sarah," Moishe whispered into the opening. "Are you there?"

Silence.

Perhaps she had a lunch engagement with the Emperor of Cipangu, or a hair appointment.

My own feathers prickling my own skin.

Fear.

What did they do to her?

Then her voice. "You shouldn't be here. It's dangerous."

"I have to ask you something."

"You can't be here. I am shamed."

"Not for me. I want to help."

Her face, a pale, smudged moon, appeared between the stones, "You must leave."

"I'm looking for your uncle. This is because of him."

"If not him, then another. Soon it will end for us. You, still, can run."

Moishe spoke quietly into the stones. "Kiss me."

Moishe. Sensitive as a barrel of pickles.

Sarah ignored him. "At the residence of the Archbishop, Diego Hurtado de Mendoza. I heard them say that he would be there."

"Kiss me," Moishe said again. "For courage."

"Not for courage," she said and stretched toward him.

Moishe tried to burrow with great enthusiasm into the side of the church, but, like traitorous crossguards on the hilt of a sword, his shoulders prevented him from plunging fully in. Only his head disappeared into the hole.

A parrot can only know what a parrot can know. In this case, a chicken-slender tuches communicating moonward with avid calligraphic perturbation. I could not read these nether words. Perhaps contact was made, for though the stones were thick, the necks of Moishe and Sarah, in proportion to their bodies, were not.

When it emerged, Moishe's face, like Sarah's, was pale and radiant.

Inside him, though this, too, cannot be known from without, adolescent blood, sperm and desire all turned bright silver and quick.

We flew into the night.

Chapter Fifteen

So, nu, if you hadn't seen the great Cathedral of Seville you might mistake the residence of the archbishop for the actual house of God.

If God had a proclivity for bull's-blood red and archways.

The Palacio Arzobispal. The residence of the Archbishop Diego Hurtado de Mendoza. It's a very large building, nu?

And in such a home, Moishe and I had to find a single treacherous Jew. A nebbish in a haystack.

We had been told that, hidden from view like a Kabbalist's God, there was an almost-forgotten door at the back of the building and far from the main gate. A small star in the tuches of the night sky. A secret entrance to the rectory.

Behind the Palacio, a rumplike hill. Moishe and I crawled up the slope. In such situations, my legs were as good as his. I'm not always a clavicle rider. We scanned for an opening and found a door tall as a dog, wide as the stern of a cow. If the stern of a cow were threshold-wide, and Rover were door tall. Moishe, creeping serpentine on his belly to avoid surveillance, reached for the handle. A door in another part of the wall opened. A grave's worth of light was thrown on the grass. A man stepped into this bright tomb. A priest carrying a lantern. We lay flat and silent as roadkill on a high street. Sometimes, there's nothing as good as two dimensions.

The priest turned and our backs were striped with lantern light. A beam-o'-nine-tails.

"The light of God is upon you," he said, looking in our direction.

We remained still as the bones of the dead. Maybe he didn't mean us. Maybe he was rehearsing a sermon.

Maybe he meant those Jewish pixie dybbuks dancing an estampie near us on the lawn.

"I see you," he said. "Do not move."

Definitely the dybbuks. We were not moving.

It would not be long before we wouldn't be able to move even if we had wanted to.

Because of fear.

Because of death.

The one not necessarily the result of the other.

He walked toward us. "Speak with me and I shall not speak of you."

Moishe stood. "Peace be with you, Father," he said. "We are lost. We are hungry. We look for help." Soon he would be telling the priest of the seven little Moishelets, his rope-thin younger brothers who were even more lost and hungry than us.

"Come inside. I will give you food," the priest said. "And you shall tell me your story."

He set his lantern on a large table and we sat around in its fringes.

"When they are angry and seek 'Padre Luis Dos Almos,' I am the one that hides. What name do you hide from?"

"Miguel," Moishe said. "Miguel Levante." He would hope to pass for this name.

The priest set out bread and wine. The official nosh of the Church.

And some pieces of cheese.

"I have not seen a parrot before, save in a painting," he said. "Who's a pretty boy?" He thrust some bread at me.

Pretty boy? Feh! I should have taken his eyes for grapes, his tongue for a red scarf. But then blindly, and without saying a word, he would have cooked me and I would be soup.

"What is your name, pretty boy?"

"Goy," I spat, naming both him and myself. I had been too long speaking only the mamaloshen to Moishe, and I was angry.

I knew my name could not be "Aaron." We were not wearing those feathers. Moishe became Miguel, I'd intended to baptise myself Christian, but not in Yiddish. A Yiddish baptism is hardly a baptism at all.

"Goy?" Padre Luis asked.

Moishe smiled at me slyly. What meshugas, what mischief, was he up to?

"Yes," he said. "He speaks but little and with limited sense. His name is Goya—in full, 'Christian Goya'—for when he was the bird of the Goya Family in Zaragoza, if they were not ever vigilant, he would dine upon Eucharist wafers stolen from the chapel. Indeed, it is because of this excess of devotion that he resides no longer with that noble family."

I smiled sheepishly.

If a parrot could be said to be sheepish.

Or to smile.

A person regarding the scene would not have known that though the bread and wine were only what they were, there had been a transubstantiation of two of the three at the table.

We had named ourselves Miguel Levante and Christian Goya.

For the padre, our Christian names were Lost and Hungry.

As we ate, I reflected that I must not again permit such an outburst of temper, or no matter the names we were known by, we would not be able to hide, would soon find ourselves tempered by fire.

What tale should Moishe relate of our history—for the priest would want details, names beyond Lost and Hungry?

At fourteen he had left the dreary shmatte-cart road-ruts of an insignificant shtetl armed only with a questionable book and a taste for the brine-tart air of the horizons beyond the horizon, only to be whipped as a cabin boy, and find driftwood escape from trade as a slave after shipwreck, then kill a priest, entomb a sexton, liberate what was bound—four sacks of heresy—and now had designs on the traitorous life of a Marrano spy working for the Archbishop and the Holy Inquisition itself, may devils make a coracle of his kishkas, his slime-white spine for a mast.

It seemed an unlikely tale, scaffolded by cloud and as fanciful as the second invisible horn of the unicorn.

Though it were true.

Surely the priest would not believe it, even were it to be scrubbed of stain in bucket water, its heresy drowned in a pail like a scrabbling kitten.

Still, of the megillah of tales that he might tell, Moishe had a sense that, spoken plainly, the authority of the truth, though shaped, sculpted, tailored and trimmed for the Church, might speak most authentically to the priest.

Truth sounds most true when it is spoken bespoke.

And it could save our lives. We were, after all, sought by the Inquisition and had been caught crawling up the leg of the Archbishop's, attempting entry at his back door. This would, we acknowledged, cause him considerable discomfort.

Moishe began:

A cabin boy from the east, he had wandered without design across water and into the history of Spain. There had been whipping, a ship-wreck, bandits, the execution lessons of the auto-da-fé, warm heaps of soft soil to sleep on, kindly farmers offering sour milk and the desiccated crusts of old bread.

Yet he should not neglect to recount the assistance of priests and the safe harbour, soft beds and fresh bread of churches.

And his faith.

Padre Luis Dos Almos sat for awhile chewing on some of that soft church bread. Tongues of lantern light worried the stumps of shadow in the kitchen's dim maw.

"An excellent tale," he said, finally. "Adventure enough for a bindlestiff of a lad in possession of but a meagre assortment of years. And what you say of history interests me. For it is true, we wander the alleys like flâneurs, sometimes finding ourselves on the main street amidst the chaos of traffic, dodging to avoid becoming flesh shoes on history's great hooves."

He poured more wine into both his own and Moishe's cups. "I observe, also, that you have, perhaps, also wandered from the narrow path of truth into the broad thoroughfare of invention. 'Miguel'—is that a name from the East? And what of the Goyas of Zaragoza and their parrot? I was born on some day's yesterday, but let me be clear that that day was not today."

Which way to run? I saw flight in Moishe's eyes.

"I requested a story and you have provided a good tale," Padre Luis said. "I warrant it is a painting with more colour than the pencil outline of the actual. Tonight you will sleep here. When the sun returns day, you will return home, returning to your parents both yourself and their sleep."

"Yes, Padre," Moishe nodded respectfully. Sculpted and trimmed, the truth was not as distant as Moishe might have imagined. Sleep and his parents had not shared a bed for some time unless it be eternal.

Padre Luis poured himself another cup of wine to water his ripening cheeks. "I myself have been the wandering I of many adventures," he began. "I was born in the city of Palma on the island of Majorca. From there, I have travelled much and seen more. The iridescent arbour of the peacock's tail, the grizzled hump on the ape's back. Great battles and tender love. Silver-hearted heroes and the mewling of cowards, though often each mistook himself for the other. I have known the jealous turnscrew of the human heart and the incomprehensible round dance of kindness. Jews, infidels, pagans and Christians. And those in between." He paused to drink again, and this seemed to inspire him. "I am drunk from the jagged edges of life's broken bottle. I have tasted the sweet blackcurrant wine of a woman's lips. But, these last several years, I have become a ghost." He imbibed now with less inhibition and more gusto, spilling wine down his cheeks and onto his cassock.

"I have become a ghost."

He did not appear to be so, though at this point, it was clear that he was comprised of a high percentage of spirits.

"This Inquisition. This Tribunal of the Farkakteh Holy Office. Shh. We must not speak with such vigour if we are to speak plainly." He leaned conspiratorially over the table and then continued in a hiss. "I am a ghost. How can I be a man? I am hollowed out by such haunting. Watching. Waiting. Not all who wander are lost."

Then he placed his soft red face on the table and closed his eyes. "How great is the darkness," he said and passed out.

If I, as Christian Goya, had supped too devoutly on the sacred body, this unconscious holy ghost of a man had too greatly sipped of the blood. Likely quarts of it before we'd arrived.

We crept into the dark hallway and were gone.

There'd be time to wonder at Padre Luis's use of a Yiddish word. I was certain that Moishe had noticed, too.

It was farkakte.

We could barely tell left from right in the dim light of the hall.

"Left," I said.

"No, right is better," he said.

"Lokshen putz," I said. Noodle dick.

"Shmeckel beak."

"Dreck shmuck."

"Seagull."

Fighting words. But he whose legs are on the ground decides which way to walk. We went right.

A long hallway. The dark shapes of doors.

Our quarry was behind one of them, asleep, we hoped, on a pallet, his nose guttural with snores, his dreams radiant hot with the burning sanbenitos of those he had betrayed. All but our prey would be in the red cassock of a priest. But soon he, too, would be robed in red: we would slit his duplicitous throat and he would become kosher meat for worms.

Behind two doors, no one. Behind another, a sleeping priest. The creak of the moving door caused him to stir and so we quickly withdrew.

The last door before a turn in the hall, a larger room, empty but for a table, a chair, and a Golem-sized bookcase filled with books. A small sconce on the wall, barely alight. A sound from down the hall. We slipped into the room, a place to hide.

There was a narrow sword, more like a skewer than a blade, resting against the wall. Moishe took it in his hand, raised it for protection. Footsteps. Some murmuring. Where could we hide?

Moishe did not yet possess the brawn of adulthood. His pisher-thick frame fit behind the shelves. And with room for a bird.

So, I hid.

There was no back to the bookcase. We had to rely on the books for cover. It would not be the first time that books had been used to obscure what might otherwise be clearly seen.

The fluttering of orange-yellow candlelight entered the room. Then a man. He put the candleholder down then looked thoughtfully at the shelves. It is impossible to know if one is invisible without asking, and we weren't going to ask.

He moved closer, either to distinguish us from shadow or to read the title on a book.

It isn't clear how the book felt, but winter came suddenly to my spine. Now we could see the man clearly. It was the very man that we sought. Abraham. The traitor. He stood in front of the books and reached out.

It happened in a single moment.

Abraham pulled a book from the shelf. As the space opened, the birth of a gapped-toothed grin, Moishe manoeuvred the skewer between the books and drove it into the soft flesh between the man's ribs. Incisive literature, the bookcase had a venomous stinger filled with revenge. Abe folded in half, clutched his chest, and then rolled to the floor. He lay on the ground in fetal position, and died. He made no sound, before or after.

Moishe stood behind the bookcase for a few minutes, his hand still protruding from between the shelf of books.

As if waiting to greet a bibliophile with a surprise handshake.

Then, waking, he retracted the hand and we quickly left the room, Moishe creeping on the toe-ends of his shoes in a silent swan-dance. We would not disturb the fathers in their beds, nor Padre Luis's wine-fuelled table-top shlof. We were soon through the door, down the rectory's sloping hill and free again to creep like shadows along the walls of Seville's sleeping streets.

Moishe returning home after another night playing Michael the Archangel, converting the living to the dead. Protecting Jews from the fiery furnace.

Chapter Sixteen

We followed another armful of bread through the back door and into the kitchen. We were hoping for a warm slice, some cheese, and a mug of hot drink. Instead, Doña Gracia was waiting for us when we returned.

Hot, bitter, steaming.

"I offer you my protection and instruct you to remain hidden but instead you creep through the night like a plague-ridden rat laying low I don't know how many men? This risk that you took, though lit bright by daring and righteousness, endangers not only yourself, but me, this household, and our people. You enrage the Church, the Inquisition, and the powerful like a toreador stabbing banderillas into the shoulders of bulls. Brave, perhaps, but also foolhardy, boy."

She led us into a room that was a small library, not unlike the library of the night before where Moishe had indeed been a banderillero, pricking another churchman.

"Doña . . ." Moishe began, but she raised her hand for silence.

"In these times," she said, "fear is a circle whose centre is everywhere and whose circumference is nowhere. A vicious circle, you might say. The Inquisition gives cause for citizens to fear even themselves."

Doña Gracia raised a brass platter and offered Moishe a dried date. He took one, rolled it around in his mouth, then extracted a damp half which he gave to me.

"As my father would say, 'It is often bitter before it is sweet,'" he said.

"If we live to see the sweetness," the Doña said. "Trust no one.

You must do only as I say and heed my plan for the rescue of the Cathedral Jews and for your exodus over the sea. Torquemada has arrived in Seville this holy week of Easter with many other Inquisitors. They come for Good Friday and now also the auto-da-fé. He has arranged this with grim logic: on the first but not Good Friday, he believes Jews murdered Christ, so, on this day, a Christian will murder Jews.

"Tomorrow, we hold a council in this house to devise a plan. Tomorrow, a Maundy Thursday that is also Passover. We will pray together that the Angel of Death will abide the blood on our doorposts and pass over both those condemned to die and those not yet condemned. That though he may not take their first-born, the escape shall be as a plague to them. But you—Moishe—shall be not our Moses, leading our people to this, if not promised, then this promising land. You will stay within the walls of my house."

She left us in the library.

We ate the remaining dates.

Then we looked at the shelves. Each book, like a living being, from hand-held sextodecimo sparrows to the ostrich torsos of folio slabs, the soft unarmoured flesh of the interior. The binding as skin. I think to myself, "Gotenyu, that could've been me."

But it's a mammal-wrapping of leather, not the feathers of birds. In Latin, these books are *incunabula*—swaddling clothes, a cradle. Every bound book a baby, dropped into the world, waiting to be understood.

And there were maps.

Moishe unrolled some of these ribbon-bound charts. Doña Gracia's library had few practical aids to navigation; instead, it was mostly maps of beautiful nonsense—a cholent of legends, ancient books, explorers' reports, and the desires and superstitions of kings, islands of real experience and archipelagos of the fanciful mixed together in a speculative and hopeful ocean.

Skinned creatures with no body. A dream of what is or might be. Some small truth stretched thin, a tattooed shade. Hope and fear transformed horses into camelbacked leopards with the wings of a dove, their riders saddled below them, feet pointing toward the sky.

"Aaron," Moishe said. "Look." He unrolled a large chart and surveyed the waters. "The world is filled with wonders." He was still the Bar Mitzvah boy, longing for adventure. His finger sailed the waves of the ocean sea. Beyond the Canary Islands to the outrigger islands of Cathay and Cipangu: Anquana, Candyn, Tristis, Java Major, Neacuram and Moabar, the possessions of the Great Khan crowding the left side of the map. Regions wickered by eel-like creatures and Antipodean half-men grimacing from their chests.

"Yet the world is as small as Columbus told us," he said. "If only because it is crammed ongeshtupted with marvels. We should take the Jews from the Catedral to this Naye Velt, these new places."

"Oh it'd have to be a bahartsteh New World to have such people as people in it."

"Bahartst—brave—why?" I said.

"Where has it gone well with people?"

We returned to our room and gave sleep to our eyes, each of my six eyelids to slumber. We'd have a night's worth of day and wake with the moon.

Chapter Seventeen

$\mathcal{M}$oishe woke me. The kitchen was empty, except for moonlight. It became emptier after we filled ourselves with food. Oranges and the delicious relic of a gumbo of stewed meat, rice and beans.

"I must tell Sarah about her uncle."

"You're meshugeh. We can't leave. Doña Gracia warned us that—"

"How can I stay here like a shmendrick, shtum silent as a blintz."

"*Azoy*, if it's filled with anything, your head is filled with soft cheese."

The street was deserted. Like our good sense, we disappeared into the night.

This path of moon shadows was becoming familiar, if more danger-ous. The Easter preparations had begun. The road had been cleared for the Good Friday processions. No dreck. No gold. No rotting food.

Moishe crawled toward the cellar of the church. There was little sound. The susurration of the wind in the leaves of trees. A distant bird. The rabbi's thin voice chanting. A subterranean muezzin calling us. We could see that he was wearing tefillin, the small boxes strapped to his forehead and arm. His shadowy figure rocked forward and back in the darkness.

He stopped. "Who's there?" He sounded both anxious and exhausted.

"Rabbi, it is Moishe. We did not mean to interrupt your prayers."

"You are not alone?"

"My parrot."

"Of course. I think he is a pinteleh—the dot of a vowel—perched on your shoulder. He helps you, no?"

"Yes. We did not mean to disturb you."

"It is good. I should rest. I have been davening since . . . well, since before I was a Bar Mitzvah. And I'm tired. . . But it puts me together with my people. I am with them. And I am near to ha-Shem, the Almighty. He gives me strength for the day. Soon I will be yet nearer to him.

"It's almost Passover and I expect you wonder *Ma nishtanah halailah hazeh?* 'Why is this night different from all others, and why do I wear the tefillin and repeat the morning prayers?'"

"Yes, I . . ."

"Well, my boy, we are like slaves in Egypt but I am not certain that the Angel of Death will pass over us this time, and so I pray as if with each prayer, it is the morning of a new day. As the Mishnah says . . ."

I could tell that Rabbi Daniel had become half fardreyt—unmoored by waiting for the upcoming storm. How would I feel two days before my expected execution?

"Rabbi, we have the books that were in the Catedral. Doña Gracia will help you and the others escape. There is a boat . . ."

"Shh. Boychik. Even Moses couldn't free our people without ha-Shem. I remember . . ."

"But I have news to tell you. Abraham is dead."

"Abraham?"

"I killed him."

"My boy . . ."

"He betrayed you. All of you. And Sarah. He—"

"Only ha-Shem can take vengeance. The Lord came down when Samson sought revenge for the loss of his eyes . . . And though Abraham died with both eyes, the Mishnah says, 'Whoever destroys a single life is as guilty as though he had destroyed the entire world; and whoever rescues a single life earns as much merit as though he had rescued the entire world.' But it is not a matter of simple mathematics, one eye given for another taken. I recall that in Leviticus . . ."

There was a voice from the front of the church.

"Shh, Rabbi," Moishe hissed. "They're coming."

The rabbi retreated into the darkness of the cell and began again to murmur prayers.

Moishe squeezed against the stone wall. We willed ourselves to be stone. I may have been the dot of a vowel, but I did my best to be both silent and invisible.

Torchlight flickered along the path. We were hidden from its illumination by a buttress.

"Anyone there?" the guard's voice said.

As if "anyone" would answer.

I wanted to say, "I'm not just anyone," but even a worthy line isn't worth death. I'd prefer my famous last words to be occasioned by my imminent and inevitable demise, not the cause of it.

I knew Moishe had expected a hero's welcome, a verbal parade in celebration of his execution of Abraham and not the Mishnah-mad ravings of a farmishteh Rabbi.

And an eight-pounder broadside of a kiss from Sarah.

The guard retreated with his light. We'd have to be even more careful. And quick.

Moishe slithered along the church-side in pursuit of a gun port behind which was the flash of Sarah.

She was curled in the straw of the corner. A seahorse, a foal.

"Sarah," Moishe whispered. "The guards are close. I must speak low if I speak."

She came to the space between stones. "You must go. It is too dangerous."

"Yes. But first . . ." He began to tell her about Abraham, but then stopped. Abraham, though he had betrayed her, had been her uncle.

This was not a time for more grief. Grief over betrayal. Over family. Over death.

"I will help you. I have a plan. I have arranged—Doña Gracia has arranged—your escape from Spain. Soon you will be sailing toward Africa."

"Disgraced. An orphan," Sarah said. "Alone."

"But I will help you," Moishe said. "I will protect you. I am also an orphan. We are bashert. Destined. Let us . . . let us be farknast. Betrothed."

She reached her hand toward Moishe. Their fingertips touched. A pretty rondeau composed suddenly in the crenelated castle of Moishe's excited brain.

But it was interrupted. Torchlight and the return of the guard's voice. Footsteps.

Moishe withdrew his hand. Turned. Ran into the shadows of dark trees. I flew above him, into the shadows of branches. The guards' voices calling. Moishe clambering over a short fence and into some kind of shit dreck.

"*Ech! Der oylem is a goylem.* The world is stupid," he muttered.

"Like Noah said to Mrs. Noah as the rain began, 'this is no time to worry about your shoes,'" I said. "Now, *drey zich.* Keep moving!"

We went at full speed down the street, turning again into an alley.

We waited. In darkness, Moishe's quick breath. Beside it, the smaller gusts of a parrot's breath, my plum-sized lungs.

He inhaled. Held his breath. Listened.

Voices and footfalls. Becoming distant.

Breathing again. Running again.

Across a wide street, along an alley of tanners' shops. We waded through the pungent tang in the dimness, Moishe careful to keep his footfall light, to look behind him. Down wide steps, a left turn, the roof of our goal. We'd soon be safe in our bed, ready to dream of the Promised Land and our Sarahs.

Then, from the shadows, a shtarker, a tough, wearing a dark robe, long sword still sheathed in its scabbard. He stepped into the middle of the alley and looked at us.

What else was there to look at, the scenery?

He drew the sword.

Death? *Azoy gich?* So soon?

Hardly time to think of famous last words, but if they have to be mine, I wish they could be: "I hope my friend's very large arquebus doesn't wake the city with the sound of your flesh spattering in a sorrowful pink rain."

When you die, you can say what you want, but for now I said, "Run."

Chapter Eighteen

Thursday. We were safe and our bed was warm. One of us may have been dreaming of a world of endless Sarahs, or of the land of but a single one. I, however, was flying through the shadow-clotted jungle to a clearing where high water spilled into lucent ponds. Monkeys nattered in the distance like idiot Shakespeares and the scent of ripe fruit came to me like song.

We ate breakfast late. The house was quiet.

Moishe had been faster than the murderous intentions of the thug—*a fayer zol im trefn*—a fire should meet him and make him crispy. The quick turn, the nimble reverse, the jumped-over fence, the dash through the oysgeshpilt outhouse. Better you're a flea than a lion when you're running from the gun.

Or that you're quick when you're a boy and he's got a sword.

And so we ate. The last leavened bread before Passover. After this, forty years of matzoh in eight days. The hardtack of exodus. Not only a covenant, but binding.

For soon we'd be bound for Eretz Africa with a boatful of Jews, books, and . . . Sarah.

Behind us, a shoreline cluttered with the fists of Inquisitors raised in a holy and impotent anger.

Unless we were all dead.

Would that be—*ek velt*—the end of the world?

We'd only know when we got there; I hear they don't take reservations.

So, after this breakfast of a bisl bread, Moishe and I, still exhilarated by our escape, became explorers, charting the unknown. At least, what was unknown to us. That's usually enough unknown for one day. Passageways, rooms, cellars, courtyards. The peninsulas, islands, caverns, and inland seas of Doña Gracia's world. We were left to ourselves to discover what we might.

I rode the thin wave of Moishe's shoulder up stairs and along hallways. We looked into the doors left ajar. Those in their beds, those sitting at chairs and before small tables. Listless, playing cards with the compulsion of a song that won't go away. Some were startled, nervous, our gaze the sudden pain of a dart, the surprise annoyance of an insect bite. Some looked with a quick smile or a vacant daze. The Doña's home was a hostel for the hurt and the hidden. And their children, charming, snot-nosed, crying, spring-like or rubbery, driftwood in the wash of parents and history.

Two men sat in a courtyard filled with ferns. I recognized one as Alonso, the man who worked in the kitchen.

"Miguel," he called to me. "Who's a pretty girl?"

"Aaron," Moishe said. "His name is Aaron."

"My father's name . . ." he said. "This old jowly rooster"—Alonso motioned—"my friend Isaac." He was stooped and chicken-thin with an abundant growth of dark moustache on his sallow face. It seemed as if this swart lip-bound earwig had sapped vital strength from the man.

The friend, almost imperceptibly, nodded in greeting.

"He has arrived at the Doña's for the seder. We eat, we tell the Passover story, we plan a Spanish exodus."

The friend again moved a few molecules in assent.

"So you will be joining us?" Alonso asked.

"Unless there's another secret meeting with good food I should know about?" Moishe said.

"My wife and I cook the food," Alonso said with pride. "It will be delicious. And secret. As the Torah says, 'Thus shall ye eat it; with your loins girded, your shoes on your feet, and your staff in your hand.'"

"I don't know about the staff, but I consider shoes and, especially, girded loins to be essential for any meal," Moishe said. "Think of the crumbs."

"Years ago, I learned from my parents. I was born a Jew," Alonso said. "When they expelled us from Seville, I did not move. It was only my Jewish name that left me. They say that God Himself drew back to make room for life. This was how it was with us, too. We had no choice. My family: children, parents, wife. I shed my skin, but even with new colours I remained a snake to them. There were riots. We are in Job's land, tested by God. Alav ha'shalom. Only my wife and I remain."

He paused and then: "So, tonight, we are Jews. What more could they take from us? 'I am that I am.' And soon we will leave Spain to where we will be safe."

"And where we can always have meals together—at Passover, Shabbos, whenever we are hungry," Moishe said.

"Next year in Jerusalem," Alonso said. "Or at least, Africa."

We continued our exploration. To an attic. Locked storerooms. Down some steps, a passageway into a cellar. It would soon be evening, but here, like Thule in the distant north, it was always dark.

Moishe lit a candle.

A room filled with spider webs, broken furniture, worn carpets, barrels, clay jugs. Spider webs. Some old swords.

A door at the back that Moishe had difficulty opening. As he struggled, we heard the bells of Maundy Thursday begin to sound.

Tonight it was both Passover and Maundy Thursday's Last Supper. It was either the devil never shites but he shites in buckets—or a good sign.

They would be holding mass in the churches, washing feet, and singing "Gloria." We went to find the dining table to begin our own last supper, our secret seder.

We'd leave the door for another time.

So.

It was a few days after Passover, and Moses and Jesus were walking together, kibitzing about this and that, remembering their glory days in Biblical times.

They came to a sea.

"Hey, Yeshua, watch this," Moses said. He raised his walking stick and parted the sea. "I still got it," he said. "Just like parting my hair. If I still had hair."

"Ok, then, Moe," Jesus said. "I can top that." And he strode out over the surface of the water, defying gravity and the physics of surface tension. Then suddenly, he began to sink. He swam to shore, spluttering.

"I don't understand," he said. "It used to be so easy."

"That was before you had holes in your feet," Moses replied.

We'd never seen such a meal. A Constantinople of food. A thousand succulent succubi threatening to make merry with our insides. A Red Sea of sauce. And soon, we'd arrive at the promised lamb.

In the centre of the table, long as a whale, bright flames surmounted two pairs of silver candlesticks that would be the prize of any pirate's booty.

The chairs were arranged for us, pillows in place, so that we could lie back as was the custom. We were once slaves, now we can recline. At each place, there was set a splendid Haggadah, the prayer book outlining the service.

Even if I had been offered a chair and a pillow, takeh, would I have been able to lean back in comfort? The seder, the Haggadah, the practice of being a Jew. These things were forbidden. In Egypt, the Jews were slaves, but they were allowed to be Jews.

Around the table, Alonso and his wife. Alonso's friend, jowly Isaac. An older man with a clipped white beard, introduced as Joshua. Two men in red cloaks both named Samuel. Let's say First Samuel and Second Samuel. One dark man known as Jacob. Near him, a portly woman—though she more resembled ship than port—named Rebecca. A Leah. A Moses. A Daniel. More names than I could remember. All told, we were likely a Jesus-and-apostles' worth of guests gathered for supper and scheming.

Presiding at the end of the table, Doña Gracia.

She introduced Moishe. The Ashkenazi and his feathered shadow.

We began the seder. First we'd all be Moses and help the Jews scramble over the Red Sea, then onto Doña Gracia's boats. Boils and frogs and locusts would give us inspiration.

We recited prayers. We drank wine. We ate bitter herbs, eggs and salt water. The mortar of apples and nut, spread between two matzoh.

We arrived at the Four Questions—the questions about the seder traditionally asked, at least in the East, by the youngest child present. *Mah nishtanah halailah hazeh.* Why is this night different than all other nights?

"My bird," Moishe said. "My bird will ask the questions."

"And then he can find the cracker. The afikomen," someone laughed.

So now I was a party trick, supposed to fly like an airborne mizinik— the family's little tousle-headed tyke—to discover the hidden matzoh?

"Jews may appear as Christians. Muhammadans as Moriscos. There may be more in heaven and feathers than are dreamt of in our philosophy," Doña Gracia said. "Ofttimes in the cage, an unexpected sage. This bird may prove useful to us."

"True," said old Joshua. "As it says in Job, 'the fowls of the air, and they shall tell thee.' So, old greybird, let's begin with some questions."

I managed to recite the first few lines before becoming fartshadet— confused. I knew much of Jewish things, but I had not been born to it. The others joined in and we asked the questions in chorus as was the Sephardi custom.

Joshua continued, leading the seder. We retold the Exodus story as he directed us, each taking turns with the telling. Even the fartshadeteh feygeleh, the befuddled bird, yours truly. As each of the ten plagues was mentioned, each person dipped a finger into his wine glass, and spilled individual drops like blood from the stone-cut palms of slaves. I dipped my beak, cut only by seeds and human words.

But we only got to the seventh plague—barad, hail—when some burly shtarkers burst through the door. Behind these oxen-browed air-suckers were two weasely-faced farshtunkeneh priests, plague-red droppings from the pestilent shvants of the church. There's a way that actions can wear heavy boots even if the actors do not.

In *flagrante delicto*. We were caught with our hand in the seder jar, our fingers in the sweet wine.

Moishe, having been on red alert for such capes dived below the horizon of the table. I remained a bird and flew to the crow's nest of a sconce, waiting to see what might transpire, how I might help or hinder.

Each burlyman grabbed someone. It was a country dance of thugs, the priests calling the tune. An arm wrapped around the throat of the old man, Joshua.

"Take my breath, I keep my belief," he said as he was pulled down.

The fabric of Rebecca's soft shoulders served as reins as she was driven into the wall then kicked. Alonso was clutched by the elbow but he knocked away the grober's gorilla hand and ran to protect his wife. Immediately he was surrounded and a fist struck him a mighty boch. He sank like a stone to the floor. His wife screamed.

"May you live to see your children die."

She lifted the long silver carving knife from the table and plunged it into the thick side of a shtarker. A short-lived revenge for they pulled her arms behind her and bound them tight. The wounded man staggered then collapsed onto a chair, clutching his pierced side. Both Alonso and his wife were weeping.

"This travesty of Easter, this Last Supper, shall indeed be your last," a priest shrieked above the tumult to no one and everyone. "I charge you in the name of the Holy Office with heresy and Judaizing. With harbouring enemies of the King and Queen, the Church, and of the Holy Father. With murder."

Doña Gracia was standing at the end of the table. Motionless, a proud statue radiating power and strength, she had both gravitas and gravitational pull. Space-time turned around her. She had not been touched by the Inquisition.

"Friend, do what you have come to do," she said, looking at the priest.

It was only a moment before it registered on the priest's face. The Gospel of Matthew. The words of Jesus to Judas.

Then they came and laid hands on her and seized her and it seemed that time began to move twice as quickly. Some ran for hallways and doors, took up chairs, knives, their own swords. An Inquisition enforcer rushed toward the woman named Leah and she thrust a Haggadah with a great zets at his head. He bent over and she ran, but she was seized by another and bound also. Daniel slashed with a dagger but was quickly overpowered. Moishe had escaped notice below the deck of the table. His dark eyes glinted from the shadows like a rat's and caught my gaze. It was time for him to make his move. I swept across the room, shrieking the excoriating cry of the harpy. Swords slashed behind my tail as they attempted to cut me from the air. I embedded my claws into a soft face and heard the raw howl.

Moishe, still a rodent, scrabbled on his knees and dove down the stairs in the direction of the cellar.

The room was a torrent of slashing sword and I feared I would soon be diced for lobscouse. In Egypt, it was Moses who burned his tongue on a coal, but here it was Aaron who would eat fire.

What is more powerful than guns or swords?

Darkness.

And in the right circumstances, it can be rendered with a bisl gob of bird spit. I swept from candle to candle, extinguishing flame. And then in that sudden night, I followed the rat I was loyal to, and went underground.

We stumbled to the cellar, Moishe feeling a path past rolled carpets, barrels and chairs. He crouched in the corner.

"I should have helped," he said. "I should have fought to save the others."

We heard a sound from outside the room, footsteps from somewhere down the passage.

They say that if a baby falls beneath an ox or an elephant, a fearful mother can find strength beyond the weight of matter or of death. And if there's a bottle of rum beneath a boulder, a shikker drunk can find his strength, too. Moishe fingered his way along the back wall of the room and found the immoveable door. He moved what had likely not been moved for lifetimes. It shifted but a rib cage's breadth, and he slid himself through the opening.

It was difficult to close the door again, but Moishe managed, hauling on the handle like a sailor hoisting anchor, the door having been reminded of its own possibility.

Chapter Nineteen

"Is this my fault?" Moishe said.

"Moishe, like they say: *Noch der chupeh iz shpet di charoteh*. After the wedding it's too late for regrets. Like any story, we must now figure what happens next."

Voices in the hall?

Only our own nervous breathing in the dark and dusty room.

Then something close clashed against metal.

A few sparks. Moishe had a small tinderbox open and was striking flint with the firesteel. On one knee, the black charcloth was spread beneath a few splinters of tinder wood. On the other, the squat nub of a candle.

With each spark, a small dim circle. Shelves of some kind, barely visible.

Finally, Moishe was able to light the cloth, transfer the fire to the tinder and then to the candle. A small thought passed about in dim whispers.

The flame was a living thing, trembling like an old rabbi.

And by its light, we could see that we were inside that rabbi's brain.

Shadows. Cobwebs. Dust.

Stacks of books and old scrolls cluttered ongevorfn everywhere. Prayerbooks, parchment, vellum. Inside a rabbi's brain after it'd been banged about by the Inquisition.

Moishe lifted a few prayerbooks from their pile. They were old and worn and their pages were ripped, stained, or fused together.

This was a hospice or tomb for the broken, the fading, the dead and the dying. I hadn't seen a binnacle list of such sieve-bodied and fissured-wounded since I watched what the Turks' cannons did during the battle for Constantinople years before.

"It's a genizah," Moishe said. "You're not allowed to destroy anything containing the name of God." He held up a page of faded writing, riddled with holes in the shape of lakes, birds, clouds and birthmarks. They store the books until they can be properly buried. But this place looks like it was forgotten. Some of these scrolls could have been made of the skins of Esau's flock."

"And, if we don't make an escape plan," I said, "they'll find us, too, sometime in the future, our words forgotten, our bones collecting dust, and they'll say, 'They're from years ago when there once was Spain.'"

"Yes," Moishe said. "Two friends: a looker and a chickenhawk."

"Nu," I said. "You can't have *a pish on a forts*—a piss without a fart."

"Takeh," Moishe said. "But we have a plan. We wait until the priests have gone, then you fly out like Noah's dove to see if it's safe. Then we rescue Sarah and the hidden Jews, then Doña Gracia and the others, and then we sail to safety—for Africa, your home."

Feh. What did I know from Africa? I wished only for my boychik's scrawny coast.

"If they put your brain inside a bird," I said, "*hi te'ofef le-achor*—it would fly backwards. How are we going to help them? Even a great captain needs a boat."

"My mother used to say, 'If one wants to beat a dog, one finds a stick.' So, nu, I'm looking for a stick."

Our first battle was with time.

We waited.

Fingers cast by candlelight wavered against the walls as Moishe examined shelves. Prayerbooks and Torahs, but also letters, leases, contracts, deeds, ketubahs, rabbinical court records, and sheaves of poems by Halevi and Moses ben Jacob ibn Ezra. Like the manifold races of man, from Ultima Thule to the lands of Prester John, the books ranged in size from those that could be held like a child's hand to those that could contain the broad lungs of an ape.

But no sticks.

The candle was becoming an even shorter thumb, a warm wax petseleh, a guttering boyhood. Moishe snuffed it like a priest and we were in the dark. How long would the shtarkers stalk Doña Gracia's? We slept for hours waiting for the waters to recede.

Finally, Moishe felt his way to the door and hauled on it to make a scupper for my exit. I crept through, found my way past the storage room and flew in darkness down the hall. I stopped at the stairs and listened.

A slurping, a chewing. An animal sound. Some chazzer on the table finishing the seder. The only toughs, twenty white soldiers on a red hill, roughing up the lamb. I climbed the last stair and looked out.

Padre Luis from the Palacio Arzobispal, now emperor of wine bottles and inquisitor of stews. There's an extra cup left for Elijah at any seder, but this ghost we could not have expected.

"Ah, Christian. Some company here in this desolate sanctuary." He'd seen me and remembered that I'd baptized myself a "Christian." "Come enjoy some strange fruit," he said, holding up the half-noshed flesh of something unidentifiable.

He appeared to be alone in his leftover kingdom and so I returned to my Noah in the bookish Ark.

We were chaleshing for a facefull. We'd eaten only the first few ritual seder foods before the table was stormed.

"A chair, Miguel," Padre Luis said, directing Moishe to a place across from him. "An oasis of food and wine for you who are hungry. And someone to break bread with."

Moishe sat at the chair that yesterday was Joshua's. He drank the remaining cup of the seder wine then piled a tall Ararat on Joshua's plate. At least two of everything.

"Your parents were not glad to see you?" Padre Luis asked, wrestling a joint of lamb with his face, the wet slap like the sea between a dock and a hull. "I am surprised to discover you here. In the house of a Jew."

Moishe motioned to the food, hoping that this would be explanation enough, relying on two of the perennial certainties of story: appetite and mystery.

Padre Luis nodded and, for awhile, the three of us pursued our appetites and allowed mystery its invisible Elijah-like place at the table. I roamed about this landscape of food, hunting the placid raisin and harvesting the gentle nut.

"You are wise, my young friend," Padre Luis said, after awhile, "to eat much and speak less." He drained a silver kiddush cup of its wine. "But I know who you are."

Moishe's gaze darted toward me. *Should we run?*

Padre Luis looked left and right about the room, as if at any moment the red capes of the Holy Office would flame from behind the tapestries.

"I know who you are because Doña Gracia told me."

Did they extract this as their hot tongs branded both her mortal flesh and her soul's thin wings?

"*Gey strasheh di vantsen*—frighten the bugs off someone else—I am called, 'Miguel,' and that is all," Moishe said with bravado. But I knew he wasn't certain if this was treachery, something to trick him into dropping his goyishe drawers and revealing the true pomp and circumcision of his Hebrew shvants.

"Miguel. Moishe. Conveyor of forbidden books. I recall little of what I said when we previously met, but I shall repeat what I believe I imprudently revealed," Padre Luis said. "I am no friend of the Holy Office. In these few years, I have become wasted, wraithlike, my faith consumed by its un-Christian fire. What I did not say was that I was an ally of the Jews, of Doña Gracia, of the rabbi, that I was to be part of the plan for the escape of those now condemned, that I would leave with them for a new life, holy yet free. Last night, I would have arrived in time to give warning to those in this house for I heard what they said in the Palacio.

It is to my eternal regret that I had first immersed myself in a blood-red sea of church wine. Its undertow pulled me under and I drowned. I woke only this noon when all was already lost. And so, what do I do? I sit at this table and eat, I who should have been a sentry at the doorpost, waiting to wave away the Angel of Death with the lamb's blood of my true Christian faith."

He filled a jug with wine and drank long and unrelentingly. Finally, he breathed.

"O *beati martyris Santiago*, Alonso is already dead. He has returned to his God. Joshua may yet still be alive, though it is unlikely that he will survive the efforts of the Holy Office to extract a confession and a list of other names. Sancta Maria mater. And what they have done to Doña Gracia? Tomorrow they all go to the quemadero to be sacrificed like Jesu Christo, our Lord . . . or at least, my Lord. Oh, all is darkness," he wailed, "All is night." He placed his head on his plate and once again, passed into a drunken sleep.

Moishe looked at me, a glance that was an ocean. Then he looked away and ate the food that was on his plate.

Padre Luis sat up suddenly, his face spackled with lamb and stew. "Hearken unto my sermon of fire for I have had a vision," he intoned. "Oh, here at this table of plenty. Oh, here in this Andalusian Gethsemane. Yea, He will rescue and redeem them for their lives are precious to him. O sweet wine! O love, who ever burnest and never consumest! O charity! O succulent lamb! O fruit abundant and moist! The beast and the false prophet will be cast into a lake of flame. The fire they kindle for their enemies will burn themselves only. Oh, for I have dreamt of the heifer-red wall of fire, I who drink deeply and stew in both regret and sorrow. O raisins and almonds! The sea shall part and they shall walk through its red flames as if through a curtain. Oh, were I a man and not a lamb or adafina stew. Though our sins be scarlet, they shall be as white as snow. For this has been written in fire and the words themselves are enflamed. Oh, shall I drink!" He reached for a jug of wine but succeeded only in overturning it. Then he rested his addle-pated head on his plate and slept again as the wine overflowed the table.

Moishe stood up. "His vision," he said. "Now I know what to do."

"Drink less," I said. "Few flagons contain as much wine as he. The only vision he has is doubled."

"He is truly farshikkered, but his pickled words have reminded me. A curtain of flame, some burning letters: fire will save them from fire."

Moishe recounted a marvel he'd seen at a shtetl wedding where a magician—a kishef-makher—had walked through a wall of fire and been unharmed. Everyone thought it was sorcery or else a propitious and divine intervention for the wedding. Like the gefilte fish. The man had chanted some obscure prayers, touched a torch to the ground, then disappeared into the burning wall of flame that he'd created. After a few horrifying minutes, he reappeared, smiling, bowing, and carrying doves. Moishe wasn't the only one in tears.

In whispers, Moishe's father had explained: it only looked like the man had walked through fire. Imagine that the magician had poured oil onto the earth in the shape of a kuf, a ק, his father had said. When the letter was on fire, he walked into the space at the bottom, waited inside for a few minutes and then slipped out from the opening at the top. The doves had been in his pocket like two pieces of bread, waiting to make a wondrous—and untoasted—sandwich. "Sometimes," said Moishe's father, "we say 'b'shin, kuf, resh,' and spell out the Hebrew word for 'lie,' sheqer. Kuf is at the heart of this lie, also, though it is a marvellous lie, like much in this world."

"With this trick," Moishe said, "we will arrange the escape."

There were three things that we needed.

Oil.

A disguise so that Moishe could appear at the lion's den of the quemadero.

Beytsim the size of lions or small ships. It would help if they would roar or at least tack into the wind.

There was a cloak and a hat on a hook in the hall outside the kitchen. Wearing these things, one could no more recognize Moishe than one could read the Mishnah between the hairs of a twilit pig.

We found lamp oil in the kitchen.

As for the beytsim, we'd have to rely on the principle that, if necessity is the mamaleh of invention, then desperation is the mother of beytsim the size of two shvitzy schooners.

I would be conspicuous and so we went in search of a means of concealment. And Moishe wanted one more look at the genizah.

There was a large thick book, the size of a gravestone. No words were stamped on its mottled rabicano binding, nothing to indicate its Hebrew insides. Moishe hauled it off the shelf, and without reading it, carried it upstairs to the seder table, pushing aside the plates and food and cups. He opened the book and began cutting at its pages with a carving knife.

I did not understand the reason for this surgery.

"Now, there's room for you. Once I close the cover, I can carry you and no one will know you're there."

It was a coffin of words and I was its hidden meaning.

"*Shver tsu zayn a Yid*," I said. "It's hard to be a hidden Jew. Just don't forget me."

Chapter Twenty

*F*rom inside the book, I could hear the shushkeh of Moishe's voice as he spoke quietly, keeping us both calm, the way one might soothe a skittish horse.

It was a long walk to the quemadero and several times, Moishe turned into an alley and opened the book a crack so that I could have fresh air. It was not difficult to know which way to go. Many had already lined the streets to witness the execution parade: the brotherhoods wearing their pointed hoods, the pasos, the elaborate floats depicting Jesus, Mary, and scenes from the Stations of the Cross. There were penitents carrying crosses, and a swarm of Inquisitors led by the Red Queen himself, the Grand Dragon Torquemada. The procession led to the quemadero and from there its route went to the Catedral. But it wouldn't arrive. Our fire, the chaos of the kuf, would create a thousand individual processions of panic and fear, in the midst of which the Jews could hide.

Moishe shuffled like an old man into the square, the jug of oil concealed beneath his cape. There were a few guards standing around, kibitzing, laughing, waiting casually for the crowds. I felt Moishe walking, pouring oil in a kuf shape. Or so I imagined.

We waited behind a stumpy wall on the edge of the square. Moishe opened the book a little, as if checking the words were still there. After some time, the sound of crowds and music increased. The procession had arrived. Moishe closed the book. Once again, everything was filtered through words.

The place would soon be thick with crosses, actual size.

The higher-ups, the balebatim, would climb up into the stands to be a little closer to God than the rest of us. Except for the condemned who would soon be nothing more than an ascending curl of dark smoke that God would inhale, then expel with the full force of His divine lungs, blowing them all to hell.

The expiration of the living.

I heard trumpets. Not the end-of-the-world trumpets of the revelation, but corporeal horns, signalling the end of some Jews.

Then singing.

> Venite, adoremus.
> Because I led thee out of the land of Egypt, thou hast prepared a
>   Cross for thy Saviour.
> Because I brought thee into a land exceeding good, thou hast
>   prepared a Cross for thy Saviour.
> O My people.

Then the sound and fury of the Grand Inquisitor, a sermon signifying voluble nothing for I could understand but few words from inside the book. Only his wrath and righteousness, the febrile excoriation of the sinful by an alter kaker.

Then the fervent jeering of the crowd.

More words.

Moishe dropped the book and stepped forward.

Its wing-like pages opened, a magician releasing a hidden dove. I flew—nu, where else?—onto his shoulder.

He bent down ready to touch the torch to the long inflammable tail of the kuf. Then without warning, those tied to the stakes began to sing as those before had sung.

Sh'ma Yisroel, they sang. Hear O Israel.

The others, chained together, waiting their own execution, sang also.

Sh'ma Yisroel Adonai Eloheinu Adonai Echad.

Sarah was bound by ropes to the stake. And she, too, sang with defiance.

The faces of the about-to-die were beatific. The world was a broken vessel and they were pouring like light from between the cracks. This was the incorporeal song of themselves, a quantum song beyond time and space.

There was shouting from the crowd, but the singers continued.

Rabbi Daniel's arms were tied to his side, but somehow he had managed to free one of his hands. Before anyone else noticed, he had reached up and clasped the tefillin box strapped to his forehead and torn it away. Tefillin, the Judaizing badge his captors were happy to have him display.

A guard ran toward him, sword raised to separate the arm from the rabbi's body.

The rabbi threw the tefillin box like a hand grenade. It was, we assumed, only filled with prayers.

It burst into flame. A yontef cocktail. He must have planned to light the kindling beneath him. He would not let them take his death from him. The fire was his own.

But his half-tied arm moved as if it were broken and he had missed the pyre beneath him.

Instead, the box landed on the ground and rolled into the trail of oil. The kuf ignited, a wall of flame that surrounded the stakes and separated the condemned from the others. The soldier was caught in between. His robes turned to fire and he ran screaming into the crowd that opened before him. He ran thirty feet and then toppled to the ground, burning like a trash heap.

Moishe dropped his torch and walked before the stands. He looked steadily into the shocked faces of the priests, nobles, the powerful. He raised his hands with the Biblical drama of a prophet.

"This is not the end, it is Ein Sof—there is no end. But I am going now. I bid you all *zay gezunt*—a fond farewell."

Then he ran into the space at the bottom of the kuf, disappearing into what looked like unrelenting hellfire.

From the outside, it appeared that the heretics—Jews and conversos—would be consumed by this lake of fire.

Inside, we were Shadrach, Meshach, and Abednego in the fiery furnace: surrounded though untouched by flame. Then a geshrey wailing. The rabbi's clothes were on fire, the pyre beneath him burning. Moishe seized the knife from his belt, thrust it through the flames and slashed the ropes binding the rabbi. He threw the rebbe to the ground. We had little time before we'd either be overcome by the heat or else the kuf would consume its fuel. Moishe cut the others free and Sarah ran to cover the rabbi in her shawl. She helped him up and guided him as he staggered.

Moishe could not separate those chained together by iron, but we could lead them to safety, escaping from the open top of the kuf. It led directly into a long alleyway, a street of weavers. Those who stood there, watching the auto-da-fé, moved quickly away, crossing themselves and muttering prayers. We were dybbuk spirits, walking ghosts, consumed by fire, beginning our God-forsaken pilgrimage to hell.

We turned a corner. There was Padre Luis sitting on a barrel.

"Good work," he said and jumped down. "Now, quick—in the barrel."

Did he expect us all to climb inside a single barrel? Na, even Ali Baba's forty thieves had one each.

But Doña Gracia—we hadn't recognized her in the line of those chained together, she was so stooped and dirty and her clothes were torn—moved forward and pulled back the lid. Inside were the stolen red robes from the Catedral. Those whose hands were free draped the robes around the others, hiding their chains and sanbenito smocks.

Moishe held me beneath his cape.

An apikoros procession—a march of heretics—walking to the water.

As much as possible, we kept to the alley's dusky arteries, though eventually we had to cross the jugular of Calle del Agua, lined with celebrants waiting for the procession to pass on its way to its final destination, the Catedral. They hadn't yet heard of the escape from fire.

Murmurs in the crowd as we went by. We were a raggle-tag procession of shlumperdik clerics wandering away from the Catedral and into the dark yard of a cobbler's shop. Rabbi Daniel wobbled unsteadily, supported by Sarah.

How to kvell with joy and relief, smooch and embrace before a singed rabbi?

"Sarah," Moishe said.

"Basherter," Sarah said, touching his soot-streaked cheek.

Then she saw something down the calle.

"Rabbi." She pulled him into the obscurity of the covered stairs behind the shop. The others quickly followed.

Two huge church bulvans—cattle-thick bruisers. Moishe strode up to them but said nothing. And he did not resist as they seized him and ox-marched him away.

Sarah had saved everyone. Moishe would waddle like a gunsel into the brig if it would continue to keep them safe.

And I would follow.

They dragged us across the city. Finally, they threw us onto the fetid shmutzy straw of a cell. I knew where we were. The Tribunal of the Holy Office of the Inquisition did not host its guests at a five-star establishment. This place was rated but one farkakteh Yiddish star. And we'd seen it from the other side.

What happened next?

Bupkes.

We waited.

Time can be a scarifying lash when your world is a small room and you've nothing to do but wait for the bullwhip of the inevitable.

Night then dawn.

Saturday. At first, we strode about the room.

"We are," Moishe said, "as my father used to say, 'Er dreyt zich arum vi a forts in rosl.' A fart blundering around in brine, not knowing what to do."

We were trying to think of a way out, of what we didn't know.

Nothing but stone walls and iron bars.

Eventually, Moishe lay in the dirty straw like a sick calf, troubled by what might have happened to the others, about what might happen to us.

Night again.

It was before dawn on the third day, Easter Sunday.

Cimmerian darkness. The hot horse breath of the Andalusian night, a fever dream heavy over the city of Seville. The faint scent of laurel, orange blossom and horse piss.

Footsteps, a distant door opening, the glow of lantern light, then someone approaching our cell. We hoped they were bringing food.

I hid in the corner, covered in darkness and straw.

A section of an old man's face appeared at the small, barred window. A watery eye, a white eyebrow, the side of a blotched and veiny nose.

The rattle of keys. With some difficulty the man pushed open the cell door with a cassock-covered, spindle-thin shoulder. A monk.

He stood at the threshold and, still in shadow, scrutinized Moishe for a long time.

Finally he shuffled forward, hung his lantern from a hook, and spoke. In the dim light, we saw who it was.

Torquemada, ancient bilious scarecrow of the Tribunal del Santo Oficio. Carrion crow of Paul the Apostle.

"I know who you are," he whispered to Moishe.

So much for a little nosh, hardtack for the empty kishkas of two heretics.

Moishe stumbled up and onto the bench. He was weak. We had not eaten for two days.

Torquemada lowered himself down onto the bench beside Moishe. In the lantern light, his sallow skin was a wasted land of shadowy hollows.

"The condemned disappear like smoke, leave no bones, no ashes. And you walk into fire and are unharmed. The people speak of miracles. I always thought you would come. Yes, I know who you are. I recognize you, though you are only a boy."

His penetrating wet eyes were small and dark, windows onto a mind that was a hurricane, its enormous power spinning everything in its path around its vacant centre.

Whatever he thought Moishe was, it was clear to me what he was.

Meshugeh.

Insane.

A small line of spittle found a desiccated fissure and rolled slowly down his chin. Moishe began, "Father, I . . ."

"'Be silent!" he said. "What could you say? I know but too well your answer . . . Besides, you have no right to add one syllable to that which you have said before. Why should you now return to impede us in our work? You've come but for that only, and you know that well. Do you know what awaits you this morning? I do not know, nor do I care to know who you might be: be it you or an image of you only. I have condemned you and you will burn at the stake, the most wicked of all heretics."

So, nu, they don't have the Egyptian fire trick out here in Spain? Every conjurer with a match is mistaken for Yeshua, the Messiah?

Though, the matchstick itself would takeh be some trick. It may not be the souls of the dead rising, but it's the splintery and sulphurous future of firestarting.

Torquemada leaned in close to Moishe. "We are not with you, but with him," he hissed. "The wise spirit. The dread one. That is our secret. For centuries have we abandoned you to follow him. The people have trusted us with their happiness, their souls, your word, their freedom. And we have helped them. Though I am an old man, a tattered cloak upon a pole, I will live for another thousand years. Oh, it is possible to become ecstatic amid destruction, to rejuvenate oneself through cruelty. You have dared to come and trouble us in our work and so deserve the Inquisitorial fires more than any."

Moishe remained silent, looking at him, calculating how he could turn this mishugas into an opportunity.

When the world is upside down, it is best to walk on your hands if you want to be king.

Moishe looked penetratingly yet tenderly at this old privateer, for that's what he was. He would not have hesitated to board Noah's boat and plunder one of every animal, two if when roasted they were choice. So, too, he was with souls. His letter of marque or holy book was from a brine-dead sea, faded, torn, illegible. The self-serving palimpsest of memory the only legible mark.

Moishe waited, allowing his silence to bloom like a wound. The old man longed to hear his voice, to hear him reply. He'd rather endure words of bitterness and scorn than his silence. I caught Moishe's sidereal glance at me, a quicksilver glint.

Then Moishe rose to his feet, slowly and solemnly. He bent toward the Inquisitor and softly kissed the bloodless, ancient lips.

The Grand Inquisitor shuddered. A convulsive twitch at the corner of his mouth. He stood up uncertainly, and hobbled to the door, pushing it open.

"Go," he said to Moishe. "Do not come again . . . never. Never!"

Moishe walked through the open door and vanished into the darkness. Torquemada shuffled back to the bench and collapsed. His head dropped to his chest and his eyes closed. I could see by the twisting runnels of his forehead that he was suffering. He touched his hand to his lips and was still.

When the sails are down, the wind runs free.

So I took my chance. I flew.

Chapter Twenty-One

*O*utside I could not find Moishe, but knew he would make for the Guadalquivir River and the ship. I would fly ahead to tell them to wait. He would soon be there.

If they had safely arrived. If they hadn't already set sail toward Cadiz and the sea.

I rose up into the pearlescent before-dawn light. Soon the sun would rise. Soon the son also: the bright rising of Easter with its banners, music and celebration. But when they rolled aside the saviour's stone in the mouth of Iberia, we'd be gone.

Even in the half-light, there were people on the street. Soldiers, too. Moishe would have to become a shadow, a ruekh—a ghost—and half-light himself, if he were to slip by unnoticed.

At the port, I circled to find our ship in a forest of masts and landed on the mainmast spar.

Below me, Padre Luis was playing with a rope beside the starboard gunwale.

The others must be keeping out of sight below deck.

Padre Luis looked up. "Salve!" he called.

I hadn't said a word when—a broch, damn it all—there was a tremendous crack. Splintered wood crashed onto the deck. Another burst. A flash from the wharf. A gunshot. Gevalt! It grazed my feathers. They were trying to separate my insides from my out, make a pretty *loch in mayn kop*, a hole in my head.

Doña Gracia shouted to the crew.

More flashes and wood-splintering.

Sailors emerged, unmoored the ship and unfurled the sails.

Another explosion and I was hit a mighty klop from Olam ha-Ba, a divine fist from the world to come. I was returned to the formless void and into complete wordless, sightless, soundless oblivion.

My last thought?

We would have to sail south for the sea and leave Moishe surrounded by gunfire. Parrotless and alone.

Sure the shvants does well without its foreskin. It grows. It prospers.

But which part was Moishe?

Which was me?

Though unlike what the moyel hath rent assunder, I would let no one keep us apart, though it might be years.

It would be five.

Part Three:
WATER

And you west wind, faithful companion
Drive my ship to that distant shore
Where my heart on eagle's wings is soaring
To the place that I've been longing for.

JUDAH HALEVI (trans. H.N. BIALIK
English text by ALLAN MEROVITZ)

Chapter One

Writing Hebrew, most of the time, you make do without vowels. Of course, when you speak, there are plenty of vowels—no matter how you mumble, you have to open your pisk eventually—unless your strudel-cave has been fully spelunked by cake, when it's better to wait. When you read, you have to imagine the vowels wheezing between the consonants' black masts. You know they exist, they're just not there. Like God to the troubled faithful. Maybe in some other disconsonant world, there are Hebrew books where all the unwritten vowels appear, like the souls of the dead, reunited with their consonant bodies, but in this world, the story goes on without them.

Atah medaber Ivrit?

Feh. I never learned Hebrew.

Moishe was like the vowels. For five years, I mumbled and the story proceeded without me.

I was blown by the wind. It was above, it was below. It came from outside, it came from inside, depending on the ratio of sea biscuit to salt pork in my three squares.

So sometimes I didn't know my insides from what's out, but sails filled and Moishe travelled from Gibraltar to Ethiopia, from the new islands of the Canaries, to Thule in the north, to the Mediterranean and back many times. Where, I didn't exactly know.

I kept myself busy, avoiding the cage and the "and so that's how the meshugeneh bird met his sorry end" chapter of my story. I sailed with the Jews. I ate. I slept. I learned a new language or two. I drank coffee, wore a beret, argued about art and life, and wrote poetry.

And when there was rum, I sang. I cursed. And there was this:

> O Moishe is out at sea again, farmisht like the farkrimter sky,
> He's a skinny ship on a farkakteh sea, with no friends to
> sail nearby,
> the rum bites and the crew shakes, their shikkereh spume
> a-flying
> and the seagulls kak on the dreck-slick deck, and always their
> meshugeneh crying.
>
> O Moishe is out at sea again, living the wandering sailor's life,
> it's a farshluginer escape, and a whip-ward flight from the
> whetted knife,
> from the mast-like stake and the smokey clouds as you begin
> to smoulder,
> but all I ask is that he lives on and, nu, to shlof again on
> his shoulder.

So Rumi, Whitman or King David I was not, though when shikkered, I sat in the warm tsimmes of my emotions and became a sloppy, weeping Bukowski of a Judah Halevi while imagining myself a psaltery-dog Solomon, a psittacine Shakespeare of the sea.

I said I would speak of treasure.

Treasure? It's everything you could hope for in the present, but just not yet.

Farshteyst?

But first: Sarah, Doña Gracia and the others.

We went south down the Guadalquivir and into the sea.

"We're not sailing into history, but out of it," Doña Gracia said. "It's safer that way."

The crew hauled and furled, jigged and swabbed. This was a common passage for them: Jews out; spices, gold, and embroidery in. A windblown railroad, not underground but over the sea. They scattered like sparrows when Doña Gracia walked the deck, a sneeze scattering flour. They weren't used to the balebosteh herself aboard ship.

She had always directed from the great house in Seville, but here as elsewhere, she took charge. As soon as we were in open water, she had the navigator bring her sea charts and compass and by the binnacle, she spoke with the captain, the Doña a conductor pointing toward the horizon and along portolan lines. She spoke to the cook and the quartermaster and held conference with the rabbi. The ship had been the Doña's trade, and it was now her home.

There was open praying on the deck as the sun rose. A minyan gathered beneath the mainmast and faced the larboard of Jerusalem. Standing close together, davening, swaying back and forth like the ship in the sea, the lapping waters of prayer a salve, a balm for the Gilead of memory.

Few who had gathered there had ever celebrated publicly, their prayers a samizdat circulated in whispers concealed below breath, in secret inter-cellar communion with their interstellar, intercellular God, whose name they dared not speak openly, until now, sailing south upon this synagogue of waves.

The rabbi reminded them that when the Jews crossed the Red Sea, there was music and Miriam sang.

It seemed as if he expected a song and dance of Biblical proportions.

And how do you measure such proportions? In ancient barbers' reckoning: shave and a haircut cubits? Nu, it is true, in making our exodus, we had had a close shave. And Moishe, I hoped, had been spared blade and bloodloss.

Though there was the chanting of prayer, the singing of psalms, the people remained sullen and quiet. They stayed below deck, or rested in the bow. Their tsuris troubled memories had not been washed away like the Tashlich casting off of sin-saturated bread at Rosh Hashannah. Not yet. They hadn't yet made the promised landing.

What were they? They were Jews and they were shul-shocked.

"My father, alav ha'shalom," Sarah said, "always wondered what it was like to travel by ship, always hoped to sail to the Holy Land. Only his books are left to cross the waves."

They had been taken from the pigsty and carried onto the ship, where they were locked in a large chest then stowed like pirates' treasure. Inside each book, the written breath, inhaled and held. A library for the future in the language of the not-yet-forgotten.

If only we could have opened the chest, spread wide the books' wings and let each letter lift from the pages, fly over the distant horizon, a murmuration of words, an escaping sigh. And if only these letters could have raised Sarah, the Doña, the rabbi and the others, lifted them from the deck on their tiny black wings. If only they could have carried them into the sky and beyond the reach of fire, if only they could have left the ship without a single word, without a single living soul.

But we were in sight of land when a ship came fast upon our starboard side. We were but a pitseleh pipsqueak with few guns and this craft, a big bulvan carrack with cannonfire bursting from its broad sides, and soon we were bleeding in reverse as wounded ships do, the brine spilling into our insides and the Jews screaming the single long vowel of the terrified.

Then the carrack hove to beside us and we were boarded. They were Turks, sent by the Sultan to defend Granada against the Reconquista salivations of the Christian crown, but what's a bisl robbery and slavery once you're farpitst—dressed to the nines—for some meshugas? I mean, na, once you're in the open ocean and you got the boots, what's a bit of freebooting?

Our crew found their swords and made to make *gehakteh leber*— chopped liver—of the buccaneers, but too often it was our swabbies' livers that were gehakt and they fell writhing upon the deck, soon to become livers no more.

I did what I could, clawing eyes and biting through the corsairs' ringed ears, but I was not much use against blunderbuss and scimitar. These cutthroats, regarding me with eponymous desire, slashed their blades at my larynx and, also, for good measure, at my flagrantly whole body.

"*Gey strasheh di vantsen*—go threaten the bed bugs," I said. "You don't frighten me."

But they did. So, nu, what should I have done—wait for these shtunks to make a half-chicken dinner of me? I needed a hole in my head like *a loch in kop*, a hole in my head. I flew up to the mainmast spar and watched. Sometimes he who watches and remembers is the best soldier. Hope without memory is like memory without hope. I planned to be an alter kaker talking a kak-storm of memories, an old bird who was also a book.

They threw Rabbi Daniel overboard. To them, he was an old man and of no value. He kicked and spluttered. Just before he went under, he looked at us, then at the sky. On his lips, a brocheh. *Baruch ata Adonai* . . . a prayer. He who had survived fire, now a victim of water. May he become the beloved rebbe of a cheder of fish, the gaon—esteemed teacher—of whales.

The pirates plundered the hold. Rolled barrels of wine onto their ship. Salt meat. Hardtack. Pickles. What stores they could carry, they carried. They carried, too, the surviving Jews. Sarah. Doña Gracia. Bound. Beaten. Bleeding.

Samuel resisted, managing to stab an elbow into a pirate's bristly pox-blotched punim, the pirate's jaw suddenly tacking in a new and extreme direction. A musketoon fired into Samuel's belly made lobscouse fireworks of his kishkas.

"*Vu sholem, dort iz brocheh.* Where there is peace, there is blessing," he said and fell to the deck, a warm nosh for rats.

A buccaneer in a tawdry blood-spattered turban, the imperious balebos of the crew, pointed an arquebus as if it were his impressively tooled shlong, and made two of our surviving sailors carry the chest of books over the gangplank and into the hold of his ship. When the Turks broke the lock, I doubted they'd be filled with bookish joy.

Can books be sold into slavery?

A broch! Zong-like, they'd toss them. The rabbi's deep-sea yeshiva would soon have a library for his scholarly fish.

Unnoticed, I flew to the Ottoman ship and hid behind the futtock shrouds. For this, I thank my grey feathers for the colours they are not.

I hid until I could be sure that their cook did not seek the sauciness of a chutzpenik parrot for a dry dish. Or that those with an arquebus had no interest in the shooting of African skeets.

⊹⊹

Twilight like bilgewater.

I flew to the hold where the Turks kept their weary Jewish cargo, bound for the slave markets of Barbary.

"Stowaways in our own world!" Doña Gracia was saying. "Not only our own ships: we need our own navy, our own soldiers, our own land, our own king."

"Next year in Jerusalem . . ." several of the old Jews murmured, repeating the words of the Haggadah.

"We shall never have Jerusalem, not in this life. Not on this earth," Doña Gracia said.

"But when the Messiah comes . . ." one man began, but then was quiet, looking over the horizon to the distant end of the world.

"Maybe in the lands of the Great Khan," another said. "Far from the Church and our kings. I hear there are Jews . . ."

"Or in Cipangu or Cathay."

"Or Ethiope."

"We'd have to travel to an entirely new world to find a land we could call our own."

"Maybe the new islands discovered in the Ocean Sea."

"Maybe," Doña Gracia said. "But I fear that even the moon would not be far enough."

For now, we remained on the Turkish ship.

"Kemal Reis," I heard the sailors sing. "Kemal Reis." It was some time before I understood that "Kemal Reis" was the admiral of their fleet, on their way to land soldiers at Malaga.

Except for those currently engaged in the delicate art of midsea brawling, enslaving and plundering.

Ech, if only we'd been captured later, we'd not have been captured at all.

"They call Ferdinand a wise ruler?" Sultan Bajazet said after hearing of the 1492 expulsion order. "He impoverishes his own country and enriches mine." Then he sent a decree to his provinces to welcome those expelled—both Jews and Muslims—to his empire.

"Excellency, how many to exclude?"

"None is too many."

Turkish death, keneynehoreh, did not await the Jews, but rather those who treated them harshly or refused them admission.

But sometimes history doesn't wait for the future. A few days after our capture, Sarah was carried onto a boat bound for the Topkapi Palace in Istanbul where she would become an exotic kaleh-moyd concubine in the Seraglio, the Imperial Harem.

Or, she'd have an audition.

She kicked and wept and clawed.

"Monsters," she said. "Devils."

I could do nothing but follow and become witness. When all was quiet, there'd be my words, and they would offer some comfort.

Once history is over, memory is all that's left.

Later, a merchant sailor who had once sailed with Doña Gracia told me what I did not know then—no one but the midwife of heaven, her sleeves rolled up in the sweet soup of stars, could have known then—but Sarah's womb was filling with Inquisition baby, its father, a Father, and killed by Moishe.

Her audition would not go well.

Feh.

May the Sultan's shmeckel become like a hedgehog or sea urchin: spiny and round and considered a delicacy when cooked and sliced thin.

The Turks sailed and prayed. Five times a day the renegadoes crouched beneath the billowing sails and spoke to their Adonai at Mecca. Starboard, larboard, toward bowsprit or rudder, as the direction of the ship changed, east moved about as if it were the sun in its orbit around the earth.

It would be another century before Copernicus had the seychl to say, "That's a tall story you tell me, Ptolemy," but for now, Sarah's world was the centre of a sorry tale told by Turks and, except for the downward davening, it was much like being on any ship.

Except that these turbaned swabs treated her well.

"I will not eat," she moaned, refusing the food that they brought on large brass platters. Yogurt, nuts, dried fruit, mutton and noodles instead of the usual shipboard salt goat. These Turkish sailors intended to keep her succulent—zaftik—for the Sultan or his princes. I'd seen the harem. It was a gold cage for birds with splendid plumage and quick brains. As long as you were happy inside such a cage, you were happy. And so if once or twice you had to shtup in the dark on a soft bed surrounded by perfume, silks and jewels . . .

So I'd help her escape. My sea-green maideleh.

To be imprisoned on a boat is to have the ocean for a jailer. We would have to wait until landfall.

I cannot read, least of all the stars, so I was unable to determine our position, but as the waves began to rise and the wind whinnied through the rigging, I could read the sails' pages and knew they foretold storm.

The sailors motioned toward an indistinct ridge of land.

"Sicily," they said.

The captain and quartermaster would not alter course for the island, one large pock out of Ferdinand's many on the pimpled face of Europe. Instead the bo'sun called, "All hands ahoy! Tumble up here and take in sail."

The clouds collected in dark scrolls. We were close-hauled on the wind, and nearly keeled over.

"*Got in Himl*," I said. "Or wherever you are."

The great hoofs of sea beat our bows like a meshugener shmid hammering at an anvil. The water shpritzing over the deck turned the crew into world champion shvitzers swimming through hell. The halyards had been let go, and the great sails filled out and backed against the masts. The wind shrayed through the rigging, loose ropes flew about. Orders were shouted from sailor to sailor.

"Tie the boom!"

"Seize the mainsheet!"

"Reef the mizzen tops'il, lad!"

A boychik of a sailor was ordered aloft the mizzen—to where I hid. He climbed and laid out on the yard with all his strength. As he did he vomited into the black sky and I saw his frightened-wide eyes look right at me. I climbed beyond the reach of his arm and his outpourings, higher up the mast, but the sharp whip of the wind lashed me and I was blown over the shuddering black back of the sea, far from Sarah, safe harbour, or solid things.

"An *umglik!*" I screamed. A disaster. "*Gey kakn af der levoneh!* Go shit on the moon!" I shouted.

Chapter Two

I thought the wind my true home, but carried by the banshee breath of the unbridled lost-its-mind middle sea I despaired of the touch of earth or gravity. Tree or silver cage, shoulder or floating corpse: I now wished for such hospitable heavens.

I was days in such windborne purgatory. Then I found myself blown over the shores of an island and able to fly into the protective maw of a cave and, thanks God, the howling finally ceased.

A great fire burned in the centre of the cave. It threw such writhing shadows as would cause Plato to kvell with pride at their form. There was a fragrance of cleft cedar and juniper. Roasting fruit and seed. A woman in long silks tended kebab skewers in the flames. I chaleshed for such food and I approached her. My storm-shaken brain was addled, for I was snatched and stuffed into a cage of wooden bars before I was able not to be snatched and stuffed into such a cage. A pale-skinned man in a dirty white kaftan grinned at me with an off-kilter, gold-toothed smile.

"Welcome," he said from the free world outside the bars.

With a quick twist of her head, a woman tossed her long hair over her shoulders, walked over and kissed him. "You are quick, Strabo."

The man looked directly at her. "There are many birds on the island, most, I'd expect, more succulent than this. If it speaks, it can be our companion. If not, our stew."

He smiled his crooked smile and left, not, I hoped, with the intent of seeking a side dish.

I would not sing for my supper, but to avoid being someone else's.

"I speak," I said to the woman, somewhat self-evidently. "I hope that excludes me from the menu."

She had turned toward the fire and did not respond.

This required some virtuoso sheyneh talking.

"I speak of the storm that has ceased," I said. "And of the luxuriant wood of alder and poplar and sweet-smelling cypress that grows outside. Of birds, long of wing, which nest there, owls and falcons and sea-crows with chattering, if meaningless, tongues. And I speak of the garden vine, richly laden with grapes, that winds about this hollow cave. Also, I speak of the four fountains in a row, the water of the first flowing into the next. And of the soft meadows of violets and parsley which bloom. And, I say also this, you are intelligent of face, beautiful of form, and your hair is bright morning woven with God's own shuttle."

The woman did not respond though this was some first-class talking.

So, nu. I'd try another tack.

"O golden-limbed Calypso, I will tell a tale of my compatriot, Moishe," I began. "He spent months teaching his parrot to pray. On Rosh Hashanah, the parrot insisted he go to synagogue.

"'Shul is not a place for a bird,' Moishe said, but the bird protested and so he took the parrot.

"'What's he doing here?' the old rebbe said.

"'Rebbe, he can daven. He knows all the prayers.'

"No one believed Moishe, but they let the bird in—as long as he wore a yarmulke. The entire congregation bet against the bird. Twenty-to-one the parrot couldn't daven. How could a bird daven?

"Service began. There was chanting and praying, but the parrot sat on Moishe's shoulder. Silent.

"'Daven, you mamzer, daven.' But the bird said nothing. After the service, Moishe was furious.

"'You putz. I'm ruined. I owe a fortune. Why didn't you daven?'

"'Don't be a shlemiel,' the parrot replied. 'Imagine the odds we'll get on Yom Kippur!'"

Still the woman said nothing. I was going to be soup.

I watched as she tended to the skewers, imagining them piercing my tender breast. I looked around the cave, planning escape. After some time, Strabo returned, covered in mud and carrying the corpse of a small brown animal, something like a rabbit or what once was one. He was singing but the woman did not turn. It has been said that the future is a woman and it is necessary, if you wish to master her, to sneak up on her from behind. In truth, I know no other way.

Strabo placed the rabbit down, crept behind the woman and embraced her, a move more amorous but as sudden as when he had snatched me.

"Strabo!" she called. "You know I cannot hear you creeping."

Strabo laughed, though this surely could not have been the first time that he had played this trick.

They fell upon each other and the meat upon the skewer burned as I watched from my cage.

This, then, was my life for five years more. My wings, though not my speech, were clipped. I became a companion of these amorous two, the king and queen, the sole servants, soldiers, serfs, bakers, hunters, fools and lovers on this otherwise humanless isle.

Sometimes I rode the shoulder of her pale king as he travelled about the island hunting and tending to the gardens, sharing a Scheherazade of stories.

Sometimes I would stay with the woman, Liliana, in her elfin grotto. Though she could read the words on the voluble pages of Strabo's lips, my immutable beak proved inscrutable. And so, for her, I was a friend without language. She sang, simply for the pleasure of singing, a meaningless Bombadil of songs as she moved about the cave, preparing food and keeping their speleological home both spic and span.

I was becalmed in this paradise, fressing on fruits only recently named, wishing to be expelled from this Eden. I wanted the salt slap of the sea, the astringent wave; to be ship-faced or in a storm and on Moishe's shoulder.

My shorn feathers grew back though I kept them under my wing. Strabo and Liliana would not know I was a flight risk, not until they saw me flapping like an epileptic "m" or "w" as I disappeared into the sky.

Then, one dawn a nub of mast appeared on the horizon. Like a sprig, it grew, sprouting sails and a ship as I watched it blossom outside the early morning mouth of the cave.

Strabo was hunting while Liliana slept. I crept from my open cage and took to the air. In the cave, the animals began to bark or bray or caw, but Liliana heard only the cloud-sounds of her dreams, Strabo's looting fingers creeping up her sleeping spine.

I flew over the beach sands and was above the open water before Strabo saw me. He ran to the shore and called out.

What did he say? *Ver veyst?* Who knows? If you put your ear to the sea, you hear only ocean. The open road of the Mediterranean thrilled in my breast and escape foamed up like a rabid wave.

"Fairwell, Strabo," I shouted. Though he had been my jailer, it was the island that was my prison and his friendship had been sweet.

I flew to the ship. It was made of solid gold and, *oy vey iz mir,* soft parrot girls purred my name and wished to preen me.

I should have such luck. It was the caravel of Andalusian privateers bound for Spain heavy with the plunder of its shnorrer mission: treasure both dry—spices, metals, jewels—and wet—wine, prisoners, and slaves, held in chains.

But sometimes God plays craps, for I discovered Moishe, pale and weak, hanging from the beams as from a gibbet. Where he was not the pallor of his own yellow eyes, he was bruise purple. He was no longer a cheder-bocher schoolboy. His fallow pisher's face was now carpeted by a patchwork of shag and his once scarecrow body was now filled with something more substantial than straw. My Moishe. My skinny shoulder. My own grown mensch of a boychik.

His eyes were closed and he moaned weakly. He was fortunate to have such misfortune just then for I had arrived and would help him. We had been diasporas of each other. Now we were home.

"Moishe, *vos machstu?*" I said, flying onto his shoulder. "Howaya?"

Chapter Three

*F*ive years. You can fit ten or twenty years into such a span, particularly when you're crossing the equator of childhood.

"So," I said. "Tell me everything from the beginning. Your breakfast the morning I left Spain. Was it eggs?"

He recounted his equinoctial transit into the tropic of young men: He had been imprisoned. Had escaped. Was imprisoned again. Had escaped and had helped others escape.

He'd stolen eggs from under others' stolen chickens. He'd stolen his own chickens and even pigs. He'd made it south to Sanlúcar on the coast and signed on with the first ship leaving Andalusia. He'd travelled the shores of Ethiope, had been to Bristol, one of the new-found Canary islands, to Genoa and other ports in the Mediterranean.

And more eggs: those of the African turtle and of the English quail. He had learned some shipcraft, some surgery, carpentry and medicine, and something of the chart reading and reckoning of the sea artist. He had navigated his naked astrolabe through the ripe nafkeh-warmth of the brothel and had had such rum as to have his green and puke-mewling flesh discover morning before he himself arrived there.

He had been Miguel Levante and Moishe ben Chaim, as well as other names. And all the while trying to find Sarah, Doña Gracia, news of the safety of the escaping Jews of Seville, and . . . me.

We wept together then like maidelehs. Young girls.

Farklemt.

But this was no time for schmaltz. Moishe was, after all, chained and starving, and I was a free bird, befriended by the crew.

I flew to the galley and schmoozed the cook for a nosh, tilting my head invitingly and nuzzling his ear. When he turned to the roiling stew, I beaked a sheet of some dun-coloured thing, perhaps salted foresail or the foreskin of whale, and brought it to Moishe.

"Es, es, my friend," I said, standing one-legged on his shoulder and holding out the food so he could gnaw the salt sheet. Later, I found him wine and hardtack. He became stronger but remembered to dangle like a nauseous and neglected marionette when members of the crew came to offer him sips of fetid water.

"Ahh, ahh," he moaned in their presence and they called him "girl."

It would be a week to Spain. We decided—after close consultation with the uncommunicative chains and the lockpicking skills of both beak and filched nail—to arrange for Moishe's escape after we arrived at port. During the commotion of arrival, we'd find a means to free Moishe while the crew patchked around readying him for transportation.

Where were they planning to take him? Why had they captured him?

"I was in the middle of the Middle Sea," Moishe said. "Actually over a barrel."

"Moishe: Admiral of a Hogshead and a fleet of fishes."

"Azoy! Rather *that* august maritime office—keneynehoreh—than goulash for sharks," he said. "He didn't know it yet, but the captain of the ship on which I was sailing and where the barrel was berthed, was about to pitch me caskless into the deep."

"Because of the Inquisition?" I asked.

"I stole extra rations of drink, got shikkered, potched the mamzer bo'sun on his shmutzik chin, and he died. And so, I sought safe passage on the barrel away from such tsuris before it was discovered."

"And this crew here—do they know this?"

"No—keneynehoreh. There's a priest on board. He saw me floating and had me netted. Though I hardly knew myself if I were man or fish, he recognized me from my quemadero performance and claimed my death for Torquemada's fire."

"So, nothing to worry about," I said. "Just execution."

"Bupkes," Moishe agreed. "*Abi gezunt.* As long as we have our health."

A week later, the ship arrived at port. Moishe and I escaped before the cargo was unloaded. The details are unimportant. So, nu, it was daring. It was full of wonder and chutzpah. Moishe, now unchained and waiting on the deck for the Holy Office, climbed the rigging and, friend to barnacles, plummeted into the dark water beneath the keel. In these times, sailors didn't swim. Better to drown immediately rather than splash about until the inevitable end. But in the last five years Moishe had become a pragmatist, a swimmer, a breath-holder. He emerged, wet as a hatchling in the dim space beneath a distant wharf, and slipped onto land like a newly grown frog. The privateers assumed he had sacrificed himself to water in order to avoid fire.

And then?

We took eggs, some bread, a wide-brimmed hat. We stole a horse, and under a crescent moon, we rode toward Granada, "the pomegranate." The Spanish wouldn't be interested in Moishe there; they were interested in the city itself. Granada: the last Muslim city in Iberia, an Islamic fruit lodged uncomfortably under the expanding tuches of Christian Spain.

As if it were ongeshnoshket, the road staggered from side to side as it climbed the Sierra Nevadas. By midday, breaded by dust, we came to a hillock. A small spring was tucked into its hip like a sidearm. It was no more than a piss-dribble soaking the gitch of the slope, but the water collected in an inviting pool. Moishe led the horse to water, and, of its own volition—for how could it be otherwise, it was a horse well versed in saws and chochmehs—it drank. Moishe stripped down and immersed his weary fleysh in the drink. I saw then the marks on his body. The red weave of whipmarks, the welts. The written weltschmerz of skin, a library of damage. And instead of his left tsitskeh nipple, there was nothing but a blind scar. His chest was a winking Creeley, a one-eyed Jack.

So, nu, he should replace it with wood as if it were a missing leg?

They say never accept a wooden nipple.

Better then to cover it with an eyepatch like a Blemmyae pirate.

There had been a fight, he said. A flash of blades slicing the air and, in this case, his chest.

"*Nisht geferlech*. Could have been worse," he said. "I wasn't using it, anyway."

We finished the last of the bread and eggs.

I'm not usually one for eggs, but they were the kinder of no one I knew.

We continued on but decided, after overhearing a group of riders, to travel to nearby Santa Fe. It was 1492 and much had changed—and was about to change—since we'd last been on the peninsula. Granada was under attack. To the crown, it was an irritating Islamic grain of sand and, currently surrounded, would soon become a Catholic pearl in the clammy hands of Ferdinand and Isabella.

They had established Santa Fe, a base several miles from the city walls, but to call it a military encampment would be to call the Great Pyramid of Giza a gravestone, or to think the Grand Canyon a gopher hole.

Santa Fe was a white city of ten thousand soldiers, horses, munitions, weaponry, chapels, and it was often visited by the King and Queen of soon—ptuh, ptuh, ptuh—all the Spains. Granada was so close that one early morning, a doughty Christian knight had left Santa Fe, slipped into the city by a secret tunnel and impaled a parchment inscribed with the words "Ave Maria!" over the doorway to the main mosque. He was back in time for breakfast.

Presiding over the other buildings of Granada was the magnificent palace of the Alhambra. The Alhambra: the world broken into a thousand pieces, then repaired, like a jigsaw puzzle assembled inside a kaleidoscope.

And soon to be a morcellated jewel in the crown of Ferdinand and Isabella.

So we travelled to Santa Fe, for as Moishe said, "A tooth is safest in the dragon's mouth."

Chapter Four

We'd been in Santa Fe for almost a week and felt the Spaniards' rising excitement. And now, in the bright morning, Sultan Abu 'abd-Allah Muhammad XII—Boabdil—was taking part in a carefully planned endgame. Dressed in silks and gold, he left the city with only a few emirs and a modest retinue of a hundred mounted men. He would bring his Moorish lips, more accustomed to dainties and the buxom delicacies of his harem, to the soft and scented hands of Ferdinand and Isabella, Los Reyes Católicos. He would surrender Spain to the Christians.

There had been a deal. They had his son. He had the key to Granada and the last remaining jigsaw piece to a completed Catholic Spain.

They met on a rise of land outside the city. The Spanish had already begun redecorating: royal banners flew from the Alhambra, the colours of Ferdinand and Isabella and the Christian cross. Boabdil climbed down from his horse and approached their highnesses. He began to get down on one knee, but Ferdinand held up his hand. No. They would not accept the key to Granada and the Sultan's proffered kiss.

This was in the script. A nursemaid guided a small boy toward him. His son. He had been a hostage since the beginning. Boabdil bowed and then he and his son walked back to the Moorish line. They climbed onto his horse and, with their dignity intact, rode away to board a ship bound for Africa.

As the unicorn said to the griffin when Noah built the Ark, "See, I told you there's nothing to worry about."

After this, the Sultan was called *el chico*, the little, or *el zogoybi*, the unfortunate.

But not to his face.

The royal party returned to Santa Fe, leading a procession of people joyfully singing "Te Deum." When they entered the central square before the church of Santa María de la Encarnación, the Royals dismounted, knelt, and kissed the torso of a huge cross. "Thanks, God. Let us snog the rood in gratitude."

Nothing excites more than the potent ragout of power and religion, particularly when accompanied by the tart spices of conquest and expulsion. The gathered crowd wept with pleasure, as did the Cardinal and Master of Santiago and the Duke of Cádiz and all the other grandees who stood there. According to what the Bishop of Leon wrote later, there was no one who did not weep abundantly.

Feh. He wasn't watching the eyes of the Jews, the conversos, the Marranos, and the Moriscos. They wept tears in disguise, the tears of the disguised, the tears of mourners as spadefuls of earth knock against the coffin, the hollow thud of regret, the sound of ending. Neither Jew nor Muslim, converted or hidden, wanted what they knew would be the inevitable next moves in this bullfight: *tercio de muerte* toward a Christian Spain.

What was abundant was the jostling of sound and colour, the cheering and kibitzing of the crowd. The streets of Santa Fe were alive with the vivid festival of its people, exuberant with change.

"Ech," Moishe said. "It's going to get bad before it gets worse."

The crowd heaved and swelled like the sea, waves of celebrants frothing toward us then being washed away. Moishe and I began in the square on the far side of the church but soon we were close to its massive doors.

We saw him on the other side of the steps.

"Oy," Moishe said. "Over there." It was the unmistakable figure of Christopher Columbus, standing taller and straighter than most, proud and haughty despite the raggle-taggle ongepatshket clothes he was wearing, as if a prince and the shmatte cart of Moishe's father had had a collision. His vivid blue eyes, his aquiline nose and high cheekbones were the same, yet he now had the wind-knurled face of a sailor. And, though it had been years since we'd seen him, his hair, long and silver, was surely white before its time. We pushed through the crowd and around the steps.

"We had not thought to see you still in this world, Admiral of the Other Side," Moishe said to him.

"Soon I shall be in the palace of the Great Khan, looking back at you from across the ocean," he said. "But I did not know they let parrots bring their servants here."

"In this way, I can say that no man is my master," Moishe replied. "You, it appears, are still looking for one that will pay you for your service."

"None but a king or queen," he said. "And that I hope for soon." The crowd surged again and for a few moments, we were pulled apart.

"But Miguel Levante," he said more quietly, "I was not able to thank you for what you did. For the rescue of my life. Since then it has been threatened many more times and I found few as ready to help as you. For that I am in your debt, if not your service."

Moishe bowed slightly.

"Join me as I sail the Ocean Sea," Columbus said. "To the Indies. To Cathay. To new worlds and the marvels beyond. To a choice land for the chosen. I wish to repay you with riches and adventure. You shall have gold in a land where gold is the common tongue and—ah—you shall spend it only in contented sighs."

Certainly, Columbus had no trouble spending words with his gilded tongue. And emes, it was a good thing for it was his only means to worm through the royal earholes and into the moneyed vaults of their pride and imagination.

More than knowledge of the sea, his adventure depended on the guileless confidence and simple optimism that not only would he bump into solid land of one denomination or another—islands, continents, isthmuses, or Asia—but that his incontinent predictions allow him to discover financing.

"How shall we decide if we will go with Columbus on this non-quest to nowhere?" I asked Moishe.

"The same nothing that is not stopping us is what we have to lose," Moishe said.

We had no script. Moishe was already a pawn who'd stepped beyond the chessboard when he'd left the shtetl and went beyond the Pale. But nu, beyond the beyond is still the beyond: perhaps an antipodean world, a world turned upside down, not converso, but inverted, where even a pawn could be king, the Jew, a citizen, and where "the land's the limit," the tsitskehs-over-tuches birds would say. For Moishe had discovered this craven old world to be built on a foundation of blood and hatred, on power and suffering, on bile and gout. Was it possible that we could leave this world behind and all its kishka-twisting memories, nothing but the bitter taste of its language in our mouths?

"I won't leave before I save Sarah, the Doña and the hidden Jews who I promised to save," Moishe said. A tree grows even after an axe is sunk into its young trunk. Sometimes it raises it high. Moishe, the boychik, the blade.

For now, we went with Columbus into a soldiers' tavern—they were all soldiers' taverns in Santa Fe—and turned, not the world, but the wine upside down.

He had a proposal. He would address the niggling matter of funding and we would retrace our route back to his brother. There we would receive maps from Bartolomeo and return with a package. What was it?

A book, but Columbus was vague.

Sha. What's ever gone wrong with a book?

But he had been granted a small stipend from Isabella, perhaps only to dissuade him from seeking sponsorship from the King of France or Portugal. He offered to lighten our load with some of this silver.

Was it a good idea? Ach, ask the silver.

Our plan. First, steal a horse. Next, steal away to Lisbon.

Chapter Five

*S*everal months later: returned from Portugal, we crept into Granada, prodigal rats skulking up a gangplank. Columbus would not be in the city until some weeks hence. He was tilting not at windmills but at moneybags, hoping that if he pricked them right, they'd plotz gold for the voyage.

Moneybags east and west:

Luis de Santángel, a converso from Aragon.

Francisco Piñelo, a Genoese living in Castile.

And from the church: not blood from a stone, but gold from atonements: indulgences sold for profit could raise more than half the necessary millions of maravedis. Columbus also ran at full tilt toward friends who dealt not in Sunday goodness but in sundry goods, such as slaves.

So what had happened since we were away?

Gornisht. Nothing important.

Some months had passed.

So, nu. They passed. It's a life.

In March, Ferdinand and Isabella had signed a decree. The Jews of Spain must leave by the end of July.

Or turn Christian.

As if that were as simple as converting from imperial to metric.

After their Catholicizing, Jew-spitting majesties had so decreed at the Alhambra, itself now converted, Don Isaac Abravanel, a Jew who had been both their advisor, tax farmer, money lender and treasurer, offered them more than a Shylock's-weight in gold to rescind the law. They were considering the plenty of his plea, when the Queen's own confessor, none other than the Grand Inquisitor Tomás de Torquemada himself, strode in, a righteous and red-caped storm, a cross in his fist.

You should know: He was descended from Jews. So, nu. We all have our cross to bear.

Torquemada was *unger bluzen* angry and his brain boiled with the fury of a witch's unbaptized brew cooking over hellfire. He looked at Abravanel, bargaining before *Los Reyes Católicos* and shouted, "I wouldn't piss in his traitorous mouth if his soul was on fire." Then he hissed at the Queen, "Judas sold his master for thirty pieces of silver. Now you would sell him again?" He pitched the cross across the room. It hit Isabella in the head.

And so, the Queen bled blue, the Edict stood, and the Jews had to leave or change from Yiddishe maggots to Christ-fearing flies.

Did Abravanel change his tune when the piper refused his money?

"Don Isaac," Isabella said, "since you have been of great service and are much loved, we would consent for you to remain in our kingdom as a Jew. We would allow nine others to remain with you to pray before your God as required by your faith."

Bowing deeply before the Queen, Abravanel advised her of his intention to travel to Naples but, ever the wheeler-dealer schacher-macher, on the way out he bargained for two extra days for the Jews in Spain and then for lenience in what they could take with them.

The Great Expectorators, Ferdinand and Isabella. They were surprised how many Jews chose to leave. Certainly, many Jews converted, especially those who had a well-heeled leg up. Who would step down and walk away from such privilege?

Some.

Abravenel, for example.

But for most it was, "you may lead a horse to holy water but soon enough, if you need glue, he'll be glue."

Foreskin and seven years ago, ach, even longer than that, a hundred years maybe, many had converted after some pogroms, but now they took to the roads and fields, shaking tambourines and beating drums, struggling, falling sick, dying. When they arrived at the shore, they wailed and shrayed, men and women, the leathery and the soft. "Adonai, merciful God, surely you will again part the seas and make a road for us out of this farkakteh land."

Nes gadol hayah poh. A great miracle happened here. The sea sloshed and sparkled, the blue crenellations of the waves were surmounted by foam. The seemingly endless sea heaved and tossed, the great ocean was a living, breathing thing, made only of water, brought to life by transcendental sighs.

A liquid Golem. A wonder.

But it did not part.

They had to take boats, wailing on the whale road, hoping for peace on the other side.

The Jews were allowed to take what they could carry: jewels, bonds, cash, children, books, their future, the old, their worries. We heard of someone whose belly was cut open because some bulvan thought he'd eaten his gold to hide it.

True, if it had been possible, many would have shouldered their houses, cows, their anvils and orchards, taken the old Spain with them. But some things are too heavy to carry, though nothing weighs as much as uncertainty.

Except, perhaps, the sea.

❦

We crept through the streets of Granada.

"We're lox-Jews, " Moishe said. "Swimming against the tide. We're sneaking back into Egypt."

"Reverse-Moses and Aarons," I said.

Moishe was concealed in a dark cloak. I flew over the moonlit roofs, keeping watch. So naturally, when he turned the corner of an alley, a face appeared.

"I see that unlike most, your shadow is above you," the face said.

"Señor," Moishe replied. "I seek only my master's door this night. I travel with but a regular kind of dark."

"But I have seen this shadow once before," it said. "This bird was at Doña Gracia's, as were my paintings. You should not be sneaking around these times, they grow ever more unsafe."

The painter.

We hadn't recognized him. There were many faces in our recent past, murderous, friendly, duplicitous and double-chinned.

"Meet me next day," the painter said. "I work on the distant horizon: the landscape in a portrait of the Queen." We would meet behind her gold-kirtled back while the Queen attended a parade in celebration of herself.

We continued to the tavern where we were to leave the sack for Columbus. What greater safety than the shtarker-shikkered shadows of an alehouse beneath a brothel? Its staggering occupants cared only for flesh, the fist and the firkin, not for a cartographer's gift to his brother. And a face-to-face with a member of the Holy Office would be unlikely. Priests did not frequent common houses. They engaged specialists to genuflect before them, to receive their sweaty and unholy secret sacrament.

We were to look for Jacome el Rico, a Genoese sailor. He had a scar down one side of his face in the shape of a zayin, though apparently the Diego who did the deed was not a master of Hebrew calligraphy for, we were told, the letter was nearly illegible.

Moishe walked down the steps and pushed open the door to the tavern.

A hairy stump of a man approached us. "I wants that Polly on your shoulder. Sell it me and these coppers are yours," he said, thrusting two dun-coloured coins into Moishe's face. "Refuse and I'll drive a hawse hole through your giblets an' wear your jawbone as me bangle." The subtle scent of unwashed rat was keen on his Sirocco breath.

So, nu, he was a humble tzadik scholar interested in the Talmud and its elaboration of righteousness.

But Moishe, having recently acquired philosophy from the hurly-burly yeshiva of the farmisht and shaken world, engaged the kishkas of this scholar with an unrelenting syllogism: the major premise of knee, followed by a minor premise of fist, resulting in the conclusion that this man, lying on his back and gazing blankly at the rafters, possessed a material reality that could be known by the senses. Except for his own, currently having being knocked out of him.

Ach, we are all in the gutter, some of us unconscious, as we look toward the stars.

We discerned in the desiccated scrubland of his face, a scar shaped like a zayin, confirming that this was the gentle soul for whom we searched: Jacome el Rico.

His resurrection was effected by baptism with a tankard of wine and the appropriate brocheh.

"Wake, you shrunken yard-arm dog," Moishe said. "Or should I kick the sleep from your eyes?"

The delicate poetry of first meetings.

Jacome spluttered.

"We have a compadre in Cristoforo Colombo," Moishe said, offering the man an arm to assist in his ascent.

Columbus's name was a magic spell. The man sprung up into a crouch like a cat on his hands and bent legs.

"Do you have it?" he said, narrowing his eyes.

We were still in the frame of light cast by the open door. Few, however, had seemed to notice our scuffle. Such things in such places were like legs in trousers, part of their very definition. Here, those who stood up often fell down, and the opposite was also true. There were also many, like the Grand Old Duke of York, who did neither, and indeed were not able to locate themselves in either the spatial or the temporal world. Ongeshnoshket. Three sheets to the wind.

We went with Jacome, now tottering on his hindquarters, to a table in shadows and effected the transfer. Jacome took the sack and concealed it beneath his shirt. Portly, he had become book-bellied. He quickly left the tavern.

After, that is, ordering a mug of ale, convincing Moishe to pay, then sloshing it down the hatchway of his greedy throat.

Chapter Six

The following morning we travelled to meet the painter in a Mozarabic palace newly collected by Isabella since the fall of Granada. Upon entering, we looked to the horizon, empty except for a few sheepish and indistinct clouds hovering above a bare and misshapen tree. The painter leaned in close, his brush twitching only slightly, his eyes only half open.

He was adding leaves.

If we had wished for blood to paint them autumn, we could have skewered him, so intent was he on each tiny leaf. Sha, we could have had children with him before he noticed and looked up.

By now, Moishe knew how to cough in at least three languages. So, he coughed. The effect was immediate. The painter twitched oily green across the edge of the sky. "Ach! May your kugel cook in hell."

Then he pointed at an ornate chair. "Sit."

Moishe looked warily around the room. He'd learned to check for exits, unless aboard ship. The sea was both escape enough and no escape. There was a door at the end of the chamber. "The Queen is not at the palace?"

"Today," the painter said, "there is another parade to celebrate the Reconquista."

"Will they also dance in the streets when the Jews are gone?" Moishe asked.

"As they did in Hamelin when the rats left," the painter said. "Now, sit." This time, Moishe sat. The painter turned and repaired the sky.

"If only such feats could be wrought outside of the canvas," he said and put down his brushes. "I am Señor Rui Fernández, painter, yes, he that painted for Doña Gracia, but together we worked on greater trickery than mere perspective and flattery. For some years, the Doña and I have arranged safe passage for oppressed and fire-bound Jews. The Doña with the ships of her late husband and brother-in-law who disappeared, likely tied to stone or iron, dropped into the deep. We could lay the foundation for new Jerusalems from such seabones as have collected there.

"I am Fernández, yes, and cousin to that Sarah who you tried to help. I, too, have spoken with this would-be world-finder Columbus. I will travel with him, through the Pillars of Hercules, across Ocean Sea and beyond history's vanishing point. With the Doña gone, there are no more rescue ships. And, in truth, this dark tide has already washed my heart to sea, and only habit keeps blood moving through me."

There was a great clattering in the courtyard.

Important people, or perhaps more correctly, the self-important, move either with preternatural silence or with profligate sound. I flew to the window. Bright colours. Hammered metal. Flourishes of cut-sleeved brocade. The landed had landed and they were coming toward us.

"Who is it?" I asked.

Fernández: "That's a clever bird."

A pageboy was on the steps of the chamber. Moishe ran to the door that he'd previously charted as a sally port for use in sudden storm.

It was locked.

I flew to the rafters. Birds and clouds can hide in the sky. Moishe would have to learn from the painter's horizon and become background. He pressed himself against the wall, miming grout or shadow.

"Señor Fernández, our queen arrives. She grants you time and her noble visage for the painting of her portrait," the page said.

The painter rose in anticipation and soon the royal cortège bustled in. A couple songbird-resplendent maidels-in-waiting, some hildagos, many pages, two priests and Torquemada, Grand biltong-dry Inquisitor of the Holy Office, and the Queen: short, strong, blue-eyed, with hair like the auburn planks of a ship. She had the self-assurance of a statue of herself, though far beneath the staid mantel of steady piety there appeared to be a fiery and excitable core.

"*Su Majestad Católica es muy generosa.* Your Catholic Majesty is most generous," Fernández said, bowing low, and with perhaps a slightly ironic curve to his painterly spine.

But it might have been artistic foreshortening.

The Queen acknowledged him with an almost imperceptible nod, then established court by enthroning the grand duchy of her regal tuches in the ornate chair. Once the seat of power was comfortable, she nodded to Torquemada who sat in a smaller chair beside her.

The pages stood against the wall beside Moishe. An invisible identification line-up. In these times, servants were deferential and soft-focus backgrounds to the prominent foreground of the powerful. It was unlikely the pages would break rank and render themselves visible by singling out Moishe, especially in the presence of the Queen. To be wrong might result in the singling out of their livers or tongues. At the very least, they would be expelled.

From a high window.

"Señor Fernández, you may begin," the Queen said, and struck a noble, world-conquering, Jew-tossing, Moor-expunging, yet humble pose.

The painter lifted his brush and palette. Soon the oval lake before him began to glow with an expression of inherited power. From amidst a shroud of mist, the face of Isabella appeared, a pious Ozymandias looking faithfully into the future.

Isabella kibitzed quietly with her ladies-in-waiting.

Torquemada, the wizened Millenarian vulture, perched on his chair silently, wondering where the Messiah was, waiting for the beginning of the end of the world, reclaiming Zion and positioning Ferdinand as "Last World Emperor." I could almost see him drying out, his alter kaker apple-doll brain collapsing in on itself like a dead star, his fearsome eyes sucking all available light from the room.

The doppelganger Isabella continued to form.

The priests and hidalgos stood waiting.

Then Columbus strode into the doorway.

A sailor with seven-league bootstraps looking for Su Majestad's permission to begin his long sail over the short sea.

He bowed but as if only to offer the Queen an exclusive vision of the pure snows that creamed the polar cap of his head.

"Señor Columbus," the Queen began. "Admiral of the distant horizon and Viceroy of what isn't there. It is a surprise."

"Su Majestad," he said.

"Doubtless, you have come to speak again of savages and kings. So, enter and prophesy." He walked into the room, a grand procession of one. There was a flicker of recognition as his eyes scanned the far wall—sailors look always to the edges of where they are—Moishe a familiar piss-pool in a lake of pages, though Columbus said nothing.

"Su Majestad, I will sail to Cathay and Cipangu," he said. "To the lands of the Great Khan. 'Most Serene Prince,' I shall say to him, 'I have travelled from where the morning begins, west from the east, and yet have arrived at the Farther East. I bring you greetings from your dearest friends, *Los Reyes Católicos*, Queen Isabella of Castile and King Ferdinand of Aragon.'"

He turned toward beef-jerky Torquemada. "And, Your Eminence," he said, "I will discover how these people are disposed and the manner whereby their conversion to our holy faith might be effected. This I do for Our Lord, enthroned above the circle of our world and who wishes it so."

He spoke again to the Queen. "Also," he said, "I will return with an Ararat of gold, spices, rare treasures, and—before the African-groping Portuguese may grasp them—new conquests of islands and mainlands in the Ocean Sea. These will provide such monies as will allow our stalwart Christian soldiers to retake Jerusalem, even as you've returned the good lamb of Granada to your Majesties' Catholic flock. It is but a small risk for great glory, both here and in the Eternal beyond."

I'm a feygeleh parrot who has sailed many seas and travelled in many languages. How would Columbus's greeting sound to the Great Khan?

I translate:

"Great Khan, or Lesser Khan, or Hardly-Khan-at-All, I am Brother Christopher and I was in the neighbourhood. Are you happy with your civilization? I bring Good News. Also, I am here to trade some magic beans for precious things, or else, ransack your house."

Torquemada and Isabella heard only Jesus, gold, glory, Jerusalem. And, "Portugal, you conquer the world in your way; we conquer it in His."

And: "first."

And: "more."

Columbus did not wait for a response but launched into a disquisition on distances, ancient Greeks and ocean currents.

"You could run a sword through their bodies," Torquemada said, suddenly emerging from his chiliastic stupor. "Though it might puncture or slice, it would not injure their hinkypink souls," he said, grinning like a chimp. "They have no souls."

"Who?" Isabella asked.

"Heathens."

"But, Padre, should we not wish to baptize them?"

"I hope thereby to win new lands for the Holy Church," Columbus said.

"And I believe all people to be human," Isabella said.

These words were fighting words then. A colourless green idea sleeping all over Europe, full of sound and fury, but, ultimately, signifying nothing.

Or, signifying plenty if you were a slave.

Isabella continued. "And some of these humans, our Lord God has chosen to allow to serve us."

Exactly.

Who wouldn't want to belong to a club that would sell some of its members? A barbecue joint that calls its ingredients "patrons"?

"And," she said, "these humans, we must teach as children."

"Then, Su Majestad," Columbus interjected, "allow me to discover these kindling gardens for Spain. I will achieve glory, gold, new land, souls, and good servants."

"These people cannot be human if being human is to mean any-thing at all. To be human is to have a soul. To be rational. To understand that there must be a Pater, Filius and a Spiritus Sanctus," Torquemada said. "Most—such as the Africans—are, at best, human in part only."

Columbus turned to Isabella. "Su Majestad," he said. "These many years, I have been petitioning your illustrious Majesties. The Reconquista has been accomplished, the Jews sent into exile. If there is to be a time for Columbus, before there is no more time in this world, surely this is that time."

He went down on one knee. "I am your humble servant, he who will bring you gold, the passage to India, the new edge of the world, great wealth, and much land, yet he who will seek, if he must, the patronage of another crown if the splendid double crown of Spain wishes to wait for the future to wash ashore like seaweed and wet sticks. Su Majestad, I believe it is God's will that a caravel and its courageous captain should sail the new sea. We wait now only for the King and Queen."

"Señor Columbus, we thank you for your words, for your ardent faith, your pressing enthusiasm, your sometime loyalty," Isabella said. "As you well know, some months ago, the King and I convened a council to discuss your plea. These learned and Godly men have decided that, though your many words stir our imagination, what is unknown is too much not known. We have watched the world unfold as you talk your way around the globe, but the calculations of our council—astrono-mers, astrologers, cartographers, mathematicians, cosmologists, priests, bishops, navigators, scholars, those with knowledge of the ancients and the lands and distances in their books—make the Ocean Sea a moon away and not some few Canary-distances as you promise. You could wish to travel to the sky with a jump, but, unless your legs were moun-tains or you had a map charting where the high blue reached close, no words could take you there, and no king or queen could, even if willing, finance such a leap.

"Señor Columbus, we ask you to leave Santa Fe. Do not tarry, but go now. Your story here has reached its conclusion. It ends on this soil, not on a field lit by the sun's far side and furrowed by Amazons."

Columbus stood. "Su Majestad," he said with simple dignity. He did not back away from the Queen, mincing into retreat, but turned and strode calmly from the room. For once, he had calculated perfectly. His full and brimming hopes in a slop bucket carried with poise and calibration as he walked steadily out of the door.

All were silent as the topography of the stairs was told by the waning tale of Columbus's footfalls.

A *broch tsu Columbusn*. A curse on Columbus. A *brocheh*. A blessing.

Then a wheezy hyena sawblade of a laugh from Torquemada's pious hole, his snail tongue pressed against his palate as he rocked back and forth in the chair and hissed. Not all people were human.

Throughout the scene, the painter had continued painting, the second smaller Isabella gazing steadfastly out from the canvas. The real Isabella posing in imitation of her portrait. Staid. Stolid. Regal.

Then a flash of colour from the back wall. Limbs suddenly moving. A luffing cape. A baggywrinkle coming alive from the distant horizon of pages. A single tree from Birnam forest sprinting toward Dunsinane.

A flashing flying fish of a blade.

Some vants nobody boychik, only the down of a duck's tuches on his chin, attempting to pay his respects to the inside of the Queen with a knife.

Assassination. It's the worst form of succession. Except for all the others.

Moishe leapt from the wall and dived toward the younger with the raised blade. The retinue around the Queen did not move.

Dios mio! A ear-wringing kvitch from the Queen. Torquemada did not react but saw only the transtemporal ghosts of his fanatic imagination.

Moishe embraced the assassin's ankles and steered him from the Queen, his knife penetrating deep into the side of a lady-in-waiting.

Wait no more, maidel, the blade is here. The knife surrounded by a dress, the page's pale sea-creature hand hanging on to its handle, Moishe hanging on the page.

Moishe grabbed the skinny wrist until the page's fingers released, then pulled the arms behind and battened them like hatches, each to the other, parbuckling him with his own cape. The knife remained buried in brocade, a flying jibboom over the Spanish lady's right hip.

If beauty is skin deep, then this mamaleh should be freylech joyful for the thick Kevlar of fashion that saved her. Her frock, a fat sheath that denied a happy ending to the shtupping knife, nevertheless granted one to its wearer.

The page hog-tied, the other pages began to flock around him. The hidalgos awoke, their swords drawn, and carried the afraid knot of youth to the cell where he would be imprisoned until execution, executed until death.

In this way, he would learn. A permanent lesson.

"Ach," as Moishe would say. "*Nifter-shmifter, a leben macht er.*"

What's it matter? As long as he makes a living.

✛

Moishe stood in the centre of a circle of the Queen's cortège. He was no longer background, nor invisible.

Moishe: Murderer. Freedom fighter. Fugitive.

Hero.

He reached over to the pierced lady-in-waiting and pulled out the dagger.

"A memento?" he said, holding it before her. "But not a memento mori."

"You have performed a great deed for me, for Castile and, I trust, for King Ferdinand," Isabella said. "What is your name and whom do you serve? Where is this lord?"

A broch. Moishe had to play this well else he share a death with the hog-tied page. And death, like music, can be shared equally by all who experience it. There is never a shortage. Life is the only thing that comes up short.

"Majesty. I am Miguel Levante," he said, bowing low. "Whether I bear wine for a priest at chapel," he said, rising slowly, "bring supper to a Duke in chambers, or lift sword to protect a ship from pirates, I serve my Lord God, my Queen, and her noble husband, King Ferdinand."

I kvelled. I was proud. I had taught him well. He stood before her, confident and gracious. His slim yet sturdy body. His dark hair and monkey-butt beard. He pronounced Spanish trippingly yet without tripping. And meant none of it.

He had grown into a real mensch.

A true parrot.

"Your Excellency," he bowed before Torquemada who had promised he would burn if seen again. But Moishe acted with such quiet calm and chutzpah that Torquemada, half fardreyt by the wash of ghosts, did not appear to recognize him.

The Queen motioned to a stunted nebbish of a man whose marmoset punim face was frozen in an expression of surprise and distaste. "Feh" seemed emblazoned on his lips.

The man reached into his doublet and procured a testicular sack that he presented before the Queen. She raised three fingers whereupon he retrieved three gold coins from within Her Majesty's scrotum and held them distastefully before Moishe.

"I shall remember your name, Miguel Levante," she said. "I give you this token of our gratitude." She nodded to the nebbish who then presented the coins. "Perhaps you serve the wind or the ocean and yet no man," she continued. "Or perhaps your master is the same as he whom you have thwarted, but yet you took a different road when the deed was close. I do not know, but God and queens forgive and reward those who choose the right path.

"This noon, our Grand Inquisitor, our sometime confessor, Torquemada, begins travel to Cordoba. I wish that you ride with him— we will provide you with a mule—and will send word to a soldier of mine who performed great service at Grenada, Gonzalo Fernández de Córdoba who is now at Loja. You will there be given a position and an opportunity."

What could Moishe do? He bowed and thanked her Majesty.

A *nar git un a kluger nemt.* A fool gives but the clever one takes.

Or gets out of town before the fool becomes clever and the clever one is skewered.

Chapter Seven

*L*ate afternoon on the road to Cordoba. Moishe, a shnook on a mule in procession with various priests, shtarkers and servants on their way to hunt hidden Jews and sundry heretical bandersnatches.

Leading them, the Imperial Red Wizard, Torquemada, a breastless wraith riding a black bruiser of an Andalusian horse with a whorl of white like a galaxy on its forehead.

"It is said to be unlucky for a horse to have a marking that it itself cannot see," he said to the Inquisitor.

"I am a Christian and so do not believe in superstition," Torquemada replied.

At this, I held my tongue, though the temptation was great.

"But, I know who you are," he continued. "Unlucky one, for whom death was not enough. You who seek to create the world anew. I have sent word to the Queen. You and this Genoese Quixote, Christophorus Columbus, shall sail into the west with the sinking sun, far from our work and those whom we serve. Perhaps this sun will not disappear but shall rise again over the Indies and Cathay. Perhaps it will burn over a new land. Perhaps, like any thousand-faced hero, in time, you shall return. This is no concern of mine as I shall be gone. Already it is only dust and disgust which hold my old bones together as I wait for the end."

Torquemada folded suddenly as if his spine had turned to sand. The wizened crab of his hand disappeared into a saddlebag.

"For you," he said, grinning with malice and cleverness, pushing something wrapped in dark cloth toward Moishe. "Take this and bury it over the Ocean Sea where it can only be found again by monsters and savages. Here it will destroy all we have worked for. Something is best hidden with those who don't need it."

Moishe took the package and began to unwrap it.

"Do not," Torquemada hissed. "Beneath the cloth is a book which teaches of life everlasting—if one learns to read its secrets. But there is another book which speaks of this, as you well know, for it is the story of your people." Torquemada's lungs were a bellows in seizure. It was a moment before I realized that this defined laughter in the sallow dictionary of his body.

"But that old scribble is but fable and ancient geography. This one reveals a new Eden on this earth where springs a fountain that refreshes both body and soul. He who bathes there will live until the world ends, which, since you have returned again, is a thousand years. A life longer than Methuselah. In this cascade, the soul is cleansed and one begins again without memory or sin. 'Sblood, I say. Without sin, everything we have worked for would be ruined."

Moishe nodded with solemnity. Let the blateration of the alter kaker continue. In a chamooleh's dreck, there may be gold.

If the chamooleh eats at the bank.

If he was to be believed, the meshugener Grand Expectorator had given us a book of directions, a Michelin guide to Paradise. Finally: the visiting hours for the Tree of Knowledge and the rules about flash photography and snakes.

"But," he said, "it's a Jewish book. And so, requires commentary. I'm told the book has four sisters," Torquemada continued, "each like a Talmud. The teachings of learned men. Interpretations. Explanations. Maps. Where these others are, I do not know. Now hide this and do not speak of it again."

Torquemada began making the sign of the cross over Moishe, but stopped midway. Instead he pointed west.

"This Columbus travels the road to France. He hopes to receive both blessing and money from the French king for his westward journey. You shall ride quickly along this road. I expect, this admiral, riding on his mule, will not have travelled further than Pinos. You shall find him and give my command that he return to the Queen. Soon, I shall have you, the book, and the viceroy of the leftmost world far from where you can interfere with our work. I cannot change heaven, but earth shall be my dominion."

He gave Moishe a great black horse and bade him ride.

✢

A story is a great city, and words are its citizens, jostling and kibitzing in its busy streets. It's these words that tell the tale, not the parrot.

But it's also *marbeh dvorim, marbeh shtus,* the more words, the more foolishness.

So I must have a sharp tongue, be a circumcising moyel, and make short what is long: We found Columbus. He returned to the Queen. He asked for the world and was granted half of it.

After three months of tideless and aimless sloshing, most spent working the monastery gardens of La Rábida, Moishe and I found ourselves with Columbus on the banks of the Rio Tinto at Palos, ready to leave one difficult world for another. Ready to transmute land to sea and then back again. To cross the trough in the centre of the atlas. To sail to the Jewless margins.

Thanks God, a godless place where God withdrew to make space and where roam those free-range souls, unfarmed by tax farmers or religion.

The unquisition.

But what would we find?

It's like they say about gatkes underwear: *zol zayn ergereh, abi andereh.* Let it be worse, as long as it's a change.

Chapter Eight

*A*ugust 3, 1492. The Port of Palos and its boat-busy river. Moishe and I watching over the larboard gunwale, suffocating in the hot canine breath of summer. Dog days when the sea convulsed, wine turned sour, hounds grew mad, and man became afflicted with burning fevers and frenzies, the brain boiling like an egg in a bone pot.

And now the end of the procession of gangplanking child- and sack-carrying Jews. A sea-crowding exodus for which we waited.

For days, Columbus's sailors had been loading sufficient nosh for an entire year. Filling small boats with supplies and then rowing to the deeper middle of the river where the ships were anchored.

Salt pork, flour, olive oil, water and manzanilla wine.

And such marvels of our ingenuity as would fill the childlike mind of a great khan or pagan chieftain with wonder, an awareness of our implied military and technological dominance, and knowledge that our God was a bigger macher and more almighty than theirs. Thus would this great leader clap his royal hands in delight and then surrender.

Such marvels? Glass beads and hawks' bells, which were carried in great quantity onto our ships.

Columbus stood beside us. "This day is Tisha B'Av in the Hebrew calendar," he said. "The ninth day of Av when we remember the destruction of the ancient temples. And when history will remember the day we made the world new."

"Me," said Moishe, "I'm hoping history will remember how I found beautiful women." In the past five years, Moishe had learned not only the maps, knots and hornpipes of sailing, but also its swagger.

Then from below deck, "Retreat, fetid piss-dribbler, or ye shall wear your red guts for ribbons in your malodorous hair." The unmistakeable poetry of Jacome el Rico, tavern-dwelling husbander of books with the zayin-scarred face. He was already claiming territory.

Columbus left the ship to confer with Martín Pinzón, local crew-procurer, captain of the *Pinta*, and second-in-command of the fleet. Pinzón stood tall on a sack of grain surveying the grand duchy of the Palos docks, a place where he was the tallest tree and could unfurl the top gallant of his pride.

Columbus hove up on the boards beside him, gesticulating in the Italian manner, flying his words like a kite. Pinzón nodded solemnly and watched the preparations of his men all around them.

There were three boats ready to sail.

The *Niña*. The *Pinta*. The *Santa María*.

The first two were extracted like teeth from the town of Palos, required by King and Queen in quittance of a fine. The *Niña*, little girl, named after Juan Niño, its owner who would sail with us. The *Pinta*, the painted or spotted one: pinta, a disease that pocks the skin. Think syphilis, bejel or yaws. But more, later, of the fleshy story of these spiralling putz-devils that travel always with sailors.

Santa María, the flagship, the largest, a carrack; the other two, caravels.

But who would sail these three nautical hand-me-downs?

Most of the crew were from Palos or other ports along the Rio Tinto. Several—including Jacome—were, like Columbus, from Genoa. There were conversos, a hidden Jew or two, some Basques, a couple Portuguese, and Fernandez, the painter. Certainly, he would haul sheets and repair rigging, but he would also fill the painted foreground with what had previously only been seen over an imaginary horizon: the peoples, creatures and lands beyond.

Columbus had also engaged the services of a translator: Luis de Torres. Torres was able to speak Hebrew and Aramaic in the event that the lost and found tribes of Israel were teeming on the beaches, awaiting contact from the mother ship, the *Santa María*, that had travelled half the world on a watery crusade to find them.

When all you have is history, everything looks like diaspora.

Columbus expected to discover these tribes in the Far East and Torres would parley with them in their common and ancient tongue.

A landing party would row up to an island in a skiff and Torres would call out, "So, nu, *vos macht ir*? How you been these last two thousand years? And breakfast before you left, was it eggs?"

Except, of course, he'd say it in Aramaic.

Sailing with us, in order to ensure that the royal interests were protected, were representatives of the King and Queen.

Or as Moishe termed them, ballast.

And though the Queen had offered pardons to criminals who would commute their sentence from land to sea, would choose the uncertain hornpipe of the waves over the inevitability of the hangman's reel, there were only four who chose to dance this freedom freylekhs.

Bartolomé de Torres had taken the local magistrate's life from his body with a knife then left the corpulent remains on the floor while he drank the deceased's flagons of wine and collapsed, like a brother beside him, thereby entering himself into evidence. A day later, rats gnawed his bleeding ear and returned him to consciousness. He found himself jailed and knew his own shlemiel life would soon be over.

But later that night of little moon, Goday, Patiño, and Foronda, three of his compadres, removed the prison bars with a rope and a mule, and the four escaped—halevay, it should happen to you—into the ever-loving arms of the jailors, returning from an evening of drink and carnal satisfaction.

These four perfectly illustrated two species of Yiddish fool. Shlemiels pass out and find themselves in hot water. Schlimazels pull their friend from the roiling pot only to get their mortal goose cooked into soup.

These hapless shmucks were now sailors making the world new. Escaping the jail of one world for another, their new digs barred only by palm trees, lagoons, and sweet fruit.

There were ninety crew. Sailors, representatives of Their Jew-horking Highnesses, but no priest.

Why would Columbus, who sang so sweetly, at least to the Queen, of discovering a new world of souls not include a single Holy Father on board?

"Who needs a priest," Moishe said, "when God chirps by the cave of your ear, huffs your sails, inks your charts, and pulls back the cover of the world as if readying it for your Vice Regal shlof. Besides, God might get to thinking He knows more than His captain. It's not good to risk mutiny by one who controls the sea."

"And everything else," I said.

"Tell that to Martín Pinzón," Moishe said.

Pinzón and his younger brother, Vicente, who captained the Niña, were khans of the Palos shore and most the crew whom they'd procured, considered them so.

"It's hard to pick your nose with another man's finger," I said.

"Unless it's very dark," Moishe said. "But what do you mean?"

"It's hard to command another man's army."

"Emes. Unless it were decreed by the King and Queen."

⟊

We set sail.

I expected ceremony. There was no ceremony save the bustling pragmatics of embarkation. The scurry of men gripping halyards, clambering ratlines, hauling hawsers and knotting sheets into Celtic alphabets of rope. The diapason of the bo'sun's whistle. The gleeful kibitzing.

"Pedro, I heard the early worm got your wife's bird and you away at sea."

"Leech-prick, may a lobster take your bowels for a lover and may you pass only starfish."

Over the entire ship, a kind of exhalation as the lamden old salts felt, once again, the wind blowing against their abraded yardang faces. As the mariners returned to marinating.

First, the *Santa María*; then, like ducklings in our wake, the *Niña* and the *Pinta*. We had leapt out the window of Europe. We had no choice but to fly or return with a sorry tale between our legs.

I flew.

Moishe was standing at the binnacle overturning an hourglass. It had to be tipped every quarter hour, like a shikker's hooch-filled flask.

At sea, time isn't money. It's position. Longitude and the reconciliation of the sun, stars, and the hour depend on these buxom jars of slipping sand.

It's important to know where you are, when you're nowhere.

Moishe looked east.

"I was thinking about Sarah and the others," he said. "We're sailing away from Spain. But we're sailing *for* Spain, also. For their execrable *yemach-shmom* Majesties and the stinking black Holy Orifice and Torquemada."

"Ptuh, ptuh, ptuh," I said at the mention of the name. And you should know, psittacine spitting, even when its muse is contempt, requires some practice.

"I don't want to be a *nochshlepper*," Moishe said. "A hanger-on. Whatever we find on the other side of this Ocean Sea, whether it's a cursed farsholtn or promised land, I want it to help—not the King and Queen and their Church—but those ground beneath their feet. We Yids have often seen the tread of those boots coming down."

The sand had run out of the top of the hourglass and so Moishe inverted it. Like many things, its name didn't reflect what it was. Hourglass. Feh. It only measured a blaychik sickly quarter of an hour.

I could say something about how each individual sandgrain makes a difference.

Just think how it feels when one gets in your shorts.

But the bo'sun rang the bell and it was time for a nosh in the mess. I hoped for a bisl seed and a snootful of wine, but emes, there are many who wait for the Messiah also.

Chapter Nine

*I*t had been more than a month since we'd left Spain. We'd had a brief sojourn on Gomera in the Canary Islands to take on more supplies—beans, goat cheese, salted beef and pork, salt cod, water, wine, garlic, olive oil, almonds, chick peas and hardtack—and to refit the lateen-rigged Niña with square sails. Then we were becalmed offshore for a few days. And now we were in the middle of nowhere.

Where was that?

Exactly.

To know if you're in the middle, you need to be able to tell where nowhere ends, assuming you still remember where it began. This much we knew: we were, as Dante, *il Poeta*, wrote, *Nel mezzo del cammin*, except the dark wood we were in the middle of was water.

We had bobbed for weeks along the deserted surface of the Ocean Sea, the closest terra firma a few miles straight down, though I wouldn't want to visit. It would be no party, poison jellyfish the only balloons, black brine the only wine. A watery firmament. Cold. Dark. Only the faint preternatural neshomeh glow of bioluminescent tentacles and urine-coloured deep-sea gerkins, jaundiced-faced death-creatures-without-faces floating around in eternal midnight. The cellar-sand of the Ocean Sea miles below whales and the secret Leviathans of the deep, the wet underside of the waves where life wears its soul on the outside.

Feh.

With no land in sight, our minds fill with cabin-fever dreams and create restless sandcastles-in-the-air mirages of thought and word.

And the crew fights, and shtups, and gambles.

And kvetches about Columbus and his futile westward tilting.

Moishe lay against a barrel amidships. I'd thought of what was below us, and having plumbed that subject dry, I dreamed of beautiful birds amourously cooing at us, the sound like wingbeats and the beach-fall of waves.

"So," Moishe began, his eyes closed. He was almost speaking to himself, "Imagine the ship gets tsekrochn—worn out—and the crew must replace the shmutzik planks one by one—though where we'd get the wood out here, *ver veyst*—who knows? After awhile, they've replaced every klots and nail with another. Is it the same ship or a different one? We'd still be on board, half-asleep against this barrel, kibitzing. But it'd be a different barrel and a different deck. And what if someone took the gantseh pile of wood and made another ship out of it? Is that our ship or a different one?"

"Depends. Which ship is closer to land?" I said.

"And what if we—or sailors not yet born," Moishe said, "continued to replace the planks? They could replace them an infinite number of times and the ship would last forever."

"But we'd still be gone. What's the use of an eternal hat if the head is dead?"

"My father said we're made of tiny specks and each of these specks changes over a lifetime. Our hair when it's shorn keeps growing, our skin when it's cut, so why shouldn't the rest of our bodies? But we're still ourselves. A shtetl is always a shtetl even if the people change."

"So there's a bisl of me scattered here and there?"

"And tiny bits of shmutz from other people all over you."

"Now I could use a bath."

"It's the same with conversos."

"They need no bath. Baptism was enough."

"No, shlemiel, how many planks can you replace and still be yourself?"

"Or how many Jews?" I said, but what I thought was, "What if you change every word that you say?"

"A broch," he said. "May each Inquisitor become a secret Jew so he can betray himself and haul himself before the Tribunal."

"May each Inquisitor burn first himself and then the others at the stake."

"May each Inquisitor host a bowelful of Jewish rats who convert in the churchy dark of his insides and then gnaw like fressers on his unkosher guts."

"May each Jew change each plank of the world until it is new."

"Omeyn," he said. "But let this new world be different than the old."

✢✢

Later.

Dark night and the ship cantered on the waves. We were in the admiral's cabin. A lantern encircled the table in honey light. Wine, cheese, dried plums and nautical charts were spread invitingly before us. Worlds hidden from the crew.

If they had once been buoyed by Columbus's chutzpah, enthusiasm and professed expertise, by now the crew believed he was meshugeh. Out of his depth and with no clue about where we were or how far we were from any kind of terra—either firma or incognito.

It was an epic and mutinous "Are we there yet?" befitting impatient children, bristle-faced tousle-heads with few teeth but many swords.

If his navigations were to be correct Columbus required the world to be 20 percent smaller than the estimation of the ancients. Perhaps since then the world had shrivelled like Eratosthenes and his friends' once ripe beytsim. Time can make between-the-leg prunes out of even the most succulent of plums.

Columbus's calculations were based on his reading a letter from a certain Toscanelli that he worried like a rosary, which agreed with his results. If your mind is a matzoh ball, then everything looks like soup.

But almost from the beginning, the canny mariner understood the measure of his men—that their patience was short—and so he acted with duplicitous and data-massaging cunning.

Mostly, Columbus kept his thoughts and schemes to himself, except when he shared them in loud sermons to the crew of the *Santa María*. Perhaps the men of the Niña and the *Pinta* also heard his speeches for he stood on the poop deck like the Pope on the balcony of St. Peter's, and declaimed them in balebos stentorian tones for all—God, the wind, the waves and the reluctant land included—to hear.

But at other times, he would confide his late-at-night thoughts to Moishe in a quieter voice.

"The truth has many façades," he said. "A man may hide his true face, or faith, with beard or mask. Some sailors taking passage on our three ships—I could mention Luis de Torres—have the skin and words of a good Christian yet Jewish blood pumps from their hearts and their heads are filled with Hebrew prayers." He had a sip from a cup of wine and continued. "A storyteller may change his tale for that which tells more true, for the truth has two sides, an inside and an outside." Columbus stood up and walked across the cabin.

"There is something I must show you."

From a shelf, he hefted a large book and laid it on the table. He ran his hand tenderly over the cover.

Ech, I thought. For a bird whose only library had been the waves, my world was becoming ongeshtupted with books. Moishe seemed to attract them the way analogies attract fools.

It was the ship's logbook, written in the hand of Rodrigo de Escobedo, the scrivener.

"Look," Columbus said, pointing to an entry.

Sailed northwest and northwest by north and at times west nearly twenty-two leagues. Sighted a turtledove, a pelican, a river bird and other white fowl; —weeds in abundance with crabs among them. The sea being smooth and tranquil, the sailors muttered that in such a region of smooth water, there

would never be sufficient wind to return them to Spain; but
afterwards the sea rose without wind, which astonished them.
The Admiral spoke on this occasion, thus: "the rising of the sea
was very favourable to me, as the waters so lifted before Moses
when he led the Jews from Egypt."

We remembered that day of waves without wind and what Columbus had said. Moishe had whispered to me, "Ech, but each day his land becomes more 'promised.'"

"Soon," I said, "he'll think himself more Moses than you."

Not long after this logbook day, we had entered a region of deep blue, thick with seaweed. The waters were of such exceptional clarity that, looking over the gunwales, it seemed as if we could stand on the fishes and eels that swam in myriad constellations far below us. This was the "sea without shores" spoken of by Portuguese *marinheiros.* The Sargasso Sea. A viscous Atlantis. Some of the crew had heard of this place. Most appeared bazorgt worried and agitated, not knowing what this plenitude of seaweed, this sea change, might mean.

Columbus now left the logbook, then unlocked a chest in the corner of the cabin and lifted out another book. He carried it to the table, and spread, too, its wings beside the other book and pointed to the entry of September 23, the same day's date.

"Twenty-seven leagues," Moishe said. The direction is the same but the distance is different."

"On this voyage," Columbus said, "as elsewhere, there are two truths. One longer than the other."

The truth and the shvants-truth, I thought.

"The first book is for the pilot and others of the crew. For now. The second is for history and the future. When we have crossed this great ocean and the men's feet walk on the shores of Cipangu or the palace paths of the Great Khan, then can the true tale be told. I tell you so that this second truth can be known by one other. Many things may befall an admiral. Sickness. Capture. Mutiny. Death."

If there were a mutiny and—Gotenyu—the admiral's journey came to a sudden and definitive end, we would be quiet. Very quiet. What second log book?

It would be no time to reveal that we were intimates of he who'd gone overboard.

Already, the sailors questioned his books, his charts and his maps.

Several weeks in, the pilots had noticed that the compass needles no longer pointed to the North Star. They muttered that even the heavens were unsure of the journey.

Columbus reassured them. The needles must have been pointing to some invisible point on earth. North was different in the west. The west that would soon become east.

For now, they accepted his explanation, deferring to his self-assurance which was, emes, astronomical.

The compass readings were critical: like all navigators of the time, he used dead reckoning. Appropriate, for as his crew reckoned it, they'd be dead soon enough.

So, when he rode the pitching deck, attempting to determine latitude by pointing his new-fangled astrolabe at the stars, such meshugas inspired even less confidence. These instruments required a steady horizontal, and relations between ship and sea most often resembled a shore-leave sailor writhing between the roiling legs of his shvitzing maideleh.

I'd heard Domingo de Lequeitio muttering with others of the crew.

They were getting restless with too much rest and not enough discovery. If Columbus would not soon agree to turn the ship around, Domingo suggested they could drop him into the Ocean where he would be admiral of an ever-diminishing quantity of air and, eventually, Viceroy of the ocean floor.

"And," he said, "the tale we sailors will well recollect is that his eyes peeped through his astry-lad only, an' he stepped into the pitchy brine without knowing. Time enough before he fell, we'd see'd him staggering about the tossing deck with no thought but the stars."

Moishe and I weren't troubled by the length of the voyage.

"Know where we're going?" Moishe asked.

"Of course," I said, shrugging my grey-wing shoulders.

"Where?"

"West toward—"

"—the west," Moishe finished. Not content with fishing for the moon, we were chasing the setting sun. Putting distance between us and Spain required time. You couldn't hurry time. We had no expectations about the unexpected. The world was large, the sea was wide, and there was still salt pork, hardtack, wine and water.

But surely even the sun must need to take a load off and rest a biseleh on a daybed of land before shlepping over the next horizon and rising.

Moishe and I left Columbus's cabin. Some of the Basque sailors were sitting abaft the forecastle kvetching and making oakum from old rope. Their blaberation concerned the captain.

"The scupper-skulled futtock is willing to die to make hisself gran señor of lands we'll not return from."

The group of them nodded in assent.

"The walty Genoese is sailing us into the barathrum of nowhere 'tils we starve an' our flesh dries to bouillon."

They nodded again. They sang the bitter shanty of kvetchers.

Moishe turned to me.

"We all have our across to bear, *azoy?*"

✢

Before long, Martín Pinzón was rowed across the scalloping water between the *Pinta* and the *Santa María*.

"The men can endure no more," he said to Columbus as he climbed on board. Columbus did not reply but ordered a lombard signal to be fired. Soon after, Martín Pinzón's brother Vicente Yañez Pinzón, captain of the *Niña*, appeared over the starboard bow. He clambered up a ladder and the three captains went into Columbus's cabin and *haken a tsheinik*, argued and flosculated late into the night.

The following day, Columbus gathered the crew. "Three more days," he said. "On the Third Day, He created Dry Land. I need only as much time as God."

"What's the difference between the great God Adonai and Columbus?" Moishe asked me.

"What?" I said, knowing the answer.

"God doesn't think he's on a mission from Columbus."

And so we passed the time.

On the second day, the sky was dark. The feathered millions of a great forest were above us, their voices like storm. A twisting hurricane of birds, as if every leaf of a great continent—or the shadow of every leaf—had taken flight and was flying west-southwest. Where there are birds, there must be land. Columbus ordered an alteration of our course to follow this migration, to sail in its shadow.

Two nights later, we could hear more birds calling overhead in the darkness. I did not know these birds or their voices. A vast crowd muttering "watermelon" in a language I had never heard.

Then the crew of the Niña found a small branch bearing delicate blossoms and soon after, the men of the Pinta collected from the sea: a cane, a stick, a piece of board, a plant that clearly was born on land, and another little stick fashioned, it appeared, with iron, so intricate was its working. We, on the Santa María, found nothing but a vast collection of waves.

Early morning, October 10. Morning watch. Two bells. Columbus high on the forecastle as if he were about to present us—Aspirin-like—with the two tablets of the law. Instead, he announced that he would award a coat of silk to the first sailor to sight land.

Just what any wind-and-salt bitten sailor wants on the other side of the world: a shmancy silk shmatte to wear when swabbing and breaming and when hauling a shroud in a skin-luffing gale.

Later that afternoon at three bells of the watch, a sailor high up in the rigging shouting excitedly, "Tierra! Tierra!" Domingo de Lequeitio pointed in frenzy to the larboard-side horizon. A scurrying of the watch to the gunwale. The admiral striding out of his cabin in the forecastle. Men on deck coming to consciousness on their straw pallets, blinking in the light, fonfering the primeval waking thought, "Huh?" Moishe, too, awakening. In a moment, I was in the air then high on the foretop yardarm. Could it be that we were somewhere, or just before?

Eyes puckered under awnings of hand in the dazzle of bright light. It didn't look like land to me.

"That," said Columbus looking toward where Domingo was pointing, "is a cloud."

I heard Jacome abaft, muttering beyond the captain's hearing, "A cloud be good land for us, for soon we be memberless as angels, our pizzles snapped like dead twigs from off a dried-out tree, else we find fresh water or solid land for our watering."

The crew, as mocking angels, flapped their crooked arms like celestial chickens then made their groins shvantsless with shielding hands. "*Tierra, tierra*," they jeered at Domingo de Lequeitio high up the foremast. The frivolity lasted only moments until, as a man, they had the realization that they yet remained landless.

Columbus had not appeared to notice this outbreak of heavenly poultry. He had installed himself on the bowsprit, straining his eyes into the Ouija-board distance, attempting, it seemed, to summon forth shore like a spirit from the Olam ha-Ba beyond. He remained like a figurehead, through three watches, willing land to appear, Columbus both dowser and dowsing stick, remembering Exodus. "'We are in the wilderness, Lord, What shall we drink?' Like Israelites, we seek 'the twelve wells of water, the threescore-and-ten palm trees. We would encamp there by the waters. Lord, bring us land.'"

Later that night, seven bells into a dog watch, Domingo de Lequeitio, Columbus and Rodrigo Sanchez observed a dim flickering. I woke Moishe who was sleeping through some kind of illness, and he saw it, too. Though the moon was but a shtikl less than full, the light was not mere moonshine. There was the orange tinge of fireblaze, small and turbulent, a bonfire on a distant shore. The men on watch took note, whispering quietly to each other, but avoiding the ostentatious mekhaye hoo-hah of hope and celebration and the eventual disappointment of the previous afternoon.

Even Columbus, usually given to chisel-worthy pronouncements spoken in doughty capital letters, only nodded to the pilot, indicating, "Sail toward the light."

The following night, two hours after midnight, after the fourth bell of the dog watch had sounded.

An arquebus fired into the night sky from the poop deck.

What happens on a ship at 2 a.m. when, without warning, there is a shot?

The rational grog-soused mariner, drowsy and hypnogogic on his pallet, can only assume a murderous infestation of ocean-borne invaders sharp with the flesh-kebabing talons of raptors and blistering with the halitosis of harpies.

Or else the sighting of land.

Under a full moon, Rodrigo de Triana, a sailor from Seville, had seen *una cabeza blanca de tierra*, a white stretch of land.

"*Tierra!*" he called. "*Tierra!*" And for good measure, he again shot the arquebus at the stars.

Perhaps I should consider it auspicious that on this day, when the prodigal halves of the earth were joined once again, no bird or other flying creature was shot from the sky, keneynehoreh.

On deck, the men exulted.

The next day, October 12, 1492, we would make landfall.

If one wants to beat a dog, one finds a shtekn, a stick.

We had found a stick. Now what kind of dog would we beat?

"A golden retriever," Moishe said and lay back on his pallet, feverish and green.

It was early morning when Rodrigo de Triana had seen land. And now we'd sailed out of night and into the next day until we were but a cannon's blast away from what we took to be an island. The crew gathered on deck.

After months sailing the featureless ocean, heading toward nowhere but the horizon and the edges of maps, how did we feel about touching tierra firma?

Nisht geferlach. Could have been worse.

We felt only the way a man lost in the desert would feel about a bucket of water. About a fountain of water. About a thimbleful of water. About a droplet of sweat on a camel's tuches.

Love at first sighting.

For a season I had perched on barren masts and now there was the prospect of a living tree, heavy with leaves. Of rivers, waterfalls, and clear pools.

And perhaps there would be parrots. The pretty feathers of zaftik island parrots warmed by both sun and desire.

The firm land.

I couldn't remember the last time.

Part Four:
LAND

My heart is in the East and
I am at the end of the West.

JUDAH HALEVI

Part Four:
LAND

*My heart is in the East and
I am at the end of the West*

—JUDAH HALEVI

Chapter One

*I*n fourteen hundred and ninety-two, Columbus sailed the ocean blue. The Niña, the Pinta, and the Santa María shlepped around the great arc of the Ocean Sea and landed in what he took to be the other side of the world. A great moment.

But Moishe and I weren't there when those of the old world first met those of the new.

Our luck. A *mensch tracht un Got lacht*. A person plans and God laughs.

Moishe was green, puking with fever and shaking with palsy. Bent heaving over the gunwales, he saw the New World, saw the sailors rowing, saw them land. He saw Columbus kneel down and kiss the reassuring shore. He saw Columbus take his sword and draw in the sand. What was it: a cross, a prayer? Was he writing, "Ferdinand and Isabella," as if labelling luggage? Was he signing his name? "Ah, yes, my pretty picture. Think I'll call it 'America.'"

Columbus, the mapmaker, the navigator. He inscribed a compass rose on the shore, the New World a map of itself.

San Salvador, he called the island. Holy Saviour.

For it had saved him: if he had sailed to the island and it was not there, he would soon enough have discovered mutiny and the empty sea floor where the island was supposed to be.

But Moishe did not land on San Salvador. Like Moses, his name-sake, he had to watch as others entered the Promised Land. And I, like

Aaron, also did not enter, though it was Columbus and his kind who worshipped golden things, who practically birthed a golden sea cow in their excitement, joined hands and danced in a ring at the thought of their true God and its value in power, prestige and purchase.

We heard the cheering of the men, heard the singing of the native people as they gathered on the beach. We heard, though we could not make out the words, the speeches given, the long prayers made by Columbus as he trod on what he thought was an older world than the one he came from. Cathay. Cipangu. India. The Indies.

There was an exchange. Food for glass beads. Shells for tchotchkes and chazerai such as little metal toys.

As night fell, there were fires. More singing. Speeches. Cheering.

Moishe slept. I stayed with him on the empty ship, my green shoulder, my blue-eyed boy. I didn't venture onto the island. Besides, who knew if these natives, or, for that matter, the farklemteh sailors, would make of me a fricassee, spiced with who knew what delicate and unfamiliar spices?

Our men rowed back from shore. Columbus opened the casks to the crew. Laughing, singing, puking, the happy buffeting of each other's ears like drunken puppies, late into the night until they all collapsed in a historic heap.

The following morning, the incessant blacksmithing of fiends inside each man's skull. Inside their bellies, thirty boiling cats, cooking in roiling bilge water. Outside, the sun like a Klieg light, branding the eyes of all who attempted vision. Moishe woke as fresh-faced and pokey as the rest, which is to say, consciousness came upon him like a mallet.

Luis de Torres stumbled down the middeck, his clothing a polyglot-stippling of vomit, wine, New World sand and tropical fruit.

"Don't tell the admiral, but the savages speak Hebrew," he said and collapsed onto a pipa-sized barrel.

Moishe opened the slit of an eye.

"How can that be?" he asked.

"I spoke the ancient tongue and they understood. They are Children of Israel—*like us*," Torres whispered. "We have found the Lost Tribes. Wherever we are."

"The savages are Jews?" Moishe said.

Noble cabbages, then, I thought. Haleshkehs stuffed with exotic meat.

"I can't believe it," Moishe said, gripping the gunwales and hauling himself onto a knee. "This, I need my own eyes to see."

But by then Torres was slumped over, brought back to sleep by the continuing effects of the previous night's revelry.

"It was probably the drink talking Hebrew, not the natives," Moishe said. "Or Torres heard himself speaking and thought it was someone else."

"Hebrew," I said. "It's always backwards."

Then it was sometime later that morning. There were no watches, no bells, only the rousing voice of Columbus ringing over the deck, and then the more strident voice of a matchlock shot, waking men from sleep, returning the ship to the regular shape of days. The men of the Niña and the Pinta, also submerged in wine-addled shlof, were woken by the shot as it reverberated off the jungle trees fringing the shore. A landing party was established to return to the island. Moishe was to carry baskets and jars to lubricate the parley. Columbus had others bring flags.

The native people were already on the beach, made restive by the matchlock shot. As we rowed closer, I could see they were almost naked, though the entire surfaces of their bodies were rudely emblazoned in black and white paint. Both men and women had coloured feathers woven into their hair, the men having feathers intertwined with their long beards. Feh. My parrot skin turned gooseflesh beneath my bristling plumage. A broch. Imagine the naked skins of the countless plucked and farkakte. The islanders jumped around in an ungainly dance, springing back and forth from skinny chicken polke leg to leg as if sandcrabs had nested in the ragged loincloths that covered beytsim or knish. Closer still, I heard their savage chanting, a disorganized ululation punctuated by guttural roars. If they were the Lost Tribes, they'd lost more than Assyria and Middle Eastern sand. Sense and civilization, for instance.

Surely what Hebrew they knew could be little more than a child's blather. They were *vilde chayes*—unruly children. Calibans of the isle. There wasn't a Yiddisher kop—a sensible mind—among them.

"How do they survive?" Moishe said. "Look at their bellies, their scrawny skillington arms." Though their hair was curly, they were not the burly-shouldered bulvans that we had expected, tall and thick-limbed as the Ethiopes bought out of Africa.

I could see by the ill-stuffed pallets of their bodies that, since they walked out of history two thousand years before, they had not learned how to hunt or harvest healthy gezunteh food.

"They are simple and wild," Moishe said. "But something *klemt mir in hartsn*—something grasps my heart."

"You should watch what you eat," I said. "Maybe fewer sardines."

The skiff's keel scudded into the sand of the shore and the men scrambled out. They crowded around us, crowing, shraying, mewling as we walked up the beach.

"Gevalt," Moishe said and froze, his eyes wide, his jaw open. His bones were replaced by the ice of ghosts.

Then, after a minute, "I . . ." he whispered to me. "I . . . I know these people."

The sailors returned to the boat and, like pallbearers, carried a large flagpole up the beach. Columbus pointed at a rise of land near the treeline and bade the crew plant it.

The first thing we built in this new world was a hole.

Soon, after some tottering, they had raised the flag. On the map of the world, a mark: you are here. You, the subject of Aragon and Castile, of the crowned F and Y that now flapped for the first time in a Caribbean wind.

The natives gathered around dancing and cheering as if the Tree of Good and Evil had suddenly blossomed on the ground before them. They made a tararam commotion of the flag-raising as if the technology of the flag were the exciting element of the story and not the part where they were being conquered. Perhaps their technology of subjugation looked different than this. A deft slit of the throat, the hull of the head staved in by handheld rock.

A stooped older man with a flourishing Brillo pad of a beard, grey yet interwoven with coloured feathers, his sagging body daubed into a dark and greasy shadow. Moishe stood close beside him and they exchanged glances. Beady eyes instead of beads.

"Rebbe Daniel?" Moishe said.

The man continued his writhing, as if he were trying to cajole the feathers into flight.

"Shh," he whispered in Spanish. "Don't speak. We talk later."

I looked around. Beneath the paint and the joyous freylech prancing and prattling, the bodies and faces of the band of secret Jews of Seville began to emerge. As if I had suddenly noticed the black-suited puppe-teers behind the puppets, the Jim Crowsowitzes behind the minstrelry.

We needed to maintain the illusion. It was unclear what the con-sequences would be if their true identity were revealed. If Columbus were deprived of his role as first discoverer. If the functionaries of King, Queen and Inquisition learned that these wild menschen of the rainforest were really wandering Jews gambolling about the newborn Spanish soil on which rested so many hopes and symbols.

For now, this carnivalesque charade was exactly what they had expected. These palsied savages had leapt, gaping and mooning out of the pages of Sir John Mandeville, Herodotus, and other tales of the exotic.

The best disguise was to be recognizable.

Moishe remained silent. He did not betray his recognition save for a cocked eyebrow and a crooked, shlemiel-faced smile.

Martín and Vicente Pinzón conferred with Columbus. Then they spoke to Luis de Torres. He, in turn, spoke a goulash of tongues, includ-ing Hebrew, to Rabbi Daniel, feathered greybeard leader of this wild island race of tropical woodwose. Torres employed a too-loud voice, the international carrier of communication between cultures, as well as a colourful Berlitz of inscrutable gestures.

The rebbe did not, or pretended to not, understand. Chimplike, he bent and leapt, then grunted like a meshugener.

Torres returned to Columbus and nodded.

"And so," Columbus announced, as if to history, "we venture into the interior. We seek villages, signs of mining and of agriculture. Gold. Silver. And, perchance, the civilized masters of these people."

Moishe went to stand with those likely to be assigned to guard the boats and thus, according to the mysterious physics of management, was so assigned. As soon as the party, led by the neoprimitive rising and falling gait of Rabbi Daniel, disappeared into the jungle, Moishe motioned to a group of Vursht Nations people to follow him. We walked the beach and found a thicket where the jungle palms grew close and Moishe and I tucked ourselves behind its leeward side.

Two of the hidden Jews, hidden now inside the painted skins covering their pale paunchy bodies, scurried along the beach after us, singing a conspicuously harmless tune.

"Benito," Moishe exclaimed. "And Samuel—can it be so?" He beamed with delight. I had told how Samuel's kishkas had been lobscoused by Turkish musketoon, how he fell dead to the deck.

They, too, smiled and regarded Moishe, now a grown man, with wonder. Years had passed since they had last seen him. He, too, had new skin.

"The Niña, the Pinta, and the Santa María sail the Ocean Sea looking for something new and the newest thing we find is you? So I have to ask: Come here often?" Moishe said.

"We could ask the same question," Samuel replied. "How far do we have to sail to elude the Inquisition? We cross half the world to get away from Spain and then Spain comes to us."

Moishe: "We must speak with haste. I fear it is but a small island and Columbus will soon return."

"Yes," Benito said. "We have discovered that there is not much to discover."

"How is it you sailed here?" Moishe asked.

"Our ship is moored in a hidden cove on the island's other side," Samuel began. "A caravel from Doña Gracia's fleet. The rebbe will keep it from the Spanish. What else they may discover, they will not discover this."

"Soon after we arrived in Morocco, a new old persecution began," Benito said. "We thought to sail to the Canaries, or perhaps the Fortunate Isles, the Ilhas Cassiterides—the islands of Tin and Silver— the Madeiras, or some new island in the Ocean Sea. Perhaps Prester John would be as kind to Jews as he is said to be kind to Mohammedans. But there was a storm and then an ocean current took us we knew not where. It seemed forty years wandering the wet desert."

He wiped his hand across his damp black forehead, revealing an olive blaze of naked skin.

"When we saw the island, we sang as Miriam sang when the Children of Israel crossed the Red Sea."

Samuel: "We did not expect the Spanish or their Inquisition."

"Columbus has no interest in Inquisition," Moishe said. "He sails only to fill his map with discoveries, his pockets with gold, and his ears with praise."

"Still, we are prisoners escaped from the Spanish crown and their attempt to bake us. We would be captured if recognized," Samuel said.

"Pitch-daubed in island haute couture as you are, I warrant you safe," Moishe said. "You cut a fine figure in such fashion."

Benito: "We had little choice seeing the Spanish ships rising over the horizon."

Samuel: "We thought our brains boiled by hunger and dread."

Benito: "We hoped the ships would sail past. When they sailed toward shore, we prepared our disguise."

"We are lost, yet do not wish to be found," Samuel said. "But how long can we pretend to be what we are not?"

"Samuel means that we are glad to see you. We are grateful that you saved us in Spain," Benito said. "But we hope you will leave. We hope your Captain Columbus hurries on his search for real islanders, the mainland, or gold."

"Ay," Samuel said. "For already, we are part found out. We were gob-struck to see the Spanish. More gobstruck still, to hear Hebrew. So one of us—Salomon—blurted back Hebrew to the translator who spoke the holy tongue."

"Let's hope his memory was drowned in wine," Benito said.

"Today, it surfaced," Moishe said. "But perhaps when sober, with no new Hebrew, he'll think it but the meshugas phantasms of wine-brained shikkery."

There was a borasco of shouts and bootfalls. Columbus had returned.

"Tell us quickly: the reb wants to know if in these last years, you have knowledge of Sarah . . . or more exactly, of her father's books," Samuel said.

"Ach, my Sarah," Moishe said wistfully. "I thought we would be married."

"First love," I said. "He carries it with him like a fracture that never properly heals. Or like syphilis."

I did not intend then to give tongue to what intelligence I had gained, but, na, there's no greater ache than an untold story.

When you need to plotz, you need to plotz: I told them what I'd heard of Doña Gracia, how she'd married a Neapolitan count so his money could help Jews. Of Sarah and her capture, of the books and theirs. I had not heard of either since they'd been carried up the gang-plank and gone south with the Turks toward an uncertain future.

I did not mention what was inside either the books or Sarah. Those were texts I did not yet know. But, I worried for the tsuris that might come to both.

The Shlepp-and-Kvetchit Jews looked at me with some surprise. They did not know that, though a bird, I was a mensch. That I could speak with intelligence.

Azoy? Were they the only ones who sometimes had needed to hide their words inside?

Down the beach, several small mammals had been hunted and hog- or perhaps opossum-tied to several sticks bridged between sailors' shoulders. These big macher huntsmen had likely blasted arquebus shot through the fist-sized kishkas of these small wild things, now as much hole as not.

The rabbi-as-island-chief led the procession, shaking his fists and frightening the clouds with a whinneying recitation of his ninnyhammer Torah.

"And," Benito said, as he scuttled back toward them. "It's not Rabbi Daniel but his brother, Nalfimay. Rabbi Daniel was pitched into the sea. A lifetime of wisdom lobbed over the gunwales like bad meat."

"Such evil." Samuel spat into the surf and ran after him.

A fire was made. Opossums were cooked.

Kosher?

Opposums have no hooves and do not chew cud.

So: not kosher.

But, nu, what's a bit of Leviticus when you're hungry, and the nearest rabbi is on the sea floor. Besides, the best way to appear as if a place is home is to eat some of it.

And so, the Jews ate.

I myself was glad to be considered companion and not poultry—keneynehoreh—and always ready to speak against the roasting of my soul, the fricassee of my mortal body for shmaltz and fislach, fat and chicken feet.

The New World Jews and conquerors gathered together on the shore. Moishe was able to signal to Samuel in a clandestine semaphore of eyebrow and finger indicating that he would communicate nothing of his true identity and yet would strive to return. And soon after, Columbus, after having stuck his colonizing toe in what he took to be the door to Cathay, Cipangu, or an outlander island to the Indies, had his men row back to the ships and ready themselves. We'd sail to stick that same toe in other and, he hoped, more golden sands.

And what else? Just a little thing. Columbus had two burly bulvans of the crew grab two islanders, Geronimovitz and Dances-with-Wolfowitz, tie them up pretty in boat ropes like powder kegs stowed in the orlop, and stick them in the bow.

When you travel, it's important to return with souvenirs.

The two said nothing to him. What should they say?

Won't you be disappointed when it rains and—you call this a gift?—all you've got is two clean Yids?

Besides, their silence would protect the others.

The skiffs were hoisted from the brine. Columbus, prophetic Ocean seer, conveyed his orders and the bo'sun—an Aaron to the admiral's Moses—was his master's voice, speaking to the hands and causing them to scuttle over the ship like crabs. The anchors heaved, the sheets hauled, the yards lifted, and the sails set. We began searching for other pearls to stud the twin diadems of Spain.

Chapter Two

$\mathcal{T}$he three ships sailed, three water-borne Magi from the east. The Ocean Sea was smooth as a river, a delicate robin's egg blue, the air scented with blossoms of island flowers.

That evening, Pedro Gutiérrez saw a great whale breaching, spouting a fountain of water high into the air. At two bells on dog watch, Rodrigo Sanchez observed several large sea creatures that resembled something between tuskless walruses and great sad bloodhounds. We'd later learn the native name, "manatí," from their word for breast. An accurate name if one expects to see breasts the size of cows, the colour of stones, floating bloated and amiable around the ocean, a forlorn and loveable expression signalling their harmlessness.

The two Jews were stowed on the *Niña*. We'd been on one of the first skiffs and so were unaware of their true identity. I flew over to see who they thought they were.

And so, I revealed to them that I could speak sense.

At least when I wasn't feather-puffed geshvollen with stultiloquent blather and narishkayt.

And so they revealed who they were. Samuel and another whom I didn't recognize named Jucef who had sailed for Doña Gracia. They were something between ongeblozn angry and befuddled.

"What will we do?" they asked.

"We'll have the chutzpah to wait until we have a plan," I said.

Six or seven leagues after we'd observed the frolicking of the sea-borne breasts pushing up against the tide, another island rose from the flat chest of the horizon. Columbus christened it Santa María de la Concepción. We continued toward it until the blood-orange sun sank, and we anchored near a cape on the island's westward end. The following dawn, Columbus sent a party ashore.

And so, the pattern continued.

Several more small islands, though no more congregations of European denomination. Instead, true island people with whom we exchanged hawks' bells, tchatchkes and chazerai for small pieces of gold and good favour.

"This pig-ringed gold in your nostils, these bangles round your arms, this nugget plugged into your earlobe—from where did they come?" Columbus gestured to the natives in a handjive of international Esperanto.

South, they'd point. South.

It was apparent that there were people who came from that direction paddling in the large boats they called "canoes," and who came bearing gold.

Or, at least, south was as good a direction as any to send the furry-faced invaders on a wild and golden goose chase.

"Midas can smooch my flea-speckled hiney for all the good this gold will do me," Jacome scowled, bending over a barrel of manzanilla wine and filling his mug. "But these swinging rope beds, these native 'hammocks.' Ah, there's something to comfort a weary sailor shaken by the tosser surf. Sleep is more good than gold to a dog-tired navvy worn-down by endless deck work and all this 'finding.'"

"Amen," Moishe said. "To invent the obvious is the mark of a true genius. To reinvent it makes one a god."

As we landed on each new island, Columbus seized a few more natives. By this time, he was calling them Indios. Indians.

Bet you can't capture just one.

Besides, what do you get for a king and queen who have everything?

We encountered cotton, silent dogs, the loincloths of pretty island maidelehs, aloe, and the unintelligible singing of birds.

"Ah. This recalls Andalusia in the spring," Columbus exclaimed, though he must have been referring to a vernal Andalusia of his own imagination. Certainly, the naked Paul Gauguin beauty of the women turned the men's Iberian peninsulas venal and warm.

There was lush fruit and talk of cannibals. There were new animals to eat.

I sat on Moishe's ragged shoulder as he rowed a skiff to the shore of what would soon be "Fernandina." Then the curdling of my own spirit: the scent of death twisted into a braid of smoke, a bloodknot round my brain.

On the beach, skewered bodies and the barbecue of souls—if indeed we parrots have such a weak thing wisped around the spindle of our spines. The native fiends were cooking parrot.

I would rescue, would resurrect those I recognized by scent alone. Their plumes radiant green and blue, their throats red, their beaks Englishflesh pink. I was seized with horror, yet also tender desire. I would salve and groom. Would nestle and preen. Ach, my sheyneh kindred. My petal-florid New World brethren. It had been awhile. I would shtup with grey cloaca your coat of many colours.

Except that you were dead.

Feh.

The soul stirs for the other that is the same.

The skiff bumped into the sand and I woke from my reverie. The beach a Dieppe of death. I threw myself into the air and up over the canopy of trees.

I left the world of men behind.

A long flight of uninterrupted green.

Then there was a river.

Falling from a cleft in the rocks, its water turned to thunder and cloud.

A waterfall.

Azoy? you say. Really?

High in the tall trees, the bright flash of feather rampiking my insides.

Another bird. A bright island parrot.

Take the gloaming shades of an African Grey. Let them be coloured vivid by Fernández the painter. From the indistinct shoals of stone to the shocking bright of the jungle. Green. Red. Blue. Take the atoms of the world and pack them closer together to make such colour.

I landed on a branch nearby.

How should I speak?

What is the green language of the birds? The pigeon's pidgin, the avian lingua franca, the conference call of the birds.

The parrot on the near branch said nothing. It lowered its head. It fanned its tail. There was deep cooing that I felt in the mortal worm of my innards. It cocked its blue-green head, exposing the hibiscus crimson of its throat.

I knew nothing.

This parrot.

Male.

Female.

Without category.

I could read the language of its colours. The riotous map of its markings. Its illegible scent.

There was a feeling of avalanche as if a great river were moving through me. As if my brain were regurgitating itself. As if a thousand thousand courtship rituals were jangling through the interstellar dulcimer flash of our wings.

I was a pirate. A lovebird. A great ship. A cannon.

The bird preened my neck and chest. My lower body span like a pinwheel.

My vent would soon explode. We rubbed beaks.

I leapt upon the parrot.

It shrieked and hissed.

We pressed our vents together. I rubbed. Azoy, I hissed. I shtupped. I shtupped. I shtupped.

Ach.

Ach.

Ach.

Oy.

Oy.

Oy.

Oy.

Oy.

Nu.

And then it was over.

I looked around. I had lost my mind. There in the shaking green leaves of the rainforest, my body mutinied and I had shtupped this parrot.

I had seen no other for many years.

He and I—for soon I would discover that he was indeed a he—had made the bird with two backs, one both grey and multi-coloured, and with wings enough for both joy and regret.

Am I, too, converso, hidden, changed? A rewritten book, a new calligraphy of desire with a few blotchy wet-spots and a misspelling or two?

I remember an old saying: "Man comes from the dust and in the dust he will end—and in the meantime it is good to drink vodka."

I wished there were some schnapps then. Some hooch to clarify things by addling me tseshtrudelt.

So. An explorer arrives on a desert island. It's uninhabited except for one old rabbi. Long white beard, rags for clothes, coconut-shell shoes, a ragged prayerbook tucked under his skinny parsnip arm. His skin is cooked dry as the prayerbook's cover. Reb Hershel lives by the shore in a lean-to of branches, leaves, bones and feathers. But, at each end of his island, there is a fine building. Each of these two synagogues is tall, smooth and well made, with a Magen David—a Jewish star—of little blue stones set into its chiselled hardwood dome.

"Tell me, Rabbi," the explorer asks. "There's only one of you. Why have you built two shuls?"

"Feh," the rabbi spits, then points at one of the synagogues. "That one I don't go to."

I thought to myself, "Is that how it's supposed to work with the sexes?"

Ach. But how could I have known? Emes. With a shvants that's tucked away inside, it's hard to tell, especially when the feathers are foreign.

So. Nu. We have no penis. It's in the mind and is mighty as a schooner. A *Flying Dutchman*, it glimmers with the iridescence of a comet riding the sky, and, takeh, is powerful and invisible as God.

The island parrot turned toward me. He tilted his head, gazed into my left eye with his right. I could see the delicate transparent third eyelid closing then opening again, the corona of tiny feathers around the eye.

Did he know?

The stutter and aphasia of our pheromones. The inscrutable whisper of our plumage. We could not speak, except in the language of shtup and gesture, and this served only to make communication more farblondzhet confused.

He bobbed his head a few times and then lifted off into the air. I watched as he rose about the treetops, the fluorescence of his great coloured wings bright against the blue sky.

I was hungry and felt like a nosh.

Nu? We had not yet learned of cigarettes.

The jungle was a fruit-bowl Eden. Below me, flesh, zaftik and luscious, hung invitingly from branches, unfamiliar fruits on strange and unfamiliar trees. Even their shadows were of a different shade.

Several fruits had fallen and split open, spilling black seeds from their yellow-green skin onto the jungle floor. Insects crawled over their soft orange insides. A sweet odour between ripeness and rankness.

I ate and sweet juice dribbled from my beak. This new world had baptized me from both ends.

Chapter Three

When I returned there were only a few pitiful molecules of burnt parrot left wafting over the beach. The air had been cauterized by death and barbecue. Moishe was standing with Columbus, Luis de Torres and a young native man.

"Diego," Columbus said. "Diego Columbus." Columbus was pointing at the young man, naming him, claiming him by sticking his finger into his thin chest. He had named the man after his own son, Diego, as he had named the islands after his king, his queen, and his God.

Luis de Torres spoke then. Diego Columbus the native had become Diego Columbus the translator. He was being taught Spanish and he was teaching Luis his native tongue. Two tongues intertwining, this French kissing of linguists.

I landed on Moishe's shoulder. Diego looked at me and said something.

Maybe it was the native word for bird.

Or lunch.

"Aaron," Moishe explained, introducing me.

"Ahh-rown," Diego said.

Shortly thereafter, the sailors gathered their tchatchkes, swords, and a selection of tropical fruits, meats, islanders, a newly made translator, and boarded the skiffs to return to the ships.

I don't know what word Diego Columbus used to describe his situation, but he might consider: stolen, shipped, transported.

Gaffled and blagged.

Crimped.

The sun sank red like a boil on the seatmeat zitsfleysh of the sky and by the next day, October 28, we had arrived at what Columbus decided was the firm land, the mainland.

Cuba, which he called Juana.

It was the same recipe.

Land. Conquer. Repeat.

Luis de Torres recorded the events for Columbus.

October 28, 1492. Here are palm-roofed houses, barkless dogs, a technology of fishing tackle, clay figurines and silver ornaments. *Los Indios* are timid and artless regarding weapons. They quake at our arquebus. Here grow sea plums, shore lavender, beach morning glory, cedar, and a riotous concatenation of roots known as mangroves. Here are placid rivers, their edge and surface teeming with small frogs and great parti-coloured birds. The natives make chairs of hardwood in a Noah's Ark of animal shapes.

And so too do they gather certain herbs that they wrap in dry leaf and then enflame. The smoke of this they inhale, by which they become benumbed and almost drunk, and so it is said they do not feel fatigue. This burning leaf we have begun to call "muskets," but they term "tabacos."

"Avast, a cloudy lungful of this fuming would be fine satisfaction after festive conjugation with a slattern," Jacome snorted after a huff of the leaf.

"Aye," said Fernández the painter, dragging the twilight air from the burning herb and exhaling slowly as if his sighs were ghosts. "Its smouldering tendrils, curling round me as I gaze into the gloaming margins of my own mind, would be a fog of sure drama for those acolytes who would watch me await the faint tintinnabulations of the muse."

When they smoked, there was always time for talk. Sometimes words can, in certain moments of grace, attain the quality of important deeds.

And emes, the men were quick to enslave themselves to this tobacco, taking to it as to drink. They sucked and posed, they gathered and kibitzed. This tobacco soon became an existential theatre of smoke and camaraderie.

Though nu, a surfeit of enthusiasm caused some to surrender their insides to the outside world in a foaming cascade of near-Iberian expulsion, some alchemy turning smoke to puke even as a zeal for wine can turn the body into the quaking spawn of hammers and swill.

Geyt gezunterhayt. Go in good health, humans.

I, too, puffed this russet leaf, but beside the polychrome tragicomedies of the Orient's hashish, it was but the poor exhaust of ferns.

And Moishe? Luftmensch no more, he engaged with the breath of the physical world and smoked himself green.

We spent the days on land, learning from *Los Indios*, for Martín Pinzón had convinced Columbus that the ships needed to be careened and caulked, barnacles riven from their soggy ballix.

Which is a good medicine for any sailor.

"I, too, would delight in doing nothing but lying on my side like a ship in cool water," Moishe said. "My gildeneh oder golden veins swabbed by a gentle team." His gildeneh oder. His hemorrhoids. "Though I'd hope for mermaids and the lithe bodies of pretty island girls instead of this stumbling and bristly crew."

Columbus was certain we were on a mainland. That Cuba was not an island. But nu, if it isn't water, all land is—eventually—an island. And all men, ultimately, islanders.

After three days in Cuba, Columbus sent explorers down the shore both east and west. And what did they find? More shore. More sons of beaches, more littoral daughters but no large villages, great khans, Cathay emperors, or gold.

After three more days, the admiral sent Luis de Torres and Rodrigo de Xerez inland with two Indians, including Diego Columbus.

Christopher Columbus paced the shore, consulted his astrolabe, his charts, his logbook, and, when it appeared that he was unobserved, the book that we had ferried from his brother. The rest of the crew worked on or under the ships and traded chazerai with the islanders. Some loincloth-chasing shiksa-trollers whose shvants were the true

admiral and viceroy of their fate contrived to engineer discreet assigna-
tions with pretty, young Indio girls in the cool murk of evening.

The music of Spanish in the deep woods:

"Come here often?"

"Anyone ever tell you you look just like that painting of Mary in the
chapel at Los Palos?"

And some afternoons, Moishe, too, would slip away into the cool of
the green canopy of trees and meet a maideleh. Maybe there was the
steady burning of memories of Sarah, but here he followed his wick
to the flame.

And sometimes, hidden under the loose calico of his shirt, he would
bring the book that hate-torqued mad-hatted Torquemada had given him.

There were five books, each of which spoke of a life everlasting.

Ach. There are some books, even with the patience of Job's boil-
wrangling dermatologist and an immortal life, few could spare the time
to read. All words and no meaning. All lid and no Yid. All Columbus
and no gold.

What were these five books?

He knew of one.

The almost translucent leather binding of Torquemada's book made
one afraid to hold it, or careful to hold it tenderly. "There, there, little
bubeleh book, everything will turn out for the best."

In the jungle, Moishe puzzled over its sigils. Its strange almost-
words. Its farmishteh calligraphy that appeared more navigation map of
a twisted Meccano alphabet than real writing.

"Why would Torquemada need to hide this? Its meaning is hidden
by its words." Moishe pointed to the opened book. "So, nu, maybe like a
women's knish, it looks strange until you know what to do with it."

Feh. This feygeleh should talk about knowing what to do.

I had mistaken up from down. Or myself for myself.

"This is different than my father's book," Moishe said, pointing to a
page. "Yet these books are cousins. Or shvester. Sisters. The same bend
in the nose. The slope of the shoulders." He turned to another page.
"Look at this . . ."

It was filled with Magen Davids. Stars.

"Some kind of constellation," Moishe said, connecting the stars with his finger.

"Above which land is the sky filled with Jewish stars?" I said.

"Emes," Moishe said. "Next year in Jerusalem."

We examined other pages under the slats of light flickering between leaf shadows.

"Somewhere there's a key, a legend that explains," Moishe said. "Maybe the other books," he said, turning to other pages. "Maybe they explain."

"Ach, who needs immortal life?" I answered. "It's but a larger sack to fill with misery."

"But it works the other way, too," Moishe said. "Trouble would scatter like ashes in the wind over a life-without-end. And anyway, it's the Fountain of Youth, so you're made young again. Younger than your memories, younger than your pain."

"Eternal relief."

"An everlasting finger to those who tried to erase us: here we are, a permanent stain on the pages of history. What's that? Wine? Jizz? Jews? Once shpritzed with Fountain water, we'll never forget because we'll never grow old."

Just then a commotion. Men calling. The trumpeting of a conch.

After four days, Luis de Torres, Rodrigo de Xerez, Diego Columbus and the other natives had returned from their colonial probe inside the island. They brought with them a procession of inland Tainos carrying several baskets and hog-tied animal carcasses. One older, highly decorated Indio appeared to be the lovechild of a warrior and several ostentatious birds: his head was plumed with tailfeathers rising like Technicolor thoughts from out of his dark scalp. The natives and their chief stood motionless in the shade of the forest while the crew approached Columbus, the viceroy of beaches and the governor of sand.

Columbus had some islanders shlepp a large carved chair onto the shore. He sat enthroned, benevolent and regal in the shade of the munificent palms. The infinite regress of power: he was an island Ferdinand and Isabella holding court before his own exploring Columbuses.

"Señor," Torres said, approaching him. He inclined his head as if to bow, but then straightened and began his report.

"Two days' walk, Admiral. Through the thickness of jungle. Along a path that was often defined only by its vagueness. Several times it appeared to disappear. But Los Indios could read it and they led us forward."

"What did you find? What of cultivated fields and of agriculture?"

"There were rivers, ponds with frogs and fish but no indication of crops. We found no large animals, but strange lizards, snakes and rodents. In the glades, gaudy parrots and bats large as foxes. Small birds drink from flowers, the murmur of their wings like bees. In a clearing, a thousand butterflies, their wings iridescent blue. We filled our baskets with specimens both live and extinguished, which we have here conveyed."

"Good, good," Columbus replied. "But tell me of villages, of mining and of gold?"

The King and Queen would not finance another voyage for glimmering wings and large bats.

Luis de Torres continued. "Far into the island's dark heart, we came upon a village: fifty large wooden huts, palm-thatched. The people came to greet us." He motioned to the older man with the avian haberdashery. "This is their chief—what they term a 'cacique.' Diego spoke with him of gold."

"Bring the man here. Let us speak with him."

The cacique, grey-haired, muscular, stepped forward. His aquiline nose and walnut-coloured ears were studded with small pieces of gold.

There was more gold, he said. In the south. Where the Caribs live.

Of course. Gold was where they weren't.

A first, pre-cinematic "they went that-a-way."

Gold?

That-a-way.

Oh, and by the way, the Caribs are the people who eat people.

You can pick your friends.

And you can pick your teeth.

And you can pick your friends from your teeth. Sometimes little bits of them get stuck there after a nosh.

Martín Pinzón stood near Columbus's carved throne, listening. Something was glistering in his rodent brain: gold.

Early next morning Pinzón comandeered the *Pinta*. He would put his own gilded island on the charts, his own hand into the open jar of the Caribbean. He would sail back to trumpets, parades, fame, and hereditary wealth and power. He would write his own chapter in the history books,

And with the persuasive eloquence of an arquebus, he press-ganged Moishe.

"Board the *Pinta*," Pinzón commanded. "You must tend to our pilot, Cristobal Garcia Xalmiento. He suffers." The *Pinta*'s surgeon was only help for the removals of either blood or limb and the *Santa María*'s physician himself lay below deck in a hypnogogic fever, yammering mishegoss about the hairy backs of sailors being sucked by teams of spine-hungry leeches and the heated mouths of glass cups.

And so Moishe, who had assisted physicians aboard Mediterranean ships and as we sailed from Spain, had helped administer salves, blood-letting, and, to be plain, medicines slippery as snakeoil became great khan of the medicine chest.

Moishe, a doctor? His mother would have been so proud.

The pilot, Cristobal Garcia Xalmiento, was splayed on a pallet below deck on the *Pinta*, the air fetid and constellated with flies.

"Drink," Moishe said and unstoppered a bottle of Madeira, pouring it between Xalmiento's dry and trembling lips.

"Jacome," Moishe called. "We must carry him on deck. He needs new air."

"Better to whore with a holeless mermaid as to think him salvage-able," Jacome spat.

"Take his legs," Moishe instructed.

"Better to toss the neargone overboard and feed me the wine," Jacome said, but still, he hove on Xalmiento's legs and helped.

Optimism and the open air, and not a frank diagnosis, appeared the best medicine for the man and he soon began to moan. Which was improvement. To feel close to death after feeling nothing was convalescence.

And to kvetch about it meant recovery was likely. Soon he would sing opera and wrest anchors from the seafloor with his teeth.

Pinzón strode about the deck, surveying his mutinous duchy. He was admiral of this floating nutshell yet considered himself king of infinite space: what was undiscovered was boundless and filled with possibility.

All about the ship, the crew was ministering to sheets and yardarms while Moishe in the bow herded Xalmiento away from fever. Pinzón went aft to his cabin. Through the small window, I saw him heave a book from chest to table.

I knew it by the pattern of its cover. We had carried this text from Lisbon—from one Columbus to another. Pinzón had thieved not only boat but book. Onboard were two of the five which spoke of the Fountain. Moishe must find means to poke his nose between the broad flanks of this tome. Such knowledge was power.

The *Pinta* sailed in search of a new island. Pinzón certainly sought gold. The yellow teeth of his acquisitive grin seemed to desire a grillework of the stuff. But perhaps he, too, sought, immortality or to become its gatekeeper.

Soon he was back at the binnacle directing the helmsman toward a distant shadow.

An island.

The native people had seen the white flukes of our sails rising from the horizon. They had gathered on the beach as if awaiting the arrival of a Leviathan or emperor. They stood shoulder-to-shoulder with little more than plaited reed loinclothes mantling their scrolls. Several wore headdresses of feathers and shells, some held gourd bowls filled with fruit, coloured stones and feathers.

Mariners and philosophers regularly state that such newly encountered natives are handsome, as if one could say that noses, beauty and nobility existed in equal quantity among all members of a people. Surely there's always an Auntie Faygel or a Zaiydee Shmuel with a nose like a tableau from Exodus played out on an anthill. But nu, these people were impressive pieces of bronze. Bright coins on the sand: their skin more lustrous than our sailors' pockdotted and leathered parchment; their strong bodies, the muscled arms and chests of the men, the smooth torsos and naked breasts of the women.

Ach. Perhaps these are but overheated words from the ajar mouths of Pinzón's gawking sailors for each member of this mutinous crew was now a sail billowing full with the Zephyrous thrill of recklessness in a kvelling gale of ambition and freedom. Each thought himself his own admiral, cut lose from the halyards of society, travelling into the unwritten margins.

Each man, now individual, thought himself impressive. The great canoe of our caravel growing into the barque of a giant as it rose from beyond the horizon, our vast mainsail like the banner of an advancing army entering a city, emblazoned with a green cross: F for Ferdinand, Y for Ysabella, large as trees surmounted with crowns broad as horses.

Pinzón: "We arrive from the East like the rising sun bringing light to the dark unknowing, these uncivilized lands on the fringes of Cipangu, Cathay, and the territories of the Great Khan. Here, each of us shall be as an emperor or king."

Of course, to the islanders we may have appeared as monkeys dressed up in silks. A hundred monkeys typing Shakespeare would seem to them to be chattering gibberish. Though they would have been impressed by the typewriters.

We dropped anchor and the men rowed to shore, sacks filled with tchatchkes, the swag of visiting gods. Moishe was in the second boat, and I travelled on his leeward shoulder. We stood like rock stars awaiting special effects: Pinzón in his furs and silk breeches, some of the men in metal breastplates, ready to stride into the Promised Land or to re-enter Eden.

All the men, armed.

Pinzón wanted to replay Columbus's landing, with himself in the role of Columbus. But this time we would not trade small talk and worthless chazerei. We were not pedlars and tinkers, but Odyssean conquerors.

The ship's master unfurled the flag of the Spanish kingdoms and planted it in the sand. For we shall have dominion over every living thing that moveth upon the earth and have a fancy brocaded flag to prove it.

The natives fell to their knees and then, their arms stretched before them, touched their foreheads to the ground.

"They think we're gods," Moishe exclaimed.

"Maybe you," I said. "Me, they think of as a bird."

The islanders rose up and surrounded us. Some held out their gourd bowls of gifts. Our men made ready to receive them. Pinzón looked warily at them, and seeing no gold and not wanting a repeat of Columbus's giltless meetings with the natives, gave the order for the men to take up their arms and make ready to fire.

What did war look like to the natives of this island—if they had war? In a war, a duel, or a chess game both sides need to know they are playing. Otherwise it's hunting. Skeet shooting. Murder.

To Pinzón, the islanders, though statuesque as rippling stallions or shapely as does, were little more than animals inside: Less-than-Calibans. Un-Christianizables. Primitive though noble Golems without souls. And like Golems or magpies, they knew how to find shiny and precious things.

The men loaded their arquebuses with powder and gunshot while the natives looked on in fascination. Pinzón's orders echoed in the stillness. "We don't need a translator to explain this," he said.

Then, "Fire."

The sound was like a rank of cannons. The vessel of the world shattered to hellflame and thunder.

Islanders dropped to the sand, ragged hibiscus-flower wounds on their bare chests and contorted heads. Some ran into the forest.

Some began to run and then collapsed. Surely not so many could have been hit. A kick and a brief inspection revealed that some had fainted in terror, while others had been slain by fear alone.

Pinzón ordered several men captured and chained to the flag-pole. Some women he had bound and carried back to the ship. A man adorned in a feather headdress and long cape, likely the cacique, lay on his back in the sand, bleeding from his mouth. Pinzón stood over him, sword pressed against his heaving throat.

"Gold," Pinzón said.

The man looked up at Pinzón, not understanding.

"Gold," Pinzón repeated.

A gloaming light in the man's eyes. Then darkness.

"Pah," Pinzón spat, then drove the sword into the dead cacique's neck.

All about us, twisted bodies amongst fallen gourds, the beach strewn with feathers, coloured stone, the bodies of women and men.

Moishe had an arquebus in his hands. When Pinzón had given orders, he, too, had fired.

"Sh'ma Yisroel," he had muttered. He had prayed. He had expected to die. "A bayzeh shu."

This was evil.

He felt that surely God would wake and come down to the island for this.

And Moishe expected that He would strike him dead.

After fireworks: smoke and ash. A bitter scent. Pinzón ordered his men over the killing field to pursue the natives who had fled. The bo'sun hoisted Moishe to standing, hauling his arm toward him like a halyard.

"Come. We hunt. And you, our surgeon: there may be a gash or two which needs your tending, a man rent asunder who'll want his two halves knitted back together."

And so we joined the slavering pack as they left their guns and strode into the foliage.

The silent woods. Even the songbirds held their breaths. All that was not rooted had fled or disappeared into stillness.

When soldiers march, all destinations hide.

Several natives were compelled to be guides and by the evening, they had led Pinzón's men into a village. The buildings were quiet, but none more quiet than the Indios, haunched in a scrubby square, staring at us toytshreken terrified. At one end of the square was a large *bohío*, a sizeable structure of tree trunks and thatch. Inside, hundreds of villagers, close-packed and fearful. They did not dare exchange shelter for unprotecting sky.

The Spanish mariners, only lately pirates and conquerors of land, stood before the village considering the art of plunder.

But few spoils are as enticing as a good nosh when a warrior's kishkas snake with hunger and so, when a steady-faced young woman rose and gathered a basket of roasted chickens—aleychem ha'shalom, peace be upon them—and walked up to the strangely bearded strangers, they accepted them as tributes.

Each fressed upon this Jeanne d'Arc meat, gnawing on the juicy poulkes with grave enthusiasm.

Alvaro Sanchez, a cousin to Pinzón, was first among the crew to finish. His thick cheeks glistened with grease, chicken pieces like burrs in his greasy beard.

He was an ox-large bruiser with a groys belly, fat as a booty sack.

A body into which the devil entered, for now, his dinner over, a fire enflamed his gaseous soul. He dropped his oily clutch of chicken bones and unsheathed his sword. This was not a spontaneous impulse toward cutlery and the graces of the table, for he howled, a monstrous beast.

As one, the twenty others seized their blades and they began to hack bellies and slice throats like crazed shochets dispatching sheep—men, women, children, and the old alteh Indios, all of whom were seated, unarmed, and caught off guard.

Within the time one could croak a single kaddish, there remained not one villager alive in the square.

The young woman leapt onto the outside wall of the bohío and scrambled up onto the thatched roof. She would leave this earth behind.

In a fever, Pinzón's men rushed through the door of the bohío and by slash and thrust began to murder all inside. The blood of an entire flock dispatched like floodwater. The girl, banshee-shrieking, emboldened those few villagers who could find their strength, to clamber up the wooden poles of the house. They birthed themselves through the thick thatch and onto the roof. From there they ascended into the trees and escaped into the canopy of leaves.

Moishe had collapsed in the square. Pulled by the tide of unhinged madness, he had drawn his sword.

Blood coloured its blade. He looked for a moment, mute with shock, as if it were a severed leg. His own. Wounded and without feeling.

"An evil spirit afflict my father. An evil spirit afflict my father's father," Moishe hissed.

A curse on where he came from. A curse on those who made him.

Then he dropped the sword and ran.

So, tell me, when did you first know you were a pirate?

Chapter Four

*D*ays or weeks or years later. What does it matter? The tide had turned long ago and we were at sea.

"Feh," I said and glided down to the mainmast.

I'd flown to the sky to sight what was hidden behind the horizon. "Ten four-pounders wait to pestle us into stew," I announced.

Before long, a galleon loaded with guns and gold rose in the distance. A ship returning to Spain, plotzing with spoils. Our gobs would soon dribble with Pavlovian glee.

We made to haul up from the cove where we'd hove to, ready to broadreach our bowsprit right up the mamzers' nether hawsehole.

L'chaim, you Spanish ladies!

"And the crew?" Moishe asked me. "How many sailors?"

"Thirty on deck. Several monks and priests . . ."

"God spare us from churchmen. When skewered, they make such a woeful noise." This was Isaac the Blind, an old sailor.

"Ha-Shlossing-Shem spare m' earwax the wheedling prayers and simpering pleas of clergy as their sickly bodies are pared from soul," he went on. Isaac the Blind. Most of him was lost. And what remained was hardly seaworthy.

His single seeing eye was a broken and bloody egg. His one grizzled hand the offspring of a spider.

Tefillin slouched over his blind eye, the box like a patch. The stump of his left arm, too, was wrapped in tefillin, the leather phylactery strap holding a fragment of anchor to serve as his hand. He was whatever he had scrounged.

Like all of us.

Except for those whose lives seemed the scratchpad of fate.

Shlomo. His body was a book of scars. We'd seen him on the island of Jews where he had settled with those who'd sailed away from Spain. Together with Isaac and the others, he had then escaped that new Zion and become part of our crew.

The Isle of Jews had been no easy billet on a sleepy pinnace. When Rabbi Nalfimay died, another quickly stripped the old rebbe of his red fez and orange-gold robes and appointed himself rebbe of the island. Unlike Nalfimay, this Reb Salomo's rule was grim and sadistic. When Shlomo questioned—when he asked for the passage in the law that explained a severity—Salomo had ordered Shlomo's arms tied to a palm tree and the words of the Ten Commandments cut into his skin. The Hebrew had scarred, red pus-crusted serpents writhing across his body as if he been flogged with a whip whose grip, you could say, was nowhere yet whose lash was everywhere.

"Ach, it's not so bad," Shlomo laughed. "When I call my own name, I'm still the one who answers. I saw a Yid who'd been flayed alive by Salomo, and you'd hardly believe how much it altered him for the worse. Skin and bones he was. Skin there, bones over there."

Our crew included an African—an Ethiope—whom we'd found floating in the sea, clinging to a barrel of olives. He was half pickled himself, his body like the wrinkled inside of a mouth.

We called him Ham, after Noah's black son who came across his father ongeshnoshket, pants down, putz rampant. His father cursed him and his children. They were punished by the five-thousand-year enslavement of those races who were also beyond the pale.

We named him because he couldn't speak. His tongue had been cut out. What we learned later, through a combination of shipboard sign language and writing, was that he had cut it from his own mouth so that he would not have to speak of what he had witnessed.

Though we came to know why Ham didn't speak, we never knew what he wasn't telling us.

Ach, but I remember Rabbi Daniel muttering that memory is useless if none of us remembers the same thing.

It was ten years since Moishe had left Martín Pinzón and his men at the village. For hours he'd run blind into the forest, then scrabbled up a tree into the dark canopy, panting, directionless, disoriented, and hungry. He had thrown his weapons and stripped most of his clothing as he sprinted in the heat. At nightfall he'd shloffed in the crook of a giant tree and I slept in the branches above him, listening always for danger.

Early morning and we found ourselves inside the boisterous mechanism of the forest. The flywheels of insects, the flap and flutter of birds. A hum, a purring, the footfalls of animals we didn't know. Then bright feathers: I was surrounded by a crowd of parrots kibitzing in a language I did not understand.

Soon they scattered. This I understood: predators.

Several natives walking, chanting, armed with bows. Their leader, the young woman from the village, spotted us immediately. I pressed myself against the tree trunk, not keen to lose a divot of flesh or to have my guts festooned in fletching. Moishe uncurled himself and sat on the branch in plain view. Pale and mostly naked. He did not appear to be a great warrior or bold sailor gluttonous for conquest. Instead, Moishe: a pallid Yiddishe Mowgli lost in the Caribbean.

"Help," he said and raised his hand.

And now, that same young woman, Yahíma, was part of our crew. Yahíma: our new Sarah. She, too, an orphan, her parents lost amidst the bohío blood.

So, nu, what about all those stories of New World Pocohonawitzes? Beautiful girls who go native in reverse. Sheyneh native maidelehs who put down their porcupine quills and tomahawks for doilies.

Yahíma was fearless and knowledgeable. Strong, nimble and lithe. But she was no beauty, though her tawny skin was the colour of Amontillado sherry and there was much of it on display. And, emes, an alter kaker would say, *Ze hot sheyneh Moishe v'Arondlach.* She had nice little Moses and Aaronses. Was Moishe the right and I the left? This, through a rigorously scientific program of manual ministrations, Moishe appeared to be keen to discern.

It should be said though, at thirty, Moishe himself was no Yohan Smith. Sunburned and scabbed like an accidental lasagne. Greasy. A scar where a scimitar had taken off his left tsitskeh. And he was a hairy yatl with a beard that was a fecund habitat for organic lifeforms, both sentient and insensible, sticks, leaves, and the oily trails of flesh.

Though of course, in the sixteenth century, that was practically dapper.

Before Yahíma, Moishe would sometimes moon about like a lover in a sonnet. "Sometimes, when I sleep on the deck under the star-pimpled prishtshevateh punim sky," he'd say, "the kitsl tickle of the breeze on my face, the rise and sigh of the waves, my cut gehakteh body aching like an Egyptian slave's, I think of Sarah, my Shulamite. How beautiful she'd be. In another world, we'd wake, husband and wife in each other's arms, early morning, the windows open, hooves on the cobbles, the scent of bread, voices in the alleys. We'd have been shtupping all night like the world was new, and now exhausted, we'd lie squeezed together like knishes, wondering what it might be like on the other side of the world. But, feh. That other world is here and where is Sarah? Lost. Murdered. Married off to someone else. A mother. And I'm left mumbling this sub-Solomon Song of Songs."

Now there was Yahíma. She of the long legs. The loincloth not much bigger than a yarmulke. The sudden eyes and blinkless smile. She who could turn a spear into a lightning flash, skewer a fish before we'd even seen. Or push Moishe into the sea when his back was turned.

Companionship is 90 percent just showing up.

Moishe had grown parrotlike: a pragmatist with the yearning neshomeh soul of a hero.

Who else was on board? Jacome, whom we'd found at sea in a coracle, spiting and cursing, hauling on the paddle with only a cutlass, a jug of water, salt meat, and his own sweet song for a crew. Pinzón had been on an island and had wanted rid of the half-cocked blunderbuss, all bile and gunpowder, that was Jacome. The usual method was to maroon a sailor who was trouble, to set them on a desert island and leave them there. *Gey gezunt.* Be well. But since they were already on an island, he was set adrift, perhaps with the idea that he would maroon himself.

His potholed punim certainly became enpurpled as he shared his thoughts regarding Pinzón.

"Next I see him, I tie the whoreson's drooping yardarm into knots," he said. "I'll weave a basket of his pizzle an' I'll fill it with crabs, black-flies and glass. An' that's tenderness besides what I'll do with his sack."

Certainly, his relations with his former employer had not remained cordial. "And look at these vittles here," he said and held up something like a dried fig tied to a string around his neck. "His bo'sun's ear."

Fernández the painter sailed with us also. He'd run as Moishe had, though it was some years before they met again.

And life aboard ship?

Lord of the yardarms, king of sails, Moishe, our captain, stood beneath the broiling sun, the radiant blade of his cutlass pointing toward the blood-red cross on the Bermudan shore, the salty wind curling through his princely hair, his preternaturally intelligent African Grey riding faithful and shotgun on the chariot of his clavicle. The crew jigged quick about sheets and halyards, singing out shanties of grog and merriment, hornpipes and contentment.

> *Oy derry,*
> *ach derry,*
> *freylich derry,*
> *may you not encounter an anchor when you sit down.*

Is this what we did? Ach, go bang your head against an onion. The rebbes say that evil spawns when we cannot tell our stories. Or if we're told to believe only in another's.

We gathered together on the deck and spoke of what to do. A pirate ship is not the house of any lord, nor the soggy fiefdom of any aspirant pharoah. Any who would believe he transmuted into gems what he pushed through his dark star would be delivered over the gunwales to become the gristle-soother of sharks within a parsec of donning even a single supercilious air.

Or as Jacome put it, "Inside our guts, it's the same worms that chaw through the same black soup."

We had signed articles, each sailor inscribing his name or as much of it as he chose to remember. Spoils were divided equally, every man, woman, or parrot—black, white, tawny, or grey—entitled to the same share. Unless there were loss of limbs. The crew's limbs. We expected some loss in our adversaries. A sailor who was injured and lost an arm or leg received additional money. Severance pay.

We were the governors of a nation that numbered only governors. Each person aboard helped draft our script. Over which horizon would we buckle, which swash, which trembling words of capitulation would we pillage from the mouths of which quaking crew? Whose kishkas would scabbard our swords, whose hatches breach for plunder?

Moishe was captain because of ballots cast by the crew. An immediate referendum could be called if his leadership was questioned. How did this cheder-bocher schoolboy turn captain? Takeh, shtetl-night was day here in the perilous land. But Moishe had wit, seychl, sense, decency, swagger, kindness, words, and the ability to pull endless treasure from behind avaricious Spanish ears. So, nu, in the country of the blind, the quick-tongued, one-nippled mensch was king. Our country: the blind, the scarred, the single-legged, the whole or half meshugeh, the mute, the lost, the faithful, the angry, those who witnessed or suffered, those who remembered or would not remember, the bereft, the curious, the other.

I haven't told about the others in our crew, but ach, the skittish nag of my tongue bolts away without the cart of sense. We are pirates and we have a profession to uphold: at this moment, there's a ship heaving up over the horizon and it's loaded with gold.

We remained cloaked by an island cove until the Spanish sailed close. "All hands," Moishe cried and we unfurled every sail so the wind could breathe life into our Golem of a ship.

Yahíma sprung up the rigging. Isaac the Blind readied the cannon, a variety of Great Turkish bombard we'd Jerez-rigged from a cauldron. Shlomo hauled up our flag, a linen tablecloth plundered from the cabin of a Spanish captain sent to Hispaniola. Through the years, we had flown under many flags.

A skull in a skullcap kippah over crossed candlesticks.

The image of the hand brandishing a curved sword, the single all-seeing eye in the centre of the palm, never blinking. Keneynehoreh. May I be protected from the evil eye. Or, nu, at least let me be on its side.

Now we sailed under the Great Eye of Providence, radiant beams like bolts of lightning flashing out from its socket, the eye itself hovering over an Egyptian pyramid. We were once slaves in Egypt. And we built this.

And now we will take apart your empire, brick by brick.

At some point, one of the crew made the eye bloodshot.

In Egypt there was sand and dust.

And here, there is such schnapps as to conjunctivate a sailor's eye.

It was a cloudless day. The waves scalloped high as a man's shoulders. There were dolphins in the cove. They had simple, shlemiel smiles and they never looked our way.

Sometimes we began with a speech from Moishe to those we intended to board. Sometimes this greeting was accomplished by the brazen sholom aleychem of cannon, and today we chose that sermon of fire. Isaac sent a tsimmes of burning fragments into the Spanish rigging and lit up the sails as if it were sunset.

Soon we were broadside and Moishe placed his boot on their gunwales.

"So maybe you could invite us in for a little something?" Then he leapt aboard. Jacome followed, calling out, "Lokshen-spined pasta-backs, we shall sauce you in your own blood."

I had a claw in the Spanish captain's eye before he had decoded the metaphor. Yahíma sent arrows into the shoulders of the crew. Fernández became a pointillist, jabbing his dirk into whatever soft flesh was before him. Ham cleared a path with a broad axe as if clearcutting Pinocchios.

There were native Taino slaves as well as Africans chained together on the foredeck.

"Nu, vos macht a Yid? Howaya?" Moishe said to them as Ham and Samuel began severing them one from another, chopping the links of the chains like pretzels.

Some panicked and jumped into the water before they had been unchained.

Moishe seized a nobleman hidalgo by the lacy throat. His cutlass sought the man's fleshy womb and there began to goulash.

As the man began his slow fall to the planks, Moishe raised the cutlass above his head; a crescent moon to be seen by all. Then he licked the blood from its blade and began, "Baruch ata Adonai . . ." The prayer for wine.

The Spanish did not end their resistance then, though much conviction drained from their fight.

Madness is more frightening than swords.

So, in this case, was feigned madness. When it came to mooning an antic disposition, Moishe was ever a Hamlet among lunatics.

Piracy is as much public relations as plunder.

It was dark before we could rest.

Blood poured from Ham's thigh. In the confusion Jacome had cleaved Ham's leg with his sword. Samuel was bereft of several fingers, his career as a maker of dog shadows cut short.

There was much gold. Silver. Meat. Wine.

Under the bright watch of our swords and arquebuses, the Spanish crew heaved our plunder into our ship while we offered the slaves some wine.

Freedom can be thirsty work.

By the end of our battle, we had new crew. Various slaves, both Ethiopian and Caribbean. An Italian cooper. We imprisoned the captain, Capitano Rodriguez, and his son in our hold.

"A bisl something for later," Moishe said.

We locked the hatches of the Spanish ship with the rest of the crew below deck and lit the ship on fire.

Was this what happened?

Certainly, there was smoke and wailing. The world was tsedreyt confused, a fog that couldn't find its own foundation. The driftnets of veins in our temples were pulsing and ready to burst with exhilaration, fear, righteousness, wonder.

Did Moishe loop a rope under a priest's arms then hang him from a yardarm over a menorah?

Did he seize a priest and say, "Afraid to die?"

"I hope to receive my eternal reward," the priest replied.

"In the meantime, thanks for everything," Moishe said and lit the seven candles.

Did the priest dance and weep and scream until his soft trotters smelt like barbecue?

I remember the general sense and the certain rage of our victory and our ardour. The cauterizing fire.

Was the treasure equally divided among our crew?

Were the dead pushed through the scuppers to be sharkmeat?

Did Moishe stand above our hatch in a haze of Spanish boat smoke and proclaim to its imprisoned captain and his son a speech for which he had hoped to find occasion?

"A broch upon your pestilient kishkas for you are a sneaking hintl puppy, as are any who submit to be governed by the chazer rich who want only their own security, for the whelps have not the beytsim otherwise to defend what they get by such dreck-mouthed knavery. And," he continued with an ostentatious wave of his hand, "a broch upon ye altogether. And damn them for a pack of crafty gazlonim thieves, and you, who serve them, for a pekel of hen-hearted shmegegges.

They villify us, the mamzers do, when there is only this difference, they rob the poor and weak under the cover of law, and we plunder the rich with no protection but our own chutzpah. You should rather join our minyan than sneak after the tucheses of villains for bread."

We were then seaborne Robin Hoods, our Sherwood a forest of waves.

Was there then silence from the captain and his son? And did we wait hours to investigate whether it was sleep, death, exhaustion, hopelessness, or villainy that kept their bodies mute?

Chapter Five

Was I surprised my hopeful pink boychik Moishe had turned pirate? Feh.

God Hisself would have turned pirate if, on bumping into the New World, He had seen that the othershtupping Spanish had discovered only a larger canvas on which to paint their murderous scenes. The same hateful fire burned inside their poxy hearts as fueled Inquisition flames. They had persecuted Jews. Now they persecuted Los Indios.

But God—being the kind of shmendrik who thinks both of everything and nothing—sailed Himself beyond the margin of the world's flat map, past the interstellar Borscht Belt, and through the quintessence into His own forever new, forever ancient and unnavigable world. Sha. One day, the oldest alter kaker of them all, Captain Yahweh, ignoring the constellations of yellow stars, pointed his metaphysical bowsprit beyond time and the page and left this world, leaving us no choice but to mutiny.

Gey gezunt, Captain.

Good riddance, you old tummeler, you cosmic stand-up.

Take all of creation. Please.

Plato, that ancient rebbe, once said we're each only half a person. And that, far back in some prehistoric Grecian dreamtime, each of us were whole, each of us pickled in an amazement of love, friendship and intimacy instead of having our kishkas roil with the burning loss of the other half of ourselves.

The New World? It was to be the Old World's other half, the earth whole and healed again. Humans to fill the empty side of the Big Macher Adonai's chest. Instead, a hollow in all of our chests, beside which the deserted island of our heart keeps beating, because it doesn't know what else to do.

A pirate? With enough pieces of eight, you can rebuild the world. One kind of chest isn't that different than another.

✛

Late afternoon. Moishe wrapping Ham's leg in a bandage fashioned from his own britches. Moishe the physician then applying medicaments to Samuel's hand. Namely, rum.

"Where to?" Jacome asked. He was bo'sun of the ship.

Our ship. What had we Jews christened it? We had adopted a Talmudic approach and continuously debated an appropriate name. And nu, maybe like the unutterable name of the captain of captains, YHVH—Yahweh or Jehovah Himself, its real name is unpronounceable, hidden, unutterable.

The *Gopherwood Shmeckel.*

The *Eleventh Plague.*

The *Meshugeneh Ship of Fools.*

"Where to?" Jacome repeated.

In an adventure, the next place is always somewhere else but in order to set the sails, we would likely need to be more specific.

We sought revenge and retribution from Spanish ships and their gold. But also: we wanted to forget, we wanted to remember. We wished for the Fountain of Youth. So first we had to find the books hidden on the mouldering shelf of some Spanish mariner that would lead us there.

"We need a human compass," Moishe said, and so the captain of our recent conquest was dragged on deck, the chains on his wrists and ankles rattling like disconsolate bells. His darkly tanned body was clothed, not in a captain's uniform but in a nest of calico rags.

"Capitano Rodriguez," Moishe said. "So, nu. What are your plans?"

Their precise nature was not clear as the captain's speech was rendered unintelligible by the venomous enthusiasm of his Spanish. We did discern, however, his suggestion of inhospitable destinations for Moishe and the rest of our crew.

"If I were you," Moishe began, "and perhaps you do see yourself in the fine silver brocade of this vest, the insouciant plenty of these silken sleeves?" Moishe displayed his newly acquired wardrobe before the captain who had good reason to recognize them. They were still warm from the heat of his body.

"So if you were me, then," Moishe said, "what would I do with you?"

The captain's frothing oaths suggested that he was not ready for such jocularities.

Time, they say, prepares one for humour. Perhaps there would be time for the captain to laugh again.

"So," Moishe said. "You guide us toward Columbus, Pinzón, and the next holdful of gold, the routes of which you doubtless know, and I grant your passage toward old age. Otherwise, you shall have brisk crossing to St. Peter or the bile-hearted devil himself in accordance with how Captain Yahweh has set your sails."

"Parasite," the captain said. "You are a pestilence well known to Spain. I forfeit my life for God, His pope, my sovereigns."

"Perhaps," Moishe said. "But know that you surrender not one life but two. Your son . . ."

Captain Rodriguez's face paled and, for a moment, he examined his bootless feet. Finally: "I understand," he said quietly. "Have you a son?"

"I know only my parents' son," Moishe said.

"Just so," the captain said. "So you understand a parent's love?"

"Well enough to thank you for guiding us wherever we so wish."

We hove our anchor up. The captive captain dejectedly directing a course, we set our sails, ran away from the bay, and bore down the coast again for Hispaniola. As we were now going to leeward, we had a fair wind and plenty of it. As I stood on the binnacle it felt as if I were flying, my imaginary beytsim kitseled by the wind. Sometimes a puff of nothing is enough.

Rodriguez, father and son, were able to roam the deck without manacles for the captain's son was collateral.

"He'll be o'er the gunwales like a hogshead o' piss—just before ye yourself be tossed, if ye think to sink us with treachery," Jacome said.

They did not join us as we kicked and palsied to the saltarellos of our new cooper's fife and drum. A delicate man with a moustache like the minge of a squirrel, Luigi del Piccolo had a lively repertory of estampies, courantes, and voltas, much needed sustenance when at sea or between pillage. Such music gave us courage, consolation, and was a convivial badhkin companion far from shore.

At length we were sated by our juddering freylich prancing and so plonked our hintns down onto the deck. The sails were set, the sheets tied, and Isaac the Blind was at the helm.

So we rested.

Fernández lay stretched against the bulwarks and looked east to where all but Yahíma were born.

"I had a brother," he said. "In Cadiz. Also a painter. Taken by the Inquisition. He had three sons. *Vilde chayes*, all three. Wild as waves. By now they must be bearded and tall. If they were spared."

Samuel passed out a few cups of rum. "My parents," he said. "In Portugal. After the expulsion. Then expelled again. They disappeared."

Ham pointed to his temple then with a resigned wave, evaporated all knowledge. He knew nothing of his parents' fate or would rather have his memories fade into sky.

"I, too, know nothing," Shlomo said from the wheel. "Bupkes. We were separated when I was a child."

Yahíma's eyes teared, remembering her parents. They had been among the first slain in the bohío and she had not known to protect them.

We shlemiels aboard spoke many languages, though Yiddish was our lingua franca. Moishe and I had taught the others. The tart sweetness of chopped liver, the spicebox tingle in the nose.

We would not speak the language of their catarrhic majesties, the Church, its words and its people. We couldn't wash the stink from those farkakte gatkes.

And so we kibitzed in mamaloshen.

Yiddish.

The perfect language for pirates, its words raggletag plundered and refitted from other times and tongues. As the Pirate Bey says, "Words belong to those who use them only till someone else steals them."

So we talked in Yiddish.

We remembered, even difficult things.

Which reminds me. There was this sailor, Yankeleh.

He leaves a pair of pants to be repaired *baym shnayder*—at the tailor's. After seven years, now covered in scars and tattoos, he returns to pick up his pants.

They weren't ready.

"Gevalt!" Yankeleh exclaims. "It only took Adonai himself seven days to make the world. You've had seven years!"

"What's to say, now that the world is done?" the tailor replies. "So, nu, your pants are a tragedy . . . but at least we can talk about them."

What could I say about Africa, of my pinfeather days and family? This ship and its crew, now baptized buccaneer, were my shtetl, my neighbours, a kind of family. These outsiders to outsiders here in the New World.

But Aaron, I said to myself. Don't be a putz.

You're a bird.

I was an outsider to all but Moishe.

And even then.

The captured Captain Rodriguez was tasked with guiding us toward a Spanish convoy of ships. He told us it would be unprotected, for what seaborne bandits roamed this distant side of the Ocean Sea?

Rodriguez would guide us to a line of ships: a wind-driven pantry, a floating larder sailing from Spain.

And what would be aboard? Clothes and food, horses and cows.

Slaves, settlers, Indians, women, guns and priests.

Accountants. It was wished that the countless desires of the Spanish should be counted. All exported loot would be recorded and taxed.

And what if the Indians returned to this new world like burning coals to Newcastle?

"They bring them back because they kill them here," Moishe said. And indeed, Indians were quickly disappearing from their own lands.

Disease. Overwork. Abuse. Starvation. The Four Grim Nag-riders of Empire.

Some Indians had been shipped across the Ocean Sea to Spain for curiosity and slavery. Many who survived were returned. Ferdinand and Isabella had changed their crowned minds: It was official, Indians were now subjects of Spain and had souls. They could not be captured or enslaved. Unless in war or by virtue of their interest in fressing upon the flesh of other subjects.

As Moishe put it, "Subject suppers are not allowed."

"Exactly," I said. "No soul food."

Indians must now be subjugated like any peasant. Africans, on the other hand, still had no soul, were strong and well adapted to working and were already used to slavery, having a rich résumé of capture by other Africans and by Arabs and Europeans. It would take thirty years for Africans to have souls. Or, takeh, souls that could be saved by the church.

It might be that Jesus saves. But Moses shops.

As we would soon shop aboard the Spanish fleet for food and clothes, animals and comforts. We would free the slaves and likely fillet the wispy souls from the mortal flesh of the priests.

"By the time this day sinks below the horizon, we will be in sight of the convoy," Rodriguez told Moishe.

"Good," Moishe said. "We'll be able to see their sails by the faint light of the stars but our ship will be invisible. I've just asked the crew to paint our own sails black."

And so we steered a shadow, the only sounds the hidden windharp of sheets and sails, the whistling nostrils and wheezing lungs of Jacome, and the heavy breathing and intermittent pickle-grepsing of the rest of the crew anticipating battle.

Between each ship of the convoy and the next, there would be space as between teeth in an alter kaker's maw. We would sail close to a single caravel, board it, bully it of plunder, and be gone before the other ships knew what hadn't yet hit them. Then we would sail into the dawn, our hold bulging, ready to plotz with spoil.

Night came fast. A sea empty of all but dark and distance.

Moishe summoned Rodriguez.

"Nu?"

"Patience, Captain."

"If there is no ship, Rodriguez, Death will need rummage through your wounds to find you."

"The ships will soon be before us," Rodriguez said steadily, though his face was pale.

Two bells. Middle watch. I flew into the dark sky. Ahead of us, a sheyneh beautiful sight.

I made a slip knot of the air and landed on Moishe's shoulder.

"Off the starboard bow."

The undulating sails of a Spanish ship, luminous in the dim light.

"Oy!" Moishe shouted to the sleeping crew. "You mangy yam gazlonim. You farkakteh Yiddishe pirates, time for a bisl Jewish flamenco."

We went to work immediately, mustering all the canvas we were able. We rigged out oars for extra yards. And, for still more speed, we wet down the sails by buckets of water whipped up to the masthead. We would run quickly toward our prey.

Surprise is best attained by those who outrun expectation.

Moishe peered into the night. We had no telescope. For such a glass we would need to squint a hundred years into the future.

Moishe could make out only that there was a ship.

At three bells, I flew again above the mainmast to observe our prey.

There was but a gloaming light, but I saw. She was armed, full of men, her sides porcupined by cannon and bristling with menace. We were a fox that had broken into a henhouse crammed with vicious hounds.

Our small caravel and four-pounders were no match. We would best attain victory through escape.

Though all light on board had been extinguished, and even the lamp in the binnacle removed, it was clear from the movements on the Spanish deck that we had been seen.

I returned to inform the crew of Rodriguez's treachery. Jacome was quick to press his pockmarked cutlass against the Spaniard.

"This man o' war is my brother's ship." Rodriguez smiled smugly. "He is the *Capitan General* of the Spanish navy."

Jacome was not pleased by this information. He thrust his mangy face into Rodriguez's and snarled, "I shall slice open your two-faced belly like a vermin-infested grainsack, then unfurl your duplicitous kishkas over the gunwales to be the living traitorwurst of sharks."

"However death finds me, my end shall be honourable," Rodriguez said.

"Your end shall be bloody as my blade shtups your dark star."

"*Halt on dem zokn*," Moishe said. "Hold your geezer beard, old man. His tuches will go nowhere without us."

Rodriguez was bound to the mizzen and we convened a painted-into-a-corner council.

"We have no choice but retreat," I said.

"It is too late," Fernández said.

"So, nu," said Isaac the Blind, raising his chicken-bone fist. "We shall fight like Maccabees."

"And our end shall be Masada." Shlomo: always ready to rouse a fatalistic cheer.

"But the Captain Rodriguez and his son," Yahíma said. "Hostages."

"Fnyeh," Samuel said. "The Spanish will only discover their false bones and teeth in the flotsam of our cannon-splintered sloop. One reads the guestbook only after battle."

A pirate ship: a barnacle-keeled kibbutz. A parliament of gonifs and rogues. Yabbering was how we decided our orders.

The Spanish were attacking?

So maybe it's time for a committee.

While we considered various ingenious nautical subterfuges, Moishe had been gazing at motes in the empty air.

"Take Rodriguez. Bind him over the pisk mouth of a leeward cannon," he said. "I will take his son in a skiff to the Spanish. Tonight, I am not a pirate but an honourable hidalgo to be received with courtesy."

Moishe had Shlomo take down our Shmuel-skull and candlesticks, and raise the Spanish flag. Young Rodriguez—Pedro—was a weedy boychik of about seventeen. He was led to the cannon over which his father was tied.

"Father!" he cried, weeping piteously. His father said nothing.

"Why so farklemt?" Moishe said. "We intend only to divide his body to match his duplicitous soul. Unless . . ."

Moishe rested his hand reassuringly on Pedro's shoulder.

"This evening, we row over to pay our respects to your uncle, the Capitan General. You will introduce me as Don Miguel de Levante, a hidalgo of Navarre. You will play this spiel of crypto-Jewry until the curtain falls, we return to our ship, then sail to safety. As long as we are betrayed by neither trickery nor chance, this cannon will not be needed and your father will remain unbageled."

That evening, Don Miguel de Levante and Don Pedro Rodriguez were rowed by some of our crew to the man o' war, the *Encarnación*. I travelled on Moishe's elaborately tailored shoulder, for Moishe was a hidden Jewish wolf in a Spanish captain's clothing, plain to see as his nose. The big macher *Capitan General* Don Luis Rodriguez stood impressively on the quarterdeck, dressed ongepatshket Rococco like a Torah in gold brocade and plush velvet. A priest stood beside him.

"Nephew," Don Luis said.

"My most respectful and loving greetings, Uncle," Pedro said. Uncle and nephew kissed and embraced. Then, "May I present Don Miguel Sánchez Villalobos de Levante of Navarre. A friend to us in these distant waters."

Moishe bowed deeply. "Capitan, I am at your service, " he said with the slick grace of a courtier.

Don Luis swept his brocaded arm and introduced the priest who stood beside him on deck. Fray Juan de Las Castillas looked briefly at Pedro and then at Moishe and me for a soul-scouringly long time. Moishe bowed courteously and remained impassive as he was surveyed. Pedro smiled weakly as if to say, "I have the face of a nebbish, how could I have the beytsim to play false?"

"Where is your father?" Don Luis asked. "So far from the land of our birth, he does not greet his own brother?"

"My father offers his most loving recollection and his deepest regrets," Pedro replied.

"Because of an oppressing fever," Moishe explained, "he must rest within his cabin."

"If my brother cannot visit me, then I shall visit him. Let us now board your skiff." The capitan began to stride aft toward the gangway.

"Don Luis," Moishe called in a low voice of much urgency, "there is great danger. Our ship is seized, the captain, your brother, held by pirates and slung over a cannon's muzzle. We dared not divulge this most important truth for the brigands watch us with murderous keen eyes. We were to play as if all were well. Betrayal means a cannonball through his midst. They have sent us on a ruse. You must move as if unaware of this."

Moishe had gone beyond the rehearsed script. We were only to have pretended to be other than who we were and then return. Don Luis looked to his nephew. The boychik Pedro's confusion was apparent on his anxious face, though certainly it reflected the tsuris of his father's plight.

"Early morning," Moishe said, "these corsairs will storm your ship when all but the watch sleeps without thought of danger."

"Some accounts of piracy in these Indies have been made," Don Luis said. "But these only in the tales of explorers—Columbus, Pinzón, others—as apt to liken a fish-filled freshet to a river of gold. We did not know there was truth in these otherwise lies."

A slight twitch of muscle in Moishe's mouth betrayed that he kvelled proud that his exploits were known in the courts of Castille and Aragon. Our piracies had left all either marooned or dead. He had not thought that either would be capable of report.

"There is perhaps a means to save your brother and return his ship to his rightful care," Moishe said.

Don Luis ordered some drink to be brought. Our visit should appear convivial to those paskudnik rogues on the surveilling ship. We toasted to King Ferdinand and to Queen Isabella. Fray Juan raised his mug in a blessing to the Pope. Then several times, he raised his mug again. Then Moishe explained his sneaky sheygets scheme.

Moishe and Fray Juan remained on the quarterdeck. The Spanish slid quietly into the leeside boats, sheltered by the sails, the dark, and by Moishe recounting a big megillah something to Fray Juan, vigorously windmilling his arms like a meshugener Don Quixote. On his shoulder, I exercised great care lest my end resemble nuggets and the feathered snow of pillowfights.

The Spanish were heavy with arquebuses and swords. They would surprise the unsuspecting pirates with a pre-emptive strike guided by the shmendrik son Pedro. For, nu, it was his father who bunged the cannon.

They began to row in dark water to the distant side of our ship.

"Don Miguel Sánchez Villalobos de Levante of Navarre," Fray Juan said, interrupting Moishe's flailing diversion as soon as the Spanish had disappeared into the murk.

"Years ago, you were a boy and 'Miguel Levante' was enough to hide you. I know who you are."

Moishe's hand went to his sword.

"Don Miguel, you need not joust with my ribs. I, too, have another name. Once I was a ghost named Padre Luis Dos Almos. You and this bird crept into the residence of the Archbishop of Seville. In the dark of the library, you dirked the inside of a Jew named Abraham."

"When one must, one can," Moishe said. "And may one tooth travel with his immortal soul always, only so it should ache forever." He released the hilt of his sword and bowed.

"So, Father, this new world, come here often?" he asked. Sangfroid was Moishe's middle name. At least when it wasn't Sánchez Villalobos.

"I travelled for many years," Fray Juan said. "I knew no solid ground. I was lost. Finally, I sought to evade the iniquity of Europe here in Orbe Novo, the New World, but it festers here, like the rot and slobber of a flax dam, with the ravenous putrefaction of greed, a negligent savagery toward natives. A new and more murderous Inquisition, we exile their blood from their very bodies. Indeed, I now return from the court at Castille where I have pleaded with both King and Queen, seeking to end the destruction of the people of these Indies. I have found myself in my own voice, speaking for those who have none."

Fray Juan was a man seized by both wine and conviction. His face, already red with drink, flushed still further as he adopted the manner of a preacher, fulminating with great volume to his man and bird congregation.

"I speak of those who collapse from hunger and toil. And we who kick and beat them to rise. We who knock out their teeth with the pommel of our swords. We who, for amusement, wager a single stroke of the sword can split them in two, slice head from neck, or spill entrails with but one plunge of the pike. We who toss infants into rivers, roaring with laughter and saying, 'Boil there, you offspring of the devil!' We who attack towns and spare neither children nor the aged, the pregnant nor women in childbed, stabbing and dismembering and cutting them to pieces as if they were sheep in the slaughterhouse. We cut off hands and hang them round the necks of our victims, saying, 'Go now, carry the message,' meaning, 'Take the news to the Indians who have fled to the mountains.' We tie our victims over smouldering fires so that, little by little, as those captives scream in despair and torment, their souls leave them. Oh, that I could describe even one-hundredth part of the afflictions and calamities that we have wrought among these innocent people! There once were many of these Indians; now there are few. May God grant enlightenment to priest and king, governor and general that they may act with justice and with wisdom. This is what I said to our Ferdinand and Isabella."

Moishe and I shuddered under such intensity, not to mention the spray of spume from Fray Juan's ardent mouth, but we knew that such things of which he spoke had truly occurred. We had seen such horrors. He was ranting to ranters.

Moishe turned to me and said, sotto voce, "He speaks of these things in court? In the shtetl, it is believed that when a wise man converses with a fool, two fools are speaking."

"Unless, like us," I said, "he speaks with sword."

"Fray Juan," Moishe asked, "what did you suggest Their Catastrophic Majesties do?"

"Transport slaves from Africa," he said.

There was a shout from our ship in the distance. They had seen the Spanish skiffs rowing toward them. Moishe went to the bell and signalled an urgent beat to quarters. Five peals repeated.

Then he grabbed Fray Juan. "A little business," he said, lowering him onto deck and binding him to the shrouds. The three other Spanish crew were soon roped like rodeo calves.

Then night flash and sky-cleaving thunder.

From our ship, the brain-severing tumult of cannons.

And it's true what is said: someone else's tuches is easy to smack. Especially when it sits in a rowboat sculling toward your cannonballs. The Spanish: we'd pissed on their backs and told them it was rain. Then we'd codswalloped them to search for umbrellas.

Now the ocean filled the holes in their bodies as they sank into the sea.

Except for Pedro and the Capitan: their kishkas remained unminced. Hostages are best when intact. Yahíma, Jacome and Shlomo paddled to the first skiff where each of their blades greeted the hostages' gullets with a silver grin.

Jacome: "Be lambs or have your apple sauced."

Yahíma laughed and shook her naked bristen in their frightened faces. And though they were fulsome fruit of Platonically perfect form, the source of many a non-Platonic thought to those who beheld them, here they were weaponry, a bitter ironic power wielded to humiliate.

Soon we had secured our captives, brought our ships broadside, thrown heaving lines over gunwales, and bound the two together.

"Have Christian mercy—release the boy's father, my brother," the Capitan said.

"Father," wailed Pedro. "Father."

"Climb down the ratlines from that cross, bubeleh, we need such lumber for masts," Moishe said to the sheygets. "But first greet your papa who filled his britches in fear."

"My father is a brave and honourable man," Pedro said.

Ham signalled to Moishe from his station near the boy's draped progenitor.

"He tells me your father is dead," Moishe said. "This I knew. Nu, I was ship's surgeon ere I was captain. Before we left the ship, your father died of fear."

"You killed him. He had much courage and was not afraid to die."

"It seems to me, he had no hesitation," Moishe said. "But I thank you for your cooperation."

The boy fainted, now realizing he had danced to a gun that had already discharged. He hung limp from the shrouds that bound him to the mast.

"When Spain learns of your infamy, you will be hunted down," the Capitan said.

"I am glad," Moishe said. "Prey that seeks me is easier to find."

The Capitan pursed his lips and launched a slobber of spit onto Moishe's cheek.

Moishe remained still and expressionless, allowing the bubbling spawn to slowly roll down his face.

"This mamzer suffers an excess of fluid," he said. "We shall correct this by withholding food and drink while he convalesces in the hold below." Moishe turned and nodded to Shlomo and Jacome who carried the Capitan to the hatch.

"History will not forget your evil," the Capitan said as they dropped him into the hold.

"History is a game played with the dead," Moishe replied. "The present actually happens. And nu, when they balance the scales, they'll find a few shlog-whomped Spanish on one side, kvetching and moaning.

And on the other, a heap of dead Jews and Indians. So, we do what we can to add to the Spanish side."

Unbound from the shrouds, Fray Juan sat on a barrel on the fo'c's'le, inhaling the smoky ghost of a large tobacco leaf.

"I, too, wish to do what I can for Los Indios," he said to Moishe. "Though by word and reason, not by murder. Allow me to return to Hispaniola where I will speak for them. I have letters signed by the King. I seek to save souls."

"As I, too, seek to save souls," Moishe said. "Our pirate souls. The Spanish will frack the insides of our mortal flesh as soon as you lead them to us. How then can I release you?"

"Because I believe you also wish to save, if not the souls of Los Indios, then at least their bodies," the priest said. "And . . . maybe you will accept a ransom for my freedom. A guarantee of my fidelity. You are not the only one who hostages something valuable aboard your ship."

"We have searched the vessel," I said. "What remains?"

"Piss buckets," Moishe said. "A fen of bilge water, black rats which dine on the wounds of the dead. We have plundered all people and goods of any worth."

"True," said Fray Juan. "But perhaps a map may be of use. Such charts have more value than gold, if they are a guide to what you seek."

"We seek only two things: revenge and gold. And, even without a map, we know how to find them aboard each Iberian sloop we encounter," Moishe said.

"The Bible commands us to forgive our enemies," Fray Juan said.

"But nowhere to forgive our friends," I said with a cynical tweet, climbing aboard Moishe's shoulder.

"Beyond what is written in the Bible, I understand little," Fray Juan said. "And even that is often mysterious. But I know you seek certain books. Books such as you would not want found by those who follow Cristóbal Colón. The Colonizers. Conquistadors of space and—if they were to find these books—time."

The mad monk knew how to get our attention.

"How do you know of them?" I asked.

"I am a priest in a place of few priests. In confession, many secrets are spoken."

"You are an honest man, if not an honest priest," Moishe said. "Lead us to these books, then."

"These books are my ransom and are hidden beyond the distant horizon," the priest said. "And aboard no ship. The first belonged to the admiral's brother and you bore it yourself from one to another. The second was given you like a curse by Torquemada, for it had made him lunatic as the vexed sea. He had it bound in the skin of a child, removed before birth from a heretic's womb. Both mother and child then sacrificed by fire. Miguel Levante, you may dowse this new world searching for this grimoire, this sanguinary, but it would be futile as seeking a camel in a stack of angels."

"So, Father, where are they?"

"There is a map." Fray Juan said. "But, ay," he said, "once you held these books in your arms. Once you caressed their words with your fingertips. Once you gazed at them longingly. But they were taken away."

Moishe looked to the sea, again gazing with longing.

He held us ransom with his words.

"The first stolen from Columbus when Pinzón first stole away. The second from your sea chest by Pinzón when you fled into Los Indios' forest. He did not find eternal youth, but eternity. By year's end, he died of a fever and was buried in the churchyard in Palos. The books became his brother's and were then passed like unlucky talismen from man to man until word of them became known by the crazed and clever, the short and ravenous governor of Coquibacoa, Francesco de Ojeda, who seeks them still like magic rings, Jewish Grails. And so they were buried by Captain Israel Manos on an island somewhere in this Caribbean sea."

"So this chart is a treasure map, then," Moishe said. "Not to the full set, but to a library of two."

"So, nu," I said. "Let's hope when we arrive, these two are not already checked out."

Chapter Six

The sun scudded above our black sails, glowering over a gloomy day of dark cumulus and wind. Most of the crew took to their hammocks while Fernández stood piloting at the wheel and splotching gaudy daubs of paint on a canvas propped against the binnacle. His many portraits were of the open sea. The frothy epaulets of its waves, the indecipherable blues of its depths. No faces, bodies, fish, or islands.

Moishe had a small cabin beneath the quarterdeck. Yahíma now joined him in a hammock where they intertwined limbs and faces and sighed. There's a language more universal than music or than memories of first love: the shvitzy harmony of shuffling bodies, the sweet tart tingling of entangled tongues. A beast with two backs but a Shiva-blur of legs and arms and bellies. The ship swayed on the waves and Moishe and Yahíma played tsung in tsingl, the uvulation of tongues like the shmeckel-in-knish gyrations down below. The cantillation of the mind in the language of the body. Or the other way round. With all this topsy-tuches-over-turvy-tsitskehs shtupping who, except for the participants, knew which way was up or where the pole star was?

And then they slept.

Dreaming of dreaming what they were dreaming, as the mystics say.

Did I watch?

Who can watch another's dreams or such conjugal hurly burly?

Ach, I knew where my end was, even if not where it belonged.

Except beneath me.

Which sweet parrot would be my dove? Man or maidel, African Grey or Red-spectacled Amazon? I'd loved many but didn't have the words.

I lived on the border. Neither man nor bird.

Feh. I'm all talk. Words only.

And nu. So maybe I looked at Moishe and Yahíma. A bisl.

The sap-sweet shout, the free-falling yawp.

Hard to ignore. Like the inexorable arrival of a bad joke.

So.

Mrs. Cohen says, "Rabbi, help me. My parrot—from morning till night, it squawks, 'I want to shmunts with anything that moves. Anything. Want to shtup? Want to shtup?' Ach, it's embarrassing."

"Oy!" the rabbi exclaims. "That's terrible. But listen, bring your parrot to shul. All day my parrot reads from his prayerbook and prays. He'll teach your parrot and in no time, it'll be praise and worship from morning 'til night."

Next day, Mrs. Cohen arrives at the synagogue. The rabbi's parrot is wearing a tiny yarmulke and davening feverishly from a little prayerbook.

Mrs. Cohen puts her parrot on the perch beside him. "I want to shmunts with anything that moves. Anything. Want to shtup? Want to shtup?" Mrs. Cohen's parrot says.

The rabbi's parrot immediately drops his prayerbook. "*Baruch ata Adonai* . . . Praise God. Praise God. My prayers have been answered!"

Distance embiggens the zeal of the heart, and far from everywhere, Yahíma and Moishe had fashioned a kind of heymishe homelike comfort in each other. A temporary autonomous zone.

With benefits.

Our ship of fools itself a shtetl beyond the Pale.

I'd shmuntsed with many birds myself since we'd first arrived here. Here—what I can't help calling—ech, the words themselves speak—the Nu World. The contingent and continental nu. Nu, as in, "so . . . what will happen here?" A dreidel with "nu" written on each of its sides. Nu, a great miracle—here? So let's see this miracle. This nu world.

So far, disease. Death. The mincing sword. The rupturing cannon. The destruction of Los Indios. In these few years, almost no Tainos remaining.

But I was speaking about yentsing.

There were many parrots.

Cockatoos, conures, macaws and Amazons.

Cherry-headed and crimson-bellied; maroon-faced and scaly naped; blue-throated, green-cheeked, and vinaceous; mealy, orange-winged, and lilac-crowned; yellow-shouldered and sulphur-breasted.

Nu, it was a world. And I was inside its varicoloured kaleidoscope.

So, not all were exactly my species, but my mother was far away, and besides, most were Pauls rather than Pollys. It began with surprise, then certainty. Across the Sundering Sea, I was purified with the water of separation.

I would rather this measure of shmuntsing heaven than any isle, save the sanctuary of Moishe's shoulder.

Both of us transmuted in the alembic of the Caribbean.

Was a map required to guide us to the map that would guide us to the book that would guide us to what we were looking for?

That would be Talmudic.

Dreaming of dreaming what we were dreaming.

But the best place to hide something is right under one's nose. Throw sniffers off the scent with another scent.

There was a chamberpot in the captain's cabin with a false bottom.

A fool chamooleh may have a false bottom, too, for in his dreck there may be gold.

Fray Juan described the pot: tin with engravings of parrots in trees, and a handle like a tropical vine. It was beneath the captain's bed, huddled coyly against the hullside. The tin parrots were idiot-eyed shmegegges. They'd clearly become meshugeh, having to bide their etched and immortal lives beneath the pungent ministrations of the empire's pimply moon. The priest didn't know how to open the secret compartment, so Jacome reached his hand into the pot's piquant lagoon and felt around for a catch or lever.

"For this I went to pirate school?"

He was unsuccessful.

We were about to pry open the secret compartments of the deceitful priest when Yahíma noticed one of the parrots' eyes was raised. Insert the point of a knife into the pupil, and the bottom of the pot fell open.

I'd noticed the eye, but thought the look was a wistful glimmer of recognition and desire.

(Note to self: schedule more time in the bird-busy bush, close to the zaftik undercarriage of your kind. Parrot-shaped scratches on chamber-pots shouldn't be causing your petseleh to tingle.)

The map was wrapped in oilcloth and we unswaddled it on the captain's large table.

There was much we recognized. The broadside islands of Hispaniola and Cuba with their fussy ongepatshket shores. Below, the pokey little skiff of Jamaica rowing up from the south. And above, the pebble-scatterings of the Bermudas, like stepping-stones to nowhere.

The map was the two-dimensional roadkill of a sorcerer's dreams, a brainbox of arcana pressed into two dimensions against the vellum. Archipelagos of eyes cluttered across the Caribbean, their preternatural gaze drawn as radiant points of a compass rose beaming across the sea. An undulating dolphin-dance of Hebrew script twisted between inky waves. And curious sigils, perhaps from Solomon's time, marks of demons, angels, cartographers, or whorehouses flocking like alchemical birds on both land and deep.

It would be hard to navigate across this mess of chazerai, but the destination was clear:

The subterranean library of two was on an island in the Bermudas. There were Hebrew letters emblazoned in the hills and Hebrew words all around it.

"Nu," Moishe said. "Always with the commentary."

Part Five:
QUINTESSENCE

why here rather than there,
why now rather than then

PASCAL

Part Five:
QUINTESSENCE

Why here rather than there,
Why now rather than then?

PASCAL

Chapter One

We were slumped around the binnacle sucking in pipesmoke and sharing a firkin of rum. We'd salvaged silver cups from Spanish pantries but drank from coconut-shell pannikins, fashioned by Yahíma in the traditional style.

Our parliamentations were made shmoozy and loud by smoke and alcohol.

"Why this map?" Isaac the Blind asked.

Jacome: "Follow that farkakteh map and we'll be futzing around the edges of the world until the Messiah hisself becomes an old geezer dribbling into both his gatkes and his mangy white beard."

"But the Fountain of Youth," Samuel said. "Could it be?"

"Like nipples on a duck. They might exist, but—gevalt—they're hard to find."

"So we plonk our tuches in this mikveh, and splash ourselves—oy, oy, oy, mayn Got, this magic vasser, such a mechayeh—but then what?" Shlomo asked. "My scars live forever? I become a boychik, maidel-soft as an unborn elbow but still I toddle around with the Bible scraped into my skin?"

"No matter where we go, there we are," Yahíma said. "We might as well follow ourselves."

"Feh. Only if we could leave ourselves behind," Fernández said.

"We'd have to sail swiftly then," Ham signed. "Quicker than words and memory."

"Or Jacome's temper," Fernández said.

Jacome raised his fist. "So quick even your mother knows your pig-ugly mieskeit snout was 'cause of the clobbering I gave you before I met you." He took a titanic swig of rum. "Because I knew you'd deserve it."

Isaac tightened the tefillin straps holding his hooked hand, and then scritched his head with the point. There was wisdom there, but also fleas. "So if this fountain is the shvitz of memory, and we walk away barnacle free, fresh like a Shabbos tablecloth and empty as the shelves in the shlemiel library of Chelm, then, without tsuris, we could go back to fressing on gold and shteching the Spanish with our swords. If we live forever, we live forever. We'd be Übermenschen who could neither be karsted by arquebus nor cratered by pox."

"*Ver veyst?* It'd takeh be a very Jewish fountain that makes a Yid immortal but not live forever," Fernández said. "I'd still look side-to-side and up-and-down before crossing the boulevard."

"Or jumping out a caravel," Yahíma added.

"But nu," Isaac continued. "If this water was good for nothing more than swabbing molluscs from the wrinkled hulls of our beytsim, it'd be worth gold when bottled and sold to the worthy shlemiels of Europe. Map. Books. Exotic puddle. Testimonials. It's the story not the steak. The brocheh not the brisket."

Finally, we voted.

Moishe taught me an old saying: *Di tsung iz nisht in goles.* The tongue is not in exile. And it was true, we'd lost everything but our accent. Takeh, many of us had gained one. We were wandering Jews and had no home. So, we might as well wander. We counted hands: We'd seek the book. It was as much home as anywhere.

⁜

We began to sail toward our treasure, following the bottom of the pannikin, the shikkering gourd, the North Star, Polaris. Our book at the end of Ursa Minor Beta. Our home at the end of the Little Bear's tail. Moishe and I would soon dishwash our hearts in the soapy,

soul-scrubbing waters of the Fountain: a map, a book, and then a quick
dunk and some bobbing for rebirth in the metaphysical lagoon.

How did we feel about this? If there's a word to describe it, ach, it's
not on this parrot's tongue.

Isaac the Blind was at the helm. Shlomo, Ham and Samuel hauled
the sheets. I flew to become the polyglot tittle—the dot—on the mainmast's "i."

As one Hebrew vowel said to the other, "Everyone's a diacritic."

I looked forward, scanning for islands, the Spanish, whales, the
Fountain of Youth, and the future.

Instead, like a punchline, I saw the horizon.

Morning. From the south, a happy-go-lucky lebediker breeze had
blown since the second half of the dogwatch. At three bells of the fore-
noon, it died away. In its place, a strong wind from the northeast, which
caused us to take our studding-sails in and brace up.

"A cheer for this glad gust from a northern rump," Jacome said.
"Somewhere the skirts of a windgod have been blown to the sky."

In a couple of hours we were bowling gloriously along, puffed-up
sailors returning victorious and carefree after their corporeal ministrations in the cat house.

We were shpritzed with the cool, northeast trade freshening up the
sea, and giving us as much as we could carry our topsails to. The bulvan
wind blew strong and steady, keeping us upon a bowline, our course
about north-north-west. Sometimes, they veered a little to the eastward,
and we unfurled a mainmast studding-sail. For a day, we scudded well
to northward.

Then the north wind left us.

Azoy gich?

So soon?

For several days after, we humbugged about in a whole gantseh
megillah of weather. Occasionally a thunderstorm.

Then the wind left us entirely. Something we said? A brocheh we
forgot? For weeks, little but hooch, kibitzing and the wind. Dreaming
of the four elements, both succulent and moist: death, revenge, sex

and feasting. Water everywhere and we almost dropped from drink. Also, dancing hornpipes as if we were lurching in heavy weather, Luigi del Piccolo trying to pipe up wind and diversion. In such ways we passed our time, watching for dolphins with their idiot savant rubber grins, and the silver sides of fish, a treasure for our supper.

"Watch for a star in the shadow of the crescent moon," Shlomo said. "It means fair winds."

"I'm told an albatross is a good sign," Samuel said.

"So, nu," said Isaac the Blind. "Watch for two."

That night, during a deep amidship shlof, Moishe's pale eyes flipped open. Often those on board had difficult sleep. Terror and keening. Night shouts. Muttering. Weeping. Shmuntsing with Neptune, a Golem, the tooth fairy, or Queen Esther.

"A dream," Moishe called. "Islands. A channel between words and no words. Pages, wings, a tongue in my ear, a knife-edge, memory, a tongue. Then many of us die." His eyes closed. Opened again. "Run," he shouted. "Run!" Then he turned with a snort and slept until two bells o' morning watch.

Weeks passed. There was neither land nor wind, fish nor albatrosses. I was the only bird near our gopherwood ship of foolhardy shmeckels.

Weeks. Perhaps if the hearty fortz of my gastrointestinally talented crewmates could be coordinated in a methane philharmonic, our sails might curve. Or the humid blasts from their cranky cursing. Water was scarce as popes in a mikveh. We'd eaten all meat fleysh but the stringy gams of Yids and the svelte feathered body of their Pollyglot familiar.

And frankly, I didn't fancy me, not to mention their sun-tarred sinews.

There was some hardtack remaining. Soon we would have to cook and eat the leather of our boots.

Fernández, the painter of empty seas, wished only for the islands flocked outside his frames. "I'd takeh sell a thousand furlongs of sea for a bisl barren ground, long heath, brown furze, anything. Adonai, follow your meshugeneh scheme if you must, but, ach, if you're asking, I'd rather a dry death."

And with plenty to drink.

He became delirious with thirst and tried to eat his paints. "This cold blue. This liquid green." Paint dribbled from his mouth and coloured his white beard. Moishe and Yahíma tied him to a post in the hold.

Together the crew had made the decision to follow the map toward the bookish grave.

But it was Moishe that they cursed.

How he had led them into this desert of thirst, this windless wanderlessness. As if it had been only he who craved youth, memory loss and immortality.

"This map is poxy with evil eyes and farkakte demon scrawl," Shlomo said.

"And nu," said Samuel, "we'll all be dead before we can live forever or get anywhere close to your poxy frantsevateh fountain." He slurped a runnel of moisture found in the fold of the sail.

"We have a covenant of articles, you pus-bloated, maggot-toothed Spanish gonif. We do not horde plunder from others in our minyan," Shlomo hissed. "Neither gold nor slaves. And especially not water." He drew his sword, ready to turn Samuel's body into its own tattered funeral shroud.

A marlinspike flash and Samuel twisted and pinned Shlomo's sword hand to a barrel.

Yahíma, perched high in a mast, leapt from a yardarm, kicking in midair, her heel realigning Samuel's jawbone and reintroducing his body to the concepts of down, horizontal, and darkness. She landed one foot nimbly on the deck, the other ready to make sauce of Samuel's gullet. After wrenching the marlinspike from the cribbage board of Shlomo's hand, she twisted his arm behind his back. Ham arrived with a rope and tied the perforated hand to its undamaged twin then bound their master to the mast. They lugged Samuel's unconscious rat-sack body over the boards, then sat it up and bollard-hitched it to the mizzen.

It had been an oratorio of shraying, grunts and gevalts. Moishe, asleep in his hammock, arrived only in time for the curtain call. By then, the rest of the rubber-gorgled crew had gathered to twist their necks and gape.

Yahíma explained what happened and Moishe considered.

On a navy ship, Samuel and Shlomo would have remained lashed to the masts. And—with a word from the captain—the captain's spiteful daughter would have ripped apart the bodice of their flesh and Kama Sutra-ed their naked spines. Or it would have been the spurs of the nine-tailed cat that sank deep into the catacomb of sinew and bone beneath the shambles of their skin.

Perhaps they would have found themselves in a dory, emigrants to death on the open sea, or Crusoed castaways on a distant island with little but a sword, some water, and a lifetime supply of exile and death.

But Moishe said, "Release them."

Perhaps if, as a boy, he had skipped a few Bible stories and read ahead a little from the future, he would not have been so lenient.

Though it's hard to look forward when your own back is scarred.

But nu, the decision should not have been his alone. Each who had scrawled their name or scribbled their mark on the articles was entitled to a vote. But none spoke.

I had made a mark on the paper. *Vos iz der chilek?* What's the difference? Was I going to disagree with Moishe? Sure, I crowed in the voice of men but, takeh, there was something stronger in my craw. Loyalty, love, companionship—these kept me quiet.

A pail of seawater was loosed on Samuel, then on Shlomo's rib-eyed hand. He and Shlomo were untied, Samuel blinking awake and confused as if rescued from a dark mine. Shlomo slinking below deck, holding his wounded hand like a newborn.

Moishe stood looking out beyond the bowsprit, squinting toward a gust from the future. Beside him, fetchingly perched on the gunwale, plumes superbly dressed in his captain's light grey shadow, his parrot, *dux volucrum*, a leader among birds, as the ancients say, and nu, I say it every time anyone eats chicken and not me.

"Nu, they're so thirsty that all they do is shecht each other's gullets," Moishe said. "Without wind, they'll kill each other before they die."

We looked down into the water and the still surface revealed a doppelganger ship barely hanging onto our hull, in danger of breaking away and falling into the antipodean chasm of the sky. A skinny parrot and a shrubby sailor stared back at us. "See? We're stand-on-our-headniks. What do we know?" I said.

"It's good you're here," Moishe said to them. "Mishpocheh. Family."

The world was still. The sails were pale papers waiting to be written on by the wind. The ocean was sky and I was a small parrot-shaped greyness, the tiniest of pupils in the infinite star-flecked eye of the entire gantseh megillah.

And Moishe—his squinty, ferkakteh missing-nipple chest covering the cracked vessel of his heart, badly in need of a cardiologist, Kabbalist, or any kind of specialist—had spoken tenderly to me. We were family.

I tried not to speak, but instead enjoy the moment.

Feh. Here I am, doorstopping the journey with words.

Then Jacome staggered toward us, his face luffing like an unsheeted sail. "We are neither dead nor alive and our dried-out souls become the wraiths our ravenous bodies now be."

What could we do? How to invoke the wind?

Sailors know never to whistle, never to say goodbye, to always drop a few coins into the sea to buy safe passage, as if Yahweh was an infinite beggar waiting for silver on the sea bed. But desperation is often the broodmare of ceremony and Moishe now rose as one of its priestly Cohanim.

"Get paper. Quill. Ink. And a small box. I know now what we must do."

The crew assembled midship, Moishe at the helm of his congregation. He raised his hand and asked for the paper. Jacome pulled it from inside his tunic.

It was a page torn from a siddur. The last words of a prayer and then the calm waters of the empty page. It was clear from Moishe's tilted brow that this was—keneynehoreh—bad mojo. Ptuh. Ptuh. Ptuh. Prayerbooks aren't usually raw material except for hope.

But he moved quickly to fold and conceal the page. Then he took the quill—from whose avian flesh was it pulled?—and dipped it in the ink.

"I write now—*Baruch ata Adonai*—the name of our farkakteh ship."

But which name? Let's hope for something that becomes apt: *The Gale-pitched Gonif, The Tempest-chuffed Tummler,* or *The Whale Road Thrill-Rider.*

"And I write our names."

And he did. Including Shlomo's and Samuel's.

Then he folded the page and placed it in a little box.

If your ship is becalmed, what seems obvious and prudent?

Lighting a fire on deck. The box burned like a pyre. The crew stood silently as it turned to ash. It could have been a lamb. The paschal paper. Wind, please don't pass over us.

Moishe gathered the ashes and stood by the gunwales. He roamed the shoals of childhood and netted some words.

"*Sh'ma ye* crew of *yam gazlonim,*" he said. Listen, Pirates. "*In zaltsikn yam fun mentshlecheh trern.* In the salty sea of human tears."

He raised the ashes above his head. "For the Lord had mind of Noah, and of all things living on the Ark; and He brought forth his breath over the face of the earth."

"Then I hope He first brushed the Black Holes of His Infinite Teeth," I said quietly into the holy sanctum of Moishe's priestly ear, but Moishe did not flinch.

He lowered the box and allowed the starling flock of ashes to fall into the sea.

"Amen," he said.

"Amen," said the crew.

Superstition may be hope in disguise.

"You think this will work?" I asked.

"Do I know the future?" he said. "I just want to be there when it happens."

Chapter Two

Yahíma lay under the still shadow of the foresail. She was telling me
stories from her island. Some involved wise parrots and two-spirited
shamans.

"In the early morning of the world, the first man greeted the first
dawn, the red and green feathers of the sun..."

But then we heard shouting and the icy metal scrape of sword.

Shlomo and Samuel were on deck. They were no longer fighting
against each other. Instead, they had laid siege to Moishe. His throat was
a bristly Masada and it seemed he was to be close shaved. Shlomo held
Moishe in a full nelson while Samuel pressed a dirk against Moishe's
jugular, threatening to swab the deck with his blood.

Yahíma and the other hands awake on this still ship ran toward
the grisly pre-op, but Ham, larger than all by half, strode in front of
us, grinned his bright crescent smile and held up his wide pink palm.
"Stop," it told us. A huge machete slung from his side.

He bounded up the mainmast shrouds, looped and knotted a halyard, then lowered himself back onto the deck, a noose now hanging
openmouthed from the yardarm. A delicate filigree of blood ran over
the blade-edge pressed into Moishe's neck. Shlomo thrust Moishe
under the noose. Samuel withdrew the blade. Then Shlomo and Ham
hoisted Moishe and placed his head into the yawning maw of the halyard. They released him into the vapourous arms of gravity and the air.

"L'chaim!" they said.

None of us breathed.

Especially Moishe.

He remained motionless, no freylecheh Tyburn jig. No headstaving kickboxing of his executioners. He gazed over the horizon. Not walking, dreamhanging.

I was considering an intervention when Fernández, having escaped his bonds, burst from the hold, shraying like a fresh crucifixion, and hurtled across the deck. In one motion, he embraced Moishe, and with a lightning flash of cutlass blade, cut the rope. Then they both disappeared over the bulwarks and into the water.

The wind rose and the sails bulged and the timbers of the ship creaked. It was the revivifying downpour of rain after a drought. We began to move.

Azoy gich? So soon?

Shlomo, the map in his hand, shouted for the crew to attend to the sheets and sails. All except Yahíma began to haul yards and position booms.

"My love is gone down to his garden," she sang quietly. A Hebrew song of Moishe's. She crept to the stern and rolled a hogshead over the bulwarks where it plunged into the pluming sea, soon bursting up like an overexcited sitting-on-shpilkes dolphin above the new waves.

She could do no more else she, too, would find herself standing on fishes.

I flew out over the ocean searching for Fernández and Moishe. There was a long trail like a fallen rainbow, a multicoloured wake stretching over the water.

I followed. It took over an hour but at the end of this arc-en-mer was Fernández. He had leapt from the ship with a sack of paints slung over his shoulder. Now, emes, he was truly painting the sea.

The waves swilled over his still face, his unblinking eyes looked toward the sky from beneath an iridescent kaleidoscope of colour.

Fernández. Painter.

A righteous man.

I repeated a psalm for him who would have wished for prayers.

"I will say of the Lord, surely he shall deliver thee from the snare of the fowler, and from the noisome pestilence. He shall cover thee with his feathers, and under his wings shalt thou trust. Blessed is the one true judge."

And then I flew high into the air.

I was reminded of a story.

Once, Rabbi Akiva travelled to the city but found no lodging. Even the mangers were full. "All that Adonai does, He does for the good!" the wise rabbi said. That night he shloffed rough between the stalks of a cornfield. He had with him a parrot, a donkey and a piece of cheese. In the night, a mouse fressed on the cheese, a cat gulped down the parrot, and a lion guzzled the donkey. When he woke up, the rabbi discovered that an army had invaded the city and slaughtered everyone.

"Nu," Rabbi Akiva nodded, glad to have been spared. "All that Adonai does, He does for the good!"

The parrot said, "What did you say, Rabbi? From inside this cat where I'm in the middle of being digested, it's hard to understand you."

And the others?

The donkey and the cheese said nothing.

I could see the ship: the billows of its sails were scudding clouds above the crimpling sea. I saw that Fernández's trail had turned crimson. Fins were circling. Fernández's gams were the nosh of sharks. He was returning to the ocean. Little by little. Not the place of his birth, but where he had imagined his future and his past.

And where was Moishe?

Gevalt. I hoped his limbs had not also become the tsimmes of sharks, that he had not become—in whole or in part—a settler of whales, a belly dweller. I scoured the sea for signs. Of the barrel. Of Moishe. For well-fed sharks and their trail of blood. Gotenyu, I did not want to be rent from him, my only mishpocheh.

The wind, lost for so long in wandering, now huffed boisterously. The waves surged through the kelpy waters, the seaweed and slime of the sea stirred in a frothing borscht. The ocean's tiger heart had woken, the waters began to leap and prowl.

The chutzpah.

Not a single purr for weeks and then this roar?

And then—*vo den*, what did you expect?—the rain.

Black skies. Lightning. Thunder.

I was not compelled to follow any route except toward Moishe. So, nu. I went with the wind.

My kishkas became quoggy in the deluge. And the inside of my kishkas? Archipelagos of guano. I flew between the blue fissures of lightning as it cracked the grim sky.

S'iz shver tsu zayn a Yid. It's tough to be a Jew.

Tougher still when such storm threatens to make barbecue of one's mortal pork. And then I spied the hogshead. A *shtik naches!* O *hetskeh zich!* I shook with joy.

Moishe?

I saw a hand emerging from the bunghole, the pale coxcomb fingers of a squid. I became a barrel-rider as I landed, the cask bucking in the breakers.

"Moishe!" I called, though both my words and myself were near drowned in the gale. "*Vi geyt dir?* How's tricks?"

The fingers curled, the hand turned, then grabbed me and pulled me in.

It was dark inside the barrel. There was the heavy breathing of a cave bear.

"I like what you've done with the place," I said.

"*Baklog zich nisht.* Don't complain," he said. "I tried decorating the sea. It's more difficult."

Water sloshed in through the hole, the spouting of an inverse whale. Moishe repositioned himself. "The cork is gone. I use my knee. But it's dukedom enough, since I'm pickled in Madeira wine."

Moishe and I in a barrel. What would you do?

Of course we spoke of metaphysics. We had the time.

Feh.

We spoke of nothing, a nothing that didn't include philosophy unless one considers the chaloshesdikeh heaving sickness-unto-death for we were thrown up and then down. Or possibly in another direction. But not at the same time. One part of my kishkas went left, another right. The rest attempted escape velocity. The only philosophy was to wait and endure.

We were tossed about like casks lobbed out of the Ark. The washed world's first trash. How long did this tempest last? Who knew? Night and day cast the same shadows in our dark cave.

But then, up and down ceased to be our world. The storm stilled and, like the captain of the *Nightingale* in the song, we smelled flowers.

We were near land.

I was about to stick my head through the bunghole, a parrotscope surveying the antediluvian sea, but our ark received a mighty wallop. I was worried that we might be stoved in like the Kabbalists' vessels, emanating Moishe, his bird, piss-diluted wine and darkness. But the barrel did not break. It was only the lid that was dislodged. Seawater flooded in. We spluttered to the surface.

We had run into the hull of a ship. There could be few boats in this part of the sea though all must be pulled by the same tide. Sha. Not fate. The Antilles current. Or perhaps the search for the same spoils.

A sailor looked over the gunwales.

"Avast, man off the larboard side."

"An Indian in a canoe?"

"A pale sea cucumber. With a bird."

"Marooned?"

"Haul in this strange fish and we shall talk turkey."

And so a ropeladder was lowered that Moishe attempted to climb. But his strength was gone. Instead, he hung like a netted crab and the sailors hove him onto the deck.

"I'faith! This sailor is known to me." The man in a cassock seemed to have some authority. He regarded Moishe with interest and spoke loudly, as if Moishe truly had the brains of a fish. "Once he saved me as I have now saved him. Sometime physician Miguel, do you know me?"

It was Columbus.

Gevalt.

Of course he found us. He was the great explorer, discoverer of what was already there.

In this case, us.

But we were pleased to be found and given a good Spanish nosh and clear, fresh drink. A little luck to go along with my handsome, brine-logged feathers.

After a few days of aboard-ship rest, Moishe recovered. We dined in the captain's cabin with the Admiral of the Ocean Seen and the Viceroy of Visions, for now, Columbus himself had been found.

"For eight days," he told us, "I was lost and despaired of hope. The sea chopped and frothed with a rage I had never known."

He looked through the aft port and into the smooth distance. "The gale enslaved us. We could not run behind headland for shelter but were washed without liberty over this accursed ocean. Never did the sky look more terrible." He turned, waving his hands to indicate the tumult.

"It blazed like a furnace, and the lightning broke with such vio-lence I wondered if it had carried off both sails and spars. The flashes came with fury and frightfulness. We were certain the ship would be blasted. I do not say it rained, for it was like Noah's deluge: the roof of sky came down low upon the dark water and we were tossed about our roiling barque. The men were so worn, they wished that death would end their dreadful suffering. I counselled them to vow pilgrimage to Holy Jerusalem if only we would survive. And then I saw light without seeing, heard voice without hearing."

He had sailed the same turvy waters as us but, takeh, he had had opportunity for metaphysics and light. Or perhaps the meshugener had greater access to Madeira than we who only bathed in it.

"A celestial voice. The light had no position but was brighter than the rays which emanate from the sun, and I could discern neither height nor depth but only God's manifest hand. And from this sparkle came words unlike any which sound from mortal mouth, but rather as dazzling flame and bright cloud moved by the pure air."

He spread his arms out as if addressing multitudes. "And I saw in this light another light, and I cannot say how I saw it, except not with these two mortal eyes, but while I beheld it, all sadness and pain was lifted from memory, so that I was as an innocent child and not the careworn mariner that I am. I know that the Last World Emperor shall reign and Jerusalem shall be returned from the heathen. The thousand-year end of the world shall soon be found, an Eden at the other side of this ocean of struggle."

"And *dernoch vos?*" Moishe asked. "What then?" Asking what came after the end of the world was like asking someone on a ledge what would happen after they fell to become dispersed dollops on the sidewalk. It wasn't really the point. At least, not yet. Of course, eventually, the dollops would rise and the buried dead would break through the sidewalks. And as long as you were a good Christian wolf, you could shmunts and cavort with the lamb. It wasn't clear what would happen with Jews, pagans, heathens, conversos, birds, beasts, and sinners, but there'd be trumpets.

Columbus had klopped into the Novo Mundo, the unfoundland. Now he must get more specific and bump into paradise. Or, at least, the terrestrial Eden. He knew from the book stolen by Pinzón that it was to be sought in the north of the Caribbean, and thence he pointed his bow in that direction.

It wasn't difficult to persuade Columbus to help regain our ship. The map that had been hidden on board would guide us both to his book and Torquemada's baby-bound tome. And these books led to the Fountain of Youth, which, takeh, surely must be the emptied Eden, its blank pages no longer inhabited by Adam and Eve, the world's first DPs.

So there's this riddle about the first couple and a character called "Vemen-Art-Es"—"What-does-it-matter?"

> *Adam and Eve and Vemen-Art-Es*
> *Jumped into the Mikveh and bathed.*
> *Adam and Eve were drowned*
> *Who do you think was saved?*

Vemen-art-es? What does it matter?

But what did happen to Adam and Eve? Did they hollow out the Tree of Knowledge, make a canoe and then paddle east to Europe?

Fnyeh.

Not these Heyerdahls.

But, if there ever were an Adam and Eve, who knows where they went?

Maybe they were Indios—or what came before Indios.

Or parrots.

I mean Adam and Eve: maybe they were birds.

I could see my great-great-great-infinitely-great-grand-parrot forebears fressing on apples, learning to name things, being too clever for their own good.

Or God's.

Chapter Three

We sailed north. The moon stuck its great shnozz through the sky, a kibitzer wondering where we were going, its glimmering trail a path across water, as if we could walk its undulating silver highway to another place. An eternal place of bodies and souls just over the horizon.

And nu, perhaps that's where we were going. Are we there yet?

To those over there, we're always somewhere else.

Especially in our words.

I sat on a yardarm.

Columbus strode about the deck in his black cassock.

I no longer pretended to have words but no understanding.

Columbus said, "St. Francis was said to preach to the birds, and so he must have believed they had understanding."

"And souls?"

"Why else would he preach?"

"And Los Indios?"

"They have understanding."

"And souls?"

"Of a kind."

"There is more than one kind?"

"Perhaps," he said.

⁂

Our problem now: how to find an uncaptained ship of Jews and the righteous among crustaceans in a vast sea. The current pulled us north and we followed its words. We would keep a clear eye for what lay before us, what lay around.

The deck was still, little sound but the soughing of the wind and the steady crosscutting of the men's snores. Columbus, ever an expectant human breaker for the transcendent fizzle of his God's unpredictable power surges, positioned himself at the convergence of the bow gunwales and waited. Moishe, grateful to be more than ballast aboard a barrel, tied a hammock between the starboard shroud and the mizzenmast, and slept. The watch slept also, save for the boy uneponymously manning the wheel.

From the fore-crosstree, I watched the phosphorescence of the sea. A mantle of blueish-white covered nearly all the dark water north of us, its edges wavering and trembling within half a mile of the ship. We floated in a sea of liquid radiance, an unearthly, blue glare. The ocean was a vast aurora of blue fire overrun by heavens of almost inky blackness. Iridescent spittle from the lips of Columbus's God on the dark velvet of a Torah mantle.

Only a moment before, the still water had reflected an entire hemisphere of spangled constellations, and the outlines of the ship's spars were projected as dusky shadows against the Milky Way. Now the sea was ablaze with opaline light, and the yards and sails were painted in faint tints of blue on a background of ebony. A vivid electrical fire was upon the ocean. As I stood farklemt upon the quarter-deck, this sheet of bluish flame suddenly vanished, causing, by its almost instantaneous disappearance, a sensation of total blindness, and leaving the sea, for a moment, an abyss of blackness. But as the pupils of my eyes gradually dilated, I saw as before the dark shining mirror of water around the ship, while far away on the horizon rose the great luminous appearance that had first attracted my attention and that was caused by the lighting up of the haze by areas of phosphorescent water below the horizon line.

I thought to call out, "Gevalt! It comes again!" but felt hushed as if in the presence of something sacred. Again the great tide of fire came sweeping up around the vessel and we floated in a sea of illumination that extended in every direction and beyond the limits of vision.

Then I heard, over the radiance, a song. A distant singing. Like the sombre keening of whales, a hollow sorrowing of such beauty that my wings felt lifted as if a sigh had gathered me in its breath and was pulling me toward the warmth of its body.

An island surrounded by phosphorescence. Women swimming near the shore, singing. Their naked bodies rising above the water, dappled in bright light, then sinking again. Brown bodies spangled with radiant life.

"Moishe," I called. "This is worth waking up for."

"What's your rush?" he grumbled. "So, nu, the farkakter Messiah will be born *shpeter mit a tog*—a day later."

The singing coiled around us, a honeyed murmuration, an undulating nigun, a writhing shimmy of smoke. It found Moishe and he woke.

"Our ship has been sighted? We've got the map? The ..." But then he slid from the hammock, and stood mesmerized at the gunwale. Columbus rose and stood beside him. Together they slipped off their clothes and fell into the sea, swimming toward the singing maidelehs.

Before long, the crew, too, glided like sleepwalkers from where they kipped and dived into the luminous dappling of dark water. Only the boy at the helm remained. The lapping water and the sinuous song lulled him to where, I imagine, he dreamed whatever populates a boy's nodding Eden and he slept with a smile.

And I, too, found my brain rippling warm with the song's phosphorescent brindling, which caused me to follow the men toward the island's shallows.

A woman, moon-luminous like the flesh of a pear, soft and glistening as kreplach in soup, stood waist-deep in water, her arms on Moishe's shoulders. Her eyes, swart and steady, transfixed him. She whispered but who could tell what she said, for her voice was the susurration of lapping water, speech without words. Columbus, too, stood before a machesheyfeh enchantress lost in a distant horizon. The crew wandered somnambulant toward the dark shadows of the forest beyond shore, where naked, both men and women stood waiting between the tangle of branches.

I heard birds—what I was sure were parrot calls—from within the trees. Then I saw, beside a fire on the beach, the extended shadow of a parrot, long and anamorphic, a smear of darkness, a shadow road. Then the pure Harlequin form of the parrot-in-itself appeared to me. I flew toward him, my brain a substance between twilight and lokshen pudding.

The women rose from the water covered in fringed prayer-shawl tallises of water and light. Water that rivered down their skin and fell in moon-bright droplets onto the sand. Moishe and Columbus followed, meek as virgins on their way to spring sacrifice, but led by their keeper's tucheses, a voluptuary prophet's round and gluteus vision of both halves of a transcendent world, suggestively tectonic as they moved.

On the beach by a fire, the bo'sun was kneeling before a broad balebosteh of a woman. More Venus of Düsseldorf than a twiggy Giacometti, she was an impressive piece of living shed-sized statuary. Higgs gazed up at her as before an altar and she smiled and kitsled tickled his ears.

Moishe and Columbus now kneeled on the sand beside the bo'sun, their eyes turned to glass. The three women had donned strange robes made of coconut shells, long reeds, mother-of-pearl, and mussels resembling the nether-part knishes of creatures of an elder world. They gathered around the fire, drinking wine.

The parrot was given its own bowl and he drank while gazing at me. Intermittently he chirruped boozily, a low vibration that I felt in my cloaca. I became shikkered drunk by proxy, grinning the idiotic shmendrick-smile of the besotted. I stood on the sand beside the others, dazed by expectation, desire, and some sorcerous variety of island legerdemain.

Then without warning, they threw their capes, which were actually sacks, over the men's heads and bound them. I woke from my stupor and flew into a tall palm away from my parrot.

I never even knew his name.

If I did, I'd beak him a thousand bespoke curses.

May an unspecified illness, vast and endless as our illusions, fress upon each of your cellwalls until you fall as miserable soup from the wretched sky.

Spanish soldiers rushed from the rainforest and seized Moishe, Columbus and the bo'sun.

"Release me for I am Admiral and Viceroy," Columbus protested from within his bag. "I am Governor of—"

A soldier paid speedy tribute by puter-kletsling him below his equator with his knee and he collapsed to the sand. Another shmitzed Moishe with a stick and he fell.

The bo'sun quickly lay down on the sand and was silent.

A Spanish captain, fussy with big macher fur and brocade, stumped out of the forest and onto the beach. Behind him, a disheartened procession of Columbus's crew, bound and led by rope.

"Buenas Noches!" the captain said, bowing slightly toward the bagged Columbus. He was a small blancmange of a man, red-bearded with but one eye, and it like the dull gallstone of a rat. He spoke as if reading the lines of a dandy stage villain. "I am known as Panfilo de Narváez, captain, commander and governor of these northern regions of Cíbola, so appointed by their most refulgent sovereigns, Ferdinand and Isabella."

He addressed the bags on the beach.

"It is a pleasure to welcome one who is so distinguished, and who has discovered so much. I trust that you will discover much more as our prisoner. And so, too, your esteemed Hebrew confrère, Moishe, the less-than-a-yardarm pirate—because, as we well know, it was not only his sail that was trimmed."

He paused for history to appreciate his bon mots.

"Ach, gey kaken afn yam," I wished to say. "May you release your bowels upon the open ocean and may sharks take interest in your sphincter. May their teeth seek hacksaw passage to the twisted phylactery of your intestines."

But I'd wait. There'd be time for bile. First I had to rescue Moishe. The captain stood over the three sacked men.

"We have played this pretty masked ball of singing sirens for two reasons. We wished to catch you alive, Master Christophorus, who is now desired at court. We shall transport you in chains, for your gubernatorial misdeeds have displeased our sovereigns. We have herded together your entire crew, who—in the unlikely event that they should have wished it—cannot now do anything to save you, but will be of help in our plantations."

He regarded the burlap sacks with disdain.

"We also wish to secure some particular charts from the circumcised circumnavigator, Moishe," he said, focussing on the bound feet that he assumed—incorrectly—to be Moishe's.

"There is a particular book—once buried like storybook treasure—which for a time was in the possession of the now-departed Grand Inquisitor," the Spanish captain said. "And there is a map. I now command you, in the name of Ferdinand and Isabella, and in the name of the Holy Father to give them to me."

From within the sack, there was only prepling muttering from the bo'sun.

"Provide me one or the other or you shall burn like kindling. Except with screaming."

Then there was more than mumbling. "It is I. Higgs."

"I do not know this name."

"The bo'sun. I led them here to you. I doused their food with the philtre that you gave me. I am your shipboard man, your spy."

"A spy who cannot be silent should be made so," the captain said. In one ampersanding motion, he drew his sword and plunged it into the loquacious sack.

Then he moved one sack to the west.

"My odds in this thimblerig shell game have just increased," he said to Moishe's sack. "The map or the books?"

"You've caught me like a cat-o'-nines in a bag," Moishe said. "So maybe we can talk?"

The captain sliced the burlap open, the newborn boychik Moishe revealed to the world in a rough C-section. The front of his smock was cut and a line of blood seeped from chin to nuts, Moishe halfway to bloodlet kosher.

Moishe stood and ducked behind the three sorcerous maidels, capeless yet still preternatural in the flickering shadows of the fire. He pushed the first one and it was distaff dominos as one fell into the other and finally knocked over the captain who fell onto Columbus.

"Oof," Columbus said.

The scene, a tropical starter kit for Chaplin and Keaton.

Then Moishe ran.

Perhaps it wasn't a noble escape but it was efficient. He sprinted down the beach, turned into the dark forest, and leapt through the brush. I sped down from the palm where I had hidden and dived at the parrot by the fire, my talons out. The mamzer didn't see what hit him. And afterwards, blinded by my claws, he saw nothing at all.

Then I, too, disappeared between the leaves.

Chapter Four

*S*ilence or speed. Moishe chose speed, bounding through the forest, his knees pumping nearly to his chin. A stampede of one disappearing into the shadows and the shadows of shadows, panting and shvitzing like the rainforest itself. I dodged branches and shadows, hovering over Moishe.

Behind us, the stomping bootfalls and shouting of the Spanish. The clatter of metal blades. A quick glance back and we could see the dim lights of their lanterns' crooked progress. They could read Moishe's bushwhacked path. A red carpet through the green. He had made it easier for them to catch him.

And then?

We'd seen how they forged compliance, how they punished resistance.

They cut off hands, pressed steaming pokers into eyes. Flayed, racked, and sliced. And that was better than what they did to Los Indios.

Moishe turned and slogged through the fetid gizzard of a swamp. Oozy shmutz creamed his thighs and thousands of insects stung his skin. I was spared the shmutz, but I, too, was the nosh of bugs. Constellations of irritation and pain formed over me as if I'd dived into a Tabasco vat and my body vibrated with sting. Moishe dunked down into the swamp, taking cover in the clotted water behind a fallen tree.

I found the dark crook of a nearby tree.

So. Those were pearls that were his eyes.

A broch.

I'd blinded the parrot without thought. Fight or flight. I could do both. If there was a playbook, I hadn't just stepped outside the text, I was thousands of miles beyond the margin. So far that I'd come around the other side to the very beginning of the game itself.

An eye for an eye.

Or two eyes for treachery.

The Spanish marched forward. Moishe's trails had disappeared, but desire imagines paths though the thicket, even when none exists. They tromped forward toward where we weren't.

We did our best to continue to not be there.

We waited for a few hours, then Moishe crawled from the swamp, a slime-covered Golem born from the ooze. The dawn sun, too, shlumped out of the star-bit night and we crept through the gloom. The shriek of monkeys and the thrilling of morning birds. The rainforest waking, beginning its workday with this racket.

Nifter-shmifter, what does it matter, as long as you make a living?

In the distance, a warm breeze and a brightness. We were near shore. We continued forward, listening for the Spanish.

I flew ahead on reconnaissance.

Gornisht. Nothing. We were safe.

Moishe crept from the trees and onto the sand. He was coated in a crust of algae, a woodwose, a greeneh, a vilder Yid of the woods.

And one who was so tired he could plotz.

He collapsed on the shadowy sand beneath a fruit tree. We noshed on the flesh of fallen fruit, soft, overripe and dribbling, and thought only of a warm bath.

Then we slept.

For an afternoon or a day, who knew, but we woke in an instant.

"Hei!" the voice said. "Hei, hei!"

I dove into the air, took refuge on a branch out of cutlass range. Moishe vaulted to his feet, crouched in fighting position, and drew the sword he didn't have.

His only weapon: chutzpah.

Before us stood the three beguiling young crones who had attempted to entrap us. The now blind parrot rested on the shoulder of the most bountiful. They, too, did not appear to be armed with anything beyond surprise and the sorcerous terror with which they had just turned our spines into gliver human jelly.

"Put the sword down," the first one said, as if Moishe were brandishing anything but air.

Moishe's hand dropped to his side. He face rested but his eyes scanned the beach for means of escape. Not for nothing was he the Yam Gazlen, the elusive Yiddish scourge of the Indies.

"*Zorg zich nit.* Don't worry," the second said.

"You have your health," said the third.

"And we have killed the governor, Panfilo de Narváez," said the first.

"*Eyn toyt iz far im veynik—iz far im veynik,*" said the parrot.

"Takeh," said the second. "As you say, we killed him only once, though he deserved to die many times."

"As he caused many deaths."

"He sat on his horse gnawing cheese and commanded his men to kill thousands from our village, even as they brought them food," the third said. "Our babies were snatched and broken against rocks. Cuffs, blows, cudgelling. They killed our families. They cut legs and arms off our sisters and mothers, our sons and daughters and fed them to their dogs."

"I cannot forget. My heart tastes it. I breathe its memory," she said.

"I, too, have seen such things," Moishe said. "In worlds both old and new."

The woman considered him.

"We escaped by hiding in a latrine pit covered by palm leaves," she finally said. "I would not recommend it. Then we travelled by night in a canoe. We travelled for many nights, not knowing where.

"Then we came to a small island. For years, we lived there alone and were silent. We did not want to remember even the words for what we knew."

The larger woman continued. "We saw where had once been a small tribe of Jews, but sometime before, they had been murdered: their houses razed, their synagogue burned, their bones, some shoes, candlesticks, all that remained. Except for this parrot." She indicated the parrot on her shoulder. "Which spoke many of their words."

"*Oy vey iz mir. Oy vey iz mir*," the parrot said with impeccable timing.

So, nu, it was a parrot, but though its feathers were brighter than mine, it strutted and fretted like an idiot, full of sound and mamaloshen, but signifying nothing.

"We also found some books of their writing hidden in a tree stump. And so we began to speak again," she said. "These strangers' words."

The women sat with Moishe in the sand. From a small sack hanging around her neck, the first woman retrieved some dried leaves and tobacco that the women assembled. The second woman removed some strands of dried grass, a small stone and a well-worn stick from a similar sack. Then she spun the stick between her palms while the first woman blew. Takeh, like this they could bring even the clay shvants of a Golem to life.

Curls of smoke, then fire. Each woman lit a cigar. The third gave one to Moishe.

They sat together for a few minutes, breathing slowly, exhaling clouds, looking out through the white, almost-creamy smoke.

Then the first woman spoke. "After some years," she said, "the great schooner of Narváez sailed to our island, anchored off the shore, and soldiers landed. We hid deep in the forest but it was a small island and they searched everywhere, digging and overturning. Finally we were found. But our skins were not their quarry. They wanted the Jews' books. We showed them such books as we had, but they threw them away. They sought others. Then they took us as prisoners."

"The devil himself would not say what they did to us," the second woman said. "How they punctured our insides with their shlechteh barbs. Who would wish to remember?"

"*Miseh meshuneh*," the third said. "Curse memory. The past poisons every future."

"And *dos hob ich oykh in dr'erd*. The hell with the present too. It fills with both the past and the bitter future," the first said.

The second woman continued. "We were taken to their ship and chained below with others. For months in the dark, they raped us. Then we were brought to this island. And this trap was set for you. We did what we were asked. They had broken our bones and picked their teeth with the splinters."

"After you escaped, Narváez and each of his sailors raped and beat us," the third said. "And fought and drank and raped and beat us again. As every day. So when they lay shikkered, asleep as if dead, we took their knives, pulled their breeches to their knees and cut off their shlongs.

"They soon woke—who would have expected it?—blood between their legs, pain rampaging through them, each tied to each and the three of us standing before them with arquebuses and swords ready to make portholes in their chests for their souls to breathe the sea air.

"'The good news,' I said to them, 'is that you do not have to eat your own shlongs. The bad news is you must eat each others'.'

"The first clamped his mouth shut and refused. So we sliced his throat and pushed the shmuck through the slit.

"After that, none refused.

"Then we took a canoe and sailed around this island. We knew we would find you."

They had left the Spanish tied together on the shore, one large, emasculated bracelet, a wounded chew toy, soon to be eaten by dogs. Or left to the retributive devices of the islanders for Columbus and his crew had taken a skiff and rowed to their ship, then set sail in search of our ship and Eden.

"It is time for us to leave this island, also," the first woman said.

So we climbed into the canoe.

Moishe. Three übermoyels. Two parrots. An African Grey and the parrot he had blinded.

Without reason.

Did that parrot have a soul?

Feh.

So, nu, I'm like the Spanish now, counting souls and deciding whose blood to spill?

Moishe and the three shiksas rowing furiously against the waves.

Where were they going?

The women were paddling to that most venerable and storied of places.

Away. A new world in this New World.

And their blind parrot knew no more where he was going than a windcock.

Did I know?

Takeh, of course: with Moishe.

Nu, some maven wrote that a book is a dictionary out of order. You ask me, it's the dictionary that's farmisht. It's a story out of order. Like when the Spanish took apart the great stones of Los Indios' temples and remade them into their houses.

And this I know: I follow Moishe.

Why? The stones of my parrot heart. Rebuilt.

❖

The susurration and rhythmic plash of the paddles. The kvetching of the breeze. We rowed in silence. Our journey was our words.

"And then what happened?"

We'd search for our crew who had the map, then find the books and the Fountain. This goal had imprinted itself on our empty insides. Both hope and hopelessness abhor a vacuum.

The ocean rose and fell, a sullen companion that said nothing of the future.

And intermittently, the air-raid siren of the nudnik parrot sounded: "Oy vey iz mir. Oy vey iz mir. Ich hob dich. Ich hob dich." Each phrase a doppelgänger of itself and thus a twin irritation.

I should have left both its eyes and ripped out its tongue.

❖

Now that we all travelled as equals, Moishe assumed his role as captain, scanning the horizon, steering the canoe from its stern, choosing which "away" was our destination.

I noticed something low in the water ahead of us, bobbing up and down with a kind of dopey and water-logged optimism. Moishe decided to investigate.

It was his old friend, the barrel in which he had spent several intimate if directionless days. Lidless, it was driftwood.

But it seemed a fated encounter, and so Moishe hauled it into the canoe, even though there was little unclaimed land in the craft and the barrel could no longer pursue its chosen career effectively. We were squeezed between various provisions that the women had brought from the island. Melons. Coconuts. Small sacks of cassava bread and tobacco. Spanish swords. Dried fish. Wineskin-like bladders filled with fresh water. A bottle that winked its green glass eye at Moishe. Drink me, it said. And he did, making a Shabbos-less kiddush with rum.

It was days without land. Between the four who paddled, two watches were established. While some slept, some wished for sleep. We shared food.

Then, on the starboard horizon: land. On the larboard: a ship.

We gazed at both intently, trying to read their indistinct shapes.

As we rowed closer: "My Yiddishe clipper," Moishe exclaimed. We recognized the flag: a bloodshot eye radiating over an unfinished pyramid.

Nu, Pharoah, we'd like to stay and finish the job, but what with these plagues and all, the working conditions for slaves have really deteriorated.

Moishe gazed at the boat and sighed. "My ship of mutinous bastard chamooleh fools."

Chapter Five

Moishe explained his plan.

Shmuntsing, mysticism, and banditry most often occur under the black chuppah of night. And, as with such things, stealth was important, so we waited until after dark. Moishe gave such a look to the parrot that even such a shlepper as that moronic cloaca-shtreimel knew to be silent. As soon as we were in the lee shadow of the boat, Moishe quietly lowered the barrel into the still water and we once again climbed in as if it were a high-gunwaled dory, a floating womb.

"Zayt gezunt. Be well," Moishe whispered to the women.

"Zay gezunt," they replied and rowed into the darkness, dipping the paddles tentatively into the water.

On deck, all was darkness, sleep or inattention.

We paddled up close to the hull, an infant elephant nuzzled against the flank of its vast and sighing mother. Shh. Sleep, mama, sleep.

The ship's hull was scarred with patches where cannonball or shallows had broken its skin. Until the ship was properly careened and the broad planks replaced, its sides were a Harlequinade of repairs. We searched for such a pockmark, small as two fingers, then Moishe worked at it with the blade of a Spanish dirk until he had reopened the wound.

A hole in the side of the hull.

He had brought the rum-bottle stuffed with a damp shmatte ripped from his ragged and swamp-ripe clothes. Now he would make fire.

In the middle of the sea, it is as simple to procure fire as it is fresh water. Both are possible if you have them already.

The women had given Moishe a firestick, a stone, and some dry grass for kindling. Moishe pressed the end of the stick into the stone with his palms and rubbed back and forth. We should only hope for a happy and propitious ending, nu? Some minutes passed. Then a splash over the rim of the barrel and the grasses were soaked. Moishe—always expecting fate to be a mamzer—removed some still dry grass from a small sack that he had kept in safety in his shirt, and began again.

Eventually, a weak smoke, and then the red spurt of fire. Quickly, Moishe dropped the burning grasses in the bottle and pushed its narrow neck into the wounded hull. The green world of the bottle teemed with smoke. Viperous tendrils would soon be fuming below-deck.

"Let's hope—keneynehoreh—we haven't lit the orlop and its store of gunpowder," Moishe said. "But we will soon know."

The ship came alive. The meshugeneh mariners aboard the *Gopherwood Shmeckel* scuttled fore and aft as a bees' nest disturbed.

We heard them buzzing, running to safety up on deck, some into the rigging.

Moishe tipped the bottle and emptied the burning wad into the ship. He manoeuvred the barrel around toward the bow and held fast to some backstay deadeyes.

Soon, as expected:

"Gevalt!" the crew shouted.

"Fire!"

"Gotenyu, get the piss buckets."

"Lower the hogshead o'er the larboard gunwale."

"Fire!"

"Flames behind the salt pork store."

"Shh! Zog's nisht oys—don't say it!"

And indeed the lovely boucan barbecue fumes of burning meat billowed invitingly from the ship along with an admixture of tar and mouldy lumber—the combined tang, an alter kaker's shvitz, his shoes, and a variety of ailing muskrat. In the fire-fighting fury and smoke-filled hoo-hah, Moishe clambered up the hull, clasping chains, deadeyes, and shrouds, then scaled the mainmast. He was a grievous and avenging angel in a fog of rum and pork-fire and from high up the cross-tree, he proclaimed:

"Nu. Look up, for I am the voice of this cloud of sulphurous and tor-menting flame. I who have turned this ship into a burning bush around which you now scurry farmisht. But don't thank me. I have returned from the dead. That's thanks enough. I whose putz is a great mast which requires no stays. Whose hair is an untamed and piratical porcupinity. Whose grepsn are the fortz of one who has dined on naught but forty years of rats. Whose eyes burn like twin stars and light up treasure maps with their reading. I who is not so easy to get rid of. But who were you expecting? Yoshkeh? The Messiah? A klog, but it is a farkakteh and scurvy world, but which other world would have us? I have returned as your captain and together we shall not perish but shall seek eternal youth and life whether in sea or fire, in earth or air or from the quin-tessence itself. Or in the sheyneh zaftikeh arms of another and their sweet knish. Remember the days that have been, the seasons we have lived, where we might sing, swear, drink, drab, and kill in vengeance as freely as cake-makers do flies, as parrots speak, or as the waves climb and fall as they seek the distant shores of the world. The white smoke—with your consent and articles—elects me again captain . . . if we are able to put the fire out."

The farklemtifying cogworks of the crew required no additional input to become yet more farklemt. Because of the obfuscating fumes of panic and smoke, they did not recognize Moishe but took his voice to be that of a dybbuk or demon of the sea. A Yiddish zombie spirit. When one is truly frightened, all fiends speak your language. In addition to their mortal fear of becoming ship-bound barbecue or drowned pickles in brine, they now felt metaphysical dread. Who was this fallen angel who had climbed the main tree? Moishe had chewed up the sails and—vo den?—overacted. He had expected his supernatural alef beytsim routine to win the hustings with eerie machismo. His crew would rec-ognize and be swayed by yet another inventive scheme of chutzpah and seyhcl by their once-and-fugitive captain, line up obediently, and await further instruction.

Plan B.

"Samuel," he called. "It's Moishe. *Vi geyts dir*—how's it going? You thought I was dead but I'm back."

"*Abi gezunt*," Samuel replied. "But what does it matter who you are. We have a fire to kill."

How do you know if you're a captain?

Moishe clutched hold of a sheet and soared down to the poop and into the midst of the tumult. He began directing the directionless.

"Shlomo, raise the hogshead. Yankel, dunk and fill the bucket then pass it to Samuel. Samuel, pass it to Yahíma. Down the hatch, Yahíma, pass it through to Ham . . ."

The ocean was thus carried below-deck, hand to hand, bucket by bucket, and so quelled the fire.

"Jacome and Trachim, take the charred barrels above-deck, break out the pork, and pitch the smouldering staves overboard."

Clothed in billows, Moishe stood amidship and became captain once again. A captain: the grammarian of ships.

His orders brought order and dinner to the deck. The fire extinguished, the crew gathered for a seder of braised pork, no longer slaves of danger and flame. Moishe, eschewing the treyf, opted for lentils on a trencher of cornbread matzoh.

Moishe did not tell the crew that he started the fire, preferring to leave mythic his sudden appearance in a cloud high above them. It seems we like our leaders to have something wondrous, strange and slightly troubling from their past on their résumé.

Isaac. Samuel. Yahíma. Ham. Shlomo. Jacome. Moishe and me. Gathered amidship around one gap-staved barrel. Yankel, Trachim, others—gathered around another.

Moishe looking into Yahíma's eyes.

The horizon.

And then what happens?

The old love in the arms of the new.

But before that, Samuel launched into: "Everything is not what it seems. Our ship is a new found land. Let me tell you the whole megillah."

His megillah, not: "Ach, so sorry—*es tut mir bang*—we mutinied and acted as shochet butcher on you, marlinspiking your jugular into a Trevi fountain."

Instead, a spiel about a battle.

Shlomo: "We spied the pennant of Spain rising from the sea and we readied for the bubo-poxed bulvans. When we smelled the bilgey rancour of their murderous Spanish breath, I called 'Fire,' and we thrust our cannons through the ports and lit the fuses, and soon cannonballs crashed through the bow-bulwarks of the Spanish *Reale*, and raked across its deck. The surprised souls of many Spanish mariners faded as do visions of baizemer bosoms fade when we wake from a dream."

"But the guns of the *Reale* did not reply," Shlomo said. "Its bow, towering over the forecastle of our ship—let's call it *Mamaloshen's Revenge*—came through the smoke cloud and struck us with a grinding crash. It dug deep, and we were so farmisht we thought we were sinking."

"Our ship—maybe we should name it the *New World Broygez*—rebounded from the shock," Samuel said. "We came alongside the *Reale* and we were like behemoths grappling and groping yardarms, rigging and masts. Then the hand-to-hand fighting began."

"Hand-to-hand?" Jacome said. "More like sword-edge to brainpan. Arquebus to thorax. Fingertip to eyehole. Though my fist followed my pike into the bo'sun's kidneys and filleted his spine so as he was gimped and could but move like a man o' war out of water."

"So," Samuel said. "We vanquished the Spanish in this chutzpenik manner just as our carrack began to plunge into the sea. We killed every one of them and just had time to retrieve our maps, our books, and some other plunder as our ship sank below the waves.

"You stand aboard *The Yellow Star. The Kike's Revenge. The Golem of the Sea*. We are in exile even from our own ship. And we don't even know what to call it. But, as with all Jews, wherever we put our yarmulke is our home. And so what if our home is usually balding? It's amazing what they can do with the desert nowadays. This ship? It's our old ship. Just newer.

"Across this new sea, we have avenged the Jews, Los Indios, and Africans with the deaths of these Christ-Colombizing Spanish. We lanced their chazer pig skinsacks to release their pustular souls to the ether where we hope they will be cauterized by stars."

"What else?" Isaac said, "We should wait for Elohim to cook them with lightning?"

"Takeh. That know-it-all sky-mucking maven?" Jacome said. "He's too busy swinging his twenty-two dimensional putz around some infinite Seraglio."

"Oy," Shlomo said. "The ineffable effing the ineffable."

"What kind of meshugener are you?" said Samuel. "The rabbis say like Cipangu or Cathay, He's just over the next horizon."

Jacome: "And in the meantime, we bump into a gantseh megillah of a continent of immoveable dirt."

"Nu," Isaac said. "He's the eternal converso, always dressed up in somewhere else."

"That's eppes a God?" Yahíma said. "My God would have my eyes shoot flame and my body glow with the warm honey of sex and eternal youth. And He'd make sure my life was catered."

"Fire, sex and food we can get you, yingeleh. And if the map isn't a shyster's sham, we can get you eternal youth, too."

"Feh. I don't have time to wait for life everlasting," Jacome said. "It's enough to have the sound of sword going through bone. And that look in their eyes." He chewed into another mouthful of pork. "If only Spaniards were kosher, I'd be happy getting fat."

"And the gold," Samuel said. "Makes my guts shake and my eyes swell. If only there were a place to spend it."

"What hoo-hah, you chazer," Shlomo said. "As the mystics say, its value is in the size of what isn't there: think of what's not in the Spanish coffers."

"Shlimazl. Think of what's not between your oysgedarteh stick-insect legs," Jacome said. "Just a dribbling thimble."

Shlomo sprung up and plunged his rigging knife toward the leather-and-brimstone body of Jacome. Moishe, who had said nothing, appeared to be drifting keellessly on an inner sea, but his hand shot out and caught Shlomo's arm and twisted it until it clicked like the chambers of a lock. At the same time, he kicked Shlomo's skinny legs out from under him. Shlomo slammed onto the deck. Moishe leapt up and held up his open hand before Jacome's scowling jowls.

"Be a mensch. Each day brings forth its own sorrows," he said, then walked over to the starboard gunwales to look out at the skiffling waves. Shlomo righted himself and sat by the barrel where he remained silent, examining the suddenly intriguing details of his own feet. Jacome glowered at the mizzen, but also said nothing.

Eventually Moishe returned to the others. "I remember the map and the island well: it resembles a tuches sticking out of the sea. And the books are buried in its valley, nu? We do not know where we are on this map—which makes it both simple and difficult to go forward. But I shall chart a course toward where this island might be. Not for nothing, my years davening over maps. I've been to the shvitz house and I'd recognize this rumpy atoll anywhere: it's like the mountainous spotted hiney of my old cheder teacher. But, *af an emes*, less hairy."

Later, we unrolled the map in the captain's quarters. Moishe had asked Shlomo and Ham to make up the morning watch. Jacome, Samuel, Isaac and Yahíma gathered around the captain's table as if we were dissecting a body.

Moishe navigated around the map. There was an island with soundings, cliffs, rivers, bays and inlets clearly indicated, and every particular that would be needed to bring a ship to safe anchorage upon its shores. It was more-or-less apple-shaped, about three leagues across, and had a sheyneh fine natural harbour where we could drop anchor. There were, as Moishe had remembered, two enticingly zaftik hills, like the twin kneydlach of a rotund tuches, which dominated the island. They were farprishtcht-poxed by three marks in red ink: one on the north part of the island, two in the southwest. Moishe explained that they were Hebrew letters. Hey. Vav. Hey. In a valley in the centre of this triangle was a small, neat letter yud written in the same red ink. Buried beneath it: the books.

On the back of the map, the same hand had written this further information:

> Tall tree, south of the valley, top o' the left hill. Bearing a point
> to the N. of N.N.E.

> Ten feet.

> Follow the trend of the east hummock, ten fathoms south of the
> black crag with the face on it.

Once we had found the island and located the valley, we would know where to go. The tree must be the yud. We wouldn't have to ask directions from indigenous birds, rodents, snakes, or the yenta know-it-all trees and their smug, trembling little leaves.

But first we had to find the island.

"See how the current flows between—*vos?*—these two-bit isles, they look like gallstones."

"A rebbe in my shtetl had moles shaped just like them."

"Of course, but *af an emes*, less hairy."

"Actually, if you want to know, he had more hairs than most Jews have tsuris."

"I don't—and I especially don't want to know where he had such troubles."

We would sail north looking for landmarks, for the distinct mole-shaped stippling of islands on either side of our passage. And the tuches would stand out plain as the undercarriage of stars.

Chapter Six

*A*n African Grey–coloured dawn, a crimson feathering near the starboard horizon. The ship sighed as the men shloffed, the breeze scuffling through the sails. Moishe stood in the bow, willing the island to appear in the ghostly translucence.

A sound like stones dropping. He turned and squinted starboard. A dark shape on dark water. The slow movement of shadowy wings or fins swimming close to the surface. The ship's skiff in the distance, rowing away. The undulation of long, tar-black hair. Further away, the obsidian silhouette of an island and the orange glow of bonfire.

"A broch," Moishe said. "Each day brings forth its own sorrows."

I stood on his ragged left shoulder. It remained steady though tears rolled steadily into the thicket of his beard. "I do not want to leave the world, but it seems my world wants to leave me."

Then: "Aaron, I'm glad you're here."

We watched as Yahíma rowed toward shore.

"I wish that we, too, could leave this meiskeit-ugly bloodletting. That we, too, could silently row out of this story and find another one, a story where more blood stayed in the body. Sha. I'm only looking for this treasure, these books, this poxy fountain, because, like a shlemiel, I still believe—keneynehoreh—in life instead of death. But, takeh, it'd be easier to be dead.

"Such pain: my parents. Spain and all those I knew there and those I didn't. Sarah, with whom I thought I could stay young and love forever.

And now this new world and Los Indios. This bellyful of spears and eyes rubbed with pepper. I don't want to forget. But I also don't want to remember.

"I'd build a hospital, a hospice for memory. I'd line its shores with gold and ale and zaftikeh half-dressed nafkehs. We'd call pirates from the seven and imaginary seas. To smash open and plunder our words and memories. Take these things, you buccaneers, spread this farkakteh hoard thin across the shoulders of the world like a pox so we can breathe again.

"And then we could forget."

I jumped from Moishe's shoulder and onto his hand. I bent my head low. Surely it would comfort him to rub the feathers of my neck, and give me pleasure.

"Perhaps the future will rewrite our stories," Moishe said, "if only the Fountain will wash out our skulls and drown our remembering."

"We have rum that does that," I said. "And coca leaves."

"Ach. Each day we scour and soak both inside and out with them. And with blood and gold. But each day we wake again. Each day, its own sorrows."

"Each day ends," I said. "Eventually. Perhaps a month later." I hopped onto the gunwale. We watched as Yahíma rowed into obscurity.

Past and future. We birds remember everything. And nothing. The only words we have are those we haven't forgotten.

We have a different forward and backward. A different up and down.

And so, too, did Yahíma. Pocahontavitz she would not be. She was free to paddle without thinking of us. To find a place where the most dramatic event was the harvesting of tubers. Or the birth of her child.

Soon it was day. We could no longer see the island or its fires. Instead we watched for the shapes of the map to emerge from the blue cerulean of the sea.

⁌⁍

We wended in and out of nights and days. Eventually we came to a region skerried with rocks and an assortment of islands. The map was a star chart and we watched for its constellations.

"Oy. Avast." Samuel said, pointing at an island off the starboard bow. "It does look a tuches—as if some sea-ogre were sticking his hairy nates up at heaven."

Thumbing his nether-nose at God and His insistence on mortality.

Moishe gave the order to sail close-hauled, working us to windward. Halyards were heaved. Sheets rose. Booms swung across the deck, and sails snapped. Our quick ship rippled and shuddered in the thrill of the wind as we approached the island from the south and were soon sailing upon the cyan-blue skirts of its white sand shores.

Some thirty fathoms away, we dropped anchor on the lee side of a small islet that—as mapped—concealed a broad and congenial lagoon. Our landing party would row in skiffs between the islet and a black cragged spit and into this lagoon. From there, we'd bushwhack to the valley, scouting for the tall marker tree, looking for the earth-bound yud under which our treasure lay.

We mustered on the deck, aft of the fo'c'sle and divided into those to come ashore and those to stay.

None stayed.

Nu, when there's treasure, go with the shmendrick who has the spade.

"So," said Moishe, climbing halfway up the fo'c'sle companionway. "I've a word to say. This land upon which our feet soon shall fall is where we find freedom from time's cat-o'-nines, where we find our treasure, those books which will lead us to that fabled freshet of life everlasting. And now, a brocheh, a little kiddush grog. Each one on board has done his duty, alow and aloft, and so let us drink *our* health and luck. And *Baruch atah*, a gantseh sea-cheer for we kings of the ocean."

Each man downed a mugful of schnapps.

The black redaction of booze: some nights disappear into mugfuls of drink and shikkereh song.

We woke, blinking in the Klieg-light of noon, the clapper of day pealing on our uninsulated skulls. Muskrats had revelled in our mouths and left their fuzzy and acrid dreck on our tongues.

"To the island," Moishe hissed, careful not to let his voice drive a spike into his own earholes.

Though far from jolly, we boarded the jolly boats, pointed the bows northeast and began pulling the oars—and the island—toward us. Then the wind blew from starboard and huffed us beyond the veil of the islet and further out to sea.

The crew's faces were furled with determination and the hammer-ache of the morning-after-the-night-before as they madly stroked the oars. I chanced to look larboard and saw the dark cloud of a Spanish ship anchored on the islet's other side. We two boats: two ships that had not passed in the night, but had slept on either side of land like a travelling swain and his farmer's daughter bedmate, separated by bundling board.

"Moishe," I said. "Look."

The Spanish had undoubtedly seen us. Perhaps they had already landed, for we had slept late. There might be a greeting party, ready to skewer us with hospitality and swords.

"Ferkakte," Jacome scowled, "as the chicken's pink nuts in the fox's gob."

We could row only where the wind might take us.

There was movement on the deck of the Spanish ship, then a skull-staving boom and a cannonball plunged into the water a single fathom from our bow.

"I'll not wait to be knacker-sausaged," Jacome said, dove into the water, and swam toward shore.

Another blast and a cannonball divoted the water close enough to Jacome to pull him under. A moment later and he emerged spluttering. Samuel reached out an oar but Jacome turned, disgusted, and resumed his churning.

Another shot from the Spanish eight-pounders.

The wind changed. It rose and with it the peaks of the waves. We lost sight of Jacome in a valley between whitecaps. Both of our jolly boats were blown across the islet's stern and now into its lee shore, closer to the Spanish ship. Still the waves pulled us from land.

Another crack of powder and a cannonball smashed the other jolly boat into eggshell halves. Blood ran into the sea. The men hung onto the two broken hulls.

The crew in our boat rowed furiously toward them.

Another iron ball plunged into the gaping mouth of the sea as we reached the other boat.

Isaac held onto the boat with his single hook.

The cannonball had removed both his legs from his already depleted inventory.

One eye, one arm.

A firkin of blood, much of it now spilling from his body.

Much suffering. We hauled him into the boat.

"I remember," he said. "My grandfather carved me a little horse. Its shmulky little shoulders, and, after a time, its broken legs. But this little wooden tchatchke looked at me with such tenderness. I kept it close to me. I had nothing . . ."

He smiled at the memory.

"It waits for me."

He closed his single eye and died.

Five sailors clung to the gunwales around us. Samuel held onto Luigi del Piccolo, who was too weak to hold on himself.

There was a long sheet coiled in the bow. Moishe passed me one end. "Fly to the island," he said. "Tie this to a tree."

I rose then fell, rose then fell. It took me three tries to rise into the air and travel the twenty fathoms to the island. It was three tries also to knot the rope around a mangrove and then alight upon its root.

Several cannonballs crashed into the foliage beside me.

Moishe and the men began hauling on the sheet. Either they would move or the island would.

It was the boat.

It approached the land, barking its nose against mangrove roots. Moishe and the crew scrambled to shore. There was no time to futz around. The Spanish continued to fire and they would soon send crewmen after us.

Samuel, Shlomo and Ham hauled Isaac's body onto the mangroves. We would hide in the interior of the islet and decide what to do next.

First, though, the wounded must be nursed. Carpentered. Or buried.

At sea, we would have wrapped Isaac in a sail, sewn it up, stitching it—according to tradition—once through the septum of his nose. When we couldn't spare a sail, we shrouded our dead in a section of Torah scroll and released them to the sea. Luigi would pipe a dirge as they were taken by the water. But now the Spanish were close by. We had but time to carry Isaac to a swamp and cover him in stones.

It's doubtful that he would have wanted us to say kaddish, but Moishe said the prayer as a stand-in for other words.

"Yisgadal veyiskadash shmey raboh," he said.

"Omeyn," we answered.

With Isaac gone, we were one short of a minyan, the required ten for prayer.

"What does it matter?" Shlomo said. "Where's our eleventh putz-finger God?"

"We speak even if no one hears," Samuel said. "So. Azoy. We hear."

"And that helps?" Shlomo said. "Let's ask Isaac and see what he hears."

Luigi waved him away from Isaac. "My father would say that we have eternal life. Until we die. And we have God. Until we look for Him."

"Perhaps," Moishe said. "But my father used to say, 'A question is its own answer.' And I'd ask, 'What does that mean?' And he'd say, 'Exactly.'"

We began again to make for the lagoon, bushwhacking our way through the mangroves and the godless synagogue of leaves.

The lagoon. Rivulets of light eeled over the rippled sand and through the turquoise water. The soughing air. One sigh fits all. Or causes a satisfied susurration so deep in the mouth, it's in your tuches.

The men dove into the water and began dog-paddling to the main island. Moishe swam on his back, kicking with fury, his arms raised above the water, holding his arquebus aloft like the Lady of the Lake brandishing a sword.

I flew.

The men clambered out of the lagoon, the water varicosing down their skin.

"Hit zich! Look out," Samuel shouted. He pointed at a dark shape that flickered between the trees like images in a flip book.

The men pulled out their wet dirks and cutlasses. Moishe loaded his arquebus, the only sailor who had had sufficient seychl to keep his weapon dry.

Was a man running in the woods? Had the Spanish already landed? The strange noises of the island became amplified by our apprehension.

"Hell is empty and the dybbuks run free," Samuel said.

"Nu," Moishe said. "We can stand tsitering quaking on the shore. Or we can hide in the woods. Where they can't see the Yids for the trees."

We crossed the beach and headed into the dark green of the forest. Our landmark for orienteering: the tall tree south of the valley.

This was finding a needle in a pine forest.

I flew above the forest canopy. The two cheeks of the island rose round and verdant. Between the two, a valley. A river quick with rapids and waterfalls.

Is the river the movement or the water? Is the story the words or what happens?

Without either one—nu—no river.

In the distance, several trees rose above the others, bodies both dark and colourful emerging from the tangle of its branches.

I saw no sign of our ship. The Spanish had either taken it and sailed away, or sank it.

I flew back into the forest and found my captain's shoulder. Which tree marked the yud under which the books would be found?

In which direction would we travel?

Forward. We could revise that later.

Shlomo walked before us, chopping through the brush with a machete-like blade. We trudged inside the forest's closed and clammy hand.

Again, the dark shape through the woods and Moishe raised his musket and fired. The forest echoed with the shot. A Gotenyu wail and then the *fshhht* of an arrow.

"Gevalt," Shlomo cried. And he fell, his shoulder punctured. The arrow had stuck him through the scar of the "Thou shalt not kill" commandment cut across his chest. Around the rough wood shaft, a tsitseh of blood began to thread down his side.

"So that settles it," Samuel said. "Man, not animal."

"But Spanish?" Luigi del Piccolo said. "With bow and arrow?"

"No matter who or what makes you bleed, the blood is still red," Moishe said.

"If your blood is red," Samuel said.

"Azoy, I'm not looking to have this confirmed," Moishe said. "And maybe we should stop so much of it spilling from Shlomo." He made a bandage from his damp clothes and bound the shoulder.

Two of the remaining able-bodied—Trachim and Yankel—helped him up and we continued toward the tree.

We shlepped on, our flesh made torpid in the heat as if replaced by a ballast of sand. The forest was a shvitz—a steambath—so thick, heavy and sluggish was the air. At this point, treasure hunting was 1 percent slogging and 99 percent perspiration.

We leaked with heat.

Ach. What am I saying? What do I know from shvitzing?

Leave it to those who have sweat glands. I panted like a dog and fanned my wings.

Our less-than-a-minyan trudged on through several grim hours. There was no joy in the honeyed shafts of light that penetrated the dark canopy. Only the gloom of overshadowed distances. From time to time, Shlomo moaned. It wasn't kvetching, but rather pain weeping from his damaged body. We felt ourselves bewitched, severed from everything we had once known—somewhere, far away, in another existence perhaps. Nu, maybe the existence where we weren't spooked.

What we remembered returned to us with the shapeless unrest of a dream, a dull and unsettling ache. We shlepped through this strange green world of unfamiliar plants and silence. Yet this stillness did not resemble peace, but the beyzeh evil redaction of an implacable force brooding over a retenish inscrutable intention.

We had thus proceeded for about half a mile and were approaching the brow of a plateau when Luigi del Piccolo, who had already ascended, began to shriek and kvitch. "Ayyy . . ."

Surely scorpions sawed his nuts while crabs made hand-shadows in his alimentary canal.

The others began to run in his direction.

"He can't 'a found the treasure," Samuel said, hurrying past us from the right, "for that's still a shlepp past the tree, and the tree is surely a good plod yet."

Indeed, as Moishe and I found when we reached the spot, it was something very different. At the foot of a big pine veined in creeping vines that had partly lifted some of the smaller bones, there was a human skeleton, with a few shmatte-shreds still clinging to its ribs.

"Once, he was a sailor," Samuel said, examining the rags. "Nu, this is good sea-cloth."

"Azoy," Moishe said. "Who were you expecting? Meshiech—the Messiah—maybe?"

"B-b-but what sort of a way is that for bones to lie?" Luigi said, still tzitering trembling in fear. "It's unnatural."

And nu, indeed, it was uncanny: but for some disarray (the work, perhaps, of the creatures that had noshed upon him or of the vines that had gradually wormed through his bones) the poor shlepper lay perfectly straight—his feet pointing in one direction, his hands, raised above his head like a diver's, pointing directly the opposite way.

Moishe stood over the bones. "What's this dead shmendrick telling us?"

"H-he's marking half past twelve o' the clock?" Luigi said.

"Could as well be quarter past nine, or any other time," Moishe said.

"As always, it's hard to know which way is up."

"That's the emes truth," Moishe said. "But this is a compass. And there," he said, pointing to a mountain crag that appeared through the trees, "is the tip-top o' the left tuches, sticking up like a fat bialy bun. Take a bearing along the line of them bones."

Samuel removed a compass from the leather bag that hung across his chest. He wiped it dry then held it over the skeleton and aligned it with the peak of the exposed tuches.

"N of NNE," he said.

"Nu?" said Moishe.

"Nu what?" I asked.

"Fly up and look for the tree."

I did. There was only one tree that stood out along the bearing marked by the skeleton.

"Nu?" Moishe asked.

"Nu." I said. "This way." I pointed with my beak.

And so we marched toward the tree.

"So," I asked quietly. "This skeleton—Spanish, I wager—is it a trap?"

"Ech. Probably a trap. But if you don't know where else to go, go toward the tumel—the action."

We came to another large tree.

But it was just a tree.

We continued descending into the valley between the two hummocks of tuches. The forest began to thin. Rainforest pattern baldness. The way ahead became increasingly clear as more island scalp was revealed.

Then before us: a behemoth of a tree, a darkwood steeple rising halfway to the sky. Hollowed out, we could have made a carrack whole from its Brobdingnagian trunk.

Or all hold hands and only just span it.

There could be no doubt. This was the tree.

Chapter Seven

I leapt from Moishe's shoulder and flew around the trunk. We would soon sing—keneynehoreh—kvelling with joy at what we had uncovered.

Beneath the vast branches of the tree, an acre of shadows. I beheld that place on the earth where the red yud—the first unutterable letter of YAHWEH—would be so inscribed. Where from beneath its imaginary calligraphy, we would cause the books to rise from their tomb, would cause them to be born.

Of course, eternal life would come from such a place: for Jews, it's all kishkas and digestion. The karkashteh darkness below. The cloaca. A hole in the ground. We would enter the divine hamantash sex of Shekinah God the mother.

Such an ark!

Thanks God it's only five hundred years till they invent therapy.

I was the first of our party who could see behind the tree.

A broch.

Es vert mir finster in di oygn: all I see is darkness and, gevalt, the darkness just got darker.

Halevay.

There was already a deep hole.

The books were gone.

The mamzer shyster chazers—pestiferous, lice-souled, pig-bastard thief-abortions. They'd taken our treasure. Whoever they were.

We needed this like God needs a nether hole.

Our lives would end in ending, and not in endless unendingness. Our souls would lisp into the void, a sulphurous fortz from the back end of our mortal hineys.

I flew up into the shade of the leaves.

Not only would our lives end, but they would end soon—after the crew discovered the books missing from their subterranean shelf. This would not be a time for a Mishnaic discussion of the intricacies of the mind/body question but a time of cleaving one from the other, ribboning with blood the flesh that festoons our mortal souls.

I signalled to Moishe. "As my last captain always said, '*Besser a miyeseh lateh eyder a sheyneh loch.*' 'Better an ugly patch than a beautiful hole.'"

Samuel, Luigi del Piccolo, Shlomo with his supporters, and the other men walked around the left side of the tree. Moishe went to the other side and emerged on the right of the excavation.

They all looked down into the emptiness.

"Nu?" Samuel said. "This, eppes, is a treasure?"

"Oy," Luigi said. "Oy." Then, "Time grows longer only to make room for more sorrow."

Shlomo said nothing, but lifted his arms from Trachim and Yankel's shoulders. He drew his sword and looked up at the sky. It was not clear who he would fight. If it were God, it would be catch-as-catch-can. Besides, it was unlikely Shlomo's blade were keen enough to slice infinity in two. Then he looked at Moishe. His eyes narrowed with the ravenous intent of a rat.

A sound from behind the treebole. An off-kilter, unmade bed of a skinny shlumper stepped out and stood twitching behind the men. If Shlomo's eyes were rats, this Spaniard's eyes were the febrile deadlights of a meshugener ferret.

A fonfetting mumble from the man's leafy beard.

Shlomo turned and swung at him with his sword.

Like an animal springing quick from a thicket of leaves, the man retrieved a stout sabre from its nest of rumpled rags and pushed it deep below Shlomo's sternum.

"Ach!" Shlomo sighed and fell backwards into the empty hole, still spitted by the Spaniard's blade.

A man's body may be scabbard for a sword.

And his life, too, may become missing treasure at the bottom of a pit.

The oysgedarteh scrawny Spaniard raised his bladeless hands in guileless surrender as he was surrounded by our crew.

Samuel retrieved Shlomo's cutlass from the lip of the hole where it had fallen. He would cleave the man's neck.

"Wait," Moishe said. He lowered himself into the hole and pulled the Spaniard's sword out of Shlomo's kishkas. Shlomo did not move.

Then, without looking back, Moishe climbed up.

"Now, kaddish."

"*Yisgadal veyiskadash shmey raboh,*" we said and pushed dirt into the pit, burying Shlomo and our hopes of finding the books and immortality.

The Spaniard was a gibbering shlimazl. Admittedly he gibbered less when Moishe requested that Samuel remove the porging blade from his gizzard.

But he gibbered enough for us to understand that he had been marooned on the island for years. A heretic, he had been condemned. But he escaped into the wilderness and was so marooned when his crew sailed. Most importantly, he had dug up the chest of books, hidden the books in a cave at the northern end of the valley, and filled in the hole.

Moishe pointed at the deep concavity, now a grave.

"This is how you shtup a hole with dirt?"

"I know—knew—they—they come back for the books. A-a-and to kill me. I who ran. I bury the chest again and f-f-fill the hole. The Spanish—"

"The Spanish who now sail from the island?" Moishe asked.

"Yesterday, with spades and with r-r-ropes they came. They dug up the chest. I w-w-watched from the m-m-mountaintop. If they saw me, you would speak now to b-b-bones, red mud, or a ghost. When they break the chest open, they will find the K-k-king, the Queen, the Grand Inquisitor. Dolls, all made of bones, my h-h-hair, my own dung."

He was encouraged to take us to the cave: a rope around his neck, a short blade pressed to his back.

If there were blazes on the trees or some discernible path, they existed only in the X-ray world of his desiccated brain. But the maroon, Luis Sera del Rojo Oscuro, led us surely between the dark trees of the valley and to a series of cave openings in the east.

As he stood before the second cave mouth, he began to twitch uncertainly.

"Nu?" Moishe asked.

Del Rojo Oscuro walked into the cave, his gaze still weaving nervously.

"Something wrong?"

Samuel pulled back on the noose. "Now is no time for meshugas. For funny business."

Del Rojo Oscuro: "Th-th-the books—they are behind these . . ." At the back of the cave, there was a scattering of rocks tumbled over some parchment-like leaves. "But . . . they were h-h-here," he said and began lifting the leaves and gazing at the baleful empty earth below. "I wrapped them like b-b-babies and hid them under rocks."

He lifted another leaf. Beneath: a gold coin like a Eucharist wafer that had seen better caves.

"Spanish," he said bitterly, picking it up. "They have entered my cave. The b-b-books. They have taken."

"Have you some boat?" Moishe said.

"A pitful coracle," he said.

"Take us there," Moishe said. "Aaron: find out if the Spanish mamzers have weighed anchor."

I flew to the sky. I would break into the quintessence, suck milk from God's fulsome moons.

Or schnapps.

I would pump my heart till it brast and my body would shisn come like the radiant feathers of shooting stars. Already I was heavy with the tsuris of humans. I needed this? I would escape like Yahíma. Though this, Moishe did not know: the thing with feathers, his pain. How I wore it like a thorn-crown.

From the sky, I could see the Spanish ship, anchored now off the eastern shore.

We ran toward the coracle. We would save the books.

Sha.

We would steal eternal life from the Spanish.

And scatter or gather what we couldn't forget into—what?—some alter kaker codger dictionary of memory.

Feh. What was that the rabbis said about writing? It's the art of remembering what you read but forgetting where you read it.

We arrived at a rock-strewn shore. A small spit stuck a tongue into the froth. Under a farvorfeneh jumble of branches, Del Rojo Oscuro had hidden his coracle on the lee side. The boat was but a small carapace of goatskin, tree branches and curved bones from the rib cage of a Leviathan. There were no oarlocks, but there was a single paddle. It, too, was made from the bone of a giant. Perhaps a whale.

There was room for one mariner only. Or one mariner and his parrot.

"Wait for us," Moishe said.

"Where were you thinking we'd go?" Samuel said.

"Azoy," Moishe said. "Then don't eat each other."

"Jews," Luigi said. "I don't touch the stuff."

"We're not even kosher," Samuel said.

"It's our cloven hooves," Luigi said. "Besides, we're stringy. Who wants Jew between the teeth?"

"I stick to unbaptized babies. They're much juicier."

We put to sea. Moishe and I. Hope may give a man strength, but not sense.

How exactly we would David the Goliath of a Spanish galleon, I didn't know.

"I once told Sarah that if the only choice is defeat, then even that is bound to fail," Moishe said.

"Make sure not to tell the Spanish," I said.

Navigating in the coracle was like walking on water. It's not that hard if you're related to God. But we ended spluttering and dunking, up to our tsitskehs in the drink. We did more spinning than moving forward. Eventually, Moishe broke its eely back and we were able to navigate—our path the path of a Celtic snake—around the island to where we expected the galleon to be.

Two cables offshore, there was a stunted forest of three bare trees.

It was the Spanish ship. Sunk beyond its crosstrees. Our fearsome Goliath resembled a sodden and frightened rat.

A shlimazl was clinging to the middle of the three trees.

Are those the books in your britches or are you just glad to see us?

He wasn't glad to see us.

He grasped the mast like the last autumn leaf in a gale. We had little to offer him.

"Should we brain you and then seize your books?" Moishe looked up at him and asked. "Batter your skull or paunch you with a stake?"

"Cut his wezand with a knife," I said.

"What's a wezand?" Moishe asked.

"Sounds like the beginning of a joke," I said.

Nu:

There was a rabbi, a priest, a shaman.

"What would you like them to say at your funeral?" one of them asks.

The priest says, "His life was a humble offering to the glory of God."

The shaman says, "He was a hawk and had the strength to eat the eyes of darkness."

"Both very nice," the rebbe said.

"And what would you like them to say at yours?" the others asked.

"'Look, he's moving!'" the rebbe said.

The shmegegge up the mast said nothing. Maybe it was a problem with terminology.

"The wezand? It's a gorgl, a throat," I said. "Come down or we will slice yours." Certainly my logic was patchy, however my delivery was impeccable and the man began to descend the timber.

He had no books, but instead a parrot in his pants. Azoy. A huge and colourful Macaw.

Love? Not "by any means necessary"—if the bird had feelings, he wasn't saying. Apparently the mamzer mariner had entroused the bird in order to have a little something to nosh on later.

We liberated the bird. He had but little thought or gaze for me but flew without hesitation to shore. Perhaps in later years, during times of reflection, there was a place for me amidst his forest of regrets and missed connections when he remembered the noble and shapely African Grey who saved him from the twilight-hued teeth and dawn-red mouth of the Spaniard.

Me: Brightly coloured Macaw down a Spaniard's pants.

You: Bedraggled grey me-liberator adrift on the goy-tormented sea.

With one hand Moishe held fast to the mast. With the other, he held a blade up to the sailor who, like most sailors, could not swim, could not escape.

But *vo den*? What did we expect?

Like sailors in the ocean, we are surrounded by life, yet do we know how to survive it? Azoy.

So now we ask this quivering tsiterdiker cabinboy, "What happened to the books?"

Having dug up the chest and finding it filled with a dreck-sculpted triumvirate of little voodoo big machers, the Spanish had blundered into the maroon's cave. How?

"We captured a shaman on another island. He read tracks that led to the cave and we found the books under some rocks. We carried them to our ship and began to sail away. But our ship began to sink. Somehow it had become full of holes.

"'All hands below deck,' our captain ordered. We thought we were to patch the hull and bail out the water, but the captain battened the hatches and locked us in. He shot holes in all the jolly boats except one. Then he took the books and the shaman, got into the jolly boat, and rowed away.

"We tried to staunch the leaks, but it was like trying to plug up a raincloud and the ship began to sink. We broke onto the deck with axes. Many leapt into the ocean and drowned.

"I climbed the mast. I could see the captain and the shaman. And a reed moving strangely across the water. Then a man surfaced near the captain's gig. He spatchcocked the captain from behind then climbed aboard, took the books, and threw the captain's body into the sea. Then he had the shaman continue to row."

Moishe took the sword from the sailor's gorgl, untied a red sash from around his own waist, and offered it to the rattled tsedreyter mariner.

As if his death would not be colourful enough.

But Moishe would row our coracle and tow the quivering trawl of the sailor behind us.

Where would we sail? Into the "And-then-what-happened." Azoy. Where was that? The man, the shaman, and the books couldn't just keep rowing. Sha. Did they think they could just Noah it across the ocean in a pea-green shifl and find eternal life? They must have made for the island. We'd catch them.

Then we'd devise some Crusoe plan to build a boat out of logs, chutzpah, chazerai and tree sap, and be gone.

And live forever.

Shoyn tsayt! It's about time.

Chapter Eight

*W*e travelled as far up and down as to and fro—for the waves rose and fell as if we were on horseback. Moishe made repeated attempts to rein in our filly, to bring her to sand, but the wind rippled in the long leaves of the palms and pulled us according to its own fickle whim. We went around a point of the island and found ourselves before the opening to a long cove.

"Well blow my briny petseleh with an onion," Moishe said. "Unless my eyes be lying shysters yabbering duplicitous yarns, there anchored in that cove is the *Gopherwood Shmeckel.*"

And there it was, our freylecheh flag flying high above our ship, snug and intact in turquoise waters. And there were sailors on board. At least two. One had colourful feathers fireworking from his kop.

Another feather in the cap of holocaust haberdashery plucked from the bright tails of birds.

This must be the shaman and the strange underwater bulvan who made *naseh arbet*—homicidal wet work—of the Spanish captain. We paddled our shifl abaft of the *Shmeckel,* hoping to remain undetected, else an arquebus make new orifices through which we might suffer.

We were able to nestle in the shadows beneath the taffrail unnoticed and preparing to board.

Then:

"You putz-faced elf-dreck. You couldn't haul flowers from your scupper hole if it were springtime in your pants."

The unmistakeable voice of Jacome el Rico. Speaking to the shaman. As was his custom, he was fostering intercultural relations with all the delicacy and sensitivity of a pitchfork.

In the eye.

Moishe called to him. "Gonif! You only live because the sharks couldn't keep you down and breched up your festering meiskeit fleysh."

There was much joy in our reunion. Also rum, good nosh, and catching up.

"I should wait with you like a putz to be blitzned by Spanish cannon-balls? So, I jumped ship and swam to shore. Then when the Spanish were close, I made a breathing tube of hollow reeds, tied stones to my feet, walked the seafloor. Then I shtupped the cutlass between the hull's wale planks and made holes."

"There's a crack in everything. That's how the outside gets in," Moishe said.

"And bilgewater," I said.

"It was my good mazel I found the captain and the shaman skiff-scarpering with the books as the ship sank," he said. "Then we rowed to the *Gopherwood Shmeckel* and sailed it into the cove. I chained this alter kaker to the mainmast just in case, but kept him well fed and in drink."

The shaman smiled affably at us, showing no indication that he understood anything, not even Jacome's saliva-spraying narrative of spice, shvitzing, sandpaper and bile.

Dusk. Sunset the vivid crimson of blood sausage.

We went into the captain's cabin. Jacome led the shaman on a rope behind us.

"*Ich hob rachmones*—pity. At night, I bring him in like an old dog."

There was an oak table, big as a shul door. Jacome lit the few candle-stubs that remained. Shadows like lost souls wavered across its surface.

And swaddled in blankets like the baby Yoshke mangered in a dark barn, our quarry finally lay before us. As if merely objects in a real world. The books.

"So now we should also expect the Messiah with his trumpets, angels, zombie line dances and horas?" Moishe said. "Maybe leave the door open."

"I don't count even hatched chickens. For beslubbering basherteh fate waits to splutter feathers," Jacome said, ever bright as rainbows shining from the hintn of a pisher pony. "And we only have two of the five books."

"Feh," Moishe said. "Our patriarch Jacob begat twelve and he had but one ball swinging in his covenantal sack. We have two."

He began to unwrap the books. Jacome brought straight-edge, compass, protractor and unintelligible kvetching.

The pale, thin skin of Torquemada's book. Onion-coloured. I thought of weeping.

Columbus's book. It seemed only weary.

Moishe opened both books to their first pages. Then, like a Ziegfeld Folly of two, turned their pages together to other pages.

There were maps, charts, diagrams. He measured. He calculated distances between letters. He counted words, the tsitskehs of demons, the tongues of fire. He read backwards, boustrophedon like an ox turning in a field, he imagined encryptions, codes and erasures. He held pages up to the light, looking for palimpsests, moon-writing, knife-cuts in the vellum. He drew maps on cloth and held them over the pages.

Once I'd been carried in a book with a parrot-shaped hole cut into it. And now, *dacht zich*, it seemed, there was a Fountain-shaped hole in these two books. Each black letter grinned like a goblin or beyzeh wicked scar but said nothing.

I remembered the old story about Rabbi Simeon who was farklemt from darkness and suffering. He davened from one twilight to another and back again until his lips cracked, his back ached, and he saw double.

"Adonai, Adonai," he said. "What should I do?" But ha-Shem said nothing. Eventually, in despair, the rebbe took an ancient scroll from a dusty shelf and rolled it open to an obscure passage. He lit some candles, scrawled prayers on the shul floor, and chanted a spell to raise spirits from the dead.

"O ruekh, ruekh, O spirit," the rebbe said. "How shall I guard against this evil and pain?"

"Give me one of your eyes and I'll tell you," the spirit said.

And so Rabbi Simeon gouged out an eye and gave it to the spirit. "Now," he said to the spirit. "Tell me."

"The secret," the spirit said, "is 'watch with both eyes.'"

What could the rabbi do? He fell to his knees and wept with his one remaining eye.

Then he said, "*Besser a miyeseh lateh eyder a sheyneh loch*—better an ugly patch than a beautiful hole," covered his socket with a patch, and became a pirate.

Ach. What did we need to sacrifice? We had lost much already.

A whole world.

Our heart was like a genizah, filled with broken things.

Sarah. Sarah's father's books. Moishe's parents. Moishe's father's book.

And I no longer had words for what I had lost. Feygl words. Bird loshen.

What had I lost?

Feh. As I said, there are no words. Except these farkakteh words.

Moishe had turned away from the table and ordered himself to splice the mainbrace: to drink. He had found a bottle of schnapps and was alternating swigs with Jacome.

"Always, we *farblondje* wander *farmisht*, confused, only ever with half a map. Farkakteh Columbuses bumping into continents. *Bereishith*—since the beginning—the world all shards. So I thought these two books would be enough."

"Like a sloop with only part of its hull," Jacome said and grepsed with the magnitude and gaseous enthusiasm of an exploding star. Then he sucked the remaining rum from the bottle and threw it to the floor.

Where it rolled balefully, impotently, beneath a chair.

"And the other books?" I asked Moishe.

"In my *finsterer cholem*—my dream-boiled brain—I imagined them among Sarah's father's books. My own father's book. And the book I cut to hide you. But *ver veyst?* In this half-baked Golem of a world, they could be anywhere. Buried, fish-knocked, in the library of a putz-faced pottle-snouted yak-sucker, or dropped in a well outside an eastern dacha.

"An umglik! So we thought that some mumbo-jumbo from a shtik-dreck Inquisitor and a shmendrick explorer would lead us anywhere? What do they know of the left-side world?"

"Azoy," I said. "We're the shlimazls who believed the whole megillah."

"You kvetch like milk-hearted piglets," Jacome scowled. "The Spanish flesh which feeds our swords will now be sweeter. The wenches batamt more delicious."

"*Ech. Vemen art es?*" Moishe said. "What does it matter? *Odem yesoydeh mey-ofor ve-soyfeh le-ofor*—man comes from the dust and in the dust he will end. In the meantime, it's good to drink."

Whatever he felt about this philosophy, Jacome obliged with another bottle.

"*L'chaim,*" he said. "To life."

"Just not immortal life," Moishe replied.

"The books?" I asked.

"Useless dreck from a rebbe's tuches," he spat. And swept them from the table. "*Yemakh shmom.* May their memory be destroyed forever."

"You know," a quiet voice said. "I could tell you. I could tell you how to find the Fountain."

Oy vey iz mir! I could have laid an ostrich egg, a rabbi's beard, and a tablesaw altogether.

It was the shaman, speaking perfectly intelligible Spanish.

"I know where it is," he said.

My tongue and the tongues of Moishe and Jacome positioned themselves as if they too were about to pronounce something intelligible.

But nothing intelligible was intelligible.

"W-w-w . . . ?"

"My people know where this Fountain is. We have always known," the shaman repeated.

Moishe, coming to, brought a chair to the old man. "Please," he said. Then: "This tsedreyter confused meshugener sailor"—he indicated Jacome—"is not a subtle man. Sometimes savage, sometimes a beast. His life has been unjust and perilous."

Moishe quickly distinguishing himself from Jacome, though he had neither untied the shaman nor offered him much beyond the most basic necessities of water and hardtack.

"He means no disrespect or unkindness. Always he has rachmones—compassion—for others. He's a mensch. Especially with a venerable alteh rov like yourself. So, please, zayt moykhl, accept my apologies as captain.

"Nu, Jacome. Something for the good rebbe to nosh on."

Purple midnight came to Jacome's face. Stars collapsed and sucked all light from the room. And he reached for his cutlass.

"A *shandeh far di goyim*," Moishe said. "You disgrace us in front of others." And before an inch of Jacome's blade had slid from the scabbard, Moishe had the point of his sword pressed against Jacome's gullet, ready to make pretty red snowflakes from his windpipe.

"You would like to be delivered to eternity, already?"

Jacome released the hilt. "So, my name is Jacome. I'll be your kelner, your server. What can I get you?"

The shaman was untied and food was brought to the table. Salt meat. Dried fruit. Hardtack. A jar of something obscure. It may have been patriarch's brain or ground and sauced unicorn tuches. But it was sweet tsimmes.

The shaman was hungry and noshed with great spiritual focus. Finally, the remedial ceremony of basic sustenance complete, he told us his name: Utina in his native language of Timucuan. He told us it meant "My land."

Later.

"You've been to the Fountain?" Moishe asked.

"I have returned from there."

"And you have eternal life?"

"I have not yet died. Let's wait and see."

Ach. It's the emes truth. We are all, af an emes, immortal. Until we die.

And maybe I'd be the world's greatest violinist. If I had fingers.

"So," Utina asked Moishe. "What would you do with your undying life?"

"There was a maidel, a girl. Nu, a woman now," Moishe said.

"Always a girl," Utina said. "Or many."

"No, I know it's meshugeh but this one I have never forgotten, and my parents dead. I would search for her: Sarah. I'd bring water from the Fountain. We could both be young again. Or, nu, in a thousand years, this old will seem young. Ach, if I find her. If she still lives."

"Cockstubble," Jacome said. "They're all dead. Or broken. All those we once knew. Or suckling grandchildren. Mad. They—"

I interrupted. "Does the Fountain bring back youth?"

"When I was a girl," the shaman said. "My mother caught a shimmering thing. Wings like blue light through rainclouds. A butterfly. I held it on my finger and watched. Then I crushed it in my fist. I always remember."

He smiled cryptically and said no more.

"When I was a girl"? Un shoyn! If my grandmother had beytsim! The shaman was a yenta.

Nu. So maybe she was a shyster only trying to escape, telling us some bubbameisse cockamamy story to buy herself more time. Extending her own mortality as long as she was able.

Or maybe she was an alter bok after all. An old goat.

Nu. Maybe the fountain was a giant hormone bath. A mikveh where you became soft. Azoy, looking closely, her skin was like paper, crumpled and recrumpled a thousand times. Soft and fissured with fractals.

But I wasn't volunteering to fly into her gatkes on a reconnaissance mission.

Gevalt. But whatever was there, she had more to say than the three books that weren't there, and was emes easier to understand than the two we had.

Besides, when you have nowhere to go, any direction is as good as another.

Chapter Nine

"*Let* the mutinous mamzers become the desiccated shlub-leather they deserve," Moishe said. "Let them become fasheydikt bewildered with loss and loneliness. I maroon them as they would have marooned me on my own ship. As they would have marooned my blood from my body. I never forget. Only a fool remains a fool."

And so we did not go back to the island for the rest of the crew. Instead, we turned our stern to the shore, and we raised sail toward the horizon. Utina nestled in the quarterdeck, navigating: watching the shape of waves, the scent of wind, the curl of cloud above us. They say that at any time, such spirit wayfarers can detect five different currents in the open water. And many more of ghosts. They draw islands out of the sea, tectonic Prosperos, reverse dowsers.

Utina imagined us a path beyond the horizon and soon we were beyond land, except as it appeared in the second sight of her internal compass.

Dawn. Immense veils of spray rose against our bulwarks and were caught by the wind and whirled away. Bars of purple cloud stretched before us and the green water frothed with delirium. The sky became mauve and scarlet in the east, kishka-coloured. Then west off the starboard bow appeared a vast mass, furlongs in length and breadth, the pale hue of a maideleh's thighs. It floated on the water, its innumerable long arms radiating from its centre and curling and twisting like a nest of snakes, a monster of flying lokshen. It had no perceptible front: like

Adonai, all was face or not-face. It seemed blind and without instinct, more island than living thing, but it undulated on the billows, an unearthly, formless, chance-like apparition. Then without warning, the water stilled and it disappeared.

"There," Utina said, pointing with her gnarled alteh kokeh finger, which was a trick finger, not pointing forward, but askew like Adam looking sneakily Eve-ways when God in Eden came down to kvetch, post-apple.

Utina with her eye fixed on an indistinct place on the long coastline.

Soon enough, Ponce de Leon would call it La Florida and bring Christianity, cattle, horses, sheep, lemons, pistachios, discount stores, disease, the Spanish language. Death.

People would come here to die or not to die. Shalom. Who could tell?

But now, there were no boats in the ocean, nor sign of people on the rock-strewn beach as we dropped anchor. We climbed into a skiff and rowed to shore.

Utina divined a trail into the seamless jungle and we followed.

"We're bilge-headed coffinwits. Soon they jump from the shadows and morcellate us for barbecue," Jacome said.

"They could," Utina said. "Or I could." And pulled back her cloak to reveal a stubby musketoon. Jacome reached for his cutlass, but Moishe raised his hand.

"Shat. Hust." Shh. Be calm.

"Why am I taking you to the Fountain?" Utina asked then smiled. "Ach, I can't help myself."

We continued to walk, Jacome glowering as we shlepped through the tangle of vines and leaves.

The sun boiling high above us, we finally came to a clearing. A thin river curled white over boulders then ran into an opening in a rocky mound.

Utina reached into deep green boughs of tree and pulled down a yellow fruit. She sat on a dry boulder, took a short knife from her cloak and began peeling it.

She speared a dripping segment on the bladepoint.

"Pond-apple?" she offered.

Sha. Was this a stalling tactic or dramatic prelapsarian irony?

Moishe looked vaguely at the river, then accepted a piece of the fruit. What was he thinking? *Ver veyst?* Who knows? One may have a head filled with boiling soup yet look like a kneydl. A dumpling. He said gornisht. Nothing.

"Where's the Fountain?" Jacome asked, not one to let catering get in the way of eternity.

"Inside the cavern," Utina said. "You find what you seek."

Still, the evasive half-answers of a tzadik.

There was a hot spring that burbled up from the cenote, its waters rising from a crack deep in the earth.

"Now," Jacome said. "Where's the door?"

On the top of the mound were several small openings. We peered in but could see nothing. Moishe dropped a rock into one. A minute passed and there was an almost inaudible splash.

The only other entrance was to follow the river into the cave, but the churning water would shlog smash you against the rocks. You'd end up the kind of immortal where you don't live forever because you're already dead. Unless you could hold your breath for ten minutes and avoid the rocks.

"The water was not always so strong," she said.

Ach. As helpful as bloodletting a corpse.

"We'll dam the river," Jacome said. "We'll move boulders."

Moishe took several sacks of arquebus gunpowder out of the bag hanging from his shoulder. They would blow their way to kingdom come.

I flew to the top of the mound. I'd squeeze myself into one of the openings.

Reverse birth.

It'd be almost entirely dark inside, the small holes like stars far above. Perhaps I could find the Fountain and bring back its waters.

One squeeze of Aaron, the immortal sponge, and they'd forget their pain. Or live forever.

I eyed a likely hole behind a jagged rock.

Perhaps if I weren't so ample. If I'd watched myself: Did I need to do all that fressing? Still, I thought I might fit inside.

I pushed myself through. How? Like anyone else, first one wing and then the other. Immediately I began to fall. I only knew which way was up because it was the direction I wasn't going. Then I found my wings and began to flap.

I saw bupkes. Nothing. Nada. I flew in little circles, not knowing where the walls were, not knowing how far was down. I heard the gurgling of water. The Fountain or the shpritzing of a kvetchy sea serpent? I could not tell.

Then a rumbling. Some kind of upset tuml in the kishkas of the cave. Then a raining down of water from above. Then—*Sh'ma Yisroel*—the vessels of the world burst open.

Gevalt. An explosion. Then another. Keneynehoreh. Suddenly it was light and I saw the outside above me.

Boulders fell. Water roared over me as if the sky had turned liquid. Up was down and I was swept into the churning of a hot current, flapping, trying not to drown. The ceiling of the cenote had collapsed. The firmament was broken. There were no stars but only the shocking blue sky.

I'd fallen into the Fountain. If I was going to die, I was going to die wet with immortality. I flapped. Each sinew and bone ached but I was able to rise.

Moishe? Where was Moishe? What had happened?

The cenote was an open volcano, but with water and air instead of fire. And falling stone. I flew into the sky above this grave pit. The river poured over the broken edge, no longer into the cave mouth where Moishe and Jacome had been.

Though I burned with pain, I searched.

My captain. My Moishe. My other.

He was gone.

Nothing but the unbridled river flowing over the open pit of the Fountain. It was a jumble of broken rock. Moses lost before he reached the Promised Land.

They all were gone.
Moishe. Jacome. Utina.
They must have been buried beneath the fallen stones.
Moishe. My captain. My shoulder.

Nu. So there's that question, And then what happened? Let me tell you. Five hundred years. It happens. It's takeh why I have these words.

Was I shpritzed by the Fountain when I fell? Or did it pish on the gantseh megillah, the whole story?

They say when I tell it, it seems as if it goes on forever. Na. I was that story, have become the whole shpiel. Have passed it down to a long line of pisher parrots who also tell it. And tell it to you now. What, they were busy being something else? Any life is just another life out of order.

As long as you have the words.

Emes, I always said: I want to live forever. I just don't want to be there when it happens.

And Moishe? I flew over the broken Fountain. Along the river. Through the gantseh jungle. For days. Weeks. Months. I could not find him.

This never leaves my farmishteh feygeleh mind.

I saw bupkes. Nothing. Emptiness. No finger reaching, no shmatte scrap of britches, no moaning voice. Maybe he thought I had died? Maybe he searched for me?

Maybe Jacome pushed him, or he jumped in and spluttered down the river and was dunked in the Fountain, his head klopped, stars prickling for a moment instead of eyes.

Maybe he searched his endless life for Sarah? If only for a second.

Ach, I can see them, hobbling old and toothless. Two zkeynim. An old bubbie and an alter kaker zadie shuffling about, forgotten by time.

"Is good?" Sarah mumbles.

"Yes, *mayn libeh*," Moishe says. "My love." He takes her hand. They wobble. "Nu, let us hodeveh cultivate our gortn. As the psalm says, 'That the spices thereof may flow out. Let my beloved come into our garden, and eat the pleasant fruits.'"

Or they fall together on the ground and shmunts, their bodies soft as alteh yidn payayas. "Oy, Sarah," he says. "Oy!"

Ei! I wish I were on his wizened pupiklech shoulder, telling these codswallop bobeh mayseh tales to his eyniklech grandchildren as if they were mine. My Moishe. I wish that the mamzer were here.

Ach but I'm getting shmaltzy. And what parrot wants to get all shmutzik with chicken-fat shmaltz?

They say I repeat myself. But I remember. Too much. Stories I would live again, keneynehoreh. Despite myself.

Not that I mind telling you. As I said, I'm glad you asked. And the zadie over there is still shloffing.

They say I'm living history. Ach. I'm the farkakteh book of geshichte stories. Some wandering siddur, a meshugener crazy Messiah, the flesh made word. So, nu, maybe someone could call an editor, *es tut mir vey*, I ache everywhere. But, azoy, I remember so that Moishe, wherever he is, doesn't have to.

Over each horizon, more horizons. From the printing press to the typewriter to the text message. I have lived long. Oy, there were years of zaftik parrots in Florida. Though no one special. Years of sailing. Shtupping. Kibitzing. Sailing. Remembering. Kibitzing. Shtupping. Remembering.

Ach, it's a life. A wonder tale. And I try not to notice that—can I help it?—all the time our tucheses are plonked in the sitz-bath of story. You think, *genug shoyn*, enough already. But nu. *Gey plotz*. What can you do? You try not to let tsuris make you old.

Which reminds me: A man goes to the theatre with his son.
"One adult and one child," he says at the box office.
"That's no child," the ticket seller says. "He looks at least thirty."
"I can help it that he worries?"

Acknowledgements

Writing this novel was a voyage into a world unknown to me and, like the fabled ursine mountaineer, I travelled to see what I could see, learning what destination I hoped for as I found it, though I had advice and encouragement on the way. The metaphor of a crew helping me build, rebuild and sail my own ship of Theseus is apt here and I'm deeply grateful.

Sculling and scouring readers and inspiriting coxswains include Craig Conley, Mike Warwick, Sandra Stephenson, Gregory Betts, Chris Piuma, Myrna Barwin (my mom), Peter Borwein, André Alexis, Martha Baillie, Stuart Ross, Emily Schultz, Brian Joseph Davis and Natalee Caple. I gained invaluable insight about parrots from Chris Pannell.

I'd like to thank the supporters of public funding for the arts, for time and assistance through grants received from the Canada Council and the Ontario Arts Council. I'm also appreciative of the opportunity to muster and buff as a result of my year as writer-in-residence at Western University.

I am grateful to Yiddish maven Michael Wex who idiom-proofed my shpritzing to make certain it was shipshape; to copy editor Angelika Glover for her perspicacious this-, that- and whichcraft; and, especially, to my remarkable editor, Amanda Lewis, whose keen insight ensured I navigated by shtern and not by shtick. I'd also like to express great appreciation to my agent, Shaun Bradley, of the appropriately named Transatlantic Agency, for, among other things, believing that this book could find land and then helping me find it when none was certain. And to my wife, Beth Bromberg: this book—as most things—would simply not be possible without her.

I have dedicated this book to my family—my wife, parents, in-laws, my children and my late grandparents. I have tried to infuse it with wonder, thoughtfulness, wit, intelligence, culture, love and compassion. If I have succeeded in this in any way, it is because I have learned these things from them.

✥

As a reader, the parrot Aaron is a polyglot, omnivore and a plunderer, and the complete sources of his learning are obscure. However, certain texts can be noted: Robert Louis Stevenson, *Treasure Island*; Fyodor Dostoyevsky, "The Grand Inquisitor" from *The Brothers Karamazov*; Capt. Charles Johnson, *A General History of the Robberies and Murders of the Most Notorious Pyrates*; Mary Johnston, *1492*; Rafael Sabatini, *Captain Blood*; Shakespeare, *The Tempest*; Richard Henry Dana, Jr., *Two Years Before the Mast*; Joseph Conrad, *Heart of Darkness*; Edward Kritzler, *Jewish Pirates of the Caribbean*; Michael Wex, *Just Say Nu*; and a great variety of books on history, language and seafaring too numerous to mention here.

Excerpts from the novel have appeared in *Joyland* (joylandmagazine.com) and *The Dalhousie Review*.

Gary Barwin is a writer, composer, multimedia artist and the author of twenty books of poetry, fiction and books for children. His recent books include the short fiction collection, I, Dr. Greenblatt, Orthodontist, 251-1457, and the poetry collections Moon Baboon Canoe and The Wild and Unfathomable Always. A PhD in music composition, Barwin has been Writer-in-Residence at Western University and Young Voices E-Writer-in-Residence at the Toronto Public Library, and has taught creative writing at a number of colleges and universities. Born in Northern Ireland to South African parents of Ashkenazi descent, Barwin moved to Canada as a child. He is married with three adult children and lives in Hamilton, Ontario.

www.garybarwin.com